The Ambassador's MISSION

By Trudi Canavan

The Magician's Apprentice

The Black Magician Trilogy
The Magicians' Guild
The Novice
The High Lord

Age of the Five
Priestess of the White
Last of the Wilds
Voice of the Gods

The Traitor Spy Trilogy
The Ambassador's Mission

TRUDI CANAVAN

The Ambassador's MISSION

Book One of the TRAITOR SPY TRILOGY

www.orbitbooks.net

ORBIT

First published in Great Britain in 2010 by Orbit

Copyright © 2010 by Trudi Canavan

The moral right of the author has been asserted.

*All characters and events in this publication, other
than those clearly in the public domain, are fictitious
and any resemblance to real persons, living or dead,
is purely coincidental.*

A CIP catalogue record for this book
is available from the British Library.

HB 978-1-84149-591-0
C format 978-1-84149-866-9

Typeset in Garamond 3 by Palimpsest Book Production Limited,
Grangemouth, Stirlingshire
Printed and bound in Great Britain by Clays Ltd, St Ives plc

Papers used by Orbit are natural, renewable and recyclable
products sourced from well-managed forests and certified
in accordance with the rules of the Forest Stewardship Council.

Mixed Sources
Product group from well-managed
forests and other controlled sources
www.fsc.org Cert no. SGS-COC-004081
© 1996 Forest Stewardship Council

FSC

Orbit
An imprint of
Little, Brown Book Group
100 Victoria Embankment
London EC4Y 0DY

An Hachette UK Company
www.hachette.co.uk

www.orbitbooks.net

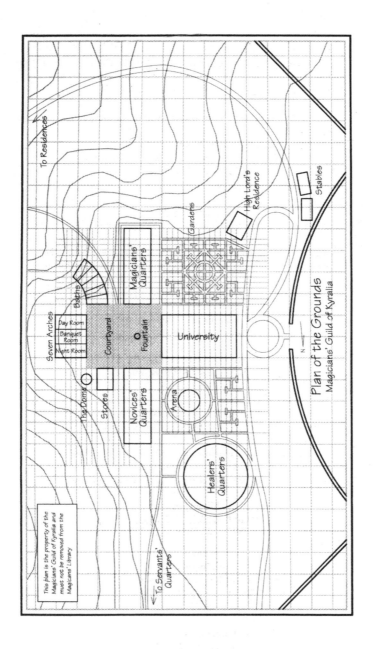

Plan of the Grounds

Magicians' Guild of Kyralia

To Residences

Baths

Seven Arches

Day Room
Banquet Room
Night Room

The Dome

Stores

Novices' Quarters

Courtyard

Fountain

Magicians' Quarters

Gardens

University

Arena

Healers' Quarters

High Lord's Residence

Stables

To Servants' Quarters

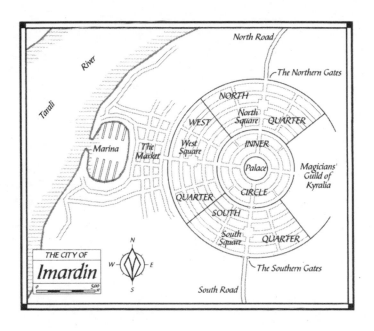

THE CITY OF
Imardin

0 _____ 500 ft

N
W — E
S

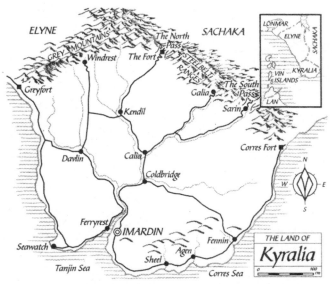

THE LAND OF
Kyralia

0 _____ 100 TM

N
W — E
S

PART ONE

CHAPTER 1

THE OLD AND THE NEW

The most successful and quoted piece by the poet Rewin, greatest of the rabble to come out of the New City, was called *Citysong*. It captured what was heard at night in Imardin, if you took the time to stop and listen: an unending muffled and distant combination of sounds. Voices. Singing. A laugh. A groan. A gasp. A scream.

In the darkness of Imardin's new Quarter a man remembered the poem. He stopped to listen, but instead of absorbing the city's song he concentrated on one discordant echo. A sound that didn't belong. A sound that didn't repeat. He snorted quietly and continued on.

A few steps later a figure emerged from the shadows before him. The figure was male and loomed over him menacingly. Light caught the edge of a blade.

"Yer money," a rough voice said, hard with determination.

The man said nothing and remained still. He might have appeared frozen in terror. He might have appeared deep in thought.

When he did move, it was with uncanny speed. A click, a snap of sleeve, and the robber gasped and sank to his knees. A knife clattered on the ground. The man patted him on the shoulder.

"Sorry. Wrong night, wrong target, and I don't have time to explain why."

As the robber fell, face-down, on the pavement, the man stepped over him and walked on. Then he paused and looked over his shoulder, to the other side of the street.

"Hai! Gol. You're supposed to be my bodyguard."

From the shadows another large figure emerged and hurried to the man's side.

"Reckon you don't have much need for one, Cery. I'm getting slow in my old age. I should be payin' *you* to protect *me*."

Cery scowled. "Your eyes and ears are still sharp, aren't they?"

Gol winced. "As sharp as yours," he retorted sullenly.

"Too true." Cery sighed. "I should retire. But Thieves don't get to retire."

"Except by not being Thieves any more."

"Except by becoming corpses," Cery corrected.

"But you're no ordinary Thief. I reckon there's different rules for you. You didn't start the usual way, so why would you finish the usual way?"

"Wish everyone else agreed with you."

"So do I. City'd be a better place."

"With everyone agreeing with *you*? Ha!"

"Better for me, anyway."

Cery chuckled and resumed the journey. Gol followed a short distance behind. *He hides his fear well*, Cery thought. *Always has. But he must be thinking that we both might not make it through this night. Too many of the others have died.*

Over half the Thieves – the leaders of underworld criminal groups in Imardin – had perished these last few years. Each in different ways and most from unnatural causes. Stabbed,

4

poisoned, pushed from a tall building, burned in a fire, drowned or crushed in a collapsed tunnel. Some said a single person was responsible, a vigilante they called the Thief Hunter. Others believed it was the Thieves themselves, settling old disputes.

Gol said it wasn't *who* would go next that punters were betting on, but *how*.

Of course, younger Thieves had taken the place of the old, sometimes peacefully, sometimes after a quick, bloody struggle. That was to be expected. But even these bold newcomers weren't immune to murder. They were as likely to become the next victim as an older Thief.

There were no obvious connections between the killings. While there were plenty of grudges between Thieves, none provided a reason for so many murders. And while attempts on Thieves' lives weren't that unusual, that they were successful was. That, and the fact that the killer or killers had neither bragged about it, nor been seen in the act.

In the past we would have held a meeting. Discussed strategies. Worked together. But it's been such a long time since the Thieves co-operated with each other I don't think we'd know how to, now.

He'd seen the change coming in the days after the Ichani invaders were defeated, but hadn't guessed how quickly it would happen. Once the Purge – the yearly forced exodus of the homeless from the city into the slums – ended, the slums were declared part of the city, rendering old boundaries obsolete. Alliances between Thieves faltered and new rivalries began. Thieves who had worked together to save the city during the invasion turned on each other in order to hold onto their territory, make up for what they'd lost to others and take advantage of new opportunities.

Cery passed four young men lounging against a wall where the alley met a wider street. They eyed him and their gaze fell to the small medallion pinned to Cery's coat that marked him as a Thief's man. As one they nodded respectfully. Cery nodded back once, then paused at the alley entrance, waiting for Gol to pass the men and join him. The bodyguard had decided years ago that he was better able to spot potential threats if he wasn't walking right beside Cery – and Cery could handle most close encounters himself.

As Cery waited, he looked down at a red line painted across the alley entrance, and smiled with amusement. Having declared the slums a part of the city, the king had tried to take control of it with varying success. Improvements to some areas led to raised rents which, along with the demolition of unsafe houses, forced the poor into smaller and smaller areas of the city. They dug in and made these places their own and, like cornered animals, defended them with savage determination, giving their neighbourhoods names like Blackstreets and Dwellfort. There were now boundary lines, some painted, some known only by reputation, over which no city guard dared step unless he was in the company of several colleagues – and even then they must expect a fight. Only the presence of a magician ensured their safety.

As his bodyguard joined him, Cery turned away and they started to cross the wider street together. A carriage passed, lit by two swinging lanterns. The ever-present guards strolled in groups of two – never out of sight of the next or last group – carrying lanterns.

This was a new thoroughfare, cutting through the bad part of the city known as Wildways. Cery had wondered, at first, why the king had bothered. Anyone travelling along it was at risk of being robbed by the denizens on either side, and probably stuck with a knife in the process. But the road was wide, giving little cover for muggers, and the tunnels beneath, once part of the underground network known as the Thieves' Road, had been filled in during its construction. Many of the old, overcrowded buildings on either side had been demolished and replaced by large, secure ones owned by merchants.

Split in two, vital connections within Wildways had been broken. Though Cery was sure efforts were underway to dig new tunnels, half the local population had been forced into other bad neighbourhoods, while the rest were split by the main road. Wildways, where visitors had once come seeking a gambling house or cheap whore, undeterred by the risk of robbery and murder, was doomed.

Cery, as always, felt uncomfortable in the open. The encounter with the mugger had left him uneasy.

"Do you think he was sent to test me?" he asked Gol.

Gol did not answer straightaway, his long silence telling Cery he was considering the question carefully.

"Doubt it. More likely he had a fatal bout of bad luck."

Cery nodded. *I agree. But times have changed. The city has changed. It's like living in a foreign country, sometimes. Or what I'd imagine living in some other city would be like, since I've never left Imardin. Unfamiliar. Different rules. Dangers where you don't expect them. Can't be too paranoid. And I am, after all, about to meet the most feared Thief in Imardin.*

"You there!" a voice called. Two guards strode toward them, one holding up his lantern. Cery considered the distance to the other side of the road, then sighed and stopped.

"Me?" he asked, turning to face the guards. Gol said nothing.

The taller of the guards stopped a step closer than his stocky companion. He did not answer, but after looking from Gol to Cery and back again a few times he settled on staring at Cery.

"State your address and name," he ordered.

"Cery of River Road, Northside," Cery replied.

"Both of you?"

"Yes. Gol is my servant. And bodyguard."

The guard nodded, barely glancing at Gol. "Your destination?"

"A meeting with the king."

The quieter guard's indrawn breath earned a glance from his superior. Cery watched the men, amused to find them both trying – and failing – to hide their dismay and fear. He'd been told to give them this information, and though it was a ridiculous claim the guard appeared to believe him. Or, more likely, understood that it was a coded message.

The taller guard straightened. "On your way then. And . . . safe journey."

Cery turned away and, with Gol following a step behind, continued across the street. He wondered if the message had told them exactly who Cery was meeting, or if it only told the guard that whoever spoke the phrase wasn't to be detained or delayed.

Either way, he doubted he and Gol had chanced upon the only corrupted guard on the street. There had always been guards willing to work with the Thieves, but now the layers of corruption were stronger and more pervasive than ever. There were honest, ethical men in the Guard who strove to expose and punish offenders in their ranks, but it was a battle they had been losing for some time now.

Everyone is caught up in infighting of one form or another. The Guard is fighting corruption, the Houses are feuding, the rich and

*poor novices and magicians in the Guild bicker constantly, the Allied
Lands can't agree on what to do about Sachaka, and the Thieves
are at war with each other. Faren would have found it all very
entertaining.*

But Faren was dead. Unlike the rest of the Thieves, he had
died of a perfectly normal lung infection during winter five years
ago. Cery hadn't spoken to him for years before that. The man
Faren had been grooming to replace him had taken the reins of
his criminal empire with no contest or bloodshed. The man
known as Skellin.

The man Cery was meeting tonight.

As Cery made his way through the smaller, lingering portion
of the split Wildways neighbourhood, ignoring the calls of
whores and betting boys, he considered what he knew of Skellin.
Faren had taken in his successor's mother when Skellin was
only a child, but whether the woman had been Faren's lover
or wife, or had worked for him, was unknown. The old Thief
had kept them close and secret, as most Thieves had to do
with loved ones. Skellin had proven himself a talented man.
He had taken over many underworld enterprises, and started
more than a few of his own, with few failures. He had a reputation for being clever and uncompromising. Cery did not
think Faren would have approved of Skellin's utter ruthless-
ness. Yet the stories most likely had been embellished during
retellings, so there was no guessing how deserving the man's
reputation was.

There was no animal Cery knew of called a "Skellin". Faren's
successor had been the first new Thief to break with the tradi-
tion of using animal names. It didn't necessarily mean "Skellin"
was his real name, of course. Those who believed it was thought
him brave for revealing it. Those who didn't, didn't care.

A turn into another street brought them out into a cleaner part of the area. Cleaner only in appearance, however. Behind the doors of these solid, well-maintained houses lived more affluent whores, fences, smugglers and assassins. The Thieves had learned that the Guard – stretched too thin – didn't look much deeper if outward appearances were respectable. And the Guard, like certain wealthy men and women from the Houses with dubious business connections, had also learned to distract the city's do-gooders from their failure to deal with the problem with donations to their pet charity projects.

Which included the hospices run by Sonea, still a hero to the poor even if the rich only spoke of Akkarin's efforts and sacrifices in the Ichani Invasion. Cery often wondered if she guessed how much of the money donated to her cause came from corrupt sources. And if she did, did she care?

He and Gol slowed as they reached the intersection of streets named in the directions Cery had been sent. At the corner was a strange sight.

A patch of green sprinkled with bright colour filled the space where a house had once been. Plants of all sizes grew among the old foundations and broken walls. All were illuminated by hundreds of hanging lamps. Cery chuckled quietly as he finally remembered where he'd heard the name "Sunny House" before. The house had been destroyed during the Ichani Invasion, and the owner could not afford to rebuild it. He'd bunkered down in the basement of the ruin, and spent his days encouraging his beloved garden to take over – and the local people to enter and enjoy it.

It was a strange place for Thieves to be meeting, but Cery could see advantages. It was relatively open – nobody could approach or listen in without being noticed – and yet public enough that any fight or attack would be witnessed, which would hopefully discourage treachery and violence.

The instructions had said to wait beside the statue. As Cery and Gol entered the garden, they saw a stone figure on a plinth in the middle of the ruins. The statue was carved of black stone veined with grey and white. It was of a cloaked man, facing east but looking north. Drawing near, Cery realised there was something familiar about it.

It's supposed to be Akkarin, he recognised with a shock. *Facing the Guild but looking toward Sachaka.* Moving closer he examined the face. *Not a good likeness, though.*

Gol made a low noise of warning and Cery's attention immediately snapped back to his surroundings. A man was walking toward them, and another was trailing behind.

Is this Skellin? He is definitely foreign. But this man was not from any race that Cery had encountered. The stranger's face was long and slim, his cheek bones and chin narrowing to a point. This made his surprisingly curvaceous mouth appear to be too large for his face. But his eyes and angular brows were in proportion – almost beautiful. His skin was darker than the typical Elyne or Sachakan colouring, but rather than the blue-black of a typical Lonmar it had a reddish tinge. His hair was a far darker shade of red than the vibrant tones common among the Elynes.

He looks like he's fallen into a pot of dye, and it hasn't quite washed out yet, Cery mused. *I'd say he is about twenty-five.*

"Welcome to my home, Cery of Northside," the man said, with no trace of a foreign accent. "I am Skellin. Skellin the Thief or Skellin the Dirty Foreigner depending on who you talk to and how intoxicated they are."

Cery wasn't sure how to respond to that. "Which would you rather I call you?"

Skellin's smile broadened. "Skellin will do. I am not fond of fancy titles." His gaze shifted to Gol.

"My bodyguard," Cery explained.

Skellin nodded once at Gol in acknowledgement, then turned back to Cery. "May we talk privately?"

"Of course," Cery replied. He nodded at Gol, who retreated out of earshot. Skellin's companion also retreated.

The other Thief moved to one of the low walls of the ruin and sat down. "It is a shame the Thieves of this city don't meet and work together any more," he said. "Like in the old days." He looked at Cery. "You knew the old traditions and followed the old rules once. Do you miss them?"

Cery shrugged. "Change goes on all the time. You lose something and you gain something else."

One of Skellin's elegant eyebrows rose. "Do the gains outweigh the losses?"

"More for some than others. I've not had much profit from the split, but I still have a few understandings with other Thieves."

"That is good to hear. Do you think there is a chance we might come to an understanding?"

"There's always a chance." Cery smiled. "It depends on what you're suggesting we understand."

Skellin nodded. "Of course." He paused and his expression grew serious. "There are two offers I'd like to make to you. The first is one I've made to several other Thieves, and they have all agreed to it."

Cery felt a thrill of interest. *All of them? But then, he doesn't say how many "several" is.*

"You have heard of the Thief Hunter?" Skellin asked.

"Who hasn't?"

12

"I believe he is real."

"One person killed all those Thieves?" Cery raised his eyebrows, not bothering to conceal his disbelief.

"Yes," Skellin said firmly, holding Cery's gaze. "If you ask around — ask the people who saw something — there are similarities in the murders."

I'll have to have Gol look into it again, Cery mused. Then a possibility occurred to him. *I hope Skellin doesn't think that my helping High Lord Akkarin to find the Sachakan spies back before the Ichani Invasion means I can find this Thief Hunter for him. They were easy to spot, once you knew what to look for. The Thief Hunter is something else.*

"So . . . what you want to do about him?"

"I'd like your agreement that if you hear anything about the Thief Hunter you will tell me. I understand that many Thieves aren't talking to each other, so I offer myself as a recipient of information about the Thief Hunter instead. Perhaps, with everyone's cooperation, I'll get rid of him for you all. Or, at the least, be able to warn anyone if they are going to be attacked."

Cery smiled. "That last bit is a touch optimistic."

Skellin shrugged. "Yes, there is always the chance a Thief won't pass on a warning if he knows the Thief Hunter is going to kill a rival. But remember that every Thief removed is one less source of information that could lead to us getting rid of the Hunter and ensuring our own safety."

"They'd be replaced quick enough."

Skellin frowned. "By someone who might not know as much as their predecessor."

"Don't worry." Cery shook his head. "There's nobody I hate enough to do that to, right now."

The other man smiled. "So are we in agreement?"

Cery considered. Though he did not like the sort of trade Skellin was in, it would be silly to turn down this offer. The only information the man wanted related to the Thief Hunter, nothing more. And he was not asking for a pact or promise – if Cery was unable to pass on information because it would compromise his safety or business, nobody could say he'd broken his word.

"Yes," he replied. "I can do that."

"We have an understanding," Skellin said, his smile broadening. "Now let me see if I can make that two." He rubbed his hands together. "I'm sure you know the main product that I import and sell."

Not bothering to hide his distaste, Cery nodded. "Roet. Or 'rot', as some call it. Not something I'm interested in. And I hear you have it well in hand."

Skellin nodded. "I do. When Faren died he left me a shrinking territory. I needed a way to establish myself and strengthen my control. I tried different trades. Roet supply was new and untested. I was amazed at how quickly Kyralians took to it. It has proven to be very profitable, and not just for me. The Houses are making a nice little income from the rent on the brazier houses." Skellin paused. "You could be gaining from this little industry, too, Cery of Northside."

"Just call me Cery." Cery let his expression grow serious. "I am flattered, but Northside is home to people mostly too poor to pay for roet. It's a habit for the rich."

"But Northside is growing more prosperous, thanks to your efforts, and roet is getting cheaper as more becomes available."

Cery resisted a cynical smile at the flattery.

"Not quite enough yet. It would stop growing if roet was

brought in too soon and too fast." *And if I could manage it, we'd have no rot at all.* He'd seen what it did to men and women caught up in the pleasure of it – forgetting to eat or drink, or to feed their children except to dose them with the drug to stop their complaints of hunger. *But I'm not foolish enough to think I can keep it away forever. If I don't provide it, someone else will. I will have to find a way to do so without causing too much damage.* "There will be a right time to bring roet to Northside," Cery said. "And when that time comes I'll know who to come to."

"Don't leave it too long, Cery," Skellin warned. "Roet is popular because it is new and fashionable, but eventually it will be like bol – just another vice of the city, grown and prepared by anybody. I'm hoping that by then I'll have established new trades to support myself with." He paused and looked away. "One of the old, honourable Thief trades. Or perhaps even something legitimate."

He turned back and smiled, but there was a hint of sadness and dissatisfaction in his expression. *Perhaps there's an honest man in there*, Cery thought. *If he didn't expect roet to spread so fast, maybe he didn't expect it to cause so much damage . . . but that isn't going to convince me to get into the trade myself.*

Skellin's smile faded and was replaced by an earnest frown. "There are people out there who would like to take your place, Cery. Roet may be your best defence against them, as it was for me."

"There are always people out there who want me gone," Cery said. "I'll go when I'm ready."

The other Thief looked amused. "You truly believe you'll get to choose the time and place?"

"Yes."

"And your successor?"

"Yes."

Skellin chuckled. "I like your confidence. Faren was as sure of himself, too. He was half right: he got to choose his successor."

"He was a clever man."

"He told me much about you." Skellin's gaze became curious. "How you didn't become a Thief by the usual ways. That the infamous High Lord Akkarin arranged it."

Cery resisted the urge to look at the statue. "All Thieves gain power through favours with powerful people. I happened to exchange favours with a very powerful one."

Skellin's eyebrows rose. "Did he ever teach you magic?"

A laugh escaped Cery. "If only!"

"But you grew up with Black Magician Sonea and gained your position with help from the former High Lord. Surely you would have picked up something."

"Magic isn't like that," Cery explained. *But surely he knows that.* "You have to have the talent, and be taught to control and use it. You can't pick it up by watching someone."

Skellin put a finger to his chin and regarded Cery thoughtfully. "You do still have connections in the Guild, though, don't you?"

Cery shook his head. "I haven't seen Sonea in years."

"How disappointing, after all you did – all the Thieves did – to help them." Skellin smiled crookedly. "I'm afraid your reputation as a friend of magicians is nowhere near as exciting as the reality, Cery."

"That's the way with reputations. Usually."

Skellin nodded. "So it is. Well, I have enjoyed our chat and made my offers. We have come to one understanding, at least.

16

I hope we will come to another in time." He stood up. "Thank you for meeting with me, Cery of Northside."

"Thank you for the invitation. Good luck in catching the Thief Hunter."

Skellin smiled, nodded politely, then turned and strolled back the way he had come. Cery watched him for a moment, then gave the statue another quick glance. It really wasn't a good likeness.

"How did it go?" Gol murmured as Cery joined him.

"As I expected," Cery replied. "Except . . ."

"Except?" Gol repeated when Cery didn't finish.

"We agreed to share information on the Thief Hunter."

"He's real then?"

"So Skellin believes." Cery shrugged. They crossed the road and began striding back toward Wildways. "That wasn't the oddest thing, though."

"Oh?"

"He asked if Akkarin taught me magic."

Gol paused. "That isn't *that* odd, though. Faren did hide Sonea before he handed her over to the Guild, in the hopes she would do magic for him. Skellin must have heard all about it."

"Do you think he'd like to have his own pet magician?"

"Sure. Though he obviously wouldn't want to hire you, seeing as you're a Thief. Perhaps he thinks he can ask favours of the Guild through you."

"I told him I hadn't seen Sonea in years." Cery chuckled. "Next time I see her, I might ask if she'll help out one of my Thief friends, just to see the look on her face."

A figure appeared in the alley ahead, hurrying toward them. Cery noted the possible exits and hiding places around them.

17

"You should tell her Skellin was making enquiries," Gol advised. "He might try to recruit someone else. And it might work. Not all magicians are as incorruptible as Sonea." Gol slowed. "That's . . . That's Neg."

Relief that it wasn't another attacker was followed by concern. Neg had been guarding Cery's main hideout. He preferred it to roaming the streets, as open spaces made him jittery.

The guard had seen them. Neg was panting as he reached them. Something on his face caught the light, and Cery felt his heart drop somewhere far below the level of the street. A bandage.

"What is it?" Cery asked, in a voice he barely recognised as his.

"S . . . sorry," Neg panted. "Bad news." He drew in a deep breath, then let it out explosively and shook his head. "Don't know how to tell you."

"Say it," Cery ordered.

"They're dead. All of them. Selia. The boys. Never saw who. Got past everything. Don't know how. No lock broken. When I came to . . ." As Neg babbled on, apologising and explaining, words running over themselves, a rushing sound filled Cery's ears. His mind tried to find some other explanation for a moment. *He must be mistaken. He's hit his head and is delusional. He dreamed it.*

But he made himself face the likely truth. What he had dreaded – had nightmares over – for years had happened.

Someone had made it past all the locks and guards and protections, and murdered his family.

CHAPTER 2

QUESTIONABLE CONNECTIONS

I t was much earlier than her usual waking time. Dawn was still some hours away. Sonea blinked in the darkness and wondered what had woken her. A dream? Or had something real brought her to this state of sudden alertness in the middle of the night?

Then she heard a sound, faint but undeniable, in the next room.

Heart beating fast, the skin of her scalp tingling, she rose and silently moved to the bedroom door. She heard a footfall beyond, then another. Taking hold of the handle, she drew magic, threw up a shield and took a deep breath.

The handle turned silently. She pulled the door inward slightly and looked beyond. In the faint moonlight filtering through the window screens she saw a figure pacing the guestroom. Male, short of stature, and instantly familiar. Relief flooded through her.

"Cery," she said, pulling the door open. "Who else would dare sneak into my rooms in the middle of the night?"

He turned to face her. "Sonea . . ." He drew in a deep breath, but said nothing more. A long pause followed and she frowned. It was not like him to hesitate. Had he come to ask a favour he knew she would not like?

She concentrated and created a small globe light, enough to fill the room with a soft glow. Her breath caught in her throat for a moment. His face was so lined. The years of danger and worry living as a Thief had aged him faster than anyone else she knew.

I'm wearing plenty of signs of my years, she thought, *but the battles for me were only the petty squabbling of magicians, not surviving in the uncompromising and often cruel underworld.*

"So . . . what brings you to the Guild in the middle of the night?" she asked, stepping into the guest room.

He looked at her thoughtfully. "You never ask me how I get here without being noticed."

"I don't want to know. I don't want to risk anyone else finding out, in the unlikely event that I must allow someone to read my mind."

He nodded. "Ah. How are things going here?"

She shrugged. "The same. Rich and poor novices squabbling. And now that some of the formerly poor novices have graduated and become magicians, we have squabbling on a new level. One we have to take seriously. In a few days we'll be meeting to consider a petition to abolish the rule against novices and magicians associating with criminals or people of low repute. If it's successful then I will no longer be breaking a rule talking to you."

"I can walk in the front gate and formally seek an audience?"

"Yes. Now that's a scenario to give the Higher Magicians a few sleepless nights. I bet they wish they'd never allowed the lower classes to enter the Guild."

"We always knew they would regret it," Cery said. He sighed and looked away. "I've come to wish the Purge hadn't ended."

Sonea frowned and crossed her arms, feeling a stab of anger and disbelief. "Surely not."

"Everything has changed for the worse." He moved to a window and parted one of the screens, revealing nothing but darkness beyond.

"And that's because the Purge was stopped?" She narrowed her eyes at his back. "Nothing to do with a certain new vice ruining the lives of so many Imardians, rich and poor?"

"Roet?"

"Yes. The Purge killed hundreds, but roet has taken thousands – and enslaved more." Every day she saw the victims in her hospices. Not just those caught up in the drug's seductions, but their desperate parents, spouses, siblings, offspring and friends.

And for all I know, Cery's one of the Thieves importing and selling it, she couldn't help thinking, and not for the first time.

"They say it stops you caring," Cery said quietly, turning to face her. "No more worries or concerns. No fear. No . . . grief."

His voice caught on the last word and suddenly Sonea felt all her senses grow sharper.

"What is it, Cery? Why did you come here?"

He drew in a deep breath. Let it out slowly. "My family," he said, "were murdered tonight."

Sonea rocked back on her heels. The edge of a terrible pain stabbed her, reminding her that some losses can never be forgotten – and should never be. But she held it back. She would be of no help to Cery if she let it consume her. He looked lost. In his eyes was an unshielded shock and agony. She strode to him and drew him into her arms. He stiffened for a moment, then slumped against her.

"It's part of being a Thief," he said. "You do all you can to protect your people, but there is always danger. Vesta left me because she couldn't live with it. Couldn't stand being locked away. Selia was stronger. Braver. After all she'd put up with, she didn't deserve to . . . and the boys . . ."

Vesta had been Cery's first wife. She'd been smart, but prickly and prone to temper tantrums. Selia had been a much better match for him, calm and with the quiet wisdom of someone who watched the world with open, yet forgiving eyes. Sonea held him as he shook with sobs, feeling tears in her own eyes. *Can I imagine what it must be like to lose a child? I know the* fear *of losing them, but not the pain of actual loss. I think it would be worse than I can ever imagine. To know one's children will never grow up . . . except . . . what of his other child? Though she must be all grown up by now.*

"Is Anyi okay?" she asked.

Cery stilled, then drew away. His expression was taut with indecision. "I don't know. I've let people think that I didn't care about Vesta and Anyi after they left, for their own protection – though I've occasionally arranged for Anyi and I to cross each other's paths so she would at least continue to recognise me." He shook his head. "Whoever did this, got past the best locks money can buy, and people I trusted completely. They did their research. They might know about her. Or they know, but they don't know her location. If I check on her I might lead them to her."

"Can you get a warning to her?"

He frowned. "Yes. Perhaps . . ." He sighed. "I have to try."

"What will you tell her to do?"

"Hide."

"Then it won't matter if you lead them to her or not, will it? She'll have to go into hiding either way."

He looked thoughtful. "I suppose so."

Sonea smiled as a look of determination hardened his face. His entire body was now tense. He looked at her and his expression became apologetic.

"Go on," she said. "And next time don't wait so long to visit me."

He managed a faint smile. "I won't. Oh. Also, there's something else. It's just a niggle, but I reckon one of the new Thieves, Skellin, fancies having his own magician. He's a rot supplier, so you better hope none of your magicians has a weakness for the stuff."

"They're not *my* magicians, Cery," she reminded him, not for the first time.

Instead of his usual grin, he responded with a grimace. "Yes. Anyway. Unless you want to know how I get in and out of here, you better leave the room."

Sonea rolled her eyes, then walked to the bedroom door. She turned back before closing it. "Good night, Cery. I'm so sorry about your family and I hope Anyi is alive and not in any danger."

He nodded, then swallowed. "I do, too."

Then she closed the door behind her and waited. There were a few faint thuds from the guest room, then silence. She counted to a hundred then opened the door again. The room was unoccupied. She could see no sign of his entrance and exit.

The darkness between the window screens was not so impenetrable now. It had gained a greyish tone, a hint of shape and form just discernible in the early morning light. She took a step toward it and stopped. Was that the square bulk of the High Lord's Residence, or was she imagining it? Either way, the suggestion sent a shiver down her spine.

Stop it. He's not there.

Balkan had lived there for the last twenty years. She had often wondered whether he felt haunted by the shadow of the former occupant, but had never asked, sure such a question would be tactless.

He's up on the hill. Behind you.

She turned and looked beyond the walls, seeing in her imagination the shiny white new stone slabs among the grey of the ancient cemetery. An old longing filled her, but she hesitated. She had much to do today. But it was early – dawn was only just breaking. She had time. And it had been a while. Cery's terrible news brought a need to . . . to what? Perhaps to acknowledge his loss by recalling her own. She needed to do more than act out the usual daily routine and pretend something awful hadn't happened.

Returning to her bedroom, she washed and changed quickly, threw a cloak around her shoulders – black over black – then slipped out of the main door to her room, walked as quietly as she could down the hall of the Magicians' Quarters to the entrance and out onto the path to the cemetery.

New paths had been laid since the first time she'd visited, with Lord Rothen, over twenty years before. Weedy vegetation had been removed, but the Guild had left a wall of protective trees around the outermost graves. She noted the smooth slabs of freshly carved stone. Some she had seen laid, some she hadn't. When a magician died, any magic left in his or her body was released, and if there was enough of it their body was consumed. So the old graves had been a mystery. If there was no body to bury, why were there graves here?

The rediscovery of black magic had answered that question. The last remaining magical energy of those ancient magicians had been drawn away by a black magician, leaving a body to bury.

Now that black magic was no longer taboo, though strictly controlled, burials had become popular again. The task of drawing the last of a magician's power fell to the Guild's two black magicians, her and Black Magician Kallen.

Sonea felt that, if she had taken the last of a magician's power at death, she ought to be present at the funeral. *I wonder if Kallen feels the same sense of obligation when a magician chooses him.* She moved to a plain, undecorated slab of stone and dried the dew from one corner with magical heat so she could sit down. Her eyes found the name carved into it. *Akkarin. You would have found it amusing to see how many of the magicians who were so against reviving the use of black magic resort to it in the end, so their flesh remains after death to rot in the ground. Perhaps you'd have decided, as I have, that allowing your body to be consumed by your last magic is more appropriate for a magician and*, she glanced at the increasingly elaborate decoration on the newer graves provided by the Guild, *considerably less expensive.*

She looked at the words on the grave she sat upon. A name, a title, a house name, a family name. Later the words "Father of Lorkin" had been added, in small, begrudging letters. But of her own name there was no mention. *And will never be, while your family has anything to do with it, Akkarin. But at least they've accepted your son.*

Pushing bitterness aside, she turned her mind to Cery and his family for a while, allowing herself to remember grief and feel the ache of sympathy. To allow memories to return, some welcome, some not. After a while the sound of footsteps roused her from her thoughts and she realised the sun had risen completely.

Turning to face the visitor, she smiled as she saw Rothen walking toward her. For a moment his wrinkled face was a mask of concern, then it relaxed into an expression of relief.

"Sonea," he said, pausing to catch his breath. "A messenger came to see you. Nobody knew where you'd gone."

"And I bet it caused a lot of unnecessary fuss and excitement."

He frowned at her. "This is not a good time to be making the Guild question their trust of a common-born magician, Sonea, considering the change of rules about to be proposed."

"Is there ever a good time for that?" She rose and sighed. "Besides, I didn't destroy the Guild and turn all Kyralians into slaves, did I? I went for a walk. Nothing sinister at all." She looked at him. "I haven't left the city in twenty years, and have only left the Guild grounds to work in the hospices. Isn't that enough?"

"Not for some. And certainly not for Kallen."

Sonea shrugged. "I expect that from Kallen. It's his job." She hooked her hand around his elbow and they started back down the path. "Don't worry about Kallen, Rothen. I can handle him. Besides, he wouldn't dare complain about me visiting Akkarin's grave."

"You should have left a message for Jonna, saying where you were going."

"I know, but these things tend to be a little spontaneous."

He glanced at her. "Are you all right?"

She smiled at him. "Yes. I have a son who is alive and thriving, hospices in the city where I can do some good, and you. What more do I need?"

He paused to think. "A husband?"

She laughed. "I don't *need* a husband. I'm not sure I even want one. I thought I'd be lonely once Lorkin moved out of

26

my rooms, but I'm finding I like having more time to myself. A husband would . . . get in the way."

Rothen chuckled.

Or be a weakness an enemy could exploit, she found herself thinking. But that thought had more to do with Cery's news sitting fresh in her mind than any real threat. While she was hardly without enemies, they merely disliked her for her lowly origins or feared the black magic she wielded. Nothing that would motivate any to the point of harming someone she loved. *Otherwise they would have targeted Lorkin already.*

As she thought of her son, memories rose of him as a child. Memories mixed together, older and younger, happy and disappointed, and she felt a familiar tight feeling that was part joy and part pain. When he was quiet and brooding, thinking hard or being clever, he reminded her so much of his father. But the confident, charming, stubborn, vocal side of him was so unlike Akkarin that she could only see a person who was unique and utterly himself and like no other. Except that Rothen claimed the stubborn and vocal part of his nature had definitely come from her.

As they emerged from the forest, Sonea looked down at the Guild grounds. Before them stood the Magicians' Quarters, a long rectangular building that housed those magicians who chose to live in the grounds. At the far end was a courtyard, beyond which another building mirrored the placement and shape of the first – the Novices' Quarters.

At the far end of the courtyard was the grandest of the Guild buildings, the University. Three storeys tall, it rose above all other Guild structures. Even after twenty years, Sonea felt a small glow of pride that she and Akkarin had saved this building. And, as always, it was followed by sadness and regret at the cost. If they had let the building fall, killing those that remained inside, and instead taken the power of the Arena, Akkarin might have lived.

But it wouldn't have mattered how much power we'd gathered. Once he had been injured he would have still chosen to give me all his power and die rather than heal himself – or let me heal him – and risk us losing to the Ichani. And no matter how much power we'd taken, I'd never have had the time to defeat Kariko and heal Akkarin as well. She frowned. *Maybe it isn't me Lorkin gets his stubborn side from after all.*

"Are you tempted to speak out in favour of the petition?" Rothen asked as they started down the path. "I know you're in favour of abolishing the rule."

She shook her head.

Rothen smiled. "Why not?"

"I might do more harm to their cause than good. After all, someone who grew up in the slums then went on to break a vow, learn forbidden magic, and defy the Higher Magicians and king to such a degree they were forced to send her into exile, is hardly going to inspire trust in lower-class-origin magicians."

"You saved the country."

"I *helped* Akkarin save the country. There's a big difference."

Rothen grimaced. "You played as great a part – and struck the final blow. They should remember that."

"And Akkarin sacrificed himself. Even if I wasn't slum-born and a woman, I'd have a hard time measuring up to that." She shrugged. "I'm not interested in thanks and recognition, Rothen. All that matters to me is Lorkin and the hospices. And yourself, of course."

He nodded. "But what if I told you that Lord Regin has offered to represent those opposed to the petition?"

She felt her stomach sink at the name. Though the novice who had tormented her during her early years in the University was now a grown man, married and with two adult daughters, and had only ever treated her politely and respectfully since the Ichani Invasion, she could not help feeling an echo of distrust and dislike.

"It doesn't surprise me," she said. "He's always been a snob."

"Yes, though his character has improved a great deal since your novice days."

"So he's a well-mannered snob."

Rothen chuckled. "Tempted now?"

She shook her head again.

"Well, you had better expect to have your opinion sought on the issue," he warned. "Many will want to know your views and seek your advice."

As they reached the courtyard, Sonea sighed. "I doubt it. But in case you're right I will consider how I'll reply to any questions that come my way. I don't want to be an obstruction to the petitioners, either."

And if Regin is representing the opposition, I had better be alert to any clever tactics. His manners may have improved, but he's still as intelligent and devious as ever.

There was a small, neat tailor's shop in West Gliar Street in the North Quarter that, if you knew the right people, gave access to small, private rooms on the second floor offering entertainment to young, rich men of the city.

Lorkin had been brought here for the first time four years ago, by his friend and fellow novice, Dekker, along with the rest of their friends. As always, it had been Dekker's idea. He was the boldest of Lorkin's friends, though that was a typical trait of most young Warriors. Of the rest of the group, Alchemist Sherran had always done whatever Dekker suggested, but Healers Reater and Orlon were not so easily led into mischief. Perhaps it was only natural for Healers to be cautious. Whatever the reason, Lorkin had only agreed to accompany Dekker because the pair hadn't refused to.

Four years later they were all graduated magicians, and the tailor's shop was their favourite meeting place. Today Perler had brought his Elyne cousin, Jalie, to visit their haunt for the first time.

"So this is the tailor shop I've heard so much about," a young woman said, looking around the room. The furniture was finely made, worn cast-offs from the wealthier houses in the city. The paintings and window screens were crude in both execution and subject.

"Yes," Dekker replied. "All the delights you might desire."

"At a price," she said, looking at him sideways.

"At a price we may be willing to pay on your behalf, for the pleasure of your company."

She smiled. "You're so sweet!"

"But not without her older cousin's approval," Perler added, giving Dekker a level look.

"Of course," the younger man said, bowing slightly in Perler's direction.

"So what delights do they offer?" Jalie asked of Dekker.

He waved a hand. "Pleasures of the body, pleasures of the mind."

"Of the mind?"

"Ooh! Let's get a brazier in here," Sherran said, his eyes gleaming. "Have a little roet to relax us."

"No," Lorkin said. Hearing another voice speak along with

his, he turned to nod in gratitude to Orlon, who was as repelled by the drug as Lorkin was.

They had tried it once before, and Lorkin had found the experience disturbing. It wasn't how it had brought out Dekker's cruel side, so that he had teased and tormented the girl who had been besotted with him at the time, but how this behaviour suddenly hadn't bothered Lorkin. In fact, he'd found it funny, but later could not understand why.

The girl's infatuation had ended that day, and Sherran's love affair with roet had begun. Before then, Sherran would have done anything Dekker had asked him. Since that day, he would only do so if it didn't come between him and roet.

"Let's have a drink instead," Perler suggested. "Some wine."

"Do magicians drink?" Jalie asked. "I thought they weren't allowed to."

"We are," Reater told her, "but it's not a good idea to get too drunk. Losing control is as likely to involve magic as much as your stomach or bladder."

"I see," she said. "So does the Guild have to make sure any of the lowies it takes in aren't drunks?"

The others glanced at Lorkin, and he smiled, knowing that it wasn't because his mother was a "lowie" but because they knew he would walk out if they made more than the occasional joke about the lower classes.

"There are probably more snooties that are drunks than lowies," Dekker told her. "We have ways of dealing with them. What wine would you like to drink?"

Lorkin looked away as the conversation turned to wine varieties. "Lowies" and "snooties" were the names that the rich and poor novices had given each other after the Guild had decided to accept entrants to the university from outside of the Houses. The nickname "lowie" had been adopted because none of the novices that had come from lower classes were actually poor. All novices were paid a generous allowance by the Guild. As were magicians, though they could supplement their income by magical or other means. A term had to be invented, and it happened to be an unflattering one, so the lowies had retorted with their own nickname for novices from the Houses. One that Lorkin had to admit was appropriate.

Lorkin did not fit into either group. His mother had come from the slums, his father from one of the most powerful Houses in Imardin. He had grown up in the Guild, away from the political manipulations and obligations of the Houses or the hard life of the slums. Most of his friends were snooties. He hadn't avoided befriending lowies deliberately, but most lowies, while not appearing to resent him like they did the snooties, had been hard to talk to. It was only after some years, when Lorkin had a firm circle of snooty friends, that he realised that the lowies had been intimidated by him — or rather, who his father had been.

". . . Sachaka like? Do they really still keep slaves?"

Lorkin's attention snapped back to the conversation, and he shivered. The name of the land from which his father's murderer had come from always sent a chill down his spine. Yet while it had once been from fear, now it was also from a strange excitement. Since the Ichani Invasion the Allied Lands had turned their attention to the neighbour they'd once ignored. Magicians and diplomats had ventured into Sachaka, seeking to avoid future conflict through negotiation, trade and agreements. Whenever they returned they brought descriptions of a strange culture and stranger landscape.

"They do," Perler replied. Lorkin sat up a little straighter.

Reater's older brother had returned from Sachaka a few weeks ago, having spent a year working as the assistant to the Guild Ambassador to Sachaka. "Though you don't see most of them. Your robes disappear from your room and reappear cleaned, but you never see who takes them. But you see the slave assigned to serve you, of course. We all have one."

"So you had a slave?" Sherran asked. "Isn't that against the king's law?"

"They don't belong to us," Perler replied, shrugging. "The Sachakans don't know how to treat servants properly, so we have to let them assign us slaves. Either that or we'd have to wash our own clothes and cook our own meals."

"Which would be *terrible*," Lorkin said in mock horror. His mother's aunt was her servant, and her family worked as servants for rich families, yet they had a dignity and resourcefulness that he respected. He was determined that, should he ever have to do domestic chores, he would never be as humiliated by it as his fellow magicians would be.

Perler looked at him and shook his head. "There'd be no time to do it ourselves. There's always so much work to do. Ah, here are the drinks."

"What sort of work?" Orlon asked as glasses of wine or water were poured and handed around.

"Negotiating trade deals, trying to encourage the Sachakans to abolish slavery in order to join the Allied Lands, keeping up with Sachakan politics – there is a group of rebels Ambassador Maron heard of that he was trying to find out more about, until he had to return to sort out his family's troubles."

"Sounds boring," Dekker said.

"Actually, it was rather exciting." Perler grinned. "A little scary at times, but I felt like we were doing something, well, *historic*. Making a difference. Changing things for the better – even if in tiny steps."

Lorkin felt a strange thrill go through him. "Do you think they're coming around on slavery?" he asked.

Perler shrugged. "Some are, but it's hard to tell if they're pretending to agree in order to be polite, or gain something from us. Maron thinks they could be persuaded to give up slavery much more easily than black magic."

"It's going to be hard to persuade them to give up black magic when we have two black magicians," Reater pointed out. "Seems a bit hypocritical."

"Once they ban black magic we will, too," Perler said confidently.

Dekker turned to grin at Lorkin. "If that happens Lorkin won't be taking over from his mother."

Lorkin gave a snort of derision. "As if she'd let me. She'd much rather I took over running the hospices."

"Would that be so bad?" Orlon asked quietly. "Just because you chose Alchemy doesn't mean you couldn't help out the Healers."

"You need to be driven by absolute, unwavering dedication to run something like a hospice," Lorkin replied. "I'm not. Though I almost wish I was."

"Why?" Jalie asked.

Lorkin spread his hands. "I'd like to do *something* useful with my life."

"Pah!" Dekker said. "If you can afford to spend your life indulging yourself, why wouldn't you?"

"Boredom?" Orlon suggested.

"Who is bored?" a new, feminine voice said.

A completely different sort of thrill ran down Lorkin's spine.

He felt his breath catch in his throat, and his stomach clenched unpleasantly. All turned to see a dark-haired young woman slip through the door. She smiled as she looked around the room. As her eyes met Lorkin's, her smile faltered, but only for a moment.

"Beriya." He spoke her name almost without wanting to, and he instantly hated how it came out in a weak, pathetic gasp.

"Come join us," Dekker invited.

No, Lorkin wanted to say. But he was supposed to be over Beriya. It had been two years since her family had taken her away to Elyne. As she sat down, he looked away as if uninterested in her, and tried to relax the muscles that had stiffened the moment he'd heard her voice. Which was most of them.

She was the first woman he'd fallen in love with — and so far the only one. They'd met at every opportunity, openly and in secret. Every waking moment she had been in his thoughts, and she'd claimed it was the same for her. He would have done anything for her.

Some people had encouraged them, some people had made half-hearted attempts to help him keep his feet on the ground — at least when it came to his magical studies. The trouble was, there was no reason for either his mother or Beriya's family to disapprove of the pairing. And it turned out that he was the sort who became so entranced when in love that no amount of sympathy or stern lectures, not even from Lord Rothen, who he respected and loved like a favourite grandfather, could keep him anchored in reality. Everyone had decided to wait until he recovered his mind enough to concentrate on something other than Beriya, then help him catch up with his training.

Then her cousin had discovered them in bed together and

her family had insisted that the two of them marry as soon as possible. It did not matter that he, as a magician, could prevent Beriya becoming pregnant. If they did not marry, she would be regarded as "spoiled" to any future suitor.

Lorkin, and his mother, had agreed. It was Beriya who had refused.

She also refused to see him. When he finally managed to ambush her one day, she had told him she had never loved him. That she had encouraged him because she had heard that magicians could make love without the danger of siring a child. That she was sorry for lying to him.

His mother had told him that the awful way he felt was the closest that most magicians came to knowing what it felt like for a non-magician to be sick. The best cure was time and the kindness of family and friends. And then she'd used some words to describe Beriya's behaviour that he could not have repeated in the company of most people he knew.

Fortunately, Beriya's family had taken her away to Elyne, so by the time the hurt subsided enough for him to feel anger she was well out of sight. He'd vowed not to fall in love again, but when a girl in his Alchemy class had shown an interest, his resolve had weakened. He liked her practical nature. She was everything Beriya hadn't been. A strange hypocrisy existed in Kyralian culture: nobody expected women magicians to remain celibate. But by the time he'd realised that he didn't love her, she was well and truly infatuated with him. He'd done all he could to end that entanglement as gently as possible, but he knew she now resented him deeply.

Love, he'd decided, was one messy business.

Beriya moved to a chair and sank into it gracefully. "So who is bored?" she asked.

36

As the others denied it, Lorkin considered her and the lessons he'd learned. In the last year he'd met a few women who were both good company and good lovers, and wanted no more than that. He'd found he preferred this sort of encounter. The seductions that Dekker undertook, which only ended in hurt and scandal – or worse – did not appeal. And the affectionless marriage that Reater had been forced into by his parents sounded like his worst nightmare.

Father's family hasn't attempted to find me a bride in a while now. Maybe they're starting to realise how much pleasure Mother gets from spoiling all their plans for me. Though I'm sure she wouldn't block anything if I wanted it.

He dragged his thoughts back to the present as the conversation turned to the exploits of mutual friends of Beriya and Dekker. Lorkin listened and let the afternoon slip by. Eventually the two Healers left to visit the new racecourse, and Beriya left for a dress fitting. Dekker, Sherran and Jalie set off on foot to their family homes, which were in the same main street of the Inner Circle, leaving Lorkin to return to the Guild alone.

Walking through the streets of the Inner Circle, Lorkin looked at the grand buildings thoughtfully. This place had been his home all his life. He had never lived outside of it. Never been to a foreign country. Never even left the city. Ahead he could see the Guild Gates.

Are they the bars of a prison to me, or a wall to keep out danger? Beyond was the front of the University, where his parents had once fought Sachakan black magicians in a last desperate battle. *Those magicians were only Ichani, the Sachakan version of outcast criminals. How would that battle have ended if they'd been Ashaki, black-magic-wielding noble warriors? We were lucky to have won that battle. Everyone knows that. Black Magician Kallen and my mother may not be able to save us if the Sachakans ever decide to invade us properly.*

A familiar figure was approaching the gates from within. As the man passed through them, Lorkin smiled. He knew Lord Dannyl through his mother and Lord Rothen. It had been a while since he'd seen the historian. As always, Dannyl wore a slightly distracted frown, and Lorkin knew the older magician could easily walk past without seeing him.

—*Lord Dannyl*, Lorkin called, keeping his mental voice quiet. Mental communication was frowned upon, since it could be heard by all magicians – whether friends or enemies. But calling another magician's name was considered safe, as doing so gave away little information to anyone listening.

The tall magician looked up, saw Lorkin, and his frown disappeared. They walked toward each other, meeting at the entrance of the street Dannyl lived on.

"Lord Lorkin. How are things?"

Lorkin shrugged. "Well enough. How's your research going?"

Dannyl frowned down at the bundle he was carrying. "The Great Library sent some records that I hoped would provide more details of the state of Imardin after Tagin's death."

Lorkin could not remember who Tagin was, but he nodded anyway. Dannyl had been caught up in his history of magic for so long he often forgot that other people did not know the details as well as he. *It must be a relief to know what you want to dedicate your life to*, Lorkin thought. *None of this wondering what to do with yourself.*

"How . . . how did you come up with the idea to write a history of magic?" Lorkin asked.

Dannyl looked at Lorkin and shrugged. "The task found me," he said. "I sometimes wish it hadn't, but then I find some new piece of information and," he smiled wryly, "I remember how important it is that the past isn't lost. History has lessons to teach us, and perhaps one day I'll stumble on some secret that will benefit us."

"Like black magic?" Lorkin suggested.

Dannyl grimaced. "Maybe something that doesn't involve as much risk and sacrifice."

Lorkin felt his heart skip. "Another sort of defensive magic? That would be a great thing to find." *It would not only free the Guild from having to use black magic, but could either provide a defence against the Sachakans, or persuade the Sachakans to give up black magic and slavery and join the Allied Lands. If I found such a thing . . . but this is Dannyl's idea, not mine . . .*

Dannyl shrugged. "I might find nothing at all. But to find the truth, record and preserve it, is achievement enough, for me."

Well . . . if Dannyl doesn't care . . . would he mind if someone else searched for an alternative to black magic? Would he mind if I did? A tingle of hope ran down Lorkin's spine.

Lorkin took a deep breath. "Could . . . could I look at the work you've done so far?"

The older magician's eyebrows rose. "Of course. I'll be interested to hear what you think of it. You might notice something I haven't." He looked down the street, then shrugged. "Why don't you join Tayend and me for dinner? Afterwards I'll show you my notes and sources, and explain the gaps in history I'm trying to plug."

Lorkin found himself nodding. "Thank you." If he went back to his room in the Guild, he'd only end up alternating between brooding over Beriya and telling himself his life was better without her. "I'm sure it'll be fascinating."

Dannyl gestured toward his house, a grand two-storey building he had rented since retiring from the position of Guild Ambassador to Elyne. Though it was known that Dannyl and Tayend were more than mere friends, little was said about it these days. Dannyl had chosen to live in the city rather than the Guild grounds because, as he said, "it's an agreement of sorts: the Guild pretends blindness, so we give them nothing to see".

"Do you need to return to the Guild first?"

Lorkin shook his head. "No, but if you need to give Tayend and the servants some warning—"

"No, they won't mind. Tayend brings unexpected visitors to the house all the time. Our servants are used to it."

He beckoned and started toward his home, and Lorkin fell into step beside him.

CHAPTER 3

SAFE PLACES, DANGEROUS
DESTINATIONS

"**H**is desk is always such a mess," Tayend told Lorkin. As Dannyl frowned at the scholar, Tayend grinned, the few lines crossing his forehead smoothing out. *Nobody would guess that he's more than forty years old*, Dannyl thought. *I'm turning into a wrinkly skeleton while Tayend . . .* Tayend looked better than ever, he noted. He'd put on a little weight, but it suited him.

"It only *looks* disorganised," Dannyl said, not for the first time. "*I* know where everything is."

Tayend chuckled. "I'm sure it's just a ploy to ensure nobody can steal his research and ideas." He grinned at Lorkin. "Now, don't let him bore you to death. If you feel your mind is starting to shrivel up, come talk to me, and we'll open another bottle of wine."

Lorkin smiled and nodded. "I will."

The scholar waved a hand in farewell, then effected a jaunty walk as he left the room. Dannyl resisted rolling his eyes and sighing, and turned back to Sonea's son. The young man was eyeing the piles of documents and books on Dannyl's desk doubtfully.

"There is order to the madness," Dannyl assured him. "It starts at the back. That first pile contains everything relating to the earliest records of magic. It's full of descriptions of places like the Tomb of White Tears, and a lot of conjecture about what the glyphs suggest magic was used for." Dannyl took out the sketches Tayend had made when they had visited the Tombs over twenty years before. He pointed out the glyph of a man kneeling before a woman, who was touching his upraised palms. "This glyph means 'high magic'."

"Black magic?"

"Perhaps. But it might be Healing magic. It may be only coincidence that our predecessors called black magic 'higher magic'." Dannyl leafed through the pile and another sketch, this time of a crescent moon and hand, flipped into view.

"What is that?" Lorkin asked.

"A symbol we found in the ruined city of Armje. It was a symbol that represented the royal family of that city like an incal symbolises a Kyralian House. Armje is thought to have been abandoned over two thousand years ago."

"What was the symbol written on?"

"It was carved above house lintels, and we saw it once on what I suspect was a blood ring." Dannyl smiled as he remembered Dem Ladeiri, the eccentric noble and collector he and Tayend had stayed with in an old castle in the Elyne mountains, near Armje. Then he felt his smile fade as he remembered the underground chamber he'd found in the ruins, called the "Cavern of Ultimate Punishment". Strange crystalline walls had attacked him with magic and would have killed him if Tayend hadn't dragged him out just as his shield had failed.

The former High Lord, Akkarin, had asked Dannyl to keep the Cavern a secret to prevent other magicians stumbling inside to their death. After the Ichani Invasion, Dannyl had told the new High Lord, Balkan, of the Cavern, and the Guild leader had ordered him to record what he knew, but also to keep it secret. When the book was finished, Balkan would reconsider whether to allow others to know of the place.

Has Balkan sent anyone there to investigate? I can't imagine the Warrior would be able to resist trying to find out how the Cavern works. Especially as it has so much potential as a defensive weapon.

"So they knew how to make blood rings two thousand years ago?"

Dannyl looked up at Lorkin, then nodded. "And who knows what else? But that knowledge was lost." He pointed to the second, smaller pile. "This is all I have relating to the time before the Sachakan Empire conquered Kyralia and Elyne, over a thousand years ago. The few records that we have only survived from that time because they are copies, and they suggest that there were only two or three magicians, and that those had limited skills and power."

"So if the people who knew how to make blood rings, and whatever high magic was, died without passing that knowledge on . . ."

". . . whether because they didn't trust anyone enough to teach them, or they never found anyone gifted enough to teach."

Lorkin looked thoughtful – and definitely not bored, Dannyl noted with relief. The young magician's attention moved to the third pile.

"Three centuries of Sachakan rule," Dannyl told him. "I've more than doubled the information we have from that time, though that wasn't hard because there was so little to begin with."

"A time when Kyralians were slaves," Lorkin said, his expression grim.

"And slave owners," Dannyl reminded him. "I believe that the Sachakans brought higher magic to Kyralia."

Lorkin stared at him in disbelief. "Surely they wouldn't have taught their enemy black magic!"

"Why not? After Kyralia had been conquered it became part of the Empire. The Sachakans didn't kill every noble, only those who would not swear allegiance to the Empire. There would have been intermarriage, and mixed blood heirs. Three hundred years is a long time. Kyralians would have been citizens of Sachaka."

"But they still fought to regain their land, and to get rid of slavery."

"Yes." Dannyl patted the top of the pile. "And that is clearly recorded in documents and letters leading up to and following the emperor's decision to grant Kyralia and Elyne their independence. Both countries abolished slavery, though there was some resistance."

Lorkin looked at the pile of books, documents and notes. "That's not what we're taught in the University."

Dannyl chuckled. "No. And the version of history you were taught was even less sanitised than what I learned as a novice." He tapped the next pile. "My generation never knew that Kyralian magicians once used black magic, taking strength from their apprentices in exchange for magical teaching. It was one of the most difficult truths for us to accept."

The younger magician eyed the fourth pile of books with cautious curiosity. "Are they the books my father found under the Guild?"

"Some of them are copies of what he unearthed. With any dangerous information about black magic removed."

"How are you going to write a history of that time without including information about black magic?"

Dannyl shrugged. "So long as there's nothing instructive, there is no danger of anyone learning how to use it from what I write."

"But . . . Mother says that you have to learn black magic from the mind of a black magician. Surely you can't learn it from books?"

"We don't think it can be, but we're not taking the risk."

Lorkin nodded, his expression thoughtful. "So . . . the Sachakan War is next? That's a big stack of books."

"Yes." Dannyl regarded the generous pile of books and records beside the "independence" one. "I sent out word that I wanted records from that time, and I've received a steady stream of diaries, accounts and records from throughout the Allied Lands ever since." At the top of the pile was a little book he'd found in the Great Library twenty years ago, that had first alerted him to the possibility that the Guild's version of history might be wrong.

"You must have that time well covered."

"Not completely." Dannyl told him. "Most of these records are from lands other than Kyralia. There are still gaps in the history. We know that Kyralian magicians drove the Sachakan invaders out and won the war, and then conquered and ruled Sachaka for a time. We know that the wasteland that weakened the country wasn't created for several years after the war. But we don't know how they kept the Sachakan magicians under control, or how they created the wasteland." *And what is the treasure that the Elynes claimed to have loaned or given to the*

45

Kyralians, which was then lost, along with its secrets? Dannyl felt a familiar, strangely pleasant frustration. There were still mysteries to be explored, and this was one of the more intriguing ones.

"Why don't you have records from Kyralia?"

Dannyl sighed. "It's possible they were destroyed when the Guild banned black magic. Or they might have been lost during the war. So much of history has been muddled. For instance: we're taught that Imardin was levelled during the Sachakan War, but I now have maps from before and after the war that show a similar street pattern. A few hundred years later, however, we have an entirely new street pattern – the one we know today."

"So . . . the age of the maps is wrong, or something levelled the city later. Did anything dramatic happen after the Sachakan War?"

Dannyl nodded and picked up the book on top of the next, much smaller pile. Lorkin hummed in recognition.

"The Guild Record." His eyes widened in understanding. "The Mad Apprentice did it!" Lorkin reached out and took the book, flicking to the final entries. "*It is over,*" he read. "*When Alyk told me the news I dared not believe it, but an hour ago I climbed the stairs of the Lookout and saw the truth with my own eyes. It is true. Tagin is dead. Only he could have created such destruction in his final moments.* His power was released and destroyed the city."

Dannyl sighed, shook his head, took the book off Lorkin and put it back on the pile. "Tagin had just defeated the Guild. He could not have had that much power left. Not enough to level a city."

"Perhaps you're underestimating him, as the Guild of the time clearly did."

46

The young magician's eyebrows rose expectantly. Dannyl almost smiled at the challenge. Lorkin had been an intelligent novice, willing to question all of his teachers.

"Perhaps I am." Dannyl looked down at the small pile of documents and books. "The Guild . . . well, it is as though they didn't set out only to wipe out all knowledge of black magic, but also the embarrassing fact that a mere apprentice had nearly destroyed them. If it weren't for Recordkeeper Gilken, we wouldn't even have the books Akkarin found to tell us what happened."

Gilken had saved and buried information about black magic out of fear that the Guild would need it for the land's defence one day. *We had five hundred years of peace in which to forget about the stash, that we had ever used black magic at all, and that over the mountains our ancient enemy, Sachaka, still practised it. If Akkarin hadn't found the stash – and learned black magic – we would now be dead or slaves.*

"The final pile," Lorkin said. Dannyl saw that Lorkin was looking at a thick, leather-bound notebook at the end of the table.

"Yes." Dannyl picked it up. "It contains the stories I collected from those who witnessed the Ichani Invasion."

"Including my mother's?"

"Of course."

Lorkin nodded, then smiled wryly. "Well, that must be the one part of history you don't need to do more research on."

"No," Dannyl agreed.

The young magician's gaze moved across the piles of books, documents and records. "I'd like to read what you have. And . . . is there a way I can help with the research?"

Dannyl regarded Lorkin in surprise. He would never have

guessed that Sonea's son had an interest in history. Perhaps the young man was bored and looking for something to put his mind to. He might lose interest quickly, especially once he realised that Dannyl had already exhausted all sources of information. There was little chance either of them would ever fill the gaps in history.

If he loses interest, there will be no harm done. I can't see why I shouldn't let him give it a try.

And a fresh eye, a different approach, might unveil new discoveries.

And it would be good to have someone here in Kyralia familiar with the work Dannyl had done so far, if he decided to leave to pursue any new sources of information.

Which might happen sooner rather than later.

Since the Ichani Invasion, Sachaka and Kyralia had been watching each other closely. Fortunately, both sides were keen to avoid future conflicts. Both had sent an Ambassador and an assistant to the other country. No other magicians were allowed to cross the border, however.

Dannyl had questioned the Guild Ambassadors sent to Sachaka over the years, asking them to seek out material for his book. They had provided some information, but they did not know what to look for, and what they sent had contained tantalising hints at uncensored records with a fresh perspective on historical events.

The position of Ambassador became available every few years, but Dannyl hadn't applied for it. Partly because he had been afraid to. The thought of entering a land of black magicians was daunting. He was used to taking for granted that he was one of the powerful people in his society. In Sachaka he would not only be weak and vulnerable, but by all accounts Sachakan higher magicians regarded magicians who did not know black magic with distaste, distrust or derision.

They were growing used to the idea though, he'd been told. They treated Guild Ambassadors with more respect these days. They'd even protested when the most recent Ambassador had to return to Kyralia, due to problems with his family's finances. They had actually grown to like him.

Which left a gap open for a new Ambassador that Dannyl found too hard to resist. He had worked in the position before, in Elyne, so he felt confident that the Higher Magicians would consider him for the place. If it did not work out he could simply come home early – and he would not be the first to do so. While he was in Sachaka he could seek records that might fill in the gaps in his history of magic, and perhaps discover new magical histories.

"Lord Dannyl?"

Dannyl looked up at Lorkin, then smiled. "I'd be delighted to have a fellow magician help me in my research. When would you like to start?"

"Would tomorrow be convenient?" Lorkin looked at the table. "I have a lot of reading to do, I suspect."

"Of course it is," Dannyl replied. "Though . . . we should ask Tayend what he has planned. Let's go talk to him now – and have that bottle of wine."

As he led the young magician to the guest room where Tayend usually relaxed during most evenings, Dannyl's thoughts returned to Sachaka.

I have run out of sources. I can think of nowhere else I might find the missing pieces of my history. The opportunity has come and I think I have the courage to take it.

But the other reason he had never sought to visit Sachaka was that it meant leaving Tayend behind. The scholar would have to gain permission from the Elyne king to go to Sachaka, and it was unlikely he would be granted it. Partly this was because Tayend wasn't well known or in favour in court, and hadn't been so even before he'd moved to Kyralia to live with Dannyl. Partly it was because he was a "lad" – a man who preferred men over women. Sachakan society wasn't as accepting of lads as Elyne society was. It was more like Kyralian society – such things were hidden and ignored. The Elyne king would not want to risk offending a land that could still easily defeat it by sending a man they would disapprove of into their midst.

But what about me? Why do I think the Kyralian king or the Guild won't reject my application for the same reason?

The truth was, Tayend wasn't as good as Dannyl at hiding what he was. Not long after settling in Imardin, the scholar had gathered a circle of friends around him. He'd been delighted to find there were as many lads in the Kyralian Houses as in the Elyne elite class, and they had enthusiastically embraced his Elyne habit of holding parties. They called themselves the Secret Club. Yet the club was not particularly secret. Plenty in Kyralian society knew of it, and many had expressed disapproval.

Dannyl knew that his discomfort came from long years of hiding his nature. *Maybe I'm a coward, or perhaps overly prudent, but I'd rather keep my personal life . . . well . . . personal. With Tayend I never got the choice. He never asked me how I wanted to live, or if I was comfortable with the whole of Kyralia knowing what we are.*

There was more to his resentment than that, however. Over

the years, more and more of Tayend's attention had gone to his friends. Though there were a few in the group whose company Dannyl enjoyed, most were spoilt higher-class brats. And sometimes Tayend was more like them than the young man Dannyl had travelled with all those years ago.

Dannyl sighed. He did not want to travel with the man Tayend had become. He was a little afraid that being stuck with each other in another land would cause them to part permanently. He also could not help wondering if some time apart would make them appreciate each other's company more.

But while a few weeks' or months' separation might do us good, could we survive two years apart?

As he entered the guest room and found that Tayend had already opened the bottle and drunk half the contents, he shook his head.

If he was ever going to fill in the gaps of this history of magic – this great work of his life – he could not sit around hoping that someone would send him the right record or document. He had to seek the answers for himself, even if it meant risking his life, or leaving Tayend behind.

One thing I'm sure of. For all that there are sides of Tayend that I don't like, I care enough about him to not want to risk his life. He's going to want to come with me, and I'm going to refuse to take him.

And Tayend was not going to be happy about it. Not happy at all.

She hadn't grown any taller since Cery had last seen her. Her dark hair had been cut badly, uneven where it barely touched her shoulders. Her fringe swept sharply to one side, covering one of her knife-slash straight brows. And her eyes . . . those eyes that had always made him weak since the first time he'd seen her. Large, dark and expressive.

But at the moment all they expressed was a ruthless, unblinking determination as she bartered with a customer almost half again her height and weight. Cery couldn't hear what was being said, but her confidence and defiance stirred a foolish pride.

Anyi. My daughter, he thought. *My only daughter. And now my only living child . . .*

Something wrenched inside him as memories of his sons' broken bodies rushed in. He pushed them away, but the shock and fear lingered. He could not let the grief distract him, for his daughter's sake as well as his own. For all he knew, someone was watching and waiting for a moment of weakness, ready to strike.

"What should I do, Gol?" he murmured. They were in a private room on the top floor of a bolhouse, which overlooked the market his daughter's stall belonged to.

His bodyguard stirred, started to turn toward the window, then stopped himself. He looked at Cery, his gaze uncertain.

"Don't know. Seems to me there's danger in talking to her and danger in not."

"And wasting time deciding is the same as deciding not to."

"Yes. How much do you trust Donia?"

Cery considered Gol's question. The owner of the bolhouse, who offered various "services" on the side, was an old childhood friend. Cery had helped her establish the place when her husband, Cery's old friend Harrin, died of a fever five years ago. His men prevented gangs from extracting protection money from her. Even if she hadn't had such a long connection with him, or she'd not been grateful for the help he'd given her, she owed him money and knew the ways of Thieves well enough to know you did not betray them without consequences.

"Better than anyone else."

Gol gave a short laugh. "Which isn't much."

"No, but I've already got her keeping an eye on Anyi, though she don't know why. She hasn't let me down."

"Then it won't seem odd if you ask for the girl to be brought to a face-to-face, right?"

"Not odd, but . . . she'd be curious." Cery sighed. "Let's get this over with."

Gol straightened. "I'll go sort things, and make sure no one's listening."

Cery considered the man, then nodded. He glanced out of the window as his bodyguard headed toward the door and noticed a new customer had replaced the last. Anyi watched as the man ran a finger across the blade of one of her knives to test its edge. "And make sure her stall is watched while she's here."

"Of course."

After some minutes had passed, four men emerged from the bolhouse and approached Anyi's stall. Cery noted that the other stallholders pretended to pay no attention. One of the men spoke to Anyi. She shook her head and glared at him. When he reached out toward her arm she stepped back and, with lightning speed, produced a knife and pointed it at him. He raised his hands, palms outward.

A long conversation followed. Anyi lowered the knife slowly, but did not put it away or stop glaring at him. A few times she glanced fleetingly toward the bolhouse. Finally, she raised her chin and, as he stepped back from her stall, strode past and toward the bolhouse, putting away her knife.

Cery let out the breath he'd been holding, and realised his stomach was all unsettled and his heart was beating too fast. Suddenly he wished he'd managed to sleep last night. He wanted to be fully alert. Not to make any mistakes. Not to miss a moment of this one meeting with his daughter that he hoped he could afford to allow himself. He hadn't spoken to her in years, and then she had still been a child. Now she was a young woman. Young men probably sought her attention and her bed . . .

Let's not think too much about that, he told himself.

He heard voices and footsteps in the stairwell outside the room, coming closer. Taking a deep breath, he turned to face the doorway. There was a moment of silence, then a familiar male voice said something encouraging, and a single pair of footsteps continued.

As she peered around the doorway, Cery considered smiling, but knew that he would not be able to find enough genuine good humour for it to be convincing. He settled on returning her stare with what he hoped was a welcoming seriousness.

She blinked, her eyes widened, then she scowled and strode into the room.

"You!" she said. "I might've guessed it'd be you."

Her eyes were ablaze with anger and accusation. She stopped a few steps away. He did not flinch at her stare, though it stirred a familiar guilt.

"Yes. Me," he said. "Sit down. I need to talk to you."

"Well I don't want to talk to you!" she declared and turned to leave.

"As if you have any choice."

She stopped and looked over her shoulder, her eyes narrowed. Slowly she turned to face him, crossing her arms.

"What do you want?" she asked, then sighed dramatically. He almost smiled at that. The sullen resignation laced with contempt was what many a father endured from youngsters her age. But her resignation came more from the knowledge he was a Thief, not any respect for fatherly authority.

"To warn you. Your life is . . . in even more danger than it usually is. There's a good chance someone will try to kill you soon."

Her expression did not change. "Oh? Why is that?"

He shrugged. "The mere unfortunate fact that you are my daughter."

"Well, I've survived that well enough so far."

"This is different. This is a lot . . . wilder."

She rolled her eyes. "Nobody uses that word any more."

"Then I am a nobody." He frowned. "I am serious, Anyi. Do you think I'd risk our lives by meeting with you if I wasn't sure not meeting could be worse?"

All contempt and anger fled from her face, but left her with no expression he could read. Then she looked away.

"Why are you so sure?"

He drew in a breath and let it out slowly. *Because my wife and sons are dead.* Pain swelled within him at the thought. *I'm not sure I can say it aloud.* He cast about, then took another deep breath.

"Because, as of last night, you are my only living child," he told her.

Her eyes slowly widened as the news sank in. She swallowed and closed her eyes. For a moment she remained still, a crease between her brows, then she opened her eyes and fixed him with her stare again.

"Have you told Sonea?"

He frowned at the question. Why had she asked? Her mother had always been a touch jealous of Sonea, perhaps sensing that he had once been in love with the slum girl turned magician. Surely Anyi hadn't inherited Vesta's jealousy. Or did Anyi know more about Cery's continuing and secret link to the Guild than she ought to?

How to answer such a question? Should he answer at all? He considered changing the subject, but found himself curious to know how she would react to the truth.

"I have," he told her. Then he shrugged. "Along with other information."

Anyi nodded and said nothing, giving frustratingly little away of her reason for asking. She sighed and shifted her weight to one leg.

"What do you suggest I do?"

"Is there somewhere safe you can go? People you trust? I'd offer to protect you except . . . well, let's just say it turned out your mother made the right decision leaving me and . . ." He heard bitterness in his voice and shifted to other reasons. "My own people may have been turned. It would be better if you did not rely on them. Except Gol, of course. Though . . . it would be wise if we had a way of contacting each other."

She nodded and he was heartened to see her straighten with determination. "I'll be fine," she told him. "I have . . . friends."

Her lips pressed into a thin line. That was all she was going to tell him, he guessed. Wise move.

"Good," he said. He stood up. "Take care, Anyi."

She regarded him thoughtfully, and for a moment the

corner of her mouth twitched. He felt a sudden rush of hope that she understood why he had kept away from her all these years.

Then she turned on her heel and stalked out of the room without waiting for permission or saying goodbye.

CHAPTER 4

NEW COMMITMENTS

The trees and shrubs of the Guild gardens cooled and slowed the late summer wind to a pleasant breeze. Within one of the garden "rooms", well shaded by a large ornamental pachi tree, Lorkin and Dekker sat on one of the seats arranged here and there for magicians to rest on. As the last shreds of his hangover began to ease, Lorkin leaned back against the back of the seat and closed his eyes. The sound of birds mingled with that of distant voices and footsteps – and the shrill sound of taunts and protests somewhere behind him.

Dekker turned to look at the same time as Lorkin. Behind them was a screen of shrubs and trees, so they both stood up to peer over the top of the foliage. Over the other side, four boys had surrounded another and were pushing their victim about.

"Stu-pid lo-wie," they sang. "Got no fam-ly. Al-ways gri-my. Al-ways smel-ly."

"Hai!" Dekker shouted. "Stop that! Or I'll get you volunteered to help in the hospices."

Lorkin grimaced. His mother had never been happy with Lady Vinara's idea of punishing novices by making them help in the hospices. She said they'd never consider the work worthwhile or noble if they were expected to want to avoid it. But she never had enough volunteers, so she couldn't bring herself to protest. Some of those sent to her for punishing had actually chosen the healing discipline because working with her had inspired them, but they were mocked quietly by their fellow novices.

The novices muttered apologies and fled in different directions. As Lorkin and Dekker sat down again, two magicians appeared in the entrance to the garden room.

"Ah! I thought I heard your voice, Dekker," Reater said. Perler's worried frown faded as he recognised his brother's friends. "Mind if we join you?"

"Not at all," Dekker said, gesturing to the opposite bench seat.

Lorkin looked from one brother to another, wondering at the reason for the frown Perler had been wearing. Reater seemed far too glad to have stumbled upon them.

"Perler got some bad news this morning," Reater said. He turned to his brother. "Tell them."

Perler glanced at Reater. "Not bad for you, I hope." His brother shrugged and did not answer, so he sighed and looked at Dekker. "Lord Maron has quit. It's going to take longer than he thought to fix his family's troubles. So I'm not going back to Sachaka."

"You don't get to assist the new Ambassador?" Lorkin asked.

Perler shrugged. "I could if I wanted to. But . . ." He looked at his brother. "I have a few family matters to take care of, too."

Reater winced.

"So who is going to replace him?" Dekker wondered.

"Someone said Lord Dannyl has applied." Reater grinned. "Perhaps he wants to check out the local—"

"Reater," Perler said sternly.

"What? Everyone knows he's a lad."

"Which doesn't make it funny when you make crude jokes about it. Grow up and get over it." He rolled his eyes. "Besides, Lord Dannyl won't want to go. He's too busy researching that book of his."

Lorkin felt his heart skip. "He told me last night that his research was going slowly. Maybe . . . maybe he's hoping to do some research there."

Reater looked sidelong at his brother. "That change your mind? Ow!" He rubbed his arm where Perler had just punched it. "That hurt."

"Which was the point." Perler looked thoughtful. "It'll be interesting to see if anyone volunteers to be his assistant. Most people might be willing to ignore Lord Dannyl's ways, but risking speculation by offering to assist him is probably beyond most."

Lorkin shrugged. "I'd go."

The others turned to stare at him. Lorkin looked around at their shocked faces, and laughed.

"No, I'm not a lad. But Lord Dannyl has always been easy to get along with and his research is interesting – and worthwhile. I'd be proud to take part in it." To his surprise, they continued to look worried. Except Perler, he noted.

"But . . . Sachaka," Reater said.

"Would that be wise?" Dekker asked.

Lorkin looked from one to the other. "Perler survived. Why not me?"

"Because your parents killed some Sachakans a few years back," Dekker pointed out in a tone suggesting Lorkin was stupid. "They tend to take exception to that."

Lorkin spread his hands to encompass the Guild. "So did all magicians during the battle, as did the novices. What difference is there in that to what my parents did?"

Dekker opened his mouth, but nothing came out and he closed it again. He looked at Perler, who chuckled.

"Don't look to me for support on this one," the older magician said. "Lorkin's parentage might make him a little more interesting to the Sachakans than other magicians, but so long as he doesn't point it out all the time, I doubt he'd be in any more danger than I was." He looked at Lorkin. "Still, I'd let the Higher Magicians decide that. There may be a reason why you shouldn't go that they've kept to themselves."

Lorkin turned to regard Dekker triumphantly. His friend looked at him, frowned, then shook his head.

"Don't go volunteering just to prove me wrong."

Lorkin laughed. "Would I do that?"

"Probably." Dekker smiled wryly. "Or just to annoy me. Knowing what your family is like, you'll turn out to be instrumental in convincing the Sachakans to give up slavery and join with the Allied Lands, and within a few years I'll find myself actually teaching Warrior Skills to Sachakan novices."

Smothering the urge to grimace, Lorkin forced a smile. *There it is again. This expectation that I'll do something important. But that's never going to happen while I sit around in the Guild, doing nothing.*

"That'll do for a start," he said. "Anything else?"

Dekker made a rude noise and looked away. "Invent a wine that doesn't cause hangovers and I'll forgive you anything."

Stepping inside the University, Sonea and Rothen passed through the rear entry hall into the main corridor. It led directly to a huge room, three storeys high, within the middle of the building known as the Great Hall. Glass panels covered the roof, allowing light to fill the space.

Contained within this room was an older, simpler building: the Guildhall. It had been the original home of the Guild, and when the grander structure of the University had been built around it the old building's internal walls had been removed and the interior turned into a hall for regular Meets and occasional Hearings.

Today's gathering was an open Hearing, which meant that while only the Higher Magicians were required to attend, any other magician was free to do so as well. Sonea was both heartened and dismayed to see the large crowd of magicians waiting at the far end of the hall. *It's good to see so many taking an interest, but I can't help doubting that many are in favour of the petition.*

The Higher Magicians were hovering around the side entrance of the Guildhall. High Lord Balkan stood with his arms crossed and was frowning down at the man speaking to him. His white robes emphasised his height and broad shoulders, but also betrayed a softness and fullness where he had once been muscular. His duties as High Lord kept him away from practising Warrior Skills, she guessed. Not that magical battles kept a magician that fit, anyway.

The man he was frowning at was Administrator Osen. Sonea could not see the blue of the Administrator's robe without remembering his predecessor and feeling a pang of guilt and sadness. Administrator Lorlen had died during the Ichani Invasion. Though Osen was as efficient as Lorlen, he lacked his predecessor's warmth. And he had never forgiven her for learning black magic and joining Akkarin in exile.

Three other magicians waited patiently together, watching

the rest and noting Sonea's and Rothen's approach. Sonea had grown to like Lord Peakin, the Head of Alchemists, in the last twenty years. He was open-minded and inventive, and as he'd grown older and settled into his role he'd revealed a wry sense of humour and compassion. Lady Vinara had survived the war and seemed determined to remain as Head of Healers for many years yet, despite advancing old age. Her hair was now completely white and her skin a mass of wrinkles, but her eyes were sharp and alert.

Seeing the Head of Warriors always roused a sour and uneasy feeling in Sonea. Lord Garrel had run the affairs of his discipline without scandal or major failure, and was always stiffly polite around her, but she could not forget that he had allowed and even encouraged his adopted novice, Regin, to torment her during their early years in the University. She might have been able to overlook that history if he wasn't also linked with the Kyralian Houses' clearing areas of the slums, involved in ruthless political manipulations, and rumoured to be profiting from dealings with Thieves.

How can I be judgemental, when I had a Thief in my rooms this morning? But Cery is different. At least, I hope he is. I hope he still has some *principles – some lines he won't cross. And I'm not involved in any of his business. I'm just a friend.*

Near to the Heads of Disciplines stood three more magicians. Two were Heads of Studies, Lord Telano and Lord Erayk, and the other was Director Jerrik. The old University Director had barely changed. He was still the same grumpy, sour man, but he was now stooped and wrinkles had made his scowl permanent, even during one of his rare smiles. She had been called to his office more than a few times in recent years, Lorkin being the perpetrator as often as the victim of some novice prank that had gone too far. *I'd wager he's relieved Lorkin and his friends have graduated.*

Rothen, as Head of Alchemic Studies, was clearly intending to join these three. It had always amused her how the Higher Magicians gravitated to those of the same rank. Yet as she caught sight of a figure striding toward them, wearing the same black robes as her, she felt no desire to do the same.

Black Magician Kallen.

After the Guild had elected new Higher Magicians to replace those that had been lost in the Ichani Invasion, they had long debated over how to tackle the issue of black magic . . . and her. They knew they must not lose the knowledge of it again, in case any Sachakans sought once more to overtake Kyralia, but they feared that anyone they allowed to have that knowledge might seek to take control of Kyralia themselves.

It had happened in the past, after all, when Tagin, the Mad Apprentice, had learned black magic and almost destroyed the Guild. The Guild of that time had felt they must ban black magic completely to prevent any individual abusing that power again.

Unfortunately, that had left the Guild and all the Allied Lands vulnerable to attack.

The current Guild's solution had been to allow only two magicians to know black magic. One could prevent the other from seizing power. Each was charged with monitoring their fellow black magician, watching for any sign of evil ambitions. Servants were regularly questioned, their minds read, for any sign that the magician they served was strengthening himself, or herself.

Sonea had no choice but to agree. It was not as if she could unlearn black magic. She had been introduced to several of the candidates for the position of her watcher, and asked for her opinion. She hadn't liked or disliked Kallen, whom she had not met before as he had been an Ambassador in Lan before the invasion. But the Higher Magicians had seen something in him that they liked, and she had soon discovered it was his unfaltering dedication to whatever purpose he was given.

Unfortunately, she was the focus of his purpose in the Guild now. While he was never rude, his scrutiny was unwavering and exhausting. It would have been flattering, if it weren't so annoying – and completely necessary. *It was a good decision. When I'm gone someone must replace me. Hopefully the Guild will choose well, but if it doesn't then perhaps Kallen's caution will save it.*

Keeping her attention on Kallen, she watched him approach. He stared back at her, face impassive. She had not been as dedicated in watching Kallen as he had been at monitoring her. It was not so easy, when you had a son to raise and hospices to run. But she effected an air of attentive watchfulness whenever Kallen was around, hoping it would reassure the few magicians to whom it may have occurred that he needed monitoring as much as the former exiled slum girl who had risen to a powerful position too early and far beyond what she deserved.

A pause in the murmur of voices around her brought her attention back to Administrator Osen.

"Novice Director Narren is in Elyne and the King's Advisers will not be attending," he told them. "Since the rest of us are present, we may as well begin."

The Higher Magicians followed him through the side entrance of the Guildhall and moved to their places. Seats had been built in steep tiers at the end of the room, the higher status positions at the top and the lesser at floor level. Sonea climbed to her place beside High Lord Balkan and watched as the doors at the far end were opened and the room filled with magicians. Two small groups gathered on either side of what was considered the front of the hall – the space before the Higher Magicians. One would be the petitioners, the other the opposition. The rest of the magicians moved to seats on either side of the hall.

Osen began the Hearing as soon as all were settled.

"I call on Lord Pendel, leader of the petitioners, to state their case."

A handsome young man, whose father ran a large metalworking business, stepped forward.

"When allowances were made for men and women of the lower classes of Imardin to enter the Guild two decades ago, many wise and practical rules were set down," Pendel began, reading from a piece of paper clutched in his hand. "But such an unexpected and necessarily rushed change to Guild practices included, not surprisingly, a few rules that have proven, in time, to be impractical."

The young man's voice was steady and clear, Sonea noted approvingly. He was a good choice as spokesman for the petitioners.

"One such rule states that novices and magicians must not associate with criminals or people of low repute," Pendel continued. "While there have been cases where novices have deservedly been removed from the Guild and denied access to magic due to continued association with unsavoury individuals or groups in the city, there are many more cases where the interpretation of this rule has led to injustice. In the last twenty years the latter cases have shown that the general interpretation of 'low repute' includes anyone of common beginnings. This has unfairly kept fathers and mothers apart from their sons and daughters, causing unnecessary grief and resentment."

Pendel paused to look around the room. "This rule paints the Guild as a hypocritical institution, as there have been no cases of higher-class magicians being punished for breaking this rule, despite them frequently being seen visiting gaming houses, brazier houses and brothels."

He looked up at the Higher Magicians and smiled nervously.

"Despite this, we do not request that the higher-class magicians and novices be more closely watched and restricted. We only ask that the existing rule be abolished so that those of us born in the lower classes be able to visit our family and friends without penalty." He bowed. "Thank you for hearing our petition."

Osen nodded, then turned to the other small gathering of magicians standing to one side of the front.

"I call on Lord Regin, as speaker for the opposers, to come forward and respond."

As a man emerged from the opposition, Sonea felt an old dislike stir. With it came memories of being taunted and tricked, of having her work being sabotaged, of being regarded as a thief after a stolen pen had been found in her possession, and of being the object of speculation when vicious rumours spread that her relationship with Rothen was more than just that of novice and teacher.

Those memories brought anger, but there were others that still made her shudder. Memories of being hunted through the corridors of the University, of being cornered by a gang of novices, of being tortured, humiliated and left magically and physically exhausted.

The leader of that gang, and mastermind of all her suffering in those early years at the University, had been Regin. Though she had challenged and beaten him in a fair fight in the Arena, though he had bravely risked his life during the Ichani Invasion, and though he had even apologised for all that he had done to her, she could not look at him without feeling an echo of the humiliation and fear she had once endured. And those emotions brought anger and dislike.

I ought to get over it, she thought. *But I'm not sure I can. Just as I don't think I'll ever stop feeling smug whenever one of the magicians from the Houses is introduced without his or her family name and title announced.*

Along with the decision to accept entrants to the Guild from outside the Houses, it had been decided that family and House names would no longer be used during Guild ceremonies. All who became magicians were expected to risk their lives to defend the Allied Lands, so all should be shown the same level of respect. Since Imardians born outside the Houses had no family or House name, the habit of stating those names for those who did was abandoned completely.

If Regin felt belittled by the omission of his family and House name, he did not show any sign of it. He was not at all unsettled by the attention that turned to him either. He almost looked bored. He carried no notes to read from, but simply scanned the room once and then began to speak.

"Before considering if this rule should be changed or abolished, we ask that all remember why it was created. Not to prevent good people from visiting their family, or even to spoil a harmless evening's entertainment, but to prevent magicians of any origin or standing being drawn into criminal acts or employment. The rule is a deterrent as much as it is a guideline for behaviour. To abolish it would be to lose a valuable motivation for magicians to resist those who seek to recruit or corrupt them."

As Regin continued, Sonea regarded him thoughtfully. She remembered the young novice who had risked his life to bait an Ichani during the invasion. Since the Ichani Invasion he had been nothing but respectful around her, and occasionally he'd even spoken out in support of her.

So Rothen thinks Regin's character has improved, she thought. *I still wouldn't trust Regin though, knowing what he was like as a novice. I'm sure, if he learned that I had met with a Thief who had snuck into the grounds of the Guild itself, he'd be the first to report me for breaking this rule.*

"It is up to the Higher Magicians to interpret whether a character is criminal or of low repute, and we should leave it that way," Regin said. "Instead of abolishing the rule, we should be more thorough and fair in investigating the activities of all novices and magicians."

The annoying thing is, he has a point, she thought. *Abolishing the rule will make it harder to stop magicians involving themselves in underworld plots. But the Guild is not applying the rule consistently enough to have much effect. It's next to useless as a deterrent because the rich novices know it's not going to be enforced in their case. If we get rid of it we'll stop wasting time and attention on novices whose mothers are whores, and then, perhaps, we'll start looking a bit harder at those magicians whose rich families have dealings with Thieves.*

Regin finished and bowed. As he walked back to join the petition opposers, Administrator Osen stepped forward.

"This is a matter which will require much discussion and consideration," he told the assembled magicians. "It is also not clear if the decision should be made by the Higher Magicians or by general vote. Therefore I am going to postpone a decision until I am convinced which course is best, and give all who wish to offer insight and information on the matter the opportunity to arrange a meeting with me." He bowed. "I declare this Hearing over."

It took Sonea several minutes to descend to the floor of the hall, as Lady Vinara decided to question her about the supplies the hospices were using. When she did finally extract herself she found Rothen standing nearby. As he stepped up to meet her, she felt her heart sink. He wore an expression she had not seen for a long time, but that she had learned to recognise instantly. The one he wore when Lorkin had got into some trouble.

"What has he done now?" she muttered, glancing around to make sure there was nobody close by to hear. The hall was all but empty now. Only Osen and his assistant remained.

"I just heard that Lord Dannyl has applied for the position of Guild Ambassador to Sachaka," Rothen told her.

That's all then. She felt relief flow through her. "That's unexpected. Yet also not surprising. He's been an Ambassador before. Has he finished his book, or abandoned it?"

Rothen shook his head. "Neither, I suspect. He's probably going there in order to explore some new lead."

"Of course. I wonder is he . . ." She stopped as she realised he was still wearing the expression of someone who had to deliver bad news. "What?"

Rothen grimaced. "Lorkin has volunteered to be his assistant."

Sonea froze.

Lorkin.

In Sachaka.

Lorkin had volunteered to go to Sachaka.

She realised she had been gaping at him and closed her mouth. Her heart was pounding. She felt sick. Rothen took her arm and led her out of the Guildhall, then away from the crowds of magicians lingering to discuss the petition. She barely saw them.

Sachakans and Lorkin. They'll kill him. No – they wouldn't dare. But family are obliged to avenge deaths. Even the deaths of outcasts. And if not on the killer, then the offspring . . .

Determination filled her. The Sachakans were not going to harm her son. They weren't, because she was not going to let Lorkin do anything so stupid and dangerous.

"Osen will never agree to it," she found herself saying.

"Why wouldn't he? He can't refuse merely on the basis of parentage."

"I'll appeal to the Higher Magicians. They must know he will be in more danger than any other magician – and that means he'll be a liability. Dannyl can't spend all his time protecting Lorkin. And the Sachakans may refuse to deal with Dannyl once they know who his assistant's father was."

Rothen nodded. "All good points. But it could be that if you say nothing, Lorkin will have time to think about all the ways this could go badly, and change his mind. I suspect the harder you try to stop Lorkin, the more determined he'll be to go."

"I can't take the risk that he won't come to his senses." She stared at him. "How would you feel, if you let him go and something happened to him?"

Rothen paused, then grimaced.

"All right. I guess we have some work to do then."

She felt a wave of affection for him, and smiled.

"Thank you, Rothen."

Dannyl looked around the dining room and sighed with appreciation. One advantage of relinquishing his room in the Guild and moving into a house in the Inner Circle had been the sudden possession of *space*. Though he now spent much of his income as a magician on rent, the indulgence of rooms was worth it. Not only did he have his own generous office, and this tastefully decorated dining room; he also had his own personal library and rooms for guests. Not that he had guests stay often – just the occasional scholar with an interest in Dannyl's history. Tayend, on the other hand, had his Kyralian and Elyne friends stay over all the time.

What are Sachakan houses like? he wondered. *I should find out before I leave. If I leave.*

Administrator Osen had said he could not see any reason why Dannyl wouldn't be given the position of Guild Ambassador to Sachaka, since he was well qualified and nobody else had applied for it.

I'll miss this place, though. I'm sure there'll be times I'll wish I could grab a book from my library, or order my favourite meal from good old Yerak, or . . .

He looked up as footsteps sounded outside the room. There was a pause, then Tayend peered around the archway. His eyes narrowed.

"Who are you, and where is the real Lord Dannyl?"

Dannyl frowned and shook his head. "What are you talking about?"

"I saw your desk." The scholar entered the room and stared at Dannyl with mock suspicion. "It's tidy."

"Ah." Dannyl chuckled. "I'll explain in a moment. Sit down. Yerak is waiting and I'm too hungry for explanations right now."

As Tayend sat down, Dannyl sent a little magic toward the dinner gong, sending the ringer gently tapping on the disc.

"You went to the Guild today?" Tayend asked.

"Yes."

"New books?"

"No, I had a meeting with Administrator Osen."

"Really? What about?"

The door from the kitchens opened, saving Dannyl from answering. Servants filed in with steaming platters and bowls of food. Dannyl and Tayend filled their plates and began eating.

"What did you do today?" Dannyl asked, between mouthfuls.

The scholar shrugged, then related a story he'd been told by another expatriate Elyne that he'd visited that morning, about some Vindo roet smugglers who'd sampled their wares and been found delirious and naked beside a river.

"So what did Administrator Osen have to say?" Tayend asked when the plates had been cleared away.

Dannyl paused, then drew in a deep breath. *I can't put it off any longer.* He looked at Tayend and made his expression serious.

"He said that there weren't any other applicants for the position of Guild Ambassador to Sachaka, so it was very likely I'd be given the position."

Tayend blinked, then his mouth fell open. "Ambassador?" he repeated. "*Sachaka?* You're not serious."

"I am."

Looking away, Tayend's eyes began to blaze with excitement. "I've never been to Sachaka! And there isn't even a sea journey involved."

Dannyl shook his head. "You're not going, Tayend."

"Not going?" Tayend turned to stare at him. "Of course I'm going!"

"I wish I could take you, but . . ." Dannyl spread his hands. "All visitors to Sachaka must be approved, either by the Guild or their king."

"I'll apply to my king, then."

Dannyl shook his head again. "No, Tayend. I . . . I'd rather you didn't. Firstly, it's a dangerous country and while magicians and most traders return alive, nobody knows yet how Sachakans will react to a non-magician noble venturing into their land."

"Then we'll find out."

"There's also decorum to consider. As far as I've been able to discover, Sachakans are neither accepting of lads, nor in a habit of putting us to death. They consider us low status, however, and they often refuse to deal with people they consider too far below them in the social hierarchy. That's not going to be helpful in my role, or in my search for historical records."

"They won't find out, if we're discreet," Tayend said. Then he frowned and turned to glare at Dannyl. "That's why you're doing this, isn't it? More research!"

"Of course. Did you think I'd suddenly manifested a desire to be an Ambassador again, or live in Sachaka?"

Tayend rose and began to pace the room. "It makes sense now." He stopped. "How long does the position go for?"

"Two years, but I can return early if necessary. And to visit home."

Resuming his pacing, Tayend tapped his chin with one finger. Suddenly he scowled.

"Who is going to be your assistant?"

Dannyl smiled. "Lord Lorkin has expressed an interest."

Tayend's shoulders relaxed. "Well, that's a relief. *He* won't have seduced you into leaving me."

"What makes you so sure?"

"Oh, Sonea's son has quite a reputation among the ladies now – since that thing with that girl blew over. Probably highly exaggerated, as always. But there's more than a few who'd like to find out for themselves."

Dannyl felt a twinge of curiosity. "Really? So why haven't they?"

"Apparently he's choosy."

Dannyl leaned back in his chair. "So will I have to keep an eye on him in Sachaka or not?"

A sly look stole over the scholar's face. "I could watch over him. It would free you up to do your research."

"No, Tayend."

Anger and frustration crossed Tayend's face, then he drew in a deep breath and let it out in a huff.

"You had better change your mind," he said. "And you should also know that if you fail to change your mind I'll . . ." He paused, then straightened his shoulders. "Then you might find I am no longer here, when you return to Kyralia in two years."

Dannyl stared at his lover, suddenly unsure what to say. His heart had lurched at the threat, but something made him stay silent. Perhaps it was the fact that Tayend wasn't trying to persuade him to stay. He only wanted the chance to go on another adventure.

The scholar gazed back at him, eyes wide. Then he shook his head, turned and strode out of the room.

CHAPTER 5

PREPARATIONS

Reaching out to touch the wall, Cery felt a wry affection. Once, the old outer city defences had been a symbol of the division between rich and poor – a barrier beyond which, after the Purge had driven all the homeless and the occupants of overcrowded safehouses out of the city and into the slums each winter, only Thieves and their friends could pass.

Now it was meaningless to Imardians except as a lingering reminder of the past. It formed part of the structure of one of Cery's properties, this time a sprawling storehouse for importers to keep their wares, both legal and smuggled. There were still a few entrances to the underground network of passages known as the Thieves' Road, but they were rarely used. He'd kept them only as possible escape routes, but these days a Thief using the Road was as likely to meet trouble as escape it.

Cery moved away from the wall and sat down. He had decided that the well-appointed apartment on the second floor of the storehouse was as good a place to settle as any. Returning to his old hideout was unthinkable. Even if it hadn't contained painful memories, it clearly hadn't been secure enough. Not that any of his other hideouts were better protected, but there was a chance, at least, that their location wasn't known by his family's killer.

But he had no intention of hiding away. As always, every time he ventured out into the city, whether in his own district or not, someone could attack him. Which made him wonder if he was wrong to assume he had been the killer's true target.

No. Even though they waited until I was gone to kill my family, the true target was me. Selia and the boys had no enemies.

His chest constricted at the thought of them, and for a moment he couldn't breathe. Somehow he took that suffocating grief and channelled it into something else: a deep, growing fury. If the killer or killers, or their employer, had intended to hurt Cery they had succeeded. And they were going to pay for it. Which meant it was more important to find out who had killed his family, and why, than how they'd managed to discover and break into his rooms.

He took a few long, deep breaths. Gol had suggested the Thief Hunter might have killed them, but Cery dismissed the idea. The legendary vigilante did not target the families of Thieves, or kill them to hurt Thieves. He only killed Thieves.

A faint chiming reached his ears in a pattern he recognised, so he rose and moved to a tube protruding from the wall, and placed his ear to it. The voice that echoed within was distorted, but recognisable. Cery moved around the room pulling levers and turning knobs until a section of wall swivelled open. Gol stepped inside.

"How did it go?" Cery asked, moving back to his chair. Gol took the seat opposite and rubbed his hands together.

"There are rumours about already. Don't know if one of our lot let it slip or the knife's been boasting." Cery nodded. Some assassins liked to own up to their high-profile targets, as it demonstrated how clever they were. "I doubt Anyi would say anything," Gol added.

"She might, if she had to. Did you do the usual rounds?"

Gol nodded.

"So how is business?"

Leaning back in the chair, Cery listened as his bodyguard and friend related where he'd been and who he'd spoken to since venturing out early that morning. It took an effort to keep his mind on the man's words, but Cery forced himself to concentrate. To his relief, business in his district appeared to be continuing as it always did. Gol hadn't found any evidence that someone was taking advantage of Cery's distraction yet.

"So," Gol said. "What are you going to do now?"

Cery shrugged. "Nothing. Obviously somebody wants me to react in some way. I'm not going to oblige them. I'll continue business as usual."

Gol frowned, opened his mouth, then closed it without saying anything. Cery managed a humourless smile.

"Oh, don't think that I'm not fired about my family's murder, Gol. I'll have my revenge. But whoever broke into the hideout was clever and careful. Finding out who and why is going to take time."

"Once we've got the knife we'll find out who paid him," Gol assured him.

"We'll see. I've a hunch it will take more than that."

Gol nodded, then frowned.

"Something else?" Cery asked.

The big man bit his lip, then sighed. "Well . . . you know how Neg thought that magic must have been used to break into your hideout?"

"Yes." Cery frowned.

"Dern agrees with him. Said there was no sign of picking. That he'd put in some putty when he made the lock so he'd be able to tell."

Dern was the lockmaker who had designed and installed the locking system on Cery's hideout.

"Could it have been a very clever lock pick? Or even Dern himself?"

Gol shook his head. "He showed me a lever that would only turn if the lock was undone from the inside – inside the lock, that is – which could only be done with magic. I asked him why he bothered, and he said to protect himself. He won't ever promise his locks are safe against magic, so he needs to prove that's the cause if they're ever broken into. I don't know. It seems a bit far to go to. Could be he's making it up to cover himself."

Or maybe not. Cery felt his skin prickle. Perhaps he had been wrong. Perhaps finding out how the killers had reached his family *was* important.

He would question Dern himself, and inspect the lock, to be sure. But if it proved to be true then he had one clue to his family's killer. A clue that, though disturbing, was a start, at least.

"I need to have a chat with our lockmaker."

Gol nodded. "I'll arrange it now."

Perler smiled and nodded at Lorkin as he entered the room. Lord Maron, however, frowned.

"Thank you for agreeing to brief us at such short notice," Lord Dannyl said. He gestured to the tables and chairs, the only furniture in the small University room Osen had arranged for the meeting, and they all sat down.

Maron's attention shifted from Lorkin to Dannyl, then he smiled. "You must be confident that the Higher Magicians will grant Lorkin his request to accompany you to Sachaka," he said. "And that Black Magician Sonea's protest will fail."

Dannyl chuckled. "Not completely confident. I never underestimate his mother's influence, and there may be factors that will sway the other Higher Magicians that none of us know about. But if we wait for the decision before briefing Lorkin then he may leave under-informed – and that would be a mistake."

"As will a replacement, if they decide Lorkin cannot go."

Dannyl nodded in agreement. "I would have brought a possible replacement, but there have been no other volunteers."

"Well, if that happens I will find another assistant, brief him for you and send him when he is ready," Maron offered.

"That would be most appreciated," Dannyl said, nodding in gratitude.

Lorkin kept his expression neutral. It was a little annoying being discussed as if he wasn't there. Still, he could easily have been left out of the meeting, and he was grateful to Dannyl for including him.

"Now, where to start?" Maron said, opening a satchel and pulling out several sheets of paper. "These are the notes I compiled last night, to add to those of my predecessors. You have all the reports of the past Guild Ambassadors?"

"Yes. And I have read them all. It makes for fascinating reading."

Maron chuckled wryly. "Sachaka is very different to Kyralia. And to all the other Allied Lands. The obvious differences stem from the common use of black magic, and from slavery, but there are subtle ones as well. How their women are regarded for instance. Though men are very protective of the women in their family, they regard all other women with suspicion and fear. They have a strange belief that women band together when away from men and plot all sorts of mischief. Some even believe there is a secret organisation or cult that steals women away from their families and alters their minds with magic in order to convince their victims of their ideas."

"Do you think it's true?" Lorkin asked.

Maron shrugged. "Most likely an exaggeration. A scary story to stop women gathering together to gossip and swap ideas on how to manipulate their men." He chuckled, then sighed and looked sad. "The few I met were meek and lonely. I came to miss the company of educated, confident women, though I suspect I'll get over that once I catch up with my sister." He waved a hand. "But I'm digressing. The important thing to know is that you must not speak to women unless invited to."

As the former Ambassador continued, Lorkin began to make notes in an unused leather-bound notebook left over from his novice days. Maron moved from the subject of women to marriage, family life and inheritance to the complex alliances and conflicts between the main Sachakan families, and finally to the protocols to follow in regard to the king.

"There used to be a Sachakan emperor," Dannyl pointed out. "Now they have a king. I've only been able to narrow down that change to the first few hundred years after the Sachakan War. Do you know when the change happened, and why the Sachakans did not return to calling their leaders 'emperor' after they began to rule themselves again?"

"I'm afraid I never thought to question anyone about it," Maron admitted. "I found it was best not to refer too openly to the fact that the Guild once ruled Sachaka. There is much resentment of it, though . . ." He paused and frowned. "I suspect it has more to do with the wasteland than the changes the Guild made – or failed to make to their society."

"Do they know how the wasteland was created?" Dannyl asked.

Maron shook his head. "If they do, they never mentioned it to me. You'll have to ask those questions yourself. Just be careful how and when you do. From what I've seen, they bear grudges a *very* long time."

Dannyl glanced at Lorkin. "Do you think it will be dangerous for Lorkin to enter Sachaka?"

Pausing at his note-taking, Lorkin looked up at the former Ambassador. His heart beat a little faster. His skin prickled.

Maron considered Lorkin. "Logically, no more than for any other young magician. I would not mention your father's name too often, though," he said to Lorkin. "They would respect him as a defender of Kyralia, but not for what happened before that. Yet at the same time they acknowledge that Dakova, the Ichani who Akkarin killed, was an outcast and a fool for enslaving a magician and foreigner, and deserved his fate. I do not think anyone but Davoka's brother would feel obliged to seek revenge – and he died in the invasion."

Lorkin nodded, feeling relief ease the tension in his body.

"Even so," Dannyl said. "Should Lorkin expect the Sachakans, or their slaves, to be uncooperative?"

"Of course." Maron smiled and looked at Perler, who grimaced. "They will be uncooperative at times no matter who you are. Aside from the general problems of status and hier-archy, the slaves take some getting used to. They may not be able to do something for you, but they won't say so because that would be refusing an order. You have to learn to interpret what they say and do – there are signals and gestures you'll pick up on eventually – and I'll tell you how best to phrase an order."

A complicated but surprisingly logical code of behaviour for dealing with slaves followed, and Lorkin was annoyed when, a while later, a knocking at the door interrupted them. Dannyl gestured at the door and it swung open. Lorkin felt his heart sink a little as he recognised the magician standing beyond.

Uh, oh. What's Mother done now?

"Sorry for interrupting," Lord Rothen said, his wrinkled face creasing into a smile. "Could I speak to Lord Lorkin for a moment?"

"Of course, Lord Rothen," Dannyl said, smiling broadly. He looked at Lorkin, then nodded toward the old magician. "Go on."

Lorkin suppressed a sigh and rose. "I'll be back as quickly as possible," he told the others, then walked to the doorway and stepped past Rothen into the corridor outside. As the door closed, Lorkin crossed his arms, steeling himself for the lecture that was bound to come.

Rothen, as always, looked both stern and amused. "Are you sure you want to go to Sachaka, Lorkin?" he asked quietly. "You're not just doing it to spite your mother?"

"Yes," Lorkin replied. "And no. I do want to go and I'm not trying to annoy Mother."

The old magician nodded, his expression now thoughtful. "You are aware of the risks?"

"Of course."

"So you admit there are risks."

Ha. Outsmarted! Lorkin found himself having to resist a smile as a wave of affection for the old man swept over him.

All the years of Lorkin's life, Rothen had been there, looking after him when his mother's duties called her away, helping him when he needed defending or support, lecturing and occasionally punishing him when he had done something foolish, or broken Guild rules.

This was different, and Rothen must know it. Lorkin wasn't breaking any rules. He had only to convince his old friend and protector that he wasn't doing anything foolish.

"Of course there are risks – there are risks to everything a magician does," Lorkin replied, mimicking something Rothen liked to say to novices.

The old magician's eyes narrowed. "But are they too great?"

"It'll be up to the Higher Magicians to decide that," Lorkin said.

"And you'll accept whatever decision they make?"

"Of course."

Rothen looked down, then when he met Lorkin's eyes again his own were full of sympathy. "I understand that you want to do something with your life. You've certainly got a lot of expectation to live up to. You know Sonea and I have never wanted anything for you but a safe, happy life?"

Lorkin nodded.

"There will be other ways you can make your mark," Rothen told him. "Ways that are as satisfying, with far less risk. You only need to be patient, and ready to grasp opportunities when they come."

"And I will. I have every intention of surviving Sachaka and returning to do whatever else comes my way," Lorkin said firmly. "But for now *this* is what I want to do."

Rothen stared at Lorkin in silence, then shrugged and took a step away. "So long as you're sure, and you've considered the full consequences . . . oh, and before I forget, your mother asked me to say she would like you to join her at dinner tonight."

Lorkin swallowed a groan. "Thanks. I'll be there."

As if I have a choice, he mused. He had learned the hard way that refusing a dinner invitation was something his mother would not easily forgive. There was one missed dinner from five years ago – not entirely his fault, either – that she still managed to make him feel guilty about.

Rothen turned to go. Lorkin turned back to the door, then paused and looked over his shoulder.

"Will you be joining us, Rothen?"

The old man paused to look back, and smiled. "Oh, no. She'll have you all to herself tonight."

This time Lorkin did not manage to suppress a groan. As he sent magic out to turn the door handle, he heard Rothen chuckling as he walked away.

Sonea regarded the man sitting across the table from her and wondered, not for the first time that evening, why he had bothered coming to see her. Seeking to sway the vote of the Higher Magicians on the petition was normal and expected for both petitioners and opposition. But surely it was obvious how she would vote, when her origins and sympathies were clearly with the lower class. Why waste the time, when his efforts would be better spent persuading other Higher Magicians to take his side?

"The rule has clearly been applied unfairly, most often in the case of lower-class novices," Regin conceded. "But the fact is, some do come from families involved in criminal activities."

"I regularly heal people involved in criminal activities," she told him. "And I know people in the city who earn money in less than legal ways. That does not make me a criminal. Neither does a magician become a criminal because a relative happens to be one. Surely it is enough that a magician – or novice – behaves as we wish them to."

"If only we could trust that they would," Regin replied. "But it is true of all novices and magicians, no matter their background and fortune, that those exposed through family or friends to dishonest people and business are more likely to succumb to the temptation of criminal involvement than those who are not." He grimaced. "I believe this rule helps them, particularly when they are unable to help themselves. It can be an excuse to back out of a situation when under pressure from others."

"Or it can drive them to rebel, when the rule is seen to be unfairly upheld. Or if it is inadvertently broken then they may reason that having broken one rule it will not matter so much if they break another. Then there are those who find what is most forbidden is the most exciting."

"For which we need the deterrent effect of the rule."

"Deterrent or, perversely, encouragement?" She sighed. "The weakness of this rule is that it is inconsistently applied – and I don't believe that can be resolved."

"I agree that is the weakness, but not that it cannot be resolved." Regin leaned back in his chair and closed his eyes. "The trouble is, things have changed. Crime has seeped up into the higher classes like damp rising through the walls. It is they we need the rule for, not the lower classes."

Sonea raised her eyebrows. "Surely you don't believe that the higher classes weren't gambling and whoring in the past? I can tell you some stories—"

"No." Regin opened his eyes and looked at her. "I'm not

talking about the usual mischief. This is bigger. Nastier. And far more organised."

Sonea opened her mouth to ask him to elaborate, but was interrupted by a knock at the door. She turned away and sent a little magic out to unlatch the door, and as it swung inward she felt her heart lift as Jonna entered the room, carrying a large platter laden with food.

Sonea's aunt and servant looked from her to Regin, then bowed politely. "Lord Regin." She set the platter down, then glanced at Sonea and took a step back.

"Don't leave for my sake." Regin rose and turned to face Sonea. "I will return another time." He inclined his head. "Thank you for hearing me out, Black Magician Sonea."

"Good night, Lord Regin," she replied.

Jonna stepped aside to allow him past. As the door closed behind him, the woman raised an eyebrow.

"Did I interrupt?" she asked.

"Yes, but it doesn't matter."

As her aunt arranged the covered dishes on the table, Sonea sighed and looked around the room.

When she had first seen inside the rooms in the Magicians' Quarters, she had been impressed by how luxurious they were, but hadn't noticed anything unusual about their size. She hadn't known that they were small compared to the houses most higher-class men and women lived in. Each suite contained two to four rooms, depending on the size of the magician's family, and the rooms were of a modest size.

Aside from the occasional complaint, most magicians were willing to live in such small quarters in order to reside within the Guild. They had adapted to the restrictions. They did not eat at a dining table, but instead meals were served on

a low table set before the guest room chairs. The only excep-
tions were the formal meals of the Guild, served at a long
dining table in the Banquet Room within a purpose-built
building.

Though there was another exception – the small dining
room in the High Lord's Residence.

A memory flashed through her mind of that room, and
flavours she hadn't tasted in years. She found herself wondering,
not for the first time, what had happened to Akkarin's servant,
Takan, the Sachakan ex-slave who had cooked such amazing
meals. Nothing had been heard or seen of him since the invasion. She had always hoped he had survived.

Jonna sat down with a heavy sigh of relief. Sonea looked
down at the cooling dishes on the table. It wasn't an exotic
meal, just the usual fare from the Guild kitchens. She frowned.
It should have been Lorkin who had interrupted Regin.

"He'll be here soon," Jonna assured her, guessing the
source of her worry. "He wouldn't dare miss a meal with his
mother."

Sonea humphed. "He seems quite prepared to defy me and
get himself killed in Sachaka. Why would a mere missed dinner
bother him?"

"Because he'd have me to answer to as well," Jonna replied.

Sonea met her aunt's eyes and smiled. "You may as well go.
I'll only end up wearing your ears out."

"My ears are robust enough. Besides, if he doesn't come we
can't let all this food go to waste."

"You know I'll wait until well after it's spoiled, so there's
no point the two of us staying hungry while we wait. Go.
Ranek must be hungry."

"He's working late tonight and will eat over at the servants' quarters." Jonna rose and examined the bookshelves, then brought a rag out of her uniform and wiped a shelf.

There's no budging her, Sonea thought. After coming to stay in the Guild in order to help Sonea through her pregnancy, birth and motherhood, Jonna and Ranek had settled in and found places as servants – Jonna as Sonea's servant and Ranek among the robe-makers. Their two children had grown up here, had played with Lorkin and eventually gained well-paid places as servants in rich homes in the city. Jonna was well pleased with this. It was the best anyone of her class could hope for. Only by becoming a magician could someone born outside the Houses enter the country's noble class.

A knock brought their attention to the door. Sonea drew in a deep breath, then sent a little magic toward the door latch. It clicked open and Lorkin stepped inside, looking contrite. She sighed with relief.

"Sorry I'm late," he said. "Mother. Jonna." He nodded to them both. "The meeting didn't finish until a few minutes ago."

"Well, you're just in time," Jonna said, walking to the door. "Any longer and I was going to eat your meal for you."

"Why don't you stay and join us?" he asked, smiling hopefully.

She gave him a measured look. "And have the *two* of us telling you what a fool you are?"

He blinked, then grinned ruefully. "Good night, Jonna."

She sniffed in amusement, before she slipped out of the door, pulling it closed behind her.

Sonea looked at him. He met her eyes briefly, and looked around the room.

"Is something different?" he asked.

"No." She gestured to the other chair. "Sit down. Eat. No point letting the food get any colder."

He nodded and they began to fill their plates with food. Sonea noted he ate with his usual enthusiasm. Or was he hurrying? Did he want this meal over with? To escape his overbearing mother and stop being reminded of things he wanted to ignore – like the risks in travelling to Sachaka?

She waited until the meal was over and he looked a bit more relaxed, before raising the subject he must know she'd invited him here in order to discuss.

"So," she began. "Why Sachaka?"

He blinked and turned to meet her eyes.

"Because . . . because it's where I want to go."

"But why do you want to go there? Of all the places, it is the most dangerous – especially for you."

"Lord Maron doesn't think so. Nor does Lord Dannyl. At least, they don't think it will be any more dangerous for me than for anyone else."

Sonea looked at him closely. "That is only because they don't believe something unless they see proof. The only way they can see proof that it is dangerous for you to enter Sachaka is to take you there and observe something bad happen to you."

His eyes narrowed. "Then you don't have proof either."

"Not that sort of proof." She forced a smile. "I'd hardly be a responsible parent if I took you to Sachaka to test my belief that it is dangerous."

"So how do you know it's dangerous?"

"From what your father told me. From what Guild Ambassadors and traders have confirmed since. They all agree that Sachakans are bound by their code of honour to seek revenge for the death of a family member – even if they didn't like that family member, and even if that family member was an outcast."

"But the Guild Ambassadors looked into it. They said the family of Kariko and Dakova did not want revenge. The brothers had been a liability to them; it was clearly a relief to them that they had died."

"They also said that the family had gained some admiration for the brother's daring invasion, despite the fact they were outcasts and the invasion failed." Sonea shrugged. "It is easier to feel gratitude and loyalty to someone after they are dead. You can't discount the fact that the Ambassadors only spoke to some family members, not all. That if the head of the family expressed one view then others who disagreed would stay quiet."

"But they wouldn't act against the head of the family, either," he pointed out.

"Not in any way that could be traced to them."

Lorkin shook his head in frustration. "Nobody is going to slip poison into my food or cut my throat in my sleep. Even if I wasn't able to use magic to treat one and shield against the other, nobody is going to risk breaking the peace between our countries."

"Or else they'll see you as the perfect excuse to spoil it." Sonea leaned forward. "They might be offended that the Guild sent Akkarin's son there. Your little sight-seeing trip might ruin everything the Guild has worked for since the invasion."

His eyes widened, then his face hardened.

"It's not a sight-seeing trip. I . . . I want to help Lord Dannyl. I think what he's trying to do is . . . is . . . it could help us. By looking into the past we might find new knowledge – new magic – that could help us defend ourselves. Perhaps we won't have to use black magic any more."

For a moment Sonea could not speak. Surprise was quickly followed by a wave of guilt.

"You're not on a quest to save me, or something, are you?" she asked, her voice unintentionally weak.

"No!" He shook his head. "If we found such magic it would help us all. It might even help the Sachakans. If they didn't need black magic they might be less resistant to ending slavery."

Sonea nodded. "It seems to me that anyone could go looking for this new magic. Lord Dannyl is already seeking it. Why do *you* have to go?"

Lorkin paused. "Lord Dannyl is only interested in filling in the gaps in history. I'm more interested in how that history – that knowledge – could be used *now*. And in the future."

She felt a chill run down her spine. A quest for magical knowledge. Exactly what had spurred Akkarin on to explore the world, and eventually enter Sachaka. And that quest had ended very, very badly.

"Such a desire for knowledge led to your father becoming a slave," she told him, "and he was lucky it only led to that, and not his death."

A thoughtful look passed over Lorkin's face, then he straightened and shook his head.

"But this is different. I'm not wandering, unwelcome and uninformed, into a hostile land. The Guild knows much more about Sachaka now. Sachakans know more about us."

"The Guild knows only what the Sachakans have allowed us to know. There must be – will be – plenty that was kept from our Ambassadors. They can't be completely sure you will be safe there."

He nodded. "I won't argue that there's no risk. But it is up to the Higher Magicians to decide if the risk is higher for me."

He has doubts, she thought. *He isn't turning a blind eye to the risks.*

"And I'm sure you'll make them consider every possible consequence," he added. He looked up at her. "If I promise that I will come home the moment Lord Dannyl or I have the slightest suspicion of danger, will you withdraw your protest?"

She smiled wryly. "Of course not."

He scowled.

"I am your mother," she reminded him. "I'm supposed to stop you harming yourself."

"I'm not a child any more. I'm twenty years old."

"But you are still my son." She met his gaze, holding it despite the anger in his eyes. "I know you will be angry at me if I succeed in preventing you going. I'd rather that than you were dead. I'd rather you joined the Lonmar cult and I never saw you again. At least I'd know you were alive and happy." She paused. "You say you are not a child any more. Then ask yourself: are you doing this, even only partly, in order to defy your mother? How much of your wanting to go comes from wanting to make your mark as an adult? If you took those two desires away, would you want to go as much?"

Lorkin said nothing, but his face was tight with anger. Suddenly he stood up.

"You don't understand. I finally find something worth doing and you . . . you have to try to spoil it. Why can't you just wish me luck and be glad that I might achieve something with my life instead of sitting around getting drunk or taking roet?"

His face red, he strode to the door and left her room.

Leaving Sonea frozen, unable to do anything but stare at the door, her heart torn between love and pride, the determination to protect him and the fear that she might fail.

CHAPTER 6

THE HEARING

There was quite a crowd outside the Guildhall, Dannyl saw as he entered the Great Hall. Thankfully Osen had decided the only magicians to attend the Hearing, held to decide whether to send Lorkin to Sachaka, would be the Higher Magicians, Lorkin, himself, and past Guild Ambassadors to Sachaka. Looking at the curious faces in the crowd, Dannyl wondered why these other magicians had bothered to come, when they wouldn't be allowed inside. What did they hope to see? Did they want to know the decision as soon as possible after it was made? Did the outcome affect them in some way?

Whether Lorkin was allowed to go to Sachaka or not might indicate if other magicians had a chance of visiting the country. *No, that can't be it. There are always few volunteers for positions there.* Dannyl noted a familiar face in the crowd. *Regin. What has he to gain if Lorkin goes or stays?* He frowned. *Perhaps some satisfaction if Sonea's protest is overruled. But Regin hasn't shown any sign of animosity or disapproval toward her since they were novices. If he is harbouring any resentment, he's hidden it well.*

The rest of the crowd might simply want to see Sonea's reaction if she failed to prevent her son going to Sachaka. Hearing that one of the Guild's black magicians was in conflict with the former High Lord's son must have generated plenty of gossip. Dannyl almost regretted slipping out of the habit of attending the Guild's social evenings in the Night Room. He'd have already known what attracted the crowd today, and what they hoped and feared to witness.

As Dannyl neared the Guildhall doors, another magician emerged from a side entrance.

Black Magician Kallen. I wonder . . . is the crowd worried that Sonea will lose her temper and use black magic if she fails to stop Lorkin going to Sachaka?

If they truly believed she might, they ought to have made themselves scarce. Dannyl knew that he would never want to be close by if a black magician lost his or her temper. But they probably assumed Kallen could stop her, and the confrontation would be more entertaining than dangerous.

Moving into the Guildhall, Dannyl saw most of the Higher Magicians were in their places. Lorkin was already waiting to one side. He walked over to the young man, who greeted him with a wary smile.

"Nervous?"

Lorkin smiled wryly. "A little."

"How did dinner with your mother go last night?"

"Not good." Lorkin's smile faded and he sighed. "I hate fighting with her. But I also hate always having to fight to do what I want to do."

"Always?" Dannyl repeated.

Grimacing, Lorkin looked away. "Well, I suppose not always. Not often, really. Just now, when it matters. When I finally find something important to take part in."

"Going to Sachaka really matters that much to you?" Dannyl asked, not hiding his surprise.

"Of course." Lorkin looked up and searched Dannyl's gaze. "Why do you think I want to go? Surely not just to defy my mother?"

"No." Dannyl shrugged. "I thought you wanted to have an adventure. Get away from a boring, restrictive Guild." He smiled. "I had no idea you truly thought the work was important."

"I do," Lorkin assured him. "Both maintaining good terms with Sachaka and researching magical history. Though with the latter I'm more interested in what we can do with what we find."

Dannyl regarded Lorkin thoughtfully. He'd hoped the young magician would be useful at the least, and a good companion at best. Now he found himself both pleased to find he might have such a willing assistant in his research as well as in his ambassadorial duties, and a little worried that he might not easily leave the lesser of those duties to Lorkin when he wanted a little time to pursue his own interests.

A low murmur filled the hall and Dannyl looked around to see what had caused it. Sonea had entered the room, but had paused to talk to – of all people – Lord Regin. She looked puzzled, but nodded and turned away. Instead of climbing the stairs at the front of the hall to her usual place, she remained standing at the other side of the front to Dannyl and Lorkin, while Regin left.

She looked calm, even a little amused. The remaining Higher Magicians had arrived now. *No doubt she had timed her arrival so that she would be one of the last, to avoid subjecting her son to the awkwardness of her presence as an adversary.* Osen began his slow pace across the front of the hall that indicated he was ready to begin, and soon the magicians quietened.

"Unless there is a reason not to, I will begin the Hearing now," Osen said. He paused, then nodded as no voice rose to stall him. "First I will outline our reasons for meeting today," he began. "Lord Lorkin has volunteered for the position of assistant to the Guild Ambassador to Sachaka, recently granted to Lord Dannyl. Black Magician Sonea has lodged a protest against our acceptance of Lord Lorkin in this role." He turned to Sonea. "For what reason do you protest?"

"That for Lorkin, as the son of the former High Lord Akkarin and myself, there will be the danger that the family of Kariko and Dakova, the latter of whom I killed during the Ichani Invasion and the former whom Akkarin killed many years earlier, will seek revenge for their deaths. Or the families of the other Ichani killed in the invasion will do so. Even if their families do not seek revenge, sending him there may be perceived as an insult. Either way his presence may hamper efforts at peace between our two countries."

Osen turned to Lorkin and Dannyl. "And what do you, Lord Lorkin, say in reply to this?"

"I leave the judgement as to whether the risk is as great as M— Black Magician Sonea believes to the Higher Magicians, and will accept whatever decision they make," Lorkin replied.

A faint smile of approval crossed Osen's face. His gaze shifted to Lord Dannyl.

"And what do you say, Ambassador Dannyl?"

Dannyl shrugged. "I trust the observations and assessment given by the former Guild Ambassadors to Sachaka. They have told me they believe Lord Lorkin's presence in Sachaka will be of no hindrance to my work and will present no danger to his life and wellbeing. His assistance is appreciated and welcome."

"Then I call upon Lord Stanin and Lord Maron to provide their opinions on the matter."

As the Administrator turned away, Dannyl could feel Sonea's gaze on him. *She's not happy with me for encouraging Lorkin, but I know her too well to be intimidated by her stares.* He looked up and met her gaze. A traitorous chill ran down his spine. It wasn't that her expression held any hint of intent or accusation. It gave away nothing, yet was filled with an intensity that made him feel as if she were stripping back his skin and reading the thoughts beneath. He looked away. *All right. Maybe her stares* do *intimidate me a little.*

Even before she'd become a novice – long before she'd become a black magician – she'd made him a little nervous. It was reasonable considering that, when just an urchin of the slums, she'd managed to stab him in the leg. If she had been capable of that then, before she'd been trained to use her powers, it was no surprise he was intimidated by her now.

He did not want to start considering what she might do to him if something did happen to Lorkin in Sachaka, so he turned his attention to the former Ambassadors who were speaking now. The Higher Magicians were asking them questions, and the answers showed that, while they conceded that no Kyralian was ever perfectly safe in Sachaka, neither man thought Lorkin would be in any greater danger than any other magician. If Lorkin was at all worried, he should avoid speaking of his parentage. But because he would be in a subordinate role normally given to a slave, the Sachakans were not likely to pay much attention to him at all.

Next, a trader was called who favoured Sonea's cautious position. He told of vendettas among the Sachakan families that had continued for decades, which he had observed during his yearly visits. The Higher Magicians questioned him closely as well.

Finally, Osen asked for all but the Higher Magicians, except for Sonea, to leave so that they might debate and come to a decision. Dannyl heard Lorkin sigh with relief when Sonea quickly turned and left, her expression suddenly distracted. As Dannyl stepped out into the crowded Great Hall, he looked for her, but she had disappeared.

The voices of the magicians milling outside the Guildhall quickly faded as Sonea hurried into the passages of the University, and were replaced by higher pitched ones as she neared the main corridor to the classrooms. The morning classes had ended and the novices were making their way to the Foodhall for the midday meal.

As she stepped out into the corridor, ready to weave her way through the novices, the voices abruptly faded to silence. She glanced about and realised all were looking at her. Those in the middle of the corridor hastily stepped out of her way and then, as one, the novices remembered their manners and bowed.

She resisted a smile, and hoped the little flush of embarrassment she felt didn't show on her face. *I know exactly what they're thinking and feeling.* A memory of a tall, frowning man in black robes striding down the University corridor, causing the same frozen moment of panic and a little fear among her fellow novices, flashed into her mind. *When I look back, I wonder at how scared we were of Akkarin, as if we knew, somehow, that he was more powerful than he ought to be.* The memory caused her chest to tighten, yet she held onto it. She treasured it for a moment, then let it fade.

Her feet took her on to the second-last classroom, which was empty but for one red-robed magician who had once made walking these corridors a torment for her.

"Lord Regin," she said. "I don't know how long I have. What did you need to tell me so urgently?"

He looked up at her and nodded politely.

"Thank you for coming, Black Magician Sonea," he said. "I'll get to the point. I've been told by someone whose word I trust that Pendel's followers are planning a raid or ambush of some sort designed to expose the criminal connections of rich novices."

Sonea sighed. "Fools. That won't help their cause. I thought Pendel was smarter than that."

"I'm not sure Pendel knows about it. The trouble is, if he doesn't he might not be inclined to believe me if I tell him, and if he does I might inadvertently expose my informant."

"You want me to talk to him?" Sonea guessed.

"Yes. But . . ." Regin frowned. "My informant was not sure of the timing. I fear it may be very soon. Today, perhaps. They said something about taking advantage of the Guild being distracted. I haven't seen the ones I suspect are involved so far today."

She looked at him. "I must return to the Hearing, Lord Regin."

"Of course. But . . ." He grimaced. "If you can speak to him as soon as you are able to I . . . I think he would listen to you."

"I will," she told him. "But now I'd better return to the hall. Can't keep Administrator Osen waiting."

The corner of his mouth twitched upward, but his gaze remained anxious. Turning away, Sonea hurried out of the classroom back into the corridor, where the remaining novices froze and didn't recover in time to bow until she was well past. Once she was out of sight she broke into a jog, slowing only when she turned from one passage into another in case she collided with someone. Finally, she made it out of the passages into the Great Hall. To her relief, Dannyl and Lorkin stood outside the Guildhall, still waiting to be called inside.

An awkward wait followed. She did not want to increase her son's discomfort by joining him and Dannyl. Nor was it appropriate for her to talk to the former Ambassadors and the trader, who were chatting together. None of the crowd seemed inclined to approach her, and she saw nobody she knew who wouldn't mind her company right now. Pendel was not among them. So she had to stand alone and wait.

After several long minutes the doors to the Guildhall finally opened. Relieved, Sonea watched as Osen gestured for Dannyl and Lorkin to enter. He looked up and nodded to her. For once his expression wasn't cold and distant. He almost appeared sympathetic.

Uh, oh. Does this mean they overruled my protest?

Her stomach sank. Then her heart began to beat faster. She kept her expression as neutral as she could manage as she walked past the crowd into the hall. Once inside, she could not help scanning the faces of the Higher Magicians. Vinara's wrinkled face seemed to express guilt. Peakin was frowning with what might be uncertainty, but Garrel's looked smug. She felt her stomach sink even further.

Looking higher, she met Balkan's gaze. His expression gave away nothing. But Kallen . . . Kallen looked annoyed. Hope filled her.

Then she looked at Rothen and her heart stopped beating. He knew she could read him too well these days, so he wasn't even trying to hide anything. His eyes were full of apology, and he was shaking his head.

"Black Magician Sonea, the Higher Magicians have considered your protest carefully. They find there is no strong evidence that Lord Lorkin will be in grave danger if he enters Sachaka, so long as he remains in the protection of Lord Dannyl and the Guild House and does not flaunt his parentage needlessly. Do you accept this decision?"

She looked at Osen, drew in a deep breath, forced her face to show no sign of the turmoil growing inside her, and nodded.

"I do."

"Then I declare this Hearing over."

Disbelief and then jubilation filled Lorkin after Administrator Osen announced the Higher Magicians' decision and he felt a sudden desire to let out a whoop. But it would not have been appropriate in the dignified surrounds of the Guildhall, and not kind to his mother.

As always, she showed little of her thoughts or feelings. How she managed that he could not guess. Long practice? He hoped that one day he would inherit the ability. Still, he saw small hints that others did not. The slight sag of her shoulders. The hesitation before she answered Osen's final question. As she walked over to him, he saw how wide her pupils were. But wide with anger or fear?

"Don't worry about Lorkin," Dannyl said quietly to her. "I will make sure nothing happens to him. I promise you that."

She looked at him and her eyes narrowed. "I'll hold you to that promise."

Dannyl actually winced. "I know."

"And *you*," she said, her eyes snapping to Lorkin. "You had better be careful. If some Sachakan murders you in your sleep I'll hunt you down and make you admit you were wrong." The smallest twitch of a smile lifted the corner of her mouth.

"I'll remember that," he said. "No getting murdered."

The smile faded and she gazed at him in silence for a moment. Then she abruptly turned to Dannyl.

"When will you be leaving?" she asked.

"As soon as possible, I'm afraid," he replied apologetically. "The Guild would rather someone had gone to Sachaka to learn from Lord Maron before taking on his duties, but Maron had to return to Kyralia in a hurry. Apparently if we leave the Guild House empty of an Ambassador too long they'll find another use for it, and we'll have to go live out in the country."

Her eyebrows rose.

"How long is too long?"

"We don't know. They've never told us."

Sonea snorted quietly. "So they're keeping you hanging on a string. Glad it's you going, not me. Not that I could if I wanted to." She turned to look at the Higher Magicians, who had nearly all descended from their seats and were making their way out of the room. Osen looked back at them.

"We'd better leave," Dannyl said.

"Yes," Sonea agreed. She frowned, her expression becoming distracted. "I have something rather urgent I need to attend to." She glanced at them both, and managed a thin smile. "Don't go leaving without saying goodbye, will you?"

Without waiting for a reply, she strode away toward the door. Dannyl and Lorkin followed, though at a slower pace. Lorkin watched as his mother disappeared through the Guildhall doorway.

"I have no intention of dying in Sachaka," Lorkin said. "In

fact, I'll be keeping as low a profile as possible. After all, if the slightest hint of foolishness gets back here, she'll come fetch me back."

"Actually, she can't," Dannyl replied.

Lorkin turned to frown at the tall magician.

"Remember, she's a black magician. She's forbidden to leave the city. If she breaks that condition, she'll be exiled from the Allied Lands."

A small but sharp stab of fear went through Lorkin. *So she can't come and save me if I get in trouble. Well, I had better not get into trouble then. Or rather, I had better be ready to get myself out of it again.* He fixed a bright smile on his face and turned to Dannyl.

"But I don't need Mother. If anything happens, I know you'll save me."

Dannyl's eyebrows rose. "Nice to know you have such confidence in me."

"Oh, nothing of the sort," Lorkin replied, grinning. "I just know you're more scared of her than of the Sachakans."

The tall magician shook his head and sighed. "What was I thinking? Of all the assistants I could have wound up with, why did I have to choose the one with the scary mother and troublemaking in his bloodlines? I am doomed."

CHAPTER 7

A JOURNEY BEGINS

As the carriage pulled up outside the front of the University, Sonea and Lorkin emerged from the building, followed by Rothen. A cluster of young male magicians lurking in the shelter of the entry hall waved and called out, and Lorkin turned to wave in reply. His wave turned into a beckoning gesture, and a servant hurried out, carrying a single, small chest.

Ah, good. The young man packs light, Dannyl thought.

Early autumn rain spattered against an invisible shield over their heads. As mother and son reached the carriage, Dannyl heard the sound of rain on the roof cease, and guessed that whichever of the magicians was holding the shield had expanded it to include the vehicle. He opened the door and climbed down to greet them.

"Ambassador Dannyl," Sonea said, smiling politely up at him. "I hope your chests are watertight. This rain doesn't look like it will ease off for some time."

Dannyl glanced up at the two boxes strapped to the back of the carriage, on top of which the servant and driver were lashing Lorkin's chest. "They're new and untested, but the maker came well recommended." He turned back to regard her. "I have no original documents in there. All copies. Wrapped in oilskin."

She nodded. "Wise." She turned to Lorkin, who was looking a little pale. "If you need anything, you know what to do."

He flashed a quick smile in reply. "I'm sure I'll be able to buy anything I've forgotten. The Sachakans might have a few barbaric customs, but it sounds like they don't lack for luxuries or practicalities."

They regarded each other silently for a long, awkward moment.

"Well, off you go then." She waved to the carriage like she was shooing a child away, spoiling the impression of a young man venturing independently into the world. Dannyl suspected she would have liked to envelop her son in a hug, but knew it would embarrass him in front of his friends. He exchanged an amused and knowing look with Rothen. They watched Lorkin climb inside the carriage, clutching a leather bag to his chest.

"I'll hold you to that promise, Dannyl," Sonea said quietly.

The urge to smile disappeared. He turned back, ready to reassure her again, but there was a glint of amusement in her gaze. He straightened his back.

"And I mean to uphold it," he said. "Though if he takes after his mother, I can't be held completely responsible if he gets it into his head to do something foolish."

From Rothen he heard a quiet snort of amusement. Sonea's eyebrows rose and he expected her to protest, but instead she shrugged. "Well, don't complain to me if he causes you trouble. You didn't have to choose him as your assistant."

Dannyl feigned worry. "Is he really that bad? I can still change my mind about taking him, can't I?"

She raised an eyebrow and regarded him closely. "Don't tempt me, Dannyl." Then she drew in a deep breath and sighed. "No, he isn't that bad. And I do wish you luck, Dannyl. I hope you find what you're looking for."

Rothen chuckled. "Goodbye again, old friend," he said. Just as Dannyl had once farewelled Rothen many years before, on this spot, before heading off to Elyne and his first ambassadorial role. *Where I met Tayend . . .*

"Farewell, even older friend," Dannyl retorted. Rothen laughed, the wrinkles on his face deepening. *He looks so* elderly *these days*, Dannyl thought. *But then, so do I.* He felt a pang of regret that he had not visited his old mentor and friend much these last few years. *I'll have to make up for that when I return.*

"Off with you then." Rothen made the same shooing motion that Sonea had. Dannyl chuckled and obeyed, climbing into the carriage to sit beside Lorkin. He turned to the young man.

"Ready?"

Lorkin nodded without hesitation.

"Driver. Time to depart," Dannyl called.

A command rang out and the carriage jerked into motion. Dannyl looked out of the carriage window to see Sonea and Rothen watching. Both wore frowns, but as they saw him they smiled and waved, as did the young men huddled under the University entrance. He waved back, then the carriage turned toward the gates and they were no longer in sight.

She won't stop worrying about him the entire time he is gone. Such is the role of a parent. He suppressed a sigh. *Why this melancholy? I should be filled with excitement at the coming adventure.* Glancing at Lorkin, he saw that the young man was gazing out of the other window. *It's not just me then. I guess all travel involves leaving somewhere, and that often involves a little sadness. Well, at least Lorkin had someone seeing him off.*

He frowned as he thought back over the previous several days. Since their argument Tayend hadn't spoken a word. Not even when Dannyl had told him he would be leaving the next day. Not a word of farewell. He hadn't been present when Dannyl had loaded his chests onto the carriage and rode away.

Why does he have to be like this? It's not as if he still wants to take part in the research. Tayend had shown less and less interest in the work over the years. He was more excited by court gossip.

Dannyl had told the silent scholar that if he judged Sachaka safe enough, he'd send a message and if Tayend was still keen to join him he could seek the Elyne king's approval. But the scholar had glared at Dannyl and left the table, his dinner unfinished.

I've never seen him this angry. It's unreasonable. My research won't progress unless I go to Sachaka. Well, I hope it will progress. I might go there and find nothing.

But he would never know that if he didn't try.

The carriage moved through the Inner Wall out into the North Quarter. Lorkin was still staring out of the window. His expression was withdrawn and thoughtful, which made him look more like his father.

Akkarin had always been brooding about something. It turned out he had a reason to be. Who'd have guessed the man so many magicians had been in awe of had once been a slave? Certainly nobody had suspected their High Lord knew black magic, and had been venturing out into the city to kill Sachakan spies.

Were there any Sachakan spies in the city now? He smiled.

Of course there were. Just not the kind Akkarin had hunted – ex-slaves sent by their Ichani masters. No, the spies here now would be the old-fashioned kind, sent or hired by the rulers of other countries to keep an eye on their neighbours. And they wouldn't bother with the poorer districts, instead looking for useful positions with access to the court and trade.

Dannyl looked out of the window. He watched as the neat stone houses of the North Quarter passed, then the carriage trundled through the Outer Wall and entered what had once been the slums.

It has changed so much, Dannyl thought. Where a shambles of makeshift building had been now neat brick houses stood. He knew there were still areas of the slums that were dirty and dangerous, but once the Purge had stopped it had quickly become apparent that the yearly forced exodus had hampered the expansion of the city as much as it had restricted access to it by the poor.

And the poor not only had access to the city, but could join the Guild as well – if they had strong enough magical ability. The wealth that came with such a privilege had lifted more than a few families out of poverty, though the influx of entrants from poor and servant classes had caused some troubles for the Guild.

Like this recent mess in which magicians and novices of the higher classes had been found in a roet and gambling house run by smugglers, but claimed to have been given directions to the place by the "lowies". What was most disturbing was that this house had been found hidden down an alley in the Inner Circle, which had always been thought to be free of such bad establishments. And it hadn't been all that far from Dannyl and Tayend's home.

But that was someone else's concern now. As the carriage moved past the last of the houses and out onto the North Road, Dannyl nodded to himself. His and Lorkin's future lay ahead of them, in the ancient land of Sachaka.

The Good Company was one of the largest bolhouses in the south of the city. As Cery and Gol walked in, they were buffeted by the heat of bodies, roar of voices and rich, sweet scent of bol. Men outnumbered women, both standing at tables fixed to the floor. There were no chairs. Chairs did not last long. The brawls that broke out here were famous throughout the city, though by the time the stories reached Northside they'd been embellished well beyond physical possibilities.

Making his way through the crowd, Cery took in the atmosphere and noted the clientele without looking at anyone long enough to draw attention. Near the back of the huge room were doorways. These led downstairs to the basement, where a different sort of company was for hire.

Sitting on a bench near one of the doorways was a plump middle-aged woman in bright, overly fancy clothing.

"Why is it that house-mothers always look the same?" Gol murmured.

"Sly Lalli is tall and slim," Cery pointed out. "Goody Sis is short and petite."

"But the rest are rather similar. Big, busty and—"

"Quiet. She's coming over."

The woman had seen them watching her, hauled herself to her feet and was making her way toward them. "You looking for Aunty? She's over there." She pointed. "Hey Aunty!" she shouted.

They both turned to see a tall, elegant woman with long

red hair swivel on her heel to regard them. At a gesture from the plump woman she smiled and strode forward.

"Here for some good company, are we?" she said. She looked at Gol, who was watching the other woman returning to her seat. "People always assume Martia runs the place," she said. "But she's here keeping an eye on her son, who works in the servery. Like to go downstairs?"

"Yes. I'm here to see an old friend," Cery told her.

She smiled knowingly. "As are we all. Which old friend would that be?"

"Terrina."

The woman's eyebrows rose. "That one, eh? Well, no man asks for her who doesn't already know what he's getting. I'll take you to her."

She led them through the doorway down a short flight of stairs into a room beneath the bolhouse. It was as large as the room above, but was filled with rows of cubicles. Paper screens were attached to the sides, and most were closed to hide the interior – and from the sounds coming from all sides most of the cubicles were being used for the purpose they were built for.

Aunty led them to a cubicle near the centre of the room. The screens were open. Inside was a single chair. It was a generously sized chair, with a large cushioned seat and sturdy arms. All of the rooms were furnished thus. The women here did not want their customers to be so comfortable they'd fall asleep and prevent them servicing more customers. Cery turned to nod at Gol, who took up a position a few steps away, outside another empty room.

As Cery moved into the cubicle, Aunty closed the screens. Sitting down, he listened to the sounds nearby, then extended his focus beyond the moans and laughs in search of sounds that didn't belong. The sound of breathing. Of footsteps. Of the rustle of cloth.

His nose caught a scent that brought a rush of memories, many years old. He smiled.

"Terrina," he murmured, turning to the back of the little room.

A panel of the wall slid aside, revealing a woman with short hair and dark clothing. *She looks just the same. Perhaps that little crease between her brows is a bit deeper.* She was a little too lean and muscular to be called beautiful, but Cery had always found her athletic build attractive. As she recognised him, her eyebrows rose and she relaxed.

"Well, well. I haven't seen you in a long time. What must it be? Five years?"

Cery shrugged. "I told you I was getting married."

"So you did." The assassin leaned against the side of the cubicle and tilted her head to one side, her dark eyes as inscrutable as always. "You also said you were the loyal type. I assumed you'd found another, shall we say, side interest."

"You were never a side interest," Cery told her. "Life is too complicated for more than one lover at a time."

She smiled. "Sweet of you to say so. I can't say the same in return – but you knew that." Then her expression grew serious. Stepping inside, she pulled the panel closed. "You're here for business, not pleasure." It was not a question; it was a statement.

"You always did read me too easily," he said.

"No, I just pretend to. Who do you need killed?" Her eyes flashed with eagerness and anticipation. "Anyone annoyed you lately?"

"Information."

Her shoulders dropped with disappointment. "Why, why, why? All the time they want information." She threw up her hands. "Or if they want the full deal they coward out of it before I can even get my knives sharp." She shook her head, then looked at him hopefully. "Will the information lead to the full deal?"

She enjoys her work far too much, Cery thought. *Always did. It was part of what was so exciting about her.*

"It might, but then I'd rather do the job myself."

Terrina's lips formed a pout. "Typical." Then she smiled and waved a hand. "But I can't grudge you, if it's that personal. So what do you need to know?"

Cery drew in a deep breath, bracing himself for the stab of pain that would come with what he was about to say.

"Who broke into my hideout and killed my wife and sons," he said quietly, so none of the other patrons would hear. "If you don't know for sure, then any gossip you've heard will do."

She blinked and stared at him.

"Oh," was all she said. She regarded him thoughtfully. The gossip of assassins rarely spread beyond their ranks. All accepted that it could be bought, for a high price, but if it led to another assassin losing trade or being killed the seller would be punished severely. "You know how much that will cost?"

"Of course . . . depending on if you have the information I need."

She nodded, dropped into a crouch so she was at eye level, and stared at him earnestly. "Only for you, Cery. How long ago did it happen?"

"Nine days."

She frowned and gazed into the distance. "I've heard nothing like that. Most assassins would have put it about by now. Getting into a Thief's hideout is impressive. He'll have tried to kill you there because it proves he's clever. Tell me how he did it."

He described the unbroken locks, the ambushed guards, but left out what the lockmaker had said about magic.

"I suppose they'd keep their mug shut if they were paid enough. It would cost. So the client is rich, or has saved up a long time. Either that or they did it themselves, or it was someone close to you who knew the way in – but I suppose you've looked into that. Or . . ." Her gaze snapped to him. "Or else it's the Thief Hunter."

Cery frowned. "But why would he wait until I went out and then kill my family?"

"Maybe he didn't know you'd gone out. Maybe he didn't know you had a wife and children. I didn't tell anyone you were getting married, though that was 'cause I didn't believe it. And if you hid them well enough . . ." She shrugged. "He got in, they saw him, he had to kill them 'cause they could tag him."

"If only there was a way I could be sure." Cery sighed.

"Every killer has their leavings. Signs. Habits. Skills. You can tag 'em from those, if you've got enough killings to compare." She sighed and stood up. "I'd tell you the details about the Thief Hunter, except we're keeping them to ourselves for now, in case one of us is the killer."

Cery nodded. When Terrina said she would not give any more information, nothing could charm it out of her.

She looked at him and shook her head. "Sorry, I haven't been much help. Can't do anything but get you spooked about someone you already know about, and I can't tell you anything useful about." She looked away and frowned. "Can't really charge you much for that."

Cery opened his mouth to start bartering over the fee he'd offer her for the trouble of meeting with him, but she looked up suddenly.

"Oh, there's one thing I can tell you, because nobody's taking it seriously."

"Yes?"

"People reckon the Thief Hunter uses magic."

Cold rushed through Cery. He stared at her. "Why do they say that?"

"I thought it was because he was so good, people thought he *must* use magic. But I had a chat to a guard at a bolhouse once, who used to work for one of the Thieves that were done, and he says he saw a streak of light, and things flying through the air. Of course, everyone says it was the knock on the head making him see things, but . . . he was so sure of it, and not a man without a bit of good sense."

"How interesting," Cery said. *It could be nothing but fancy and rumour. If I hadn't seen for myself the lockmaker's evidence I wouldn't believe it.* But added to other rumours of magic occurring where it should not, he was beginning to wonder how much truth there was in it.

If it was true, then either a Guild magician was getting involved in things he or she shouldn't be, or there was a rogue magician in the city. Either way, they could have been involved in the murder of his family.

He suddenly thought of Skellin's obvious desire to hire his own rogue magician. *If this Thief Hunter is a rogue, he'll have no problem getting close to Skellin. Hmm, should I warn Skellin?*

But surely he's already heard of the rumours of magic . . . Ah! Maybe that's why he asked about magic. He knew I'd had connections to the Guild in the past and was testing me to see if I still did. Which would mean he suspected I'd hired the Thief Hunter.

Then another possibility occurred to him.

Had a Thief come to this conclusion and sent an assassin to kill me, not realising they'd hired the very same magic-wielding assassin they fear so much? He frowned. *At least I know it couldn't have been Skellin, as he wouldn't have arranged to meet with me and sent an assassin to kill me in* my *home at the same time.*

He shook his head. The possibilities seemed endless. But here was this mention of magic again. It had been used to open the lock of his hideout, and it was believed to be used by the Thief Hunter. Coincidence? Perhaps. But it was the only clue he had, so he may as well pursue it.

Every time Sonea entered the Administrator's office, memories wormed their way into her thoughts. Though Osen had rearranged the furniture and kept the room bright with globe lights, she could still remember how it had looked when Lorlen was alive. And she always wondered if he was aware there was an entrance to the secret passages of the University behind the panelling.

Lorlen didn't know, so I doubt Osen does.

"Tell me how you came to be at the Nameless?" Osen asked of the two young magicians standing to the left of his desk.

All turned to look at Reater and Sherran. Sonea had been dismayed to realise the two magicians found at the house were Lorkin's friends. The pair glanced at each other, then at the floor.

"We were given a slip of paper," Reater said. "It gave

directions to the best new playhouse in the city. There'd be free things for the first fifty customers."

"And it was in the Inner Circle, so we assumed it was safe," Sherran added.

"Where is this slip of paper now?" Osen asked.

One of the two older magicians standing to his right, Lord Vonel, stepped forward and handed over a tiny strip of white. Osen frowned at it as he read, then felt the thickness of the paper and turned it over to examine the back.

"Good quality. I will have the Alchemists who run the printing machines examine it and see if they can tell us the source."

"Hold it up to the light," Vonel suggested.

Osen did as he suggested and his eyes narrowed. "Is that part of the Guild's mark?"

"I believe so."

"Hmm." Osen put the slip down, then looked up at Vonel again.

"So how did you learn of the Nameless?"

"A novice brought that to me," Vonel replied, nodding toward the paper.

"And?"

"I asked Carrin to accompany me to the place, so that we could see what manner of establishment this 'playhouse' was, and if any members of the Guild had taken advantage of the offer."

"And what did you find on arrival?"

"Gambling, drinking, roet braziers and women for hire," Carrin replied. "Lord Reater here losing badly in some new game, Lord Sherran near comatose from inhaling roet smoke. Overall, these two plus twelve novices were engaged in sampling the full range of products on offer."

Osen picked up a sheaf of paper. "Those listed here."

"Yes."

The Administrator scanned the list, then put it aside and looked up at Regin and Sonea.

"And what part did you take, Lord Regin and Black Magician Sonea?"

"I was informed by a concerned novice who had overheard that there may be some mischief taking place, though not of the specifics," Regin replied. "Knowing that Black Magician Sonea has been taking an interest in the debate over the rule against magicians associating with criminals, I told her what I'd heard in the hopes she had clearer information. She did not."

"But I went looking for it, when I was free to," Sonea added. "And I was given an address. I sought permission to leave the Guild and investigate, but by the time it was given several novices and magicians had already been lured to the playhouse."

"Why did you not arrange for somebody else to go?" Osen asked.

Sonea felt a flare of annoyance. Why shouldn't she leave the grounds if all she was doing was trying to prevent a few novices and magicians falling into a trap? But plenty of magicians, Osen included, still thought she deserved having her move-ments restricted as punishment for learning black magic and defying the Guild all those years ago.

"We thought the fewer who knew of this place the better," Regin replied. "Only yourself and Lord Vonel and Lord Carrin."

She felt a wave of gratitude, then wry amusement that it was toward Regin, of all people.

Osen was now looking at the list of novices again. "It is too late for that. The Guard have shut down the playhouse, so it is no longer a temptation to anyone. All that remains is to decide the punishment." He turned to Reater and Sherran, who cringed and looked everywhere except at the other magicians. "You, like all magicians, are supposed to be an example of restraint and appropriate behaviour to those still in their years of learning. You also have a duty to present the Guild as an honourable and trustworthy institution. But it is not long since your graduation, and we all carry some of the foolish tendencies of novices into our first years as magicians. I will give you both another chance to mend your ways."

The two young men visibly sagged with relief. *If they'd had the misfortune of coming from low-class backgrounds the result would have been very different*, Sonea thought darkly.

"The novices . . ." Osen tapped the list. "Should be punished under the rules of the University. I will refer the matter to the University Administrator."

Oh great, Sonea thought. *Knowing my luck they'll end up at the hospices, where all the vices that got them into trouble are available mere streets away. They'll slip away as soon as they get a chance and I'll be blamed for it.*

"You acted as you were charged to," Osen said, nodding to Vonel and Carrin. "I have sent a letter to the Guard thanking them for acting so quickly." He looked at Regin. "In future we should all work together in order to prevent this sort of thing happening again. You may go."

Turning away, Sonea walked to the door, opening it with a little magic, and stepped out into the corridor. Regin followed, and they both stopped outside the door and waited until the two young magicians appeared. Sonea moved forward to block their path. Reater and Sherran stared at her in dismay.

She smiled sympathetically. "So you only went there for the

roet. What is it about roet, then? What's so appealing about it that you'd put yourself in the hands of obvious criminals for it?"

Reater shrugged. "It makes you feel good. Not a care."

Sonea nodded, but she had noticed that Sherran's expression had shifted to one of longing while Reater only looked resigned. She leaned closer, keeping her voice to a murmur.

"Did Lorkin ever . . .?"

Sherran looked at her, then hastily down at the floor again. "Once. He didn't like it."

Sonea straightened. He could be lying, afraid she would blame him if he answered otherwise. *But then he'd have told me Lorkin had never tried it. I think this is the truth.*

"You two are lucky Administrator Osen has chosen to be lenient on this. I wouldn't test his willingness to be so again."

They both nodded quickly. She gestured to indicate they could go, and they hurried away.

"Lorkin's too smart to be caught up in roet-taking," Regin murmured. "And the same good sense will keep him out of trouble in Sachaka." He sighed. "I only wish my own daughters had half his maturity."

She glanced at him, surprised and amused. Lorkin wasn't any more mature than other young magician his age. But judging by the small amount of gossip she had heard about Regin's daughters, they were very childish young women. "Still causing you trouble?"

He grimaced. "They take after their mother, though there's enough cruelty in their rivalry to remind me of myself at their age." He shook his head. "It's bad enough looking back and regretting your youthful arrogance without having to then regret your offspring's as well."

Sonea chuckled, then started down the corridor. "I hope I never have to experience that for myself. But considering the sort of things I did in my youth, I'd say Lorkin has a long way to go before he makes as great a disgrace of himself as I did."

CHAPTER 8

SIGNS

After two days in the carriage on increasingly bumpy roads, Lorkin felt as if his bones had been shaken into new and impractical arrangements. He kept having to Heal the aches of his body and soothe away headaches, but most of all he was bored. Hours of discomfort had left him too tired and grumpy for conversation, and he'd discovered that the jostling of the carriage on the roads made him ill if he tried to read.

Clearly, the excitement of travel wasn't in the actual travelling part. It was more likely in the arriving part. Though he suspected by the time they got to Arvice he'd feel more relief than excitement.

Lord Dannyl – or Ambassador Dannyl as he must remember to call him now – endured the ride with a strange kind of happy resignation, which gave Lorkin some hope that it was all worthwhile. Or else this was nothing compared to the discomfort of sea travel, or the chafing of saddles, both which Dannyl had survived during his travels over twenty years before.

Lorkin knew that, over twenty years ago, Dannyl had been ordered by the former Administrator to retrace Akkarin's journey in search of ancient magical knowledge. The stories

Dannyl told were fascinating, and made Lorkin want to visit the Tomb of White Tears and the ruins of Armje himself.

But I am going where neither my father nor Dannyl have been before: the capital of Sachaka.

It would be a completely different Sachaka to the one his father had stumbled into. There would be no Ichani waiting to enslave him. If anything, from what Perler had described, the powerful men and women of the capital, especially the Ashaki patriarchs, would deign to notice an Ambassador's assistant only reluctantly.

Still, he was reassured by the slight weight of the ring buried deep in the pocket of his robe. He'd found it in his chest that morning, in a small box buried deep among his belongings. There had been no note or explanation, but he recognised the plain gold band and the smooth red gemstone set within it. Had his mother slipped her blood gem ring into his chest secretly because she did not have permission to give it to him, or because she didn't want to risk that he would refuse to take it?

He and Dannyl had begun each day's journey by listing off the members of the most powerful Sachakan families several times, recalling key characteristics and alliances, correcting and helping each other memorise them. They had gone over what they knew of Sachakan society, and speculated where there were gaps in their knowledge. Lorkin noticed signs of nervousness and uncertainty in his companion. He felt almost an equal to the older magician, but he was sure that would change once they arrived and had to assume their roles.

The swaying of the carriage changed and Lorkin looked up. Only darkness lay beyond the windows, but the dull rapping of hoof on road had slowed. Dannyl sat up straighter and smiled.

"Either there's an obstruction on the road or we're about to be released from our cage for the night," he murmured.

As the carriage came to a stop, it swayed gently on its springs, then stilled. Lorkin could see a building lit by the glow of lamplight outside the left window. The driver made an incomprehensible noise, which Dannyl somehow interpreted as a signal to get out. The magician opened the door and climbed outside.

Following, Lorkin breathed in fresh night air and felt his head start to clear. He looked around. They had arrived in a tiny village, just a few buildings on either side of the road. It probably existed only to service travellers. The largest, which they had pulled up beside, was a Stayhouse. A stocky man stood within the entrance, beckoning and bowing.

"Welcome, my lords, to Fergun's Rest," he said. "I am Fondin. My stable workers will look after your horses, if you drive them around the back. We have clean beds and good food, all served with a smile."

There was a look of surprise and amusement on Dannyl's face, but the magician said nothing and led the way inside. Lorkin wondered if it was from wondering if the man had meant to suggest his beds were served with a smile. *Possibly he did. These roadside Stayhouses do have that sort of reputation.*

Dannyl introduced them and asked for a meal to be served to them and the driver. The owner ushered them to a pair of seats inside a large guest room. Only one other group of visitors occupied the room. Traders, by the look of them. They were talking quietly and only cast a few curious glances at Lorkin and Dannyl.

It was not long before the meal arrived. A young woman arrived with a platter containing meats, savoury buns, well-sautéed vegetables and small, probably local fruit. She smiled politely at them both, but her gaze brightened as she looked at Lorkin. When she returned with two complimentary cups of bol she paused to give him a coy look as she handed him his. As she walked away, her hips swayed invitingly. She glanced over her shoulder and smiled as she saw him watching her.

"I wonder if Sonea expects me to protect your virtue while we are away from the Guild," Dannyl said.

Lorkin chuckled and turned back to the other magician. Dannyl was filling his plate from the platter, and didn't look up.

"Virtue?"

"Yes, well, I figure your virtue is your own to protect. But as an older and wiser companion I feel, at this moment, a strange urge to steer you away from temptation for the sake of your health and wallet."

"Your concern is noted," Lorkin said, smiling. "Should I offer the same service in return?"

Dannyl looked up at Lorkin, his expression guarded and serious for a moment. Then he smiled. "Of course. We shall look out for one another." Then he gave a short, quiet laugh. "Though I suspect you may have a much easier task than I."

The ground vibrated in a way that brought a rush of memories to Cery's mind. Once, he would have passed this section of the Outer Wall via the city's sewers below. It had been an unpleasant and sometimes dangerous route. The city guard had discovered the sewer being used as a route into the city and started flushing it at intervals. An arrangement made between the Thieves to post watchers, who would signal if a flush was starting, got around that problem. It had been a reliable system, and he had used it to take Sonea to see the Guild many years ago, before she had become a magician.

But now the sewers were divided up among the Thieves whose territory they crossed, and many of these were rivals. It cost a fortune to gain access to them, and the watchers were no longer reliable. It was rumoured that this was how the Thief who'd drowned had been killed. A watcher upstream had been murdered by the Thief Hunter, and not only had the Thief died but all the watchers downstream as well.

There's not much reason to use the sewers now that the Purge has ended, Cery thought. *It's only useful if you have a powerful need to travel unseen.*

Since he no longer used the Thieves' Road to travel long distances either, Cery walked the streets of Imardin, in the daytime, like most of its citizens. It was safer, despite the risk of robbers or gangs. Gol's bulk deterred the former, while Cery's status still protected him from the latter.

I probably shouldn't rely on it so much. Or on poor Gol to intimidate possible attackers. Some day, one or the other won't work as a deterrent, and we'll be in trouble. But unless I want to go everywhere in a crowd of guards, that's a risk I have to take.

Passing through one of the new archways cut into the old wall, Cery started toward his own part of the former slums, Gol walking beside him.

"What did you make of Thim's story, Gol?"

The big man scowled. "We heard nothing new. Nobody's got any information, but plenty of the same old rumours."

"Yes. But at least they are the same. Everyone thinks it's the same person. Everyone has the same ideas about that person's skills."

"But everyone has a different reason for coming up with those ideas," Gol pointed out.

"Yes. Things moving through the air that have no right to be. Strange scorch marks. Shadowy figures that can't be stabbed. Flashing lights. Invisible walls. What do you believe, Gol?"

"That it's always better to be over-careful than dead."

Cery felt a flash of amusement. He stopped walking and turned to face his bodyguard. "So we act like the Thief Hunter is real and uses magic and has already had a go at me."

Gol frowned and glanced around to see if anyone had heard Cery. "You heard what I said about being over-careful?" he asked, a touch of annoyance in his tone.

"Yes." Cery sighed. "But what difference does it make if someone hears us? If my enemy is a magician I'm doomed."

The big man's frown deepened. "What about the Guild? They'd want to know if . . . about this. You could tell . . . your old friend."

"I could. But unless I have something real to tell her, she won't be able to do anything. We have to know for sure."

"Then we've got to lay a trap."

Cery stared at Gol in surprise, then shook his head. "And how do you think we're going to keep that sort of prisoner in it?"

"Not to catch him." Gol shrugged. "Just to confirm that's what he is. To lure him somewhere and into using what he can use, with us watching. Better still if he doesn't realise it was a trap."

Starting to walk again, Cery considered the idea. It wasn't a bad one. "Yes. Wouldn't want him getting mad . . . and if he doesn't realise he's walked into a trap the first time then we could trap him again – with my friend around to see."

"Now you're catching up," Gol said with an exaggerated sigh. "Sometimes you can be so slow to see—"

"Of course, I'd have to be the bait," Cery said.

Gol's teasing tone vanished. "No you won't. Well, you will, but you don't actually have to *be* there. The bait'll be the *rumour* that you will be there."

"It'll have to be a pretty convincing rumour," Cery told him.

"We'll sort something out."

They fell silent as they continued on their way. Cery found himself plotting out the details. *So where can we lure the Thief Hunter to? It will have to be somewhere people would expect me to be. Terrina said he struck the hideout because it was more clever to kill me in my safest place. So I need to set myself up in a new hideout, and arrange for some people to blab about it and how much safer it is than my old one. It'll have to have a few good spy holes, and an escape route or three. And it has to make the Thief Hunter use his powers in an obvious way.*

For the first time in weeks Cery felt a tingle of excitement and anticipation ruffle the surface of the gloom and suffocating pain that had settled on him. Even if the trap didn't lead to him avenging his family's deaths, planning and setting it up would keep him from brooding over them. He needed to act, not sit around feeling sorry for himself, frustrated at the lack of clues to their killer.

The steep, winding mountain road leading toward the Pass reminded Dannyl of those that he and Tayend had travelled to the city of Armje so many years before. Which was not surprising, since the peaks here belonged to the same range dividing Sachaka from the Allied Lands. Here, too, the forest

130

that edged the mountains thinned and gave way to stunted plants and rocky slopes.

The carriage travelled slowly as the horses hauled it steadily uphill. Lorkin had a now familiar look of boredom in his eyes, staring out of the window with a gloomy, resigned expression. They were both beyond conversation already, though it was not yet midday, and the silence only made the crawling pace more unbearable.

Then, without warning, the carriage abruptly turned and gained speed as the road levelled out. They began moving between two smooth walls of rock. Lorkin straightened, unlatched the window beside him and peered out.

"We're here," he said.

Dannyl felt excitement prickle his skin. He smiled with relief, and Lorkin grinned in reply. They sat in tense expectation, all attention on the movement of the carriage, the passing walls, and the sound of the hoof beats, until the driver called out and the vehicle slowed to a stop.

A face appeared at the window beside Lorkin. A man in red robes looked from Lorkin to Dannyl and nodded politely.

"Welcome to the Fort, Ambassador Dannyl and Lord Lorkin. I am Watcher Orton. Will you be staying for the night or continuing into Sachaka?"

"Unfortunately we cannot linger, as Administrator Osen is anxious to see us settled in Sachaka as quickly as possible," Dannyl said.

The man smiled sympathetically. "Then I invite you to stretch your legs and look around as we change your horses for fresh ones."

"We will gladly accept."

Lorkin unlatched the door and then followed as Dannyl

stepped out of the carriage. As soon as the young man set foot on the ground, he looked up and gave a little gasp.

"Ah, yes. It is an impressive structure," Orton said, following Lorkin's gaze.

Dannyl looked up and felt a shiver run up his spine. The face of the Fort towered over him, stretching from one side of the narrow ravine to the other. It was smooth and unblemished except where the shadows of huge cracks, filled in with more stone, showed where repairs had been made.

"Was that damage from the Ichani Invasion?" Lorkin asked.

"Yes, though it was worse inside," Orton replied. He started forward, leading them into a cavernous opening. It took a few moments for Dannyl's eyes to adjust, then he was able to make out tunnel walls stretching before them, lit by lamps. Slight variations in colour showed where sections had been filled with new stone. In some places there were gaps that went up several floors.

"Did we replace the traps that were originally here?" Dannyl asked.

"Some." Orton shrugged. "Most were simple barriers, designed to delay and use up an attacker's strength. We have installed more complex systems of defence to replace them. Tricks that might catch an invader if their guard was lowered. Illusions that will waste his power. But nothing that could hold off a group of powerful Sachakan black magicians for long, which is why we have spent as much time and energy creating means of escaping the Fort as well. Too many died in the Invasion who need not have, for lack of escape routes. Ah – here we have a memorial to those who gave up their lives bravely defending the Pass."

Between two lamps a list of names had been carved into

the wall. Dannyl felt a mix of disquiet and amusement as he caught a familiar name. *From what I recall, Fergun was dragged out of some hiding place by the Sachakans. Hardly what I'd call bravely defending the Pass. But the rest . . . they died not understanding what they faced, because the Guild did not believe Akkarin's warning. It could not comprehend the threat he described, having forgotten what black magic could make a magician capable of.*

They stood in silence for a while, then the sound of hooves and the creak of wheels and springs echoed in the tunnel. Turning, Dannyl saw that the driver was leading a new set of horses, harnessed to the carriage, toward them.

"You must see the Fort from the Sachakan side," Orton told him, continuing down the tunnel.

Dannyl and Lorkin followed. The sound of the carriage was loud in the confined space, so none of them spoke until they had emerged from the tunnel. Once again, high ravine walls rose on either side. They curved away in front of the Fort, giving no view of Sachaka. As Orton turned around and looked up, Lorkin and Dannyl followed suit. Another smooth wall stretched between the ravine walls, broken by many small windows. Two huge slabs of stone that had clearly once been a single square lay against the ravine wall to one side.

"That was once a door of sorts," Orton told them. "It was dropped down to block the tunnel." He shrugged. "I do wonder why the magicians who built the Fort, who were black magicians themselves, thought such things would slow down an invader."

"Every little bit of power used by the enemy might be a life saved," Lorkin said.

Orton looked at the young man and nodded. "Perhaps." The carriage emerged from the tunnel and the driver pulled the horses to a stop beside them. Orton turned to Dannyl. "Fresh horses, plus feed and water for the three days it will take you to cross the wasteland, are on board. There are also supplies for yourself in the cabin, and I asked the cook to throw together something nicer for your next meal. Nothing fancy, but it might be the last Kyralian meal you have for a while."

"Thank you, Watcher Orton."

The man smiled. "My pleasure, Ambassador Dannyl." He looked at Lorkin. "I hope you and Lord Lorkin have a safe journey, and that you will stop for a while on your return to Kyralia."

Dannyl nodded. "We'll do our best to keep any invaders from testing out those new defences."

Orton chuckled and turned to the carriage. "I know you will."

The carriage door swung open, no doubt by Orton's magic. Dannyl climbed aboard and sat down, bracing himself against the sway of the vehicle as Lorkin eagerly followed him. They waved goodbye and called out thanks as the carriage rolled away and Orton moved out of sight.

Dannyl looked at Lorkin, who grinned back.

"I suspect Watcher Orton doesn't get many visitors," Lorkin said quietly.

"No. You look a lot more cheerful than you were this morning," Dannyl remarked.

Lorkin's grin widened. "We're in Sachaka now."

A shiver ran down Dannyl's spine. *He's right. The moment we stepped out of the tunnel we were no longer in our own land. We're in exotic Sachaka, the heart of the former Empire that once included Kyralia and Elyne. The land of black magicians. All so much more powerful than me . . .*

This must be what it felt like to be a trader or diplomat who dealt with magicians in the Allied Lands, always aware how helpless they'd be in the face of magic, but relying on diplomacy and the threat of retaliation from their homeland to keep them safe from harm. Dannyl thought of the blood ring Administrator Osen had given him, made by Black Magician Kallen out of Osen's blood so that Dannyl could contact him. *For monthly reports, otherwise only to be used in emergencies. As if he could stop a black magician killing me from all the way—*

Suddenly the wall of rock beside him was gone, and in its place was a great, pale expanse. Lorkin made a wordless exclamation, changed to the seat opposite Dannyl and moved close to the window to look out.

"So that's the wasteland," he breathed.

A treeless slope fell steeply from the edge of the road down to rocky, eroded hills below. Lapping around them like a frozen sea was a desert, dunes rippling across the land. The air was dry, Dannyl noticed suddenly, and tasted of dust.

"I guess it is," he replied.

"It's . . . bigger than I thought," Lorkin said.

"We are taught that it was meant to be a barrier," Dannyl said. "But the older records only comment that it *might* act as one. That suggests the wasteland wasn't entirely deliberate. At least, not what the Guild had planned."

"So nobody knows for sure why it was created, let alone how?"

"There are some records that state that those who made it intended to weaken Sachaka by ruining its most productive land. I've found letters in which magicians support the idea, and others who thought it an appalling idea. But the letters

135

have the tone of people reacting to rumour and gossip, not an official decision."

Lorkin grimaced. "It wouldn't be the first time in history someone acted independently of the Guild."

"No." Dannyl wondered if Lorkin was referring to his parents. His tone had been wry.

They sat and stared at the wasteland for several minutes without speaking. Then Lorkin shook his head and sighed.

"The land has never recovered. Not after seven hundred years. Has anyone tried to restore it?"

Dannyl shrugged. "I don't know."

"Maybe it's a good thing nobody knows how it was done. If we ever face a proper war – rather than a bunch of outcasts – we'd be in some serious trouble."

Looking out over the ruined land, Dannyl had to agree. "From all accounts, the Sachakans were furious at the devastation. If they'd known how to strike back, they would have. I don't think they know any more than we do."

Lorkin nodded. "It's probably better that way." He frowned and looked at Dannyl. "But if we do find anything . . ."

"We will have to keep it a secret. At least until we can pass on the information to the High Lord Balkan. It would be even more dangerous than the knowledge of black magic."

CHAPTER 9

SEEKING TRUTHS

L ike many low-born novices from the poorer parts of the city, Norrin was of small stature. But he looked even smaller walking between the two Warriors escorting him into the Guildhall. Sonea felt her heart twist in sympathy as he glanced up at the rows of magicians staring down at him on either side, turned white, then set his gaze on the floor.

It is cruel to drag him before the entire Guild, she thought. *A Hearing before the Higher Magicians would have been intimidating and humiliating enough. But someone wanted to make an example of him.*

By Guild rules, any novice who failed to attend the University or reside in the Grounds without permission to live elsewhere was considered a potential rogue, and must be brought before the assembled Guild to explain themselves, even if only the Higher Magicians were to judge their actions and decide on a punishment.

If he hadn't been found right before a Meet day, he might have been spared this. But it is much easier to tack a Hearing onto the end of a Meet than arrange a separate one. I suspect if Osen had been faced with getting the whole Guild together just for this Hearing, he'd have bent the rules and kept it to the Higher Magicians.

The escorts stopped at the front, Norrin halting beside them and bowing to the Higher Magicians. Administrator Osen glanced back at the Higher Magicians – at Sonea. For a second their gazes locked, then he looked away.

Others had noted his glance, and she found herself the subject of speculative looks from High Lord Balkan, Lady Vinara and Director Jerrik. She resisted the urge to shrug to indicate she had no idea why Osen had chosen that moment to look at her, instead ignoring them and keeping her attention on the novice.

The Administrator approached Norrin, whose shoulders hunched, but he didn't look up.

"Novice Norrin," Osen said. "You have been absent from the Guild Grounds and University for two months. You have ignored requests that you return, forcing us to take you into custody. You know the law restricting a novice's movements and where he or she may reside. Why have you broken it?"

Norrin's shoulders rose and fell as he took a deep breath and let it out again. He straightened and looked up at the Administrator.

"I don't want to be a magician," he said. "I'd want to, if I didn't want to look after my family more." He stopped and looked down again. Sonea could not see Osen's face, but his posture was all patient expectation.

"Your family?" he prompted.

Norrin looked around, then flushed. "My little brothers and sisters. Mother can't look after them. She's sick."

"And nobody else can take on this responsibility?" Osen asked.

"No. My sister – next oldest after me – died last year. The rest are too young. I didn't use magic once," he added quickly. "I know I'm not supposed to if I'm not gonna be a magician."

"If you do not wish to be a magician – if you wish to leave

the Guild – you must have your powers blocked," Osen told him.

The novice blinked, then looked up at the Administrator with such hope that Sonea felt a pain in her chest. "You can do that?" Norrin said in a barely audible voice. "Then I can go look after my family and nobody will mind?" He frowned. "It doesn't cost a lot, does it?"

Osen said nothing, then shook his head. "It costs nothing, except in lost opportunities for yourself. Can't you wait a few more years? Wouldn't it be better for your family if you were a magician?"

Norrin's face darkened. "No. I can't see them. I can't get money to them. I can't make Mother's . . . sickness go away. And the others're too young to look after themselves."

Osen then turned to the Higher Magicians. "I suggest we discuss this."

Sonea nodded her agreement along with the others. The Administrator indicated that the escort should take the boy out of the hall. As soon as the doors closed, Lady Vinara sighed loudly and turned to face them.

"The boy's mother is a whore. She is not sick, she is addicted to roet."

"It is true," University Director Jerrik said. "But he has not picked up the habits of his mother. He is a sensible young man, studious and well mannered, with strong powers. It would be a pity to lose him."

"He is too young to know what he is giving up," Lord Garrel added. "He will regret sacrificing magic for the sake of his family."

"But he would regret it more if he sacrificed his family for magic," Sonea could not help adding.

Faces turned toward her. She had not made a habit of partici-
pating in the debates of the Higher Magicians these last twenty
years. At first, because she felt too young and inexperienced
in Guild politics to contribute, later because it had become
clear to her that her position among them had been bestowed
not out of respect but out of a begrudging acknowledgement
of her powers and assistance in defending the country.

*Yet whenever I speak I seem to attract a lot more attention than
is warranted.*

"You have much in common with Norrin, Black Magician
Sonea," Osen began. "In having not wanted to join the Guild
– though not due to family circumstances, of course," he added.
"What would you suggest we do to persuade him to stay?"

Sonea resisted the urge to roll her eyes. "He wants to visit
and help his family. Grant him that and I'm sure he'd be
delighted to remain with us."

The Higher Magicians exchanged glances. She looked at
Rothen. He grimaced, communicating in that one look how
unlikely it was the Higher Magicians would agree to that.

"But that would result in Guild money going to a whore,
and no doubt feed her addiction," Garrel pointed out.

"Plenty more Guild money goes toward hiring the services
of whores each night than would be required to keep Norrin's
family fed and accommodated for the year," Sonea replied, then
winced at the tartness in her voice.

The magicians paused again. *And this, too, always seems to
happen when I dare to speak*, she mused. Lady Vinara had covered
her mouth with a hand, she noticed.

"It will have to be up to Norrin to ensure that the money
he gives his mother does not go toward roet," Sonea told them
in what she hoped was a more conciliatory tone. "It is clearly

not his aim to kill his mother." Then she had a flash of inspiration. "If he agrees to stay, send him to the hospices to work – as punishment if you must. I will arrange for his family to visit. That way he can see them *and* be seen to be disciplined for breaking the law."

There were nods all around.

"An excellent solution," Lord Osen said. "Perhaps you can persuade his mother to give up the drug at the same time." He looked at her expectantly. She said nothing, just met his gaze levelly. *I'm not stupid enough to make any promises, when it comes to roet.*

Osen looked away, turning to the others. "Does anyone object, or have another suggestion?"

The Higher Magicians shook their heads. Osen called in the escorts and Norrin. When Sonea's suggestion was offered to him, he gazed up at her with open gratitude. *That's a little too much like adoration*, she thought. *I had better make sure I keep him working hard, so he doesn't start idolising me – or, more importantly, thinking that breaking rules leads to him getting his way.*

As Osen announced the Hearing and Meet concluded, and Sonea rose and started descending the stairs, Lady Vinara stepped out to block her path.

"It is good to see you speaking your mind at last," the elderly Healer said. "You should do so more often."

Sonea blinked in surprise, and found she could think of nothing to say that wouldn't sound trite. Vinara's smile changed to a more serious look. She glanced down at where Norrin had been standing.

"This case clearly demonstrates the need to make a prompt decision on whether to change or abolish the rule against associating with criminals and characters of low repute." She lowered her voice. "I am in favour of a clarification. The rule is too easily interpreted in a way that would restrict the work of my Healers."

Sonea nodded and managed a smile. "Mine even more so. When do you think the Administrator will call for a decision?"

Vinara frowned. "He has not yet concluded whether it should be a decision for us or the Guild. It may be perceived as unfair, should it be the former, as you are the only Higher Magician who might be seen to represent the magicians and novices of lower-class origins. But if we open it up to the entire Guild . . ."

"It may not make that much difference," Sonea finished. "And there are sure to be remarks made that, stated publicly, may cause lasting resentment."

Vinara shrugged. "Oh, I don't think we can avoid that. But it will cause a lot more fuss and work, and Osen is not sure the issue warrants that."

"Well, then." Sonea smiled grimly and stepped past the woman. "Perhaps Norrin's case will convince him otherwise."

Lorkin gazed out at the fields beside the road, wondering how long it would take for him to get used to the greenness of it all. For three days they had travelled across the wasteland, and it felt as if the dry dustiness of the place had filled every crease in his skin and hollow of his lungs. He was looking forward to a bath more than he had ever before in his life.

At night they had taken turns keeping watch for the approach of Ichani, or sleeping in the carriage. The wasteland was considered the most dangerous part of their journey – hence the precautions – but no attacks by outcast Sachakan magicians had ever been made on Guild magicians since the invasion. Previous Guild Ambassadors had seen figures in the distance watching them, but none had ever approached.

Lorkin doubted they could have held off an attack by Ichani bandits for long, but the previous Ambassador had told them that they'd always relied on the hope that looking like they were prepared for a fight was deterrent enough. The Ichani roaming the wastes and mountains knew that the Guild had managed to kill Kariko and his gang, though not *how* they had, and so kept a cautious distance from any robed visitors.

On the second day a sandstorm had forced Dannyl to sit beside the driver and protect horse and carriage, as well as keep the road visible, with a magical barrier. On the third day the sands gave way to tussocks and stunted bushes. As the vegetation thickened, grazing animals had appeared. Then those gave way to the first struggling crops, which slowly improved in health and lushness until all looked appealingly rural and normal — so long as one didn't look too closely at the south-western horizon.

Now and then clusters of white buildings and walls appeared several hundred paces from the road. These were the estates of Sachaka's powerful landowners, the Ashaki. Only when they passed the first of these did Lorkin realise that the ruins the carriage had passed in the wasteland had probably once looked just like them.

Tonight, Lorkin and Dannyl were to visit and stay with an Ashaki. Lorkin was not sure how much of the nervous tingle of anticipation he felt at finally meeting a Sachakan was excitement or dread. Dannyl had met with the Sachakan Ambassador in Imardin, but Lorkin had not been confirmed as his assistant at the time and so was not invited to the meeting.

I want us to hurry up and get there, but how much of that is due to hunger and wanting a comfortable bed and a whole night's sleep?

The carriage slowed, then turned off the main road. Lorkin's heart began racing. Leaning close to the window he saw white buildings at the end of the narrow road the carriage was following. The walls were smooth and curved, with no sharp edges. As they drew closer, he could see, through an archway ahead, thin figures moving about inside a space beyond the wall. One stopped within the archway, then turned to wave at the others before moving out of sight.

When they passed through the archway they found themselves in a near-deserted courtyard. Whoever the people were, they had made themselves scarce. A single figure stepped out of a narrow doorway as the carriage drew to a halt, and dropped smoothly face-down on the ground.

Clearly he was a slave. Lorkin looked at Dannyl, who smiled grimly and moved to the door of the carriage. As the Ambassador climbed out, the man on the ground did not move. Lorkin followed. He looked up at the driver. The man wore a frown of disapproval.

Well, we were told to expect this. It doesn't make it any less discomfiting. And it feels a bit rude, too. Still, they do things differently here. The master of the house does not emerge to greet his guests. He welcomes them once they're inside.

"Take us to your master," Dannyl ordered. His tone was neither commanding, nor did it sound like a request. Lorkin decided this was a good compromise and resolved to do the same when addressing a slave.

The prone man rose and, without looking up or saying anything, moved back through the doorway into the building.

Dannyl and Lorkin followed. They entered a corridor. The interior walls were the same as the exterior, though perhaps a little smoother. Looking closely, Lorkin saw that there were fingermarks in the surface. The walls had been coated with some kind of paste. He wondered if there was a solid stone or brick core to the walls, or if they had been made entirely of some sort of clay, built up in successive layers.

Reaching the end of the corridor, the slave stepped aside and threw himself on the floor. Dannyl and Lorkin entered a large room, the white walls decorated with hangings and carvings. A man was sitting on one of three low stools, and now he rose and smiled at them.

"Welcome. I am Ashaki Tariko. You must be Ambassador Dannyl and Lord Lorkin."

"We are," Dannyl replied. "It is an honour to meet you and we thank you for inviting us to stay in your home."

The man was a head shorter than Dannyl, but his broad stature gave the impression of strength. His skin was the typical Sachakan brown – lighter than a Lonmar's but darker than an Elyne's honey-brown. From the wrinkles about his mouth and eyes Lorkin guessed he was between forty and fifty years old. He wore a short jacket covered in colourful stitchwork over some sort of plain garment, and a pair of trousers in the same cloth as the jacket, but not as elaborately decorated.

"Come sit with me," Ashaki Tariko invited, gesturing to the stools. "I set watchers on the road to alert me when you were near, so I could have a meal prepared ready for your arrival." He turned to the prone slave. "Alert the kitchen that our guests are here," he ordered.

The man leapt to his feet and hurried away. As Lorkin followed Dannyl to the stools, he caught a flash of something metallic at Tariko's waist and looked closer. An elaborately decorated knife sheath and handle hung from his belt. It was quite beautiful, set with jewels and inlaid with gold.

Then Lorkin felt a chill run down his spine.

It's a black magician's knife. Ashaki Tariko is a black magician. For a moment he felt a rush of fear that was strangely exhilarating, but it faded as quickly and left behind a disappointing cynicism. *Yeah, and so's your mother*, he found himself thinking, and he suddenly knew that living in a land of black magicians wasn't going to be as thrilling and novel as he'd thought it would be.

His thoughts were interrupted by a stream of men and women, dressed simply in cloth wrapped about their torso and bound with a length of rope about their waist. They bore either a platter laden with food, or pitchers and goblets. Exotic smells assaulted his nose and he felt his stomach rumble in response. Each slave approached Ashaki Tariko, burden held out before them and head bowed, then knelt before him. The first held the utensils with which the host and guests would eat: a plate and a knife with a forked tip. Then goblets were offered and filled with wine. Finally there were successive dishes, the master of the house selecting first, then Dannyl, then Lorkin. Tariko dismissed each slave with a quiet, "Go".

The master of the house first, Lorkin recited silently. *Magicians before non-magicians, Ashaki before landless free men, age before youth, men before women.* Only if a woman was a magician *and* head of her family would she be served before men. *And women often eat separately from men anyway. I wonder if Ashaki Tariko has a wife.*

The food was richly spiced, some so hot he had to stop and cool his mouth with a mouthful of wine every few bites. He resisted as long as possible, both in the hope he would grow used to the heat sooner, and because he did not want to end up insensible from drink – especially not on his first night as a guest of a Sachakan black magician.

While Dannyl and their host discussed the journey across the wastes, the weather, the food and the wine, Lorkin watched the slaves. The last of them to offer their burdens had waited the longest, but their arms were steady. It was strange to have these silent people in the room, all but ignored as Tariko and Dannyl talked.

These people are Tariko's possessions, he reminded himself. *They are put to work and bred like livestock.* He tried to imagine what that would be like, and shuddered. Only when the last of the food had been offered and the last slave dismissed was Lorkin able to pay attention to the conversation.

"How does it affect you, living this close to the wasteland?" Dannyl asked.

Tariko shrugged. "If the wind comes from that direction it sucks the moisture out of everything. It can ruin a crop if it blows too long. Afterwards there will be a fine sanddust coating everything, inside and outside." He looked up, beyond the walls toward the wasteland. "The wastes grow a little larger each year. One day, maybe in a thousand years, the sands will meet those in the north, and all Sachaka will be desert."

"Unless it can be reversed," Dannyl said. "Has anyone here attempted to reclaim land from the wastes?"

"Many." *Of course we have*, Tariko's expression seemed to say. "Sometimes successfully, but never permanently. Those who have studied the wastes say that the fertile top layer of the land was stripped away, and without it water is not retained and plants cannot return."

Dannyl's gaze sharpened with interest. "But you have no idea how?"

"No." Tariko sighed. "Every few years it rains in the northern desert, and within a few days the land turns green. The soil is rich with ash from the volcanoes. It is only the lack of rain that keeps it a desert. We have plenty of rain here but still nothing grows."

"That sounds like a wonder to see," Lorkin added in a murmur. "The northern desert in flower, that is."

Tariko smiled at him. "It is. The Duna tribes come south to harvest the desert plants and sell the dried leaves, fruit and seeds in Arvice. If you are lucky, such an event will happen during your stay, and you will have the opportunity to enjoy some rare spices and delicacies."

"I hope so," Lorkin said. "Though I can't imagine anything more exotic and delicious than the meal we just enjoyed."

The Sachakan chuckled, pleased at the flattery. "I have always said that of all slaves, good cooks are worth the extra expense. And horse trainers."

Lorkin just managed to stop himself wincing at such a casual reference to buying people and was glad that Tariko said no more about it. After a discussion about foods native to Sachaka, in which Tariko recommended they try some dishes and avoid others, the Ashaki straightened his back.

"You must be tired and now that I have fed you I won't keep you from a bath and bed any longer."

Dannyl looked disappointed as their host rose, but to Lorkin's relief did not protest. A gong rang out and two young women hurried into the room to throw themselves on the floor.

"Take our guests to their rooms," he ordered. Then he smiled at Dannyl and Lorkin. "Rest well Ambassador Dannyl and Lord Lorkin. I will see you again in the morning."

Lifting the cover, Cery leaned close to the spy hole and squinted at the room beyond. It was narrow, but very long, so the overall space was generous. He hadn't liked the shape, but it could be divided into a string of smaller rooms, and escape routes spaced along the length.

Several men were working within the room, covering the brick walls with panelling, building the framework for the dividing walls, and tiling the floor. Two were working on the fireplace, clearing a blockage. As soon as they were finished and the mess cleared, work would start on decorating, and Cery's new hideout – and trap for the Thief Hunter – would become a tasteful, luxurious space.

"Are you sure you want to use the same lockmaker?" Gol asked.

Cery turned to see his bodyguard's eye illuminated by a small circle of light from beyond another spy hole.

"Why wouldn't I?"

"You said you didn't think Dern betrayed you, and if nobody betrays you then the Thief Hunter will never fall into our trap."

Turning back to the spy hole, Cery watched the men working. "I don't want people thinking I'm blaming him."

"I'm still a bit suspicious about the lock. Why would Dern build into it a way to tell if magic had been used, if it was so unlikely magic *would* be used on it?"

"Maybe he thought it *was* likely. After all, I'm a Thief. Thieves have been getting murdered for some years now."

"Then he must have reason to suspect they were killed with the help of magic."

149

"Perhaps he has. Perhaps he's heard the rumours about the Thief Hunter. But I've always found Dern to be habitually thorough to the point of ridiculousness and I think that's why he made it like that, not that he knew anything about the Thief Hunter and his methods."

Gol sighed. "Well . . . yes, he does seem that way at times. And while he was thankful to get more work from you, he seemed, well, nervous. Twitchy. Kept saying if the Thief Hunter and the Rogue turned out to be real and the same then what other legends might be true? Like the one about the giant ravis that eat people alive if they go into the sewers, or come up and drag people off the Thieves' Road."

"He would have to wonder." Cery shook his head. "I always thought the Rogue was a myth, too. People have been saying there's a magician hiding in the city for twenty years, even though Senfel rejoined the Guild after they pardoned him, and died of old age . . . what? Is it nine or ten years ago?"

"Senfel put the idea into people's heads – as did Sonea. Now every strange occurrence that could be magical is evidence that more rogues are about."

"Seems they might have been right about that." Cery scowled. "But that's more reason why we need to be sure before we tell Sonea."

Gol grunted in agreement. "Do you think we should tell Skellin what we're doing?"

"Skellin?" For a moment Cery wondered why, then he remembered the agreement he'd made with the other Thief. "We don't know for sure if the person we're baiting is the Thief Hunter. If we find evidence that he is, we'll tell Skellin. Otherwise . . ." he shrugged. "He never asked me to tell him if I found a rogue."

For a while they both looked through the spy holes in silence, then Cery let the cover of his hole swing back. The workmen knew of the escape routes they were building, but not of the ones that already existed, or of the spy holes Cery and Gol were watching them through.

"Let's go."

The hole of light before Gol's eye vanished. Cery began walking, trailing a hand along the wall.

I wonder which one of the workmen I've hired will leak the location of my new hideout. Though Cery always treated workers well, paying them fairly and without delay, he could never be completely sure of their loyalty or ability to keep secrets. He found out everything he could about them: if they had family, if they cared about that family, if they had debts, who they had worked for in the past, who had worked for them, and if there was anyone, the Guard especially, they'd rather not encounter.

Not this time. Gol has set the information gathering in motion, but there isn't enough time to be thorough, and that's fine. For the trap to work Cery needed someone to leak information about it. *But if I don't take some precautions the Hunter might think it out of character, and become suspicious.*

The passage turned, then turned again.

"You can open the lamp now," Cery murmured.

There was a pause, then a faint squeak, and the tunnel was suddenly bathed in light.

"You know, any of those workers could be the Hunter."

Cery glanced over his shoulder at his friend.

"Surely not."

Gol shrugged. "Even the Hunter needs to eat and keep a roof over his head. He's got to have a job of some sort."

"Unless he's rich," Cery pointed out, turning back again.

"Unless he's rich," Gol agreed.

Once, it would have been a safe bet to assume the Hunter was rich. Only rich people learned magic. But these days, people of all classes could join the Guild. And if the Hunter couldn't afford to bribe people, he could always blackmail and threaten them – possibly more effectively using magic to scare people.

I wish I could ask Sonea if any magicians or novices have gone missing. But I don't want to risk meeting her again until I have proof there is a rogue in the city.

And in the meantime, he had best make sure he got that proof without getting himself killed.

CHAPTER 10

A NEW CHALLENGE

The former Guild Ambassador to Sachaka had told Dannyl that no walls surrounded Arvice. No defensive walls, that was. There were plenty of boundary walls in Sachaka. Taller than a man, or so low they might be stepped over, and always rendered and painted white, they marked the boundaries of property. The only indication that he and Lorkin had reached the city was that high walls now lined the roadside instead of low ones, except in places where they had collapsed and not been repaired.

There have been a lot of ruins, he noted. *Out in the wasteland, and then the occasional clusters of broken walls within estates that looked like they might once have been mansions. And now this . . .* The carriage passed another collapsed wall and through the gap he could see the scorched and crumbling remains of a building. *It's as if the Sachakan War only happened a few years ago, and they haven't had time yet to rebuild.*

But if the creation of the wasteland had cut Sachaka's food production by half, as Ashaki Tariko claimed, then perhaps the population had shrunk accordingly. Houses wouldn't be rebuilt if there wasn't anyone to live in them.

The war happened seven hundred years ago. Surely the houses abandoned then would be long gone. These ruins must be more recent. Perhaps the population is still slowly diminishing. Or maybe the owners are too poor to afford repairs or rebuilding.

The carriage neared a young woman, walking barefoot along the street and wearing the plain, belted wrap of a slave. She glanced up as the vehicle approached, then her eyes widened. Veering away, she hunched over and fixed her eyes on the ground as it passed.

Dannyl frowned, then leaned closer to the window so he could see ahead. More slaves populated the road in front of them. They, too, reacted with fear as the carriage approached. Some turned and ran in the other direction. Those near side streets took advantage of them. Others froze and shrank against the nearest wall.

Is this normal slave behaviour? Do they shrink away from all carriages, or is it because this is a Guild carriage? If the latter, why do they fear us? Have any of my or Lorkin's predecessors given them reason to? Or do they fear Kyralians only because of past events?

The carriage turned into another street, then crossed a wider thoroughfare. Dannyl noticed that the slaves here were not as fearful, though they did give the carriage a wide berth. After it rounded a few more corners it abruptly turned between two gates into a courtyard, and stopped. A glint of gold caught his eye, and he saw that a plaque on the side of the house stated: *Guild House of Arvice.*

Dannyl turned to regard Lorkin. The young man was sitting straight, his eyes bright with excitement. He looked at Dannyl, then waved at the carriage door.

"Ambassadors first," he said, grinning.

Moving across the cabin, Dannyl opened the door and

climbed down. A man was lying on the ground nearby. For a moment Dannyl felt a flash of concern, worried that the stranger had collapsed. Then he remembered.

"I am Guild Ambassador Dannyl," he said. "This is Lord Lorkin, my assistant. You may rise."

The man climbed to his feet, keeping his gaze on the ground. "Welcome, Ambassador Dannyl and Lord Lorkin."

"Thank you," Dannyl replied automatically, remembering too late that such social habits were seen as amusing and foolish to the Sachakans. "Take us inside."

The man gestured to a nearby door, then turned and walked through it. He glanced back to ensure they were following as he led the way down a corridor. Just as in Ashaki Tariko's house, it led to a large room – the Master's Room. But this room was abuzz with voices. Dannyl was surprised to find at least twenty men standing there, all in the highly decorated short jackets that Sachakan men wore as traditional formal attire. All turned to regard him as he entered, and the voices immediately fell silent.

"Ambassador Dannyl and Lord Lorkin," the slave announced.

One of the men stepped forward, smiling. He had the typical broad-shouldered stature of his race, but there was a little grey in his hair and the wrinkles around his eyes and mouth gave his face a cheerful expression. His jacket was a dark blue with gold stitchery, and there was an ornate knife in his belt.

"Welcome to Arvice, Ambassador Dannyl, Lord Lorkin," he said, glancing at Lorkin briefly before turning his attention back to Dannyl. "I am Ashaki Achati. My friends and I have been waiting to greet you, and give you your first taste of Sachakan hospitality."

Ashaki Achati. Dannyl felt a small rush of excitement as he recalled the name. *A major political player, and friend to the Sachakan king.*

"Thank you," Dannyl replied. "I . . ." He looked at Lorkin and smiled. "We are flattered and honoured."

Ashaki Achati's smile widened. "Let me introduce you both to everyone."

Voices filled the room again as Achati called over the rest of the men, individually or in pairs, to meet Dannyl. One portly man was introduced as the king's Master of Trade; a short, stooped man turned out to be the Master of Law. The Master of War seemed a strange choice – thin for a Sachakan, and overly flippant in manner for such a weighty and serious role. The Master of Records' friendliness seemed forced, but Dannyl picked up no dislike in his manner, just a hint of boredom.

"So do you have any plans to entertain yourself, when not buried in ambassadorial duties?" a man named Ashaki Vikato asked after they were introduced.

"I find the past fascinating," Dannyl replied. "I would like to know more about Sachaka's history."

"Ah! Well you should talk to Kirota." The man waved toward the Master of War. "He is always talking about some obscure bit of the past, or reading old books. What is a chore to most Sachakan boys is a pleasant pastime to him."

Dannyl looked across at the thin man, who was grinning at something he was being told.

"Not the Master of Records?"

"No," Ashaki Achati said, shaking his head. "Not unless you're having trouble sleeping."

Ashaki Vikato chuckled. "Old Richaki is more interested in recording the present than dredging up the past. Master Kirota!"

The thin man turned and then smiled as Vikato beckoned. He wove his way across the room.

"Yes, Ashaki Vikato?"

"Ambassador Dannyl has an interest in history. How would you suggest he go about satisfying it while he is in Arvice?"

Kirota's eyebrows rose. "You do?" Then he frowned as he considered. "It isn't easy to gain access to records or libraries," he warned. "All our libraries are privately owned, and you have to get permission from Master Richaki to view the palace records."

Achati nodded. "I'm on good terms with most of the library owners in Arvice." He looked at Dannyl. "If you'd like, I can introduce you and see if we can gain access to some of them."

"I would be most grateful if you did," Dannyl replied.

Achati smiled. "It'll be easy. They'll all want to meet the latest Guild Ambassador. Only trouble you might have is getting them to leave you alone long enough to read anything. Is there any aspect of history that you are most interested in?"

"The older, the better. And . . ." Dannyl paused to consider how to phrase what he wanted to say. "While I'd like to fill the gaps in my knowledge of Sachakan history, I'm also interested in anything that might fill some of the gaps in Kryalian history as well."

"You have gaps?" Kirota's eyebrows rose again. "But then, don't we all?" He smiled, the lines on his thin face deepening and making Dannyl realise the man was older than he'd first guessed. "Perhaps you can help me fill some of the gaps in ours as well, Ambassador Dannyl."

Dannyl nodded. "I'll do what I can."

As Achati looked around the room, perhaps to check if he'd neglected to introduce anyone yet, Dannyl realised that, despite being surrounded by black magicians, he felt perfectly at ease. These were men of power and influence, and he'd had plenty of dealings with such men in the past. *Perhaps this role should not be much harder than it was in Elyne. Not that that one was easy. And it seems black magic is no obstacle to having scholarly interests, too.* He felt a tingle of anticipation, thinking of the records he might stumble upon in these private libraries Achati had mentioned. Then he felt a twinge of guilt and sadness. *It would have been good to share the discoveries with Tayend. But I'm not sure he'd be that interested now. And for all that these men seem friendly, he is safer back in Kyralia.*

The crowd outside the Northside Hospice was smaller than usual. Pale faces turned toward the carriage, eyes bright with hope but expressions guarded. As the vehicle turned and passed between the gates, Sonea sighed.

When the hospices had first opened, hordes of sick had gathered outside the doors, along with those hopeful of seeing the legendary slum magician, former exile and defender of Kyralia. Those not intimidated by her black robes had surrounded her, begging or babbling, making it difficult to get inside the hospice and do the work she needed to do. She could not bring herself to push them away with magic. Other Healers had experienced similar problems, as the sick not yet admitted to the hospice, or their families, begged and pleaded for help.

So enclosed carriageways had been built beside the hospices, with guards to man the gates, and a side entrance. They allowed Healers to arrive and get from carriage to hospice without being harassed.

Sonea waited until the guards called out to indicate all was clear, then climbed out of the carriage. As she turned to smile in thanks, the two guards bowed. She heard the side door to the hospice open.

". . . and it's about time – oh!"

Sonea turned to see Healer Ollia staring at her in horror.

"Sorry, er, Black Magician Sonea. I was . . . we were . . ."

"It's I who should be apologising." Sonea smiled. "I'm late. Or rather, Healer Draven is. His mother has fallen ill, suddenly, so I'm stepping in for him." She stepped aside and nodded to the carriage. "Go on. You must be tired."

"Um. Thank you." Flushed, Ollia hurried past and climbed into the vehicle.

Turning away, Sonea entered the hospice. A large room full of supplies with a central area of seating for exhausted Healers and helpers formed a sanctuary of privacy between the carriageway entrance and the public rooms. A young woman in green robes was sitting in one of the chairs, the edge of her mouth quirked up in a wry smile.

"Good evening, Black Magician Sonea," Nikea said.

"Healer Nikea," Sonea replied. She liked Nikea. The young Healer had first volunteered to help in the hospice not long after joining the Guild, and discovered a love of both healing and helping people. Her parents were servants for a family of one of the less powerful Houses. "Looks quiet here tonight."

"More or less." Nikea shrugged. "Did I hear right? You're replacing Healer Draven?"

"Yes."

Nikea rose. "Then I had better let Adrea know you're here."

"I'll come with you."

Sonea followed her through the door to the main part of the hospice, locking it behind her with magic. As they walked down the corridor, she listened to the sounds escaping the treatment rooms. Rasping breathing told her there was a patient with respiratory problems in one room, and groans from another doorway told of a painful condition. All rooms, as always, were occupied – some with both patient and the two family members that were allowed to stay with and help tend to them.

There were too few Healers willing to work in the hospices to treat the multitudes of sick visiting them, and between them they did not have enough power to meet the demand. But if all of the Healers of the Guild were made to work at them daily there still would not be enough. Sonea had known she would have to run these places with a limited supply of Healing power.

So they treated Healing power like a rare and powerful medicine. Only those people who would not survive without it were Healed with magic. The rest were treated with medicine and surgery.

This had revealed that the Guild's Healers did not know as much about non-magical healing as they'd thought they did. Those Healers who had joined Sonea in treating the poor had begun to expand and develop fields of knowledge that had been long neglected. Some Healers still regarded non-magical healing as primitive and unnecessary, but Lady Vinara, Head of Healers, was not inclined to agree. She now sent novices favouring the Healing discipline to Sonea to learn both how to apply non-magical healing, and why it was still needed.

Turning into the main corridor, Nikea led Sonea to the front room of the hospice. A short, plump woman with grey in her hair paced the room, watching the people seated on benches around the walls with her arms crossed and a stern expression. Sonea suppressed a smile.

Adrea. One of our first non-magician helpers.

When the first hospice opened, Healers had spent as much of their time talking with everyone who entered to find out who was sick and who wasn't as they did treating people. They had to decide how serious the illness or injury was, and pass the patient on to a Healer with the appropriate experience and knowledge. Soon Healers were complaining that they spend their time there herding people, not Healing them. They tried allocating the task instead to novices, but new novices were either too young or inexperienced to deal with distressed patients and their families, and older ones needed to learn something more than how to diagnose illnesses and ferry people about.

It had been Lady Vinara's idea to circulate a request among the Houses for volunteers to help in the hospices. Sonea had expected no response, so she was surprised when three women had appeared at the door a few days later. She'd suddenly had to come up with useful tasks that weren't too menial for women of the higher classes, but would not cause too many problems or damage if done badly.

Only one of those women had returned to the hospice after the first day, but after a few weeks Adrea had not only proven herself capable of being helpful but soon persuaded three other women – friends and relatives – to try out being "hospice helpers".

A few weeks later more helpers began to arrive. Gossip about the original helpers had spread, and general opinion was that they should be admired for their noble sacrifice of time and willingness to risk personal safety for the benefit of the city. Suddenly it was fashionable to be a hospice helper and there was a flood of volunteers.

The reality of the work soon dampened the enthusiasm of fad-followers and the number of new volunteers settled to a steady rate. The helpers that remained not only continued to work at the hospices but organised themselves into shifts and held meetings to discuss new and better ways that non-magicians could help the poor and the Healers.

"Adrea," Nikea called.

The woman turned and, seeing Sonea, bowed deeply. "Black Magician Sonea," she said.

"Adrea," Sonea replied. "I'm taking Healer Draven's place tonight. Give me a few minutes, then send the first one in."

The woman nodded. Turning back to face the corridor, Sonea took a step toward the Examination Room, then stopped and looked at Nikea.

"Nothing needs any special attention out here?" she asked, gesturing down the corridor to the patient rooms.

Nikea shook her head. "Nothing we can't handle. There are three of us working the rooms. All the patients have been fed and half of them are probably asleep already. I'll let you know if anything comes up."

Sonea nodded. She moved to the first door to the left and opened it. The room inside was large enough for two chairs, a locked cupboard and a narrow bed along one wall. It was dark, so she created a globe light and sent it hovering near the centre of the ceiling.

Sitting down on one of the chairs, she took a deep breath and readied herself for the first of the patients. Adrea would ring a gong if anyone arrived who needed immediate treatment. The rest came to the Examination Room, where a Healer examined and questioned them before either Healing them with magic or treating them with medicine or minor surgery.

If major surgery was needed but not urgent they arranged for the patient to return another day.

A knock came from the door. Sonea drew a little magic and sent it out to the handle, turning and tugging it inward. The man standing beyond looked surprised as he saw nobody standing behind the door, despite having visiting the hospice several times before.

"Stoneworker Berrin," Sonea said. "Come in."

He looked relieved to see her. He bowed, closed the door, moved to the chair and sat down.

"I was hoping you'd be here," he said.

She nodded. "How are you?"

Rubbing his hands together, he paused to think before answering.

"I don't think it worked," he finally said.

Sonea regarded him thoughtfully. He had first come to the hospice nearly a year before, refusing to say what was wrong with him. She'd assumed something embarrassing and private, but what he'd revealed, slowly and reluctantly, was an addiction to roet.

It had taken some courage to admit it, she knew. He was the sort of man who worked hard and prided himself on doing "honest" work. But when his wife had died bearing their first child, which hadn't survived, he had been so wrapped up in grief and guilt that he'd tried the wares of a rot-seller with a persuasive tongue. By the time the pain had receded enough that he could resume his former work he found he could not give up the drug.

At first she had encouraged him to reduce the amount he took and endure the aches, cravings and bad moods that came over him. He had done well, but it had exhausted him. The desire for the numbing, freeing sensation of roet did not diminish, however. Eventually, after several months, Sonea took pity on him and decided to see if magic could speed the process.

All Healers had agreed that roet addiction was not an illness, so to use magic to cure it was a waste of a precious resource. Sonea had agreed, but Berrin was a good man who had been taken advantage of when most vulnerable. She had Healed him in secret.

"Why do you think it didn't work?" she asked him.

He looked down, his eyes wide with distress. "I still want it. Not as bad as before. I thought the need would grow less and less. But it hasn't. It's like . . . a tap dripping. Quiet, but if it's quiet it's there, nagging at you."

Sonea frowned, then gestured for him to move closer. He shuffled the chair toward hers. Reaching out, she placed a hand on either side of his head and closed her eyes.

Healing him had been a strange experience. There had been nothing obviously wrong with him. No break or tear or infection that his body was already trying to deal with. Most of the time a Healer could pick up from the body what was wrong and let it help guide the application of magic to repair damage. Sometimes the problem was too subtle, but allowing the body to use magic to return it to its right state nearly always worked.

In Berrin there had been a feeling of distress coming from several directions. It resided in the paths of sensation, and in his brain, but was so subtle she could not comprehend how to fix it. So she had let his body guide her, and when the feeling of distress had gone she knew her work was done.

The aches had gone, and his mood had lifted. He hadn't said anything about a lingering craving for roet, however. But maybe it had been too subtle for him to notice initially. *Or maybe he had started taking it again.*

Sending her mind forth, she sought the feeling of distress within his body. To her surprise, she found nothing. Concentrating harder, she detected natural healing around blisters on his hands and some muscular soreness in his back. But as far as his body was concerned, he was fit and well.

She opened her eyes and removed her hands.

"There's nothing wrong with you," she said, smiling. "I can't feel any of the indicators I felt before."

His face fell and he searched her gaze. "But . . . I'm not lying. It's still there."

Sonea frowned. "That's . . . odd." She considered his steady gaze and what she knew of him. *He's not the type to lie. The very idea that people might think he'd lie is distressing to him. In fact, I expect his next question to be—*

"Do you think I'm making it up?" he asked in a low, fearful voice.

She shook her head. "But this is puzzling. And frustrating. How can I heal what I can't detect?" She spread her hands. "All I can say is, give it time. It could be there's some echo of the craving there. Like the memory of someone's touch or the sound of a voice. In time, if you don't refresh that memory, your body may forget it."

He nodded, his expression thoughtful now. "I can do that. That makes sense." He straightened and looked at her expectantly.

She rose, and he followed suit. "Good. Come back and see me if it gets worse."

"Thank you." He bowed awkwardly, then moved toward the door, glancing back and smiling nervously as it swung open at a tug of her magic.

As the door closed behind him, Sonea considered what she had found – or failed to find – in his body. Was it possible that magic couldn't heal away addiction? That roet made some sort of physical change that was permanent and undetectable?

If that is the case, can a magician's body heal away the effects of his or her own roet addiction? A magician's body healed itself automatically, which meant he or she was rarely ill and often lived longer than non-magicians. *If it can't, then it's possible a magician could become addicted to the drug.*

But not straightaway, surely. Plenty of magicians and novices had tried roet and not become addicts. Perhaps only some people were susceptible to addiction. Or perhaps it had an accumulative effect – they had to take it several times before permanent damage was done.

Either way, it could have both tragic and dangerous consequences. Magicians addicted to roet might be bribed and controlled by their suppliers. And the suppliers are most likely criminals, or linked to the underworld.

Suddenly she remembered Regin's assertion that novices and magicians of the highest classes were associating with criminals more often nowadays. She had believed the situation was no worse than it had always been. But was he right? And was roet the reason? A chill ran down her spine.

As another knock came from the door, she took a deep breath and put the thought aside. For now her concern was the sick of the lower classes. The Guild would have to deal with the consequences of the Houses' more foolish members.

But it wouldn't hurt to see if any of the other Healers – and even the hospice helpers – had heard of magicians becoming addicted to roet, or being drawn into the world of criminals. And it might be useful to have them ask a few questions of their patients, too. There's nothing bored patients and their families like doing more, to pass the time, than gossiping.

Lorkin had no idea what time it was when the visitors finally left and he and Dannyl were free to retire for the night. Once the last guest had gone, they looked at each other and grimaced in relief.

"They're friendlier than I expected," Dannyl said.

Lorkin nodded in agreement. "I could sleep for a week."

"From the sounds of it we'll be lucky to have a day to recover from the journey. Best get some sleep while we can." Dannyl turned to a slave — a young female who promptly threw herself face down on the floor. "Take Lord Lorkin to his rooms."

She leapt up again, glanced at Lorkin once, then gestured to a doorway.

As Lorkin followed her through into a corridor, he felt his mood sink a little. *Every time they do that it feels so wrong. But is that only because I know they're slaves? People bow to me because I'm a magician, and I don't mind it. What's the difference?*

The people who bowed to him had a choice. They did so because it was considered good manners. Nobody was going to have them whipped or executed or whatever the Sachakans did to disobedient slaves.

The corridor curved to the left, following the odd circular shape of the Master's Room. Now it split into two and the slave took the right-hand divergence. *I wonder why they don't make their walls straight. Is it easier to construct them this way? Or harder? I bet it leads to some odd little nooks here and there.* He reached out to touch the smoothly rendered wall. *It was strangely appealing. No harsh edges.* The slave abruptly turned through a

167

doorway. Lorkin followed and stopped in the middle of another oddly shaped room.

It was almost but not quite circular. It was lit by small lamps placed on stands around the room. The walls were decorated with hangings or carvings set within alcoves. Between each was a doorway. The centre of the room was furnished with stools and large cushions. His travel chest lay on the floor beside one of the doorways. The room beyond was also lit by lamps, revealing a bed which looked, to his relief, no different to an ordinary Kyralian bed.

The slave had stopped beside a wall and remained standing, head bowed and eyes downcast. *Is she going to stay there, or leave? Perhaps she'll go away once I indicate I'm happy with the rooms.*

"Thank you," he said. "This will be fine."

She did nothing, said nothing. Her expression – the little he could see of it – did not change.

What will she do if I go into the bedroom? He walked past her through the doorway and looked at the bed. *Yes, it definitely looks like a normal bed.* Turning, he saw that she was now standing against the wall inside the bedroom, in the same pose. *I didn't even hear her follow me.*

He could probably tell her to go away, but as he opened his mouth to speak he hesitated. *I should take the opportunity to find out how the master–slave situation works. Is she my personal servant, or do a range of servants have different tasks?*

"So," he said. "What is your name?"

"Tyvara," she replied. Her voice was unexpectedly deep and melodic.

"And what is your role here, Tyvara?"

She paused, then looked up and smiled. *That's better*, he thought. But looking into her eyes, he saw that they did not match the smile. They gave nothing away. They were so dark he could barely tell where the pupils began and the colour ended. It sent a sensation down his spine that was not quite a chill of disquiet, nor was it entirely a thrill of excitement either.

Pushing away from the wall, she walked toward him. Her eyes dropped to his chest. She reached out and took hold of the sash of his robe and began to untie it.

"Wha-what are you doing?" he said, taking hold of her wrists to stop her.

"One of my duties," she said, frowning and letting go of the sash.

His heart was racing. His body had decided to favour the side of excitement over disquiet. *I can't jump to conclusions here*, he told himself. *Besides, it's disturbing enough having someone serve me without any choice; I suspect bedding someone who has no choice would be even more off-putting.* He imagined looking into those dark, empty eyes and all interest fled.

"We Kyralians prefer to undress ourselves," he told her, letting her hands go.

She nodded and stepped back, her mysterious eyes expressing confusion and acceptance. *Better that than nothing.* Retreating to the wall, she resumed her former position. He suppressed a sigh.

"You may go," he told her.

She paused for the slightest moment, her eyebrows twitching upward, then she moved rapidly, turning away from the wall and disappearing through the doorway. Her footsteps were silent.

Lorkin moved to the bed and sat down.

Well, that was awkward and uncomfortable. And a little odd.

She hadn't answered his question. But then, perhaps asking a female slave what her role was when standing in a bedroom was a big obvious hint that you wanted her to come to bed.

I'm an idiot. Of course it is. He sighed. *I have much to learn,* he thought ruefully. *And with Dannyl the only other free person here, the only option is to learn from the slaves. If Tyvara is my personal servant then I will see her the most of all the slaves. And if I'm going to question a slave I had better do it privately, where no Sachakan can overhear me revealing how ignorant I am.*

Next time he had the opportunity, he decided, he was going to question her on master–slave etiquette.

And hopefully we can set a few rules between us. Lessen the whole obeisance thing to the point where it's not so disturbing for me, without going so far that it's uncomfortable for her.

Simply put, he was going to have to befriend her. And that should not be too hard. He'd never found it difficult to form friendships with women. It was romantic entanglements that caused him more trouble than they were worth. Working out how to befriend a Sachakan slave woman might be a new challenge, but surely one well within his abilities.

CHAPTER 11

TANTALISING INFORMATION

A lone in the new hideout, Cery listened to the silence.
When it was quiet like this, when Gol was out attending
to business, Cery could close his eyes and let the memories
rise to the surface. First there came sound of his children's
voices and laughter. Akki, the eldest, teasing Harrin. Then the
gentle scolding from Selia.

If he was lucky he saw them, smiling and lively. But if not
the memory of their bodies arose, and he cursed himself for
having looked at them despite knowing the images would
torture him forever. *But they deserved to be seen. To be farewelled.
And if I hadn't seen them I might cling to that notion that comes to
me, when I first wake up, that they're still there, alive and waiting
for me.*

A rude, jangling noise interrupted his thoughts, but as he
roused himself he decided it was all for the better. He could
not let grief distract him from his task, or he might not get
the chance to avenge them.

The sound was a signal that someone was approaching the
hideout. *Is this the Thief Hunter at last?* Cery rose from his chair
and paced the room slowly. The first sound had died away
now, and a new sound replaced it. Each step of the stairway

leading down from the bol brewery above the hideout would depress slightly under a person's weight, setting off a mechanism that sent a clunk echoing through the rooms below. Cery counted the clunks, feeling his heartbeat quicken to match the beat.

He eyed the panelling behind which the closest secret escape route lay. *It's been over a week. That's not very long. I'd want to plan carefully if I intended to kill off a Thief. I'd take as long as I thought I could get away with, researching my victim. I'd let them settle into their new hideout, and allow time for the guards to relax and get lazy.*

He frowned. *But I don't want to spend weeks here waiting. If this isn't the Thief Hunter . . . maybe there's a way we can make him think he doesn't have much time . . .*

There was a pause, then a chime rang in a familiar pattern, and Cery let out the breath he hadn't realised he'd been holding. It was Gol's signal.

Walking over to the other wall, Cery pushed aside one of the paper screens mounted on the walls to imitate windows and ease the oppressive feeling of being underground. Behind it was a ventilation grille in a shallow alcove. He swivelled that open and pressed the lever inside. Then he peered through some darkened glass to check that the approaching person was indeed Gol.

As the figure stepped into the corridor beyond the glass, Cery recognised him as much from his movements as his stature and face. The big man walked to the end of the corridor and waited. Cery moved back to the grille and lifted the lever up again.

A moment later the hideout door swung open and Gol stepped into the room. The big man raised his eyebrows.

"No visitors while I was out?"

Cery shrugged. "Not one. Mustn't be as popular as I used to be."

"I've always said it is better to have a few good friends than many bad ones."

"Someone like me doesn't have much choice." Cery moved to one of the cupboards and opened it. "Wine?"

"This early?"

"The only alternative is to lose at tiles again."

"Wine, then."

Taking a bottle and two glasses from the cupboard, Cery carried them to the small table set between the luxurious chairs in the centre of the room. Gol sat down opposite him, took the bottle and began to work the plug out of the top.

"I heard some good news, today," Gol said.

"Oh?"

"I heard that you've got a new hideout, and it's more secure than any Thief's in the city." The plug came free and Gol began to pour some wine into the glasses.

"Is that right?"

"Yes, and that you're not as smart as you think. There's a way to break in, if you know how." Gol held out a glass to Cery.

Cery feigned concern as he took it. "How terrible. I must get around to fixing that. Eventually." He took a sip. The wine was sharp and rich. He knew it was excellent, but it didn't thrill him. He'd never gained a true liking for wine, preferring a warming mug of bol. But it paid, in some company, to know how to tell a good wine from a bad one, and good vintages could be a profitable investment.

He put the glass down and sighed. "I think I know how

Sonea felt, all those years ago, stuck in Faren's hideout. Though I'm not trying to learn to control magic and setting the furniture on fire instead."

"No, but it is still all about magic." Gol took a sip of the wine and looked thoughtful. "I got to wondering about this Thief Hunter the other night. How good at magic do you think he is?"

Cery shrugged. "Good enough to open a lock." He frowned. "He must be in control of it, since he's been using it for years, if the rumours are right. It would have killed him a long time ago if he wasn't."

"Someone would have to teach him, right?"

"Yes."

"Then either there's another rogue who taught him, or he was taught by a Guild magician." Gol blinked as a thought occurred to him. "Maybe Senfel did, before he died."

"I don't think Senfel would have been that trusting."

Gol's eyes widened. "Have you considered that the Thief Hunter could be a Guild magician trying to get rid of all the Thieves?"

"Of course." A chill ran down Cery's spine. The late High Lord had hunted Sachakan black magician spies in the city for years without the Guild knowing. A vigilante magician trying to wipe out the criminal underworld leaders was not so outlandish an idea in comparison.

Well, when the Hunter falls into my trap we'll find out.

"I wish it wasn't going to take so long," Cery said, sighing. He considered his earlier thought: that perhaps he could give the Thief Hunter reason to think he didn't have much time. *Perhaps let out some gossip that I'm about to leave Imardin.*

Such a rumour was as likely to put the Thief Hunter off,

though. The man must be prepared to take his time, as he'd been killing Thieves over many years. *I'm the sort of bait that has to be patient. Nobody is going to attack a Thief without plenty of planning.*

Was there some other kind of bait that the Thief Hunter might not be so cautious or patient in approaching? Something that could be left somewhere less protected without it seeming uncharacteristic and suspicious?

What would a magic-wielding vigilante rogue be tempted to hunt down or steal?

The answer came with a rush of excitement and Cery sucked in a quick breath.

Magical knowledge! Cery sat up straight in his chair. *If our Hunter is a rogue magician, he must have learned magic outside the Guild. Even if he is an ex-Guild magician, he must lust after the great store of knowledge the Guild has. And if he is a vigilante Guild magician, he's obliged to investigate and remove any magical knowledge that falls into the wrong hands.*

"What's wrong?" Gol asked. He cast about. "Has one of the alarms gone off?"

"No," Cery assured him. "But I don't think that's going to matter any more. I've thought of an even better – and faster – way to lure our quarry into revealing himself." He began to explain, watching Gol's expression change from surprise to excitement to dismay.

"You look disappointed," Cery noted.

Gol shrugged and waved a hand at the room. "I guess we won't be needing all this now. Such a lot of work and money went into it. And we built in all those flaws, so you can't come back and stay here later. Seems a shame."

Cery looked around thoughtfully. "It is, I guess. Perhaps

when all this is over, and people have forgotten about it, we can fix the flaws. But for now it's no good as a location for our new bait. We need something less secure, so he'll strike sooner."

"I guess I had better go buy you some books on magic," Gol said, putting his glass down.

"You won't find them that easily. If you did there'd be no point in us using them as bait."

Gol smiled. "Oh, I never said they'd be the real thing. We'll get some fakes made."

"That will take time. Maybe all we need is the *rumour* that there are books somewhere."

"Do you think the Thief Hunter would risk exposure as a magician for the sake of the *rumour* of books on magic? He'll only investigate if he knows someone has laid eyes on them."

"All right, get some fakes made." Cery grimaced. "Just . . . don't let them take as long as real book-copiers do, or I may as well stay here and wait for the Thief Hunter to come find me."

Dannyl surrendered his plate to the slave and resisted the urge to pat his stomach contentedly. He was beginning to like the strange manner in which meals were served in Sachaka. By having guests select food from the offered plates it allowed them to eat as much or as little as they liked. At first he had felt obliged to try every dish, but he noticed that other guests did not – if anything they affected an air of fussiness which the host did not appear to mind.

Nobody ever commented on the food, he'd noted. Which was a relief, because some of the dishes had been laced with spices so hot, or else unexpectedly bitter or salty, that he'd not been able to finish what he'd taken. Sachakans did not appear to serve dessert, though if receiving a visitor during the day they made sure there were dishes of nuts, sweet fruit or confections laid out on tables.

Dannyl's host for the night was a portly Sachakan named Ashaki Itoki. He knew that the man was one of the most powerful in Sachaka, and cousin to the Sachakan king. It appeared Ashaki Achati, the man who had greeted Dannyl and Lorkin when they had arrived at the Guild House, had been given the task of ensuring Dannyl was introduced to the right people in the right order. Though he had not told Dannyl this plainly, he had hinted at it.

"What shall we do now?" Itoki asked, glancing from Dannyl to Achati. "My baths are large enough to accommodate guests and my slaves are well trained in the art of massage."

"Ambassador Dannyl might be interested in seeing those ancient maps you collect," Achati suggested.

Dannyl felt a flash of hope. He had always found old maps intriguing, and it was always possible they might contain information relevant to his research.

"I would not like to bore my guest," Itoki said doubtfully.

"Remember, I told you earlier that Ambassador Dannyl is a historian. I'm sure he will find them very interesting."

Itoki looked at Dannyl hopefully. Dannyl nodded in agreement. "I would."

The man smiled broadly, then rubbed his hands together. "Oh, you'll be impressed, I'm sure. Most advanced maps ever drawn." He rose, and Achati and Dannyl followed suit. "I'll take you to the library."

They made their way through curved white corridors to a cluster of rooms similar to those Dannyl had been given at the

Guild House, and those he and Lorkin had used while staying with Ashaki hosts on their journey to Arvice. It was interesting to see that another Sachakan house followed the same pattern. Were they all the same? How long had Sachakans been building their homes in this way?

The central room held a few stools and a large pile of cushions in the centre, and several cabinets stood against the walls. Through the doorways leading out on all sides Dannyl could see several more. Itoki moved to a cabinet and drew a key out of an inner pocket of his jacket. He unlocked it and pulled open the doors.

Several metal tubes stood on end within. Itoki ran his fingers along them reverently, then chose one and drew it out. He moved to the cushions, nudged several aside to clear an area of floor, then lowered himself onto a stool with a grunt of effort.

"If you position yourselves there and there," he said, pointing, "we can hold a corner each and weigh the other down." Achati moved a stool into one of the indicated positions, and Dannyl shifted another to the second. They sat down and watched Itoki remove the cap of the tube and pull out a roll of yellowed paper.

"This isn't the original, of course," the man said. "It's a copy, but it's still over four hundred years old and a bit delicate." He laid the roll on the floor and began to unroll it. Dannyl automatically caught the edge closest to him, preventing it from springing back. Achati did the same. At a glance from Itoki a stool rose and floated over to weigh down the last corner with one of its legs.

A great swirling mass of lines was revealed. Blue rivers wound across them, and beside several of them roads matched and reflected every curve. Tiny drawings of buildings, fields and the low walls of estate boundaries covered the map. *Contour lines on a four-hundred-year-old map? The Guild didn't develop the use of contour lines until two hundred years ago. But . . . this is a copy.*

"How old was the original map?" he asked.

"Over seven hundred years," Itoki replied, with a note of pride. "They've been passed down through my family since the Sachakan War."

"Do you have the originals?"

"Yes," Itoki grinned. "But they are in fragments, and are too delicate to handle."

Dannyl looked down at the map again. "What is this map of?"

"A region in western Sachaka, near the mountains. Let me show you the others." Itoki rose again and collected another two metal tubes from the cabinet. The map he unrolled next was of a coastal area, with tiny boats drawn in the water parts and warnings written next to rocks and reefs. It was followed by one of another rural area.

"This is – was – in the south," Itoki told him.

Where the wasteland lies, Dannyl thought. *He doesn't state it. He doesn't have to.* The fields and estates hinted at a fertile, green land where sand and dust now dominated.

They examined the maps for some time until, at a signal from Achati, Itoki began rolling them up carefully and sliding them back into their tubes.

"What areas of history are you interested in?" he asked Dannyl.

Dannyl shrugged. "Most of them. Though I suppose the older the better, and naturally any reference to magic is interesting to me."

"Naturally. That would include Guild history, or is that already well recorded?"

"Yes and no. There are some gaps in Guild history that I am trying to fill."

"I doubt I could help you there, though I do have some records from the short time that Kyralia ruled Sachaka." Itoki rose and returned to the cabinet to replace the map tubes, locked the cabinet, then beckoned and moved into one of the side rooms. Dannyl and Achati followed. The tall, heavy cabinets around the room stood like guards on duty, still and silent. Itoki moved to one and opened the doors. *Which aren't locked*, Dannyl noted. *What's in them obviously isn't as valuable.*

The familiar smell of old paper and binding wafted out. Inside were several books with missing or tattered covers, frayed rolls of paper and envelopes of leather wrapped around stacks of paper. Itoki rifled through gently, then took out a stack of papers and a book.

"These are letters and records of a Guild magician who lived in Sachaka during the years of occupation. I rescued them from an old estate at the edge of the wasteland that fell into the king's hands after no legitimate heir came forward to claim it."

He handed the book to Dannyl. Opening it, Dannyl leafed carefully through the first few brittle old pages. Like many of the old records of Kyralian magicians, they contained both accounting lists and diary entries. Conscious of the two men watching him, he started to skim the contents.

"*. . . offer to purchase our House. I refused it, naturally. The building has belonged to my family for over two centuries. Though the price was tempting. I explained that if we do not own a House in Imardin we will lose the right to call ourselves Lord and Lady.*

180

He said land ownership is as important to power and influence here in Sachaka as well."

Dannyl frowned. *This was written after the war, yet here is a reference to a building that is at least two hundred years old and still standing. It is proof that Imardin wasn't levelled during the war, as our history books claim.* His heart skipped. He looked up at the two Sachakans. Clearly he was not going to be able to read the whole book, and make notes, while they waited.

"Do you mind if I copy this passage out?" he asked.

Itoki shook his head. "Not at all. You found something noteworthy?"

"Yes," Dannyl drew out the notebook and a wrapped stick of compressed charcoal he always carried in his robes. "It confirms something I've suspected."

"That is?" Achati asked.

Dannyl paused to write down the record entry, then looked up. "That Imardin wasn't destroyed in the Sachakan War."

Itoki's eyebrows rose. "I've never heard such a thing. According to our histories the final battle happened before the gates, and our armies were defeated."

Dannyl paused. "Armies? There were more than one?"

"Yes. They came together for the final confrontation. You'd have to ask Master Kirota for the full story, but I can show you some maps drawn after the war that show the three paths of the armies. They are not that old, or relating to magic, though."

"No, but it sounds like they'd be very interesting."

As the man took the book from Dannyl and placed it and the stack of letters back in the cabinet, Dannyl felt a pang of disappointment. In a few short moments' access to this man's library he'd confirmed something that had nagged at him for years. How much more could he learn?

But it was late and he could not impose on his host too much. And no doubt Ashaki Achati would like to return home soon. *Perhaps I can return some time.* Then he felt his heart sink. *But not for a while, because I have to visit all the other powerful Sachakans wanting to meet the new Guild Ambassador to Sachaka first, or I might show too much favour for one over the rest. Curse the politics of this place!*

He would do his best to arrange another visit. In the meantime he must take advantage of any opportunities that came his way. As Ashaki Itoki led the way out of the room to show him the battle maps, Dannyl swallowed his impatience and followed.

Healer Nikea met Sonea at the door of the hospice.

"I've arranged a room for us, Black Magician Sonea," she said, smiling and turning to lead Sonea away. "It's small but we'll all squeeze in."

"All?"

Nikea glanced over her shoulder. "Yes. A few of the Healers I talked to had some interesting stories that we all agreed you should hear first-hand."

Sonea smiled wryly at the young woman's back. *Most of the time it's a relief to be around someone who isn't intimidated by or wary of me, but sometimes there are drawbacks. I wish Nikea had asked me about this first. I don't want too many people knowing I'm asking questions about rich magicians associating with criminals.*

The room the young Healer led her to was a narrow storeroom, worryingly low in supplies. Several chairs had been arranged around the walls. Nikea did not enter, but waited until another Healer stepped into the corridor and then called out to the man.

"Healer Gejen, could you gather the others?"

He nodded and hurried away. After a few minutes he returned with five other women. Two were helpers, Sonea noted. All filed into the room and sat down, then Nikea gestured for Sonea to enter, moved inside and closed the door behind her.

A globe light filled the room with sharp brightness. All but Nikea watched Sonea expectantly.

"Well then," Nikea said. "Who wants to go first?"

After a short pause, one of the helpers cleared her throat. She was Irala, a quiet middle-aged woman. An efficient helper, though a little cold with the patients sometimes.

"I'll speak," she offered. Her gaze shifted back to Sonea. "It's about time the Guild stopped ignoring this problem."

"What problem exactly?" Sonea asked.

"Roet. And those who sell it. It's everywhere. In the Houses they say it spread from the slums like a plague, but out here they say it's spread by the Houses to control the poor and reduce their numbers. Nobody really knows where it comes from. I've heard gossip and stories, though, that say that the ones selling it are rich and as powerful as the Houses, but have their toes rooted in the underworld."

"I've heard plenty say the Thieves are using it to take over the city," Gejen added. "One person told me it was imported by foreigners to weaken us before they invaded Kyralia. They suspected the Elynes." The others smiled at this. Clearly none of them believed it.

"Have any of you heard of novices or magicians who crave roet? Who can't stop taking it?"

The other helper and one of the Healers nodded. "A . . . a relative of mine," the helper said. She shrugged apologetically.

183

"He made me swear never to tell anyone so I won't say his name. He says no matter how long he resists, the need won't go away. I tell him he just needs to stop long enough for his body to heal properly, but he won't."

Sonea felt her heart sink. "Do you know who he buys the roet from?"

"No, he won't tell me for fear I'll stop his supply somehow." The woman frowned. "And he said something about the source being a friend. If he had to find another seller, that person might ask for more than money."

Sonea nodded. She looked at the others. "Have any of you heard of novices or magicians becoming involved with criminals – whether roet sellers or not? I don't mean visiting pleasure houses. I mean trading through or with them, doing magic for money or favours?"

"I have," the other Healer said. In her thirties, she had a young family which her non-magician husband watched over while she worked at the hospice – a practical arrangement that only Healers seemed to find unremarkable. "A few years ago, before I married Torken, a friend I'd known since our University days stopped spending time with us – my University friends, that is. He preferred some non-magician friends in the city, who met in one of these pleasure houses. He told us he wasn't interested in the things people bought there, just the arrangement he had with the owners. Some sort of importing arrangement. He would never tell us what. Now he doesn't even live in the Guild. He moved out into a house in the city and spends all his time helping his new friends."

"Do you think the trade is illegal?"

She nodded. "But I don't have proof."

"Is he addicted to roet?"

The Healer shook her head. "Too smart for that."

Sonea frowned. This was bad news, and something Regin would be interested to hear about, but it didn't prove that roet was being used to lure magicians into criminal activity.

"Well, it's always been known that some novices from the Houses have dealings with Thieves," the other woman said. She was a thin woman named Sylia, who was a powerful and skilled Healer.

"But is that rumour or is there evidence?" Sonea asked.

"There is never evidence." Sylia shrugged. "But young novices have always bragged about it. Often to bluff their way out of trouble with other novices, but if you asked enough questions there were always some rumours that stuck more than others."

The others were nodding. "There's truth in those rumours," Gejen agreed. "It's just difficult to know which rumour has truth in it."

"So . . . do you think the rule against novices and magicians associating with criminals or unsavoury types has any effect at all on higher-class novices?"

"Yes and no," Gejen replied. "There's no doubt that it prevents some from taking the risk, but those who are foolish, or whose families are already involved in crime, won't be dissuaded." The others nodded in agreement, some smiling knowingly.

"And if the rule was abolished, would more be tempted?"

The five exchanged glances.

"Probably," Sylia said. She shrugged. "Since the Thieves are involved in everything, and rich and powerful enough to offer tempting payment."

"Like payment in roet," Irala added.

"Any rule that reduces the number of novices and magicians caught up in gambling, drink and roet is good, as far as I'm concerned," Gejen said. The others hummed in agreement.

"But the rule is unfair and ineffective as it is," Sylia added. "It shouldn't be abolished, just changed."

As the five began discussing how, some quite passionately, a shiver of realisation ran through Sonea. *They've all been thinking about this. And debating it. Have other magicians given the rule this much consideration? Are they all discussing it?* Then she felt her heart skip. *Can I gauge from them how the vote might go, if it's put to the entire Guild?*

She listened to them carefully, and while they talked she began devising another set of questions to ask them. This was going to be a more useful information-gathering exercise than she had planned or expected.

CHAPTER 12

DISCOVERIES

As Lorkin followed the slave down the corridor of Ashaki Itoki's home, he took a deep breath and let it out slowly. Despite everything that his friend Perler had told him, he was still not entirely sure how to behave around the Ashaki. To be a magician and a landowner gave one the highest status in Sachakan society aside from the king. A magician who did not own land but was an heir to an Ashaki was one level lower in status than the Ashaki. A magician who was not an heir was next, then any free non-magician – both of whom were dependent on an Ashaki for an income and to broker trade deals or marriages.

If lower-status Sachakans were given important duties – such as Master Kirota holding the role of Master of War – they gained enough extra status to circulate among more powerful men. Dannyl did not own land, but his role as Ambassador boosted his status to the point where the Ashaki would deal with him. Lorkin, on the other hand, was a mere assistant – not quite equal to a non-heir Sachakan magician because he didn't know black magic. Perler had warned him that some Sachakans thought the role of assistant was not much better than a servant's, and had actually treated him with less respect than a free non-magician.

Ashaki Itoki is one of the most powerful men in Sachaka. I have no idea how I should behave around him. And, if that isn't enough, I still can't get used to the idea these men are black magicians who might hold immense magical power and could probably fry me to ashes if I happened to offend them.

The slave reached the end of the corridor, took a few steps into the room and threw himself onto the floor. Lorkin felt his stomach lurch and a crawling, uncomfortable feeling run up his spine. *I can't get used to seeing people do that, either. And it's worse when they do it to me.*

He looked up to see a large man, his flashy, overly decorated clothes stretching tightly around his ample girth. As the slave informed him of Lorkin's identity, the man smiled thinly.

"Welcome, Lord Lorkin. You have a long task ahead of you, so I will not delay you. My slave will take you to my library and do his best to supply you with anything you need."

Lorkin inclined his head. "Thank you, Ashaki Itoki."

"Ukka. Take Lord Lorkin to the library," the Sachakan ordered. The man leapt to his feet, beckoned to Lorkin with his eyes lowered, then moved away toward a doorway. Lorkin nodded to Itoki again, then followed the slave out of the room.

Out of the Ashaki's presence, Lorkin let out a sigh of relief. He would not relax completely until he had left the man's house. And then maybe not until he was back at the Guild House. *But I'm not here in Sachaka to relax or feel safe and comfortable. I'm here to help Dannyl in his research.*

The slave turned into a cluster of rooms similar to those Lorkin had use of in the Guild House, and moved into one of the side rooms. He stopped before a cabinet.

"My master says the records you want to see are in here,"

he said, extending a hand toward it. Then he moved to the wall beside the door and stood with his back to it, just as the slaves at the Guild House did when not engaged in a task or dismissed.

Ready to serve me if required. And perhaps to keep watch and make sure I don't look at anything I wasn't invited to. Or steal anything.

Opening the double doors, Lorkin examined the piles of papers wrapped in leather satchels, the rolls of parchment and the books. He found the book Dannyl had described and took it out, then drew his notebook out of his robes. Casting about, he realised there was nowhere to sit and no table to work on. He turned to the slave.

"Is there something I can sit on?"

The slave hesitated, then nodded. *Curses, I've done it again. I must remember to phrase requests as an order rather than a question.*

"Bring it to me," he said, biting back the "please" that he would usually have added, which he'd discovered sounded lame, and both free Sachakans and slaves seemed to find strange and amusing.

The man moved into the main room and brought in one of the simple stools Sachakans preferred. *Strange that a people with so much power and all the country's wealth use such basic furniture. I'd expect them to be reclining in chairs as big and over-decorated as they are.*

There didn't appear to be anything resembling a table in the main room, so Dannyl drew out one of the sturdier books from the cabinet. He sat down, rested the book on his knees and placed his notebook on it. Then he began to read.

Within a few pages of the record book Lorkin began to struggle with uncertainty. Clearly he could not copy the entire contents in the time he had. Dannyl hadn't told him to copy out any particular passage, just to note anything that might be relevant. It was flattering that the magician trusted Lorkin to judge what was relevant – *or else he had no choice but to leave it to me* – but that didn't make the task any easier.

The book wasn't the rich source of information that Lorkin had hoped, either. It was part accounting, part diary, as record books of landowning magicians often were in those times. He could not afford to skim anything, or become distracted, or he might miss something. But the lists of household purchases and descriptions of trade agreements were hardly fascinating reading.

He noted any reference to magic and the names of visitors to the magician's home. When he had finished he put the book away and began to read a bundle of letters. They were old but in good condition, written on small squares of paper that hadn't been folded, so they did not break into pieces. They had been sent to the magician from a friend in Imardin. Lorkin couldn't tell if the friend was a magician or not, as he knew that the title "Lord" had been used only by landowners and their heirs at the time. The friend enquired in most letters on progress toward ending slavery in Sachaka, which he and others in Imardin were anxious to achieve.

From the sounds of it, that was a matter of great urgency, Lorkin thought. *But I suppose it hadn't been that long since Kyralians had been slaves.*

Finishing the letters, he examined the rolls of parchment, which proved to be accounting charts. Other satchels contained more letters, this time from the magician's sister. She seemed more interested in how the slaves who had been freed were faring, and Lorkin found himself liking her for her compassionate yet practical suggestions.

190

I wish I could read his replies. I'd like to know the answers to the questions she asks about the Guild's plans for Sachaka. Maybe that would give us clues as to why Kyralia relinquished control of the country it had conquered.

A slave arrived with food and drink. Lorkin ate quickly, then launched into his work again. When he'd finally read everything in the cabinet, he realised several hours had passed. He looked at his notebook and felt a vague disappointment. *I'm not sure I found anything particularly useful, but perhaps Dannyl will see something I haven't.*

As he reached out to close the cabinet doors, he realised he was still holding the book he'd been using as a support for his notebook. Opening it, he saw it was another record book. It appeared to continue where the last one had ended, but only a third of the pages contained text. Lorkin started to read the last entry. Immediately his skin began to prickle. The writing was short and hurried.

"Terrible news. The Storestone is missing. Lord Narvelan has also disappeared and many believe he is the thief. The fool knows it is essential to our control over the Sachakans. I must leave now and join the search for him."

The blank pages after the entry were suddenly rife with questions and possibilities. Why hadn't the magician resumed his record-keeping? Had he died? Had he confronted this Lord Narvelan and perished as a result?

And what is this "Storestone" that is so essential to the Guild's control of Sachaka? Was it recovered? If it wasn't, was that the reason Kyralia gave control of Sachaka back to its people?

And if it was never recovered, what happened to it? Did some magical object exist that was powerful enough to keep a nation – a feared *empire* of black magicians – subjugated?

Lorkin sat back down on the stool and began to copy out the entry.

I'm right. There is some sort of ancient magic that could help protect Kyralia. It's been lost for over seven hundred years, and I'm going to find it.

Gol had done his research well. The shop was the kind that bought and sold the belongings of debtors and the desperate. It was also located in a part of the city where Cery was unlikely to be recognised. In one corner, paper window screens of all sizes and shapes leaned against the wall. Coats and cloaks hung on racks and shoes sat in pairs below them. All manner of pottery, glass, metal and stone domestic vessels and objects crowded shelves behind the owner's chair and side bench. And a heavy, decorative ironwork cage protected trays of jewellery – though from the look of it most was badly made or fake.

Another set of shelves held books of all sizes. Some were bound with paper, the threads of the binding exposed and fraying. Some were bound in leather and, of those, most were worn and cracked, but a few gleamed with newness.

"Books on *magic*, then?" the pawnshop owner said, his voice rising in volume but dropping in tone. He chuckled. "I get a few from time to time. Oh, you won't find any there, young man."

Cery turned to find the man looking at him. The man's smile faltered for a moment as he realised his error.

"The Guild takes them off you?" Cery asked.

The man shook his head. "No, the Guard come by now and then to check but I'm not fool enough to put something like that on display. And the books go too quickly. In and out. My regular customers know they have to come quick when I let them know something's arrived, if they want to be the one that gets it."

"How do you get hold of them – if you don't mind me asking?"

The man shrugged. "Mostly I get 'em from novices. The ones that come from around here. For some reason they can't send money direct to their families, so they steal books and sell them to me, and I pass on the money."

"For a fee," Cery finished.

The man shook his head. "Oh, I make a good enough profit on selling them. I treat my novices good, 'cause there's plenty of others they could go to if I didn't." He scowled. "Of course, some of 'em try to get me to pass the money on to rot sellers instead. I won't have any of that. Nasty people, those. Don't want anything to do with them."

"Me neither," Cery replied. "How do you know if a book is real or a fake?"

The man straightened. "Many years' experience. And a couple spent working in the Guild when I was a young man."

"Really? You worked for the Guild?" Cery leaned toward the man. "What you get kicked out for?"

The man crossed his arms. "Did I say I got kicked out?"

Cery gave the man a hard look. "You *left* a job like that?"

The seller hesitated, then shrugged. "Didn't like being told what to do all the time. As my late wife said, it doesn't suit everyone. 'Makkin the Buyer' is a name that suits me best. Better to be Makkin my fortune than Makkin anyone's dinner or beds." He chuckled.

"Fair enough," Cery said. "I don't think I could put up with it either. So . . . when do you think you might get some new books? And what sort can I get?"

Makkin's eyes gleamed with pleasure. "They arrive when they arrive. Sometimes you wait days, sometimes weeks. I can try to get my novices to steal what you want, but it's not always possible – or else it takes longer. Price depends on difficulty, and I have to warn you, sometimes one of my more, erm, influential customers takes an interest and buys out everything I have, no matter who ordered it." The man rubbed his hands together. "What were you after in particular?"

"Something . . . unusual. Rare. On a particular subject. I don't care what, just not beginner's books."

The man nodded. "I'll see what I can do. Call back in a few days and I'll tell you what my boys have or can get." He beamed at Cery. "Always nice to have a new customer."

Cery nodded. "Always." He tilted his head to one side a little. "I don't suppose you can tell us who your other customers are. Just so I know who I'm up against."

Makkin shook his head. "Wouldn't be in business long if I did that."

"No, I suppose not." Cery turned toward the door, then looked thoughtful and turned back. "Just curious, but how much would a man have to offer you to be worth risking it?"

"I like being alive too much to even think about it."

Cery raised his eyebrows. "You must have *very* influential customers."

The man smiled. "I look forward to doing business with you."

Holding back a laugh, Cery turned away. Gol strode forward to open the door for him, and they both stepped out into the street.

It was nearing sunset, and the people still out and about were walking with a hunched and intent stride, no doubt looking forward to getting to their destination. A few steps past the shop, Cery crossed the road and moved into the shadow of the opposite buildings. Then he stopped and looked back.

"What are you thinking?" Gol asked. "You have that look."

"I'm thinking that Makkin and his shop might be a good location for our trap."

"So do we arrange for something special to fall into his hands and see who comes to get it, or do we wait until something real comes in?"

"I doubt he'd tell us first, if he got real books. We need to be in control of the transaction as much as possible, and by arranging for the fakes to reach him we can time it to our plans. Though . . . we have to give our quarry reason to use magic to get hold of it. I wonder . . . he said he keeps them out of sight. A safebox, perhaps?"

"I'll find out. It would make it easier to be sure Makkin doesn't sell the books to anyone else. Hopefully that'll force the Hunter to break in to get it."

"And use magic." Cery nodded. "We'll need a safe place to watch from. And make sure we can get away if things go wrong or Makkin works out what's going on."

Gol nodded. "I'll look into it."

It was late when Dannyl finally walked through the door to his rooms at the Guild House. He'd spent the evening visiting an old Ashaki who insisted on filling Dannyl in on the trading exploits of all his ancestors, and was overly gleeful at their success at cheating other traders to the point of ruin.

He glanced into the side room he and past Ambassadors used as an office and, seeing something new on the desk, stopped and looked closer. A notebook lay there. He walked

into the room and picked it up. Opening the pages, he recognised Lorkin's handwriting and suddenly the weariness he'd
felt these last few hours lifted.

At some point a previous Ambassador had purchased or had
made for the office an ordinary chair with a back. Dannyl sat
down with an appreciative sigh and began to read. The first
passages Lorkin had copied out were from the record that
Dannyl had skimmed through. There weren't many entries,
he noted, and he felt a pang of worry as he realised the young
man hadn't copied out the entry about the house in Imardin.
Dannyl hadn't mentioned it, curious to see if Lorkin would
notice.

*But it wasn't an obvious clue. Lorkin will, no doubt, see different
things. While he won't pick up everything I would have, he may find
things I wouldn't.*

Sending Lorkin in Dannyl's place had been a brilliant solution to the problem of being unable to visit important Sachakans
twice in a row for fear of showing undue political favour.
Nothing would be the same as doing the research personally,
but having Lorkin do it for him at least gave him some material to examine and consider until he was free to do it himself.

Reading on, he felt his excitement at having new information slowly ebb. There was little more here of use. Then Lorkin's
handwriting suddenly became bolder and angular, with one
word repeatedly underlined. Dannyl read and then reread the
copied-out record, and Lorkin's speculations, and felt his mood
lift again.

*Lorkin is right. This "storestone" is clearly important. Though he
is assuming it is a magical object. It might be something with political value – an object that states the possessor is important, like a
king's band or a religious leader's treasure.*

196

The name "Narvelan" was familiar, but he could not remember why. He rubbed his forehead and realised he had a growing headache and was thirsty. The meal had been excessively salty, and the only drink offered had been wine. Looking through the doorway into the main room, he saw that there was a slave standing against the far wall.

"Fetch me some water, will you?" he called.

The young man hurried away. Dannyl turned back to Lorkin's notes, rereading and trying to remember where he'd heard the name "Narvelan" before. Hearing the slave return, he looked up. Instead of the previous young man, a boy stood there, holding out a jug and a glass.

Dannyl hesitated, then took them, wondering why he was now being served by a different slave. The boy looked down, avoiding his eyes. Not for the first time, he wondered who decided which slaves did what. Probably the slave master, who had introduced himself on the first day. Lord Maron had explained that the slaves actually belonged to the king, but were "on loan" to the Guild House. This prevented the Guild from breaking the law against Kyralians enslaving others while in Sachaka – a rule that was designed to prevent Kyralians getting to like the idea and trying to introduce it in their homeland.

The boy bit his lip then took a step toward Dannyl.

"Does my master wish for company in bed tonight?" he asked.

Dannyl felt his insides freeze, then a wave of horror rushed over him.

"No," he said quickly and firmly. Then he added: "You may leave, now."

The boy left, showing neither relief nor disappointment in

his walk or posture. Dannyl shuddered. *Just when I'm getting used to seeing slaves everywhere . . .* But perhaps it was better not to grow too comfortable. Perhaps it was good to be reminded of how barbaric the Sachakan people could be.

But why a boy? None of the female slaves have been so forward. It was likely the Sachakan king's spies would have looked into his background and picked up on his scandalous but not-so-secret preference for men in his bed instead of women. *But that does not mean I'd take a mere child to bed. Or a slave, who had no choice in the matter.* The latter thought repelled him, but the former filled him with disgust.

Has Lorkin received a similar offer? The question filled him with anxiety for a moment, but then he remembered the expression Lorkin always wore whenever a slave prostrated themselves in front of him. *If he had, I don't think he'd have taken it up. Still, I need to keep an eye on him.*

But not tonight. It was late and Lorkin was probably long asleep. Dannyl ought to retire, too. There would be another Ashaki to visit and listen to tomorrow night, and the night after, and the list of matters of trade and diplomacy to sort out during daylight hours was starting to grow as well.

Yet when he did finally settle in his bed, he dreamed he was arguing with Tayend – who had somehow become a Sachakan Ashaki – about the stunningly handsome male slaves he owned. *Do as the locals do,* Tayend told him. *We'd expect the same from them if they came to Kyralia. And remember, I'm not the first Guild magician to own slaves. Remember that, in the morning.*

CHAPTER 13

THE TRAP

As the carriage stopped before the door to Regin's home, Sonea felt a reluctance steal over her. She remained seated, while memories rose of being exhausted and helpless, tormented by a young novice and his friends in the depths of the University late at night.

Then she remembered that same novice backing away from a Sachakan Ichani, having volunteered to be the bait in a trap that could have easily gone wrong. And his words: *". . . if I live through all this, I'll try to make it up to you."*

Had he? She shook her head.

After the war, many of Imardin's powerful Houses had been anxious to replace the family members who had died in the battle, knowing that the more magicians each House had the greater the prestige. Regin had married soon after graduating, and the gossip about the Guild suggested he did not much like the wife his family had chosen for him.

He had done nothing unpleasant to Sonea since those early University days. Certainly none of the petty pranks of a novice, but also no moves against her as an adult. Twenty years had passed. So why did she feel this reluctance to face him in his own home? Was she still wary of him? Or was she worried that she would be rude out of her old habit of dislike and distrust of him? It was childish to resent him for things he'd done to her when he was young and foolish. Rothen was right that Regin had matured into a sensible man.

But old habits are as hard to shift as old stains, she thought.

Forcing herself to rise, she climbed out of the carriage. As always, she paused to take in her surroundings. She did not have the opportunity to see the city streets often.

Naturally, this street was a part of the Inner Circle, since Regin's family and House were old and powerful and only the most rich and influential could afford to live this close to the Palace. It looked much the same as streets in the Inner Circle always had, with large two- and three-storey buildings – many showing subtle signs of repair work, or entirely new facades, completed soon after the Ichani Invasion.

Sonea turned her attention to the people walking the street. A few men and women strolled along it, their high status obvious from their clothing, and one magician. The rest were servants. But then she noticed a group of four men leaving a building at the end of the street and entering a carriage. Though they wore the finery of the rich, there was something about their stature and movements that brought to mind the confident brutality of street gangs.

I could just be imagining it, she told herself. *Could be making connections only because I've heard Regin talking about criminal connections in the Houses so much lately.*

Turning away, she walked up to the door of Regin's house and knocked. A moment later the door opened and a slim, sour-faced servant bowed deeply before her.

"Black Magician Sonea," he said in an unexpectedly deep voice. "Lord Regin is expecting you. I will take you to him."

"Thank you," she replied.

He guided her through a large hall and up a curving stair-case. Crossing a hall, they entered a large room filled with cushioned chairs, sunlight streaming in through tall windows on one side. The cloth covering the chairs, the paint on the walls and the paper screens were in bright, clashing colours.

Two people rose from their seats – Regin and a woman Sonea guessed was his wife. The woman approached Sonea with outstretched arms as if she meant to envelop her visitor in them, but at the last moment she clasped her hands together.

"Black Magician Sonea!" she exclaimed. "Such an honour to have you in our home."

"This is Wynina, my wife," Regin said.

"A pleasure to meet you," Sonea told Wynina.

The woman beamed. "I have heard so much about you. It's not often we have a historical figure in our home."

Sonea tried to think of something appropriate to say in reply, but couldn't. The woman flushed, then put a hand to her mouth. "Well," she said, looking from Regin to Sonea. "You two have serious matters to discuss. I'll leave you be."

She moved to the door, turned back to smile at Sonea, then disappeared into the corridor beyond. Regin chuckled.

"She's quite intimidated by you," he said in a low voice, gesturing to the chairs in an invitation to sit.

"Really?" Sonea moved to one of the chairs and sat down. "She didn't seem it."

"Oh, she's normally much more verbose." He smiled thinly. "But I imagine there is something more important you have come to discuss?"

"Yes." Sonea paused to take a deep breath. "I have been questioning Healers and helpers at the hospices, and it has led me to agree with you: it would be harmful to abolish the rule against associating with criminals."

She had decided not to mention her suspicions about roet's potential to permanently affect magicians' bodies. When she had mentioned her suspicion to Lady Vinara the woman had been politely disbelieving. It would take a lot more than one stoneworker's claims to convince magicians that they couldn't Heal away the drug's effects. Until Sonea had the time to test her theory, she would have to keep the idea to herself. And even if she did prove it, there were some in the Guild who would blame the lower classes for the problem, and that would only worsen the situation the rule had put the "lowies" in.

Regin straightened, his eyebrows rising slightly. "I see."

"But I still believe the rule is unfair to novices and magicians from the lower classes," Sonea continued, "and that we must do something to resolve that, or we are going to lose talented and powerful novices – or worse, invite rebellion."

Regin nodded. "I have come to agree with you on this. And for quite opposite reasons I feel we must ensure that those magicians charged with ensuring the rule is obeyed and punishing those who break it do so fairly and without favour."

"The rule must be changed, not abolished," Sonea concluded.

"I agree."

They regarded each other in expectant silence, then Sonea found herself smiling. "Well, that was easier than I thought."

He chuckled. "Yes. Now we face the hard part. How should the rule be changed and how are we going to convince the Higher Magicians – or the rest of the Guild – to vote the way we want them to vote?"

"Hmm." Sonea frowned. "It might be easier to plan our approach if we knew who was going to be voting."

Regin steepled his fingers together. "Osen will be more likely to decide the way we want him to swing if we both suggest the same thing. We must go to him, separately, and tell him our preference. Or you must persuade Lord Pendel to, as he is the leader of those seeking the abolition of the rule."

Sonea nodded. "I think he will listen to me. But I will have to give him a good reason to suggest one way or the other. And you?"

"I will do what I can to soften the stance of the opposed. We must explore the advantages and disadvantages of both possibilities thoroughly, so we are ready for all arguments raised against us."

"Yes. Though we need to consider a different approach according to who we need to convince: either the Higher Magicians or the whole Guild. I suspect, given the choice between abolition of the rule, retaining it or changing it, most of the Higher Magicians would vote to keep things as they are."

"You're probably right. Putting the vote to the whole Guild may have a less predictable outcome, but will most likely lead to seeking a compromise – which will be to change the rule. How to change the rule will be the main focus of the debate."

"Yes." Sonea smiled crookedly. "Which brings us back to the hardest question: how do we want to change the rule?"

Regin nodded. "Well, I have a few ideas. Shall I go first?"

She nodded. "Go ahead."

As he began to explain the changes he'd considered, Sonea could not help feeling a reluctant admiration for the careful thought he'd put into the problem. It was clear he'd been thinking about it for much longer than the few weeks the issue had been debated around the Guild. Yet, unlike some of the women and men she had questioned, the solutions he was suggesting were practical and unbiased. *Where is the arrogant, prejudiced snob that I knew as a novice? Is he simply better at hiding it now?*

Or had he changed? Even if he had, it would take more than a few clever solutions to a class problem within the Guild to convince her to trust him. No matter what he said, she would always be waiting for the cruel side she knew Regin possessed to surface again.

After Dannyl had left for the evening, and the slaves had served dinner, Lorkin had returned to his rooms. There wasn't a lot of work for him to do as Dannyl's assistant yet. Apart from the one visit to Ashaki Itoki's home, he hadn't left the Guild House. Only a small part of the work that Dannyl tackled during the day could be handed on to Lorkin.

He spent the evenings reading or questioning the slaves. The latter was proving harder than he expected. While the slaves always responded to his questions, they offered no more than the most basic answer. If he asked them if there was anything else he needed to know they looked confused and anxious.

But it's probably impossible for them to know what I need to know, he thought. *And they're reluctant to guess in case they get it wrong and it angers me. Initiative is probably a trait discouraged in a slave.*

He had a feeling that the dark-eyed girl who had first taken him to his room – Tyvara – might be more receptive, though he wasn't sure why. She hadn't served him since that first night, however. Tonight he had nothing pressing to do, so he'd asked the slave serving him to bring her to him.

They probably all think I want to bed her, he mused, remembering her misunderstanding the first night. *Tyvara probably will, too. I'll have to reassure her that isn't my intention. Is there any way I can encourage her to talk freely?*

He looked around and his eyes settled on the cupboard containing wine and glasses for his own use or entertaining guests. Before he could cross the room to collect them, he saw a movement in the doorway. Tyvara stepped into the room and approached him, stopping several steps away to prostrate herself.

"Rise, Tyvara," he told her. She stood, and her gaze remained on the floor. Her face was expressionless, and he was not sure if it was his imagination that made her seem a little tense. "Fetch me two glasses and some wine," he ordered.

She obeyed, her movements quick but graceful. He sat down on one of the stools in the centre of the room and waited for her. She placed the glasses and a bottle on the floor, then knelt beside them.

"Open it," he instructed. "And fill both of them. One is for you."

Her hands had begun to reach toward the bottle, but now hesitated. Then they continued in the tasks required of them. When both glasses were full she lifted one and handed it to him. He took it and gestured to the other.

"Drink. I have some questions for you. Only questions," he added. "Hopefully nothing that will compromise you in any way. If I ask anything that will get you in trouble by answering, tell me that instead."

She looked at the glass, then picked it up with obvious

reluctance. He sipped. She followed suit, and the muscles around her mouth twitched into a faint grimace.

"You don't like wine?" he asked.

She shook her head.

"Oh." He cast about. "Then don't drink it. Put it aside."

There was a definite air of dislike to the way she set it down as far away from herself as she could stretch. He took another mouthful from his own glass, considering what to ask next.

"Is . . . is there any way I should be behaving toward the slaves here that I am . . . I am neglecting . . . or getting wrong?"

She shook her head quickly. Too quickly. He reconsidered the question.

"Is there any way I could improve my interaction with the slaves here? Make things more efficient? Easier?"

Again, she shook her head, but not as quickly.

"Am I making a total fool of myself when interacting with slaves?"

The slightest hint of a smile touched her lips, then she shook her head once more.

"You hesitated then," he pointed out, leaning toward her. "There's something, isn't there? I'm not making a fool of myself, but instead I'm doing something unnecessary or silly, aren't I?"

She paused, then shrugged.

"What is it?"

"You don't need to thank us," she said.

Her melodic, husky voice was a revelation after all the silent gestures. He felt a shiver run down his spine. *If she wasn't a slave, I think I'd find her immensely fascinating. And if she wasn't dressed in that awful wrap dress, probably quite attractive as well.*

But he hadn't called her here to romance her.

"Ah," he said. "That's a habit — what we consider good manners in Kyralia. But if it makes things easier, I'll try not to do it."

She nodded.

What next? "Other than thanking slaves unnecessarily, is there anything I or Dannyl have been doing in our interaction with slaves that would make us look foolish to free Sachakans?"

She frowned, and her mouth opened, but then she seemed to freeze. He saw her eyes roaming about the floor, focusing as close to him as his feet, then flickering away. *She is afraid of how I'll respond to her answer.*

"The truth will not anger me, Tyvara," he said gently. "Instead it may be a great help to us."

She swallowed, then bowed her head even further.

"You will lose status if you do not take a slave to bed."

He felt a flash of shock, then of amusement. Questions flooded his mind. Did he and Dannyl care about losing status for such a reason? Should they? But then, how damaging was their inaction? Had previous Guild Ambassadors and assistants bedded the slaves here?

But, more importantly, how would free Sachakans know if the new Guild Ambassador and his assistant bedded their slaves or not?

Clearly such information isn't kept a secret. The slaves here are, after all, the Sachakan king's possessions. It would be stupid to think our prowess in the bedroom wasn't discussed and judged.

And then he smiled, thinking of all those powerful Sachakan Ashaki gossiping like old women.

He should find out what the consequences were, while he had Tyvara talking.

"How much status will we lose?" he asked.

She shook her head. "I cannot say. I only know they will not respect you as much."

Does that mean none of the previous Guild House occupants found this out, because none of them refused the opportunity? He looked at Tyvara. *If only she would look at me. And look at me without hesitation or subservience. To see her stand straight and tall with confidence and fearlessness, or for those dark eyes to express true, willing desire, I would take her to bed without hesitation. But this . . . I couldn't do it. Not even to help Dannyl gain respect in the Ashaki's eyes.*

And it was unlikely Dannyl was taking any of the female slaves to bed either.

"I don't care about status," he told Tyvara. "A man should be judged by his integrity, not by how many women he takes to bed – slave or free, willing or otherwise."

She glanced up at him for the briefest moment, an intense look in her eyes, but quickly dropped her head again. He saw her teeth flash as they pressed against her lower lip, then she grimaced.

"What is it?" he asked. *She is afraid. How does this affect her? Of course! She will be punished if it is thought she didn't please me.* "What will they do to you?"

"They will . . . they will send someone else. And another." *And they will all be punished*, her words seemed to hint.

He bit back a curse. "If they do, I will ask for you. If you want me to, of course," he added. "We will talk. Tell each other about ourselves and our countries, or something. I don't see how I'm going to learn about Sachaka otherwise, shut up in the Guild House – and I'd really like to know more about your people. And yourself. How does that sound? Will it work?"

She paused, then nodded. Relieved, he took in a deep breath

and let it out again. "So tell me something about yourself, then. Where were you born?"

Even as she began to describe the breeding house where she had been raised, he felt the horror of her story eased by something inexplicable. She was *talking* to him. Finally a Sachakan was actually communicating with him beyond orders and answers. It had never occurred to him that he might be lonely in Sachaka. Listening to her, he realised she suddenly seemed much more human – something he might come to regret later. But for now he relaxed and listened to the beautiful, hypnotic voice of this slave woman, and savoured every word.

The roof of the pawnshop was surprisingly well constructed. Cery and Gol had crawled out on it a few hours ago, when the full darkness of night had set in. They'd separated the tiles they'd sent a street urchin up to loosen for them earlier that day, and now were looking through cracks between them down at the room where Makkin the Buyer kept his safebox.

Inside that safebox were Makkin's most valuable books, including a new volume about Healing magic. After visiting the shop, pretending to view the book for the first time and making sure Makkin didn't sell it before Cery could return with the money for it, Cery had visited a few of the drinking establishments they patronised to boast about the special volume he'd be buying just as soon as someone paid their debt to him – which would probably be tomorrow.

It could be a long night, Cery thought, carefully stretching the stiffness out of one leg. *But if all goes to plan we won't have to lie out here in the night air for more than one. We just have to hope the Thief Hunter is a magician . . . and has the hunger for knowledge we assume he has . . . and has heard about my boasting today . . . and hasn't got something more important to do tonight.*

Cery had to admit he was acting on only rumour and guesses. He could easily be wrong about a great number of things. The magician that had opened the locks in Cery's hideout might not be the Thief Hunter. He might have been in the employ of the Thief Hunter, or someone else. He might not be a customer of Makkin's.

But this is not so wild an idea that it's not worth trying. And it's the only lead we have.

Shifting his weight, he stretched the other leg. At times like this he was all too aware that he was getting older. He could not climb up the sides of buildings using only a few handholds or a rope, or leap the gaps between them so fearlessly. His muscles stiffened up quickly in the cold air, and took longer to recover from exertion.

And I don't have a beautiful Sachakan woman nearby to catch me with her magic if the roof collapses.

Old, pleasant memories flashed through his mind. *Savara.* Mysterious. Seductive. Dangerous. A skilled fighter. The practice bouts he'd had with her had been challenging and exciting, and he'd picked up more than a few new tricks. She'd known too much about the deal he'd made with High Lord Akkarin to kill off the freed Sachakan slaves that the Ichani had sent to Imardin as spies, and to expose the Guild's weaknesses. But he'd also sensed that he'd not easily get rid of her. That it was better to keep her occupied thinking she was helping him, without letting her get too close to the truth.

She'd worked that one out pretty fast. And then there was that night when they'd watched Sonea and Akkarin fight and kill an Ichani woman. The battle had caused the roof to collapse under them, but Savara had stopped him falling with magic. And then things had become much more personal . . .

After the Ichani Invasion she'd left, returning to the people she worked for. He'd never seen her again, though he'd often wondered where she was and if she was alive and safe. She would most likely have ventured into dangerous situations again and again for the sake of her people, so it was easily possible one had led to her death.

I was never in love with her, he reminded himself. *Nor was she in love with me. I admired her, for both her body and mind. She found me a useful and entertaining ally and distraction. If she'd stayed we wouldn't have . . .*

A sound below drew his attention back to the present. Peering through the crack between the roof tiles again, Cery saw two people climb the stairs into the small room below. One he recognised instantly: Makkin, carrying a lamp. The other was a dark-skinned woman.

"Is that it?" she asked. Her voice was strangely accented and had the hoarseness of age, but she moved with the vitality of a younger person. *The Thief Hunter is a woman?* Cery thought. *That's . . . interesting. It seems I'm doomed to know or be the target of very powerful and dangerous women.*

"Yes," Makkin replied. "That's it. They're in there. But—"

"Open it!" the woman ordered.

"I can't! They took the key. Said that way I couldn't sell it to anyone else before they came back with the money."

"What? You're lying!"

"No! Nonononono!" The pawnshop owner threw up his arms and cringed away from her. His behaviour was a little extreme for someone a head taller than the woman stalking toward him. *As if he knows she is more dangerous than she looks.*

The woman waved her arms. "Get out," she ordered. "Leave the lamp, get out of this shop and don't come back until tomorrow."

"Yes! Thank you! I'm sorry I couldn't—"

"OUT!"

He tore back down the stairs as if a wild beast were in pursuit. The woman waited, listening to Makkin's footsteps. The sound of the shop door slamming echoed up to Cery's ears.

The woman turned to look at the safebox, then her shoulders straightened. She approached it slowly, then squatted before it and went still. Cery could not see her face, but he saw her shoulders rise and fall as she breathed deeply.

A moment later the lock clicked open.

Gol let out a quiet gasp. Cery smiled grimly. *Locks don't just open of their own will. She must have used magic. I have the proof I need that we have a rogue in the city.* It wasn't proof that she was the Thief Hunter, though, but what if she was? He felt a chill run up his spine at the thought. Was the woman below really the murderer who had killed so many Thieves?

She was examining the books within the safebox now. He recognised the one on magic. Opening it, the woman flicked through the pages, then muttered something and tossed it aside. Picking up another book, she examined it as well. When she had looked at all of the tomes she slowly stood up. Her fists clenched and she uttered a strange word.

What did she say? He frowned. *Wait a moment. That was a different language. She's foreign.* But she hadn't said enough for him to recognise the language or even her accent. *If only she would speak again. A whole sentence, not only a curse word.*

But the woman remained silent. She rose and turned her

back on the safebox and its contents, now strewn about the room. Walking away, she reached the stairs and disappeared into the darkness of the shop below. The door slammed again. Faint footsteps faded in the street beyond.

Cery remained still and silent, waiting until they were sure that if anyone had heard the woman shouting they would have lost interest and stopped watching the shop. He considered his plan. *We have the information we need. The only surprise is that the magician is a woman and a foreigner. That doesn't make her any less dangerous, whether she is the Thief Hunter or not. And if foreign magicians are taking up residence in Imardin, Sonea will definitely want to know about it.*

And Skellin. Should he tell the other Thief?

I don't have proof that she is the Thief Hunter. I only have proof that she is the Rogue. I'd rather Skellin didn't know that Sonea and I still communicate. If the Guild captures this woman they'll read her mind and find out once and for all if she is the killer. If she isn't, then there's nothing to tell Skellin.

And if she was . . . well, once the Guild found and dealt with the Rogue there'd be no Thief Hunter to worry about any more.

CHAPTER 14

UNEXPECTED ALLIES

"So who am I meeting tonight?" Dannyl asked Ashaki Achati as the carriage set out from the Guild House.

The Sachakan magician smiled. "Your ploy of not nagging to see the king has worked. He has invited you to the palace."

Dannyl blinked in surprise, then considered all that Lord Maron had told him about the Sachakan king and protocol. The former Ambassador had said that the king refused an audience as often as he granted one, and that there was no point Dannyl seeking one unless he had something to discuss. "I wasn't aware that I should have been nagging. Should I apologise for that?"

Achati chuckled. "Only if you feel you must. As I am the liaison between the Guild House and the king, it is up to me to advise you how and when to seek an audience with him. I would have told you to wait until he invites you. Since you weren't making any mistakes, there was little reason to raise the subject."

"So it wasn't a mistake to *not* ask to see him."

"No. Though showing no interest might have caused offence eventually."

Dannyl nodded. "When I was the Second Guild Ambassador

in Elyne I was required to present myself to the king once, which was arranged for me by the First Guild Ambassador. After that it was only to be for important matters, most of which the First Ambassador took care of."

"That is interesting. You have two Ambassadors in Elyne, then?"

"Yes. There is too much work for one person. Somehow we wound up with as much work that didn't relate to the Guild and magic as work that did."

"Your work here is even less related to magic and magicians," Achati pointed out. "You are not assessing new recruits or keeping track of graduated magicians. You're mostly dealing with issues of trade."

Dannyl nodded. "It is entirely different, yet so far it has been very pleasant. I expect once I have met all of the important people I will no longer be treated to nightly meals and conversations."

Achati's eyebrows rose. "Oh, you may find yourself even more in demand once I am no longer required to escort you. Entertaining another Sachakan can be an exhausting and politically perilous exercise. You are both exotic and not too easily offended, so an easy guest to entertain." He gestured to the carriage window. "Look outside as we turn the corner."

The vehicle slowed and the wall beside them ended. A wide road came into sight. Long beds of flowers appeared, sheltered by enormous trees. Where these gardens ended, a large building stood. White walls curved out from a central archway like carefully draped curtains. Shallow domes rose above them, glittering in the sunlight. Dannyl felt his heart lift at the sight.

"That's the palace? It's beautiful," he said, leaning forward to keep the building in view as the carriage turned into the road. But soon he could only see the white walls of the mansions to the side. He turned back to Ashaki Achati to see the man smiling in approval.

"It is over a thousand years old," the Sachakan said, with pride. "Parts had to be rebuilt over the years, of course. The walls are doubled so that defenders can hide within and strike at invaders through holes and hatches." He shrugged. "Not that they have ever been used for that purpose. When Kyralia's army arrived here ours had already been defeated, and the last emperor surrendered without resistance."

Dannyl nodded. He had learned as much from basic history classes during his University years, and his research had confirmed it.

"The third king had the domes plated with gold," Achati continued. He shook his head. "A frivolous indulgence in what was a time of starvation, but they are so beautiful that nobody has ever removed them, and from time to time a king will see that they are cleaned and mended."

The carriage began to slow and turn, and Dannyl watched eagerly as the palace came in sight again. Once he and Achati had alighted, they stopped to gaze up at the building in admiration for a moment before starting toward the central archway.

Guards at either side of the entrance remained frozen, their gaze set on the distance. They weren't slaves, Dannyl remembered, but were recruited from the lowest ranks of the Sachakan families. *I suppose having your palace guarded by slaves wouldn't be particularly effective. Guards who throw themselves on the ground whenever someone important walks by are hardly going to react quickly to defend anything or anyone.*

They passed through two open doors, then followed a wide corridor with no side entrances. At the end of this was a large room filled with columns. The floor and walls were polished stone. Their footsteps echoed as they walked. Toward the back of this room was a large stone chair, and in it sat an old man wearing the most elaborately decorated clothes Dannyl had seen on any Sachakan since he'd arrived.

He doesn't look comfortable, he noted. *And he looks like he'd like to get off that throne at the first opportunity, too.*

Men stood about the room, alone or in twos and threes. They watched silently as Dannyl and Ashaki Achati approached. About twenty paces from the king, Achati stopped and glanced at Dannyl.

The glance was a signal. Achati bowed deeply. Dannyl dropped to one knee.

Lord Maron had explained that Sachakans felt that nothing less than the gesture considered most respectful by an individual – especially a foreigner – was what their king deserved. So the traditional Kyralian and Elyne obeisance to a king was the most appropriate, despite the fact that Sachakans did not kneel before their own king.

"Rise, Ambassador Dannyl," an elderly voice spoke. "Welcome, to you and my good friend Ashaki Achati."

Dannyl was grateful the contact with the floor had been brief. The stone was cold. He looked up at the king and was surprised to find the man had left the throne and was walking toward them.

"It is an honour to meet you, King Amakira," he replied.

"And a pleasure for me to meet the new Guild Ambassador at last." The old man's eyes were dark and unreadable, but the wrinkles around them deepened with a genuine smile. "Would you like to see more of the palace?"

"I would, your majesty," Dannyl replied.

"Come with me and I'll show you around."

Ashaki Achati waved a hand to indicate that Dannyl should walk beside the king, then followed behind as the ruler led them out of the hall through a side entrance. A wide corridor ran alongside the hall, before curving off in another direction. As the king repeated what Achati had told Dannyl of the age of the palace, he led them through more sinuous corridors and odd-shaped rooms. Soon Dannyl was completely disorientated. *I wonder if that is the point of all the curved walls. And if the entrance corridor and greeting hall are the only square rooms in the building.*

"You have an interest in history, I have been told," the king said, looking at Dannyl with one eyebrow raised.

"Yes. I am writing a history of magic, your majesty."

"A book! I would like to write a book one day. How close are you to finishing?"

Dannyl shrugged. "I don't know. There are some gaps in Kyralia's history that I'd like to fill before printing the book."

"What gaps are they?"

"According to the history taught in the Guild University, Imardin was levelled during the Sachakan War, but I've found no evidence of it. In fact, I have found some evidence to the contrary in Ashaki Itoki's collection."

"Of course it wasn't levelled!" the king exclaimed, smiling. "We lost the final battle!"

Dannyl spread his hands. "It might have been destroyed during the battle, however."

"There's no mention of it in our records. Though . . . few Sachakans survived the last battle and even fewer returned home, so most of the information was gleaned from the Kyralians who conquered us. I guess they could have painted a better picture than the reality." The king shrugged. "So where do you think this idea that the city was levelled came from?"

"Maps and buildings," Dannyl replied. "There are no buildings older than four hundred years, and the few maps we have from before the Sachakan War show an entirely different street plan."

"Then you should be looking at events from four hundred years ago," the king concluded. "Was there any battle fought in the city at that time? Or a disaster such as a flood or fire?"

Dannyl nodded. "There was, but few magicians believe it was drastic enough to level the city. Many records from that time were destroyed." He paused, hoping the king wouldn't ask why. The event he referred to was the story of Tagin, the Mad Apprentice, which was the story of why the Guild had banned black magic. He could not help feeling reluctant to remind the Sachakan king that most Guild magicians did not learn black magic.

"If this event was great enough to ruin a city it would have destroyed any records within the city as well."

Dannyl nodded. "But the Guild wasn't destroyed. I've found many references to the library it contained. By all accounts, it was well stocked."

"Perhaps those books had been moved."

Dannyl frowned. *I guess it's possible Tagin had the contents of the Guild library brought to the palace. He was only an apprentice, so there must have been gaps in his learning that he was eager to fill. I'd assumed the books were all destroyed deliberately. But if they were destroyed when Tagin died then most of the work had been done already.*

"I am surprised Kyralian history is so muddled. But we have gaps in our history as well. Come in here." The king ushered Dannyl and Achati into a small, round room. The walls and floor were polished stone, as was the ceiling. There was only one entrance. In the centre stood a column about waist high.

"Something important once lay here," the king said, running a palm over the flat top of the column. "We don't know what it was, but we do know two things: it was a thing of power, either political or magical, and the Guild stole it."

Dannyl looked at the king, then back at the column. *The storestone that Lorkin found references to?* The king's expression was serious and he watched Dannyl closely.

"I've encountered a reference to an artefact taken from this palace," Dannyl told him. "But I'd not heard about it before coming to Sachaka. That reference also stated that the object had been stolen from the Guild magicians here."

The king shrugged. "Well, that is what palace folklore says. Our records say nothing more than that something called a "storestone" was stolen by a Guild magician." He drummed on the column top with both hands. "Not long after it was taken, the wastes appeared. Some believe that the removal of the talisman lifted some sort of magical protection over the land that had kept it fertile and productive."

"Now that's a new and interesting idea," Dannyl said. *Lorkin will be intrigued to hear this.* "I have been told that attempts have been made to return the wastes to their former state, but they were unsuccessful."

The king's eyebrows rose. "Oh, yes. Plenty have tried; all have failed. Even if we knew how to replace the protection that was removed, I suspect it is too big a task for a few magicians. It would take thousands." He smiled wryly. "And Sachaka no longer has thousands of magicians to call upon. Even if we had, trying to unite magicians is like trying to prevent the sun rising or the tide's ebb."

Dannyl nodded. "But there was only one talisman, wasn't there? Sometimes all it takes is one man and a little knowledge to do great things."

The king smiled crookedly. "Yes. And sometimes it only takes one man and a little knowledge to do a great deal of harm." He stepped away from the column and gestured toward the door. "You don't seem that kind of man, Ambassador Dannyl."

"I'm glad you feel that way," Dannyl replied.

The king chuckled. "As am I. Come. It's time I showed you the library."

From her seat high at the front of the Guildhall, Sonea watched the room filling up with magicians. A few patches of purple, red and green had formed, which was a recent phenomenon. Magicians from the Houses tended to sit with family members and allies rather than those of their own discipline, and that led to a mix of robe colours. But magicians from outside the Houses tended to form friendships with those of the same discipline, and the collective effect was a patch of the same robe colour in the audience.

As the last stragglers took their seats, she drew in a deep breath and let it out slowly. *How will they vote today? Will they act out of fear that "lowies" may rebel against the Guild if rules are too restrictive? Will they act out of fear of criminal groups gaining too much influence on magicians and novices? Or will they want to abolish the rule so that they can indulge in pleasure houses and other enter-tainments run by Thieves without restriction? Or in order to continue to benefit from their own illegal enterprises with less danger of discovery?*

A gong rang out. Sonea looked down to see Osen striding

across the front of the hall. The buzz of voices immediately began to diminish, and when all had quietened the Administrator's voice rang out.

"Today we have gathered to decide whether or not to grant the request, made by Lord Pendel and others, that we abolish the rule that states: 'No magician or novice may associate with criminals and people of unsavoury character.' I have decided that this is a decision that should be made by all magicians, by vote. I now request that the side for abolition of the rule sum up their position and reasoning, beginning with Lord Pendel."

Lord Pendel had been standing at the side of the room, and now stepped forward. He turned to face the majority of magicians and began to speak.

Sonea listened closely. It had not been easy persuading him to offer a compromise to the Guild, and even now she was not completely sure if he would. He began by pointing out where the rule had failed, or had been applied unfairly. Then he tackled the reasoning of those opposed to the rule's abolition. Then he began to paint a picture of a more unified Guild in conclusion. Sonea frowned. *He is going to wind this up without even a suggestion that a compromise may be possible.*

"If there is to be a rule to prevent magicians and novices from involving themselves with criminal enterprises – and I do think there should be one – then it should be *designed* to achieve that. What is clear from the cases I have described is that this is not a rule suited for that purpose. It is ineffective and should be abolished."

I suppose the message is in there, though it's very subtle, Sonea thought. *Now let's see if Regin keeps his side of our agreement.*

As Lord Pendel bowed to the audience and stepped aside, Administrator Osen returned to the front.

"I now call upon Lord Regin to speak for the opposition to the abolition of the rule."

Regin strode forward. If he was disappointed with Pendel's effort at suggesting a compromise, he didn't show it. He turned to face the hall and began to speak.

Knowing what she did about the corruption among the higher-class novices, Sonea could not help admiring how Regin managed to avoid saying anything that would directly reveal who the culprits and victims were. Yet he didn't shy from claiming such corruption existed, and Sonea heard no more than a few protests from the watching audience of magicians.

I wish I could have given him proof of the permanent effects of roet for magicians. It might have helped us persuade everyone that the rule should be changed, instead of abolished.

As Regin concluded his speech, Sonea felt her heart skip a beat. He hadn't suggested a compromise. But as he summed up, she realised there was a hint of admission in his words that the rule was ineffective as it stood. A subtle shift in position, but no stronger or weaker than Pendel's.

Had he anticipated that or did he change tack in response? Or did he have different approaches planned in case of different eventualities? She shook her head. *I'm glad it's not me down there, speaking in his place.*

"I now call for ten minutes of discussion," Osen said. The gong rang out a second time and immediately the hall filled with voices. Sonea turned to watch and listen to the Higher Magicians.

At first none spoke. All seemed hesitant and indecisive. Then High Lord Balkan sighed.

"There is merit in both arguments," he stated. "Do any of you favour one or the other?"

"I favour keeping the rule," Lady Vinara said. "These are bad times for relaxing control over magicians. The city is more corrupt than it has ever been, and keeping ourselves immune is more complicated now that we no longer all have similar strengths and weaknesses."

Sonea resisted a smile. *"Strengths and weaknesses". A clever way of pointing out we have different backgrounds without making one sound better than the other.*

"But it is clear the rule is unfair, and we do risk rebellion at the worst, or the loss of much-needed talent at the best," Lord Peakin argued.

"It is only the application of the rule that is at fault," Vinara replied.

"I don't think the lowies will accept a promise we'll be fairer," Lord Erayk pointed out. "They need something stronger. A real change."

"Change sounds like the solution to me," Lord Peakin said. "Or a clarification. What is an 'unsavoury character', after all?" His eyebrows rose and he looked around. "I'd find someone who smells bad unsavoury. That's hardly justification for punishing a magician."

There were a few chuckles.

"Black Magician Sonea."

Sonea felt her heart sink as she recognised Kallen's voice. She looked past High Lord Balkan at the man.

"Yes, Black Magician Kallen?" she replied.

"You have been meeting with the representatives of both sides. What have you concluded?"

The others were looking at her expectantly now. She paused to consider how to answer.

"I am in favour of the rule being changed. Of removing the

reference to 'unsavoury characters', which not only eases the restrictions and perceived prejudice against novices and magicians from poorer backgrounds, it strengthens the emphasis on 'criminals' as those we don't want Guild members associating with."

To her consternation, none of the Higher Magicians looked surprised. Not even Rothen. *Clearly they expected me to take this position. I hope that is because it is fairer, not because I grew up in the old slums.*

"Even with this change, the weakness of the rule is the ambiguity in what a criminal is, or whether an activity is a crime," Lord Erayk said.

"The king might not appreciate you calling his laws 'ambiguous'," Lord Peakin pointed out, chuckling. "His laws clearly state what is a crime."

"I agree that certain activities need to be defined," Lady Vinara said. "As the laws stand, it is difficult for us to prevent criminals taking advantage of magicians when those magicians are in their pleasure houses – whether by luring them into debt through gambling, addling their minds with drink, rewarding them with free whores or poisoning them with roet. If I had my way, roet selling would be a crime."

"Why roet?" Lord Telano asked. "It is little different to drink, and I'm sure none of us would like wine to be declared illegal." He glanced around, smiling and getting many nods in reply.

"Roet does far more harm," Vinara told him.

"How so?"

She opened her mouth, then shook her head as a gong rang out. "Come to the Healer's Quarters – or Black Magician Sonea's hospices – and you will see the truth of it."

Sonea's heart skipped. Had Vinara investigated the effects of roet since Sonea told her of them? She looked at Vinara, but the woman's attention was on Telano. He had turned away, scowling. *I wonder why he is so bothered by Vinara's position. And surely, as a Healer, he's seen the effect of roet on its victims – even if he hasn't realised it could be permanent. I must have a closer look at our Head of Healing Studies and talk to Lady Vinara again.*

Administrator Osen announced the end of discussion time, and all returned to their seats. "Does anybody have anything they wish to say on this subject that has not been raised yet?" he asked.

A few magicians raised their hands. They were called to the floor. The first suggested that magicians should be subject to the same laws as ordinary Kyralians and there be no Guild rules at all. His proposal was met with a rumble of disagreement from all sides. The second magician declared that the rule should be changed, but his suggestion was that the rule should forbid magicians from involvement in or benefiting from criminal activity. This roused a thoughtful murmur. The last magician said only that the decision should be the king's.

"The king knows and has acknowledged that Guild rules, as opposed to laws, are for the Guild to make," Osen assured them all. He turned to the front. "Do any of the Higher Magicians have anything further to add?"

Nobody had suggested the simple change of removing "unsavoury characters" from the rule yet. Sonea drew in a deep breath and braced her feet, ready to rise.

"I do," High Lord Balkan said. Sonea glanced at him, then relaxed. He stood up. "A small change can make a great difference. I propose that we change the wording of the rule, leaving out the reference to unsavoury characters, since it is ambiguous and open to unfair interpretation."

Osen nodded. "Thank you." He turned back to the hall. "Unless there is majority disagreement, we have four viable choices: abolish the rule in its entirety, leave it as it is, change it to remove reference to unsavoury characters, or change 'associating with criminals and unsavoury characters' to 'involvement in and benefiting from criminal activity'. If we have a vote for change we will all vote again for our preference of the two choices. Form your globe lights now and move them into position."

Concentrating a little power, Sonea created a globe of light and sent it up, with the small cloud of globe lights belonging to the Higher Magicians, to float near the Guildhall ceiling. Hundreds of other lights joined it. The effect was dazzling.

"Those in favour of abolition change your light to blue," Osen ordered. "Those in favour of changing the rule make your light go green. Those favouring no change at all change to red."

The dazzling whiteness shifted to a brilliant mix of colours. Sonea squinted at the globe lights. *There aren't many red ones. A few more blue than red. But there are clearly more green than any other colour.* She felt her heart lift with hope.

"Now, those in favour of removing 'unsavoury characters' from the rule move your light to the front end of the hall, those in favour of changing it to forbid magicians from involvement in or benefiting from criminal activity move to the back."

Balls of light surged in different directions. There was a long pause while Osen stared upward, his lips moving as he counted. Then he turned to the Higher Magicians.

"How many of each do you count?"

"Seventy-five to the back, sixty-nine to the front," Lord Telano replied.

Sonea felt her breath catch in her throat. *But that means . . .*

Osen nodded. "My count agrees with Lord Telano's." He turned to face the hall. "The vote is cast. We will change the rule so that it forbids magicians to 'be involved in or benefit from criminal activity'."

Staring up at the globe lights, Sonea watched them flicker out of existence until one was left. Hers. She extinguished it, then looked down at Regin. His expression matched what she felt. Surprise. Perplexity. *They chose an option introduced at the last moment, which changed the rule completely. Which both weakened and yet narrowed the focus of it. Magicians and novices can no longer be punished for indulging themselves in pleasure houses, because they're no longer forbidden to associate with criminals. But at least they can't be lured into criminal activity, which is what the rule was meant to prevent in the first place.*

Regin looked up at her and raised his eyebrows slightly. She lifted her shoulders a little and let them drop. He looked away and she followed the direction of his gaze to Pendel. The young man was smiling and waving at his supporters.

It's all the same to him, Sonea thought. *He's gained a better result than he was hoping for. But Regin looks worried now. Oh dear. I can't believe I'm actually eager to meet with him again and find out what he thinks about this.*

But she'd also never thought she'd ever consult and plot with him. *I guess it's the price you pay for getting involved in Guild politics. Suddenly you have to be civil to old enemies. Well, thankfully it's all decided now. I don't have to talk to Regin again if I don't want to.*

She looked down at him a second time. He definitely looked worried. She sighed.

I guess one more chat wouldn't hurt.

CHAPTER 15

LATE-NIGHT VISITORS

The room's walls were round, like the inside of a sphere. *Like the Dome at the Guild,* Lorkin thought. *Are we home already?*

A large rock lay on the floor, at the lowest point of the curved surface. It was about the size of a small child curled up, but when he reached out to it he found it was small enough to fit into his palm. As he cupped it in his hand, it shrank rapidly, then vanished.

Oh, no! I found the storestone, but I've lost it again. I've destroyed it. When the Sachakans find out they're going to be furious! They'll kill me and Dannyl . . .

Yet the feeling of fear faded quickly. Instead he felt good. No, he felt *very* good. As if the sheets on his bed were moving across his skin, and getting rather personal in a nice way with parts of him that—

Suddenly he was wide awake.

And someone else was there, very, very close to him. Crouched on top of him. Smooth skin brushed against his. A pleasant scent filled his nostrils. The sound of breathing caressed his ear. He could see nothing. It was utterly dark in the room. But the sound of breathing was somehow recognisable as coming from a woman's throat.

Tyvara!

He could feel that she was naked. And she now let her weight settle onto his body. He ought to be dismayed – to push her off – but instead a rush of interest went through him. She chose that moment to take advantage of his arousal and he gasped at the unexpected pleasure of her body and his locking together. *Traitor*, he admonished his body. *I should stop her.* But he didn't. *It's not as if she isn't willing*, came another thought.

He thought briefly of the time they'd spent talking, and how he had grown to like the glimpses he'd seen of a smart, strong woman under the forced submissiveness. *You like her*, he assured himself. *That makes it all right, doesn't it?* But it was getting harder to think. His thoughts kept dissolving under waves of sheer physical pleasure.

Her breathing and movements began to quicken and sensation intensified. He stopped trying to think and gave in. Then her body stiffened and she stopped moving. Her chest lifted away from his as she arched back. He smiled. *Well, that proves that she is enjoying it, too.* She gave a muffled cry.

Muffled?

Brilliant light suddenly dazzled his eyes. He squinted as his eyes adjusted, then realised two things.

There was a hand covering Tyvara's mouth.

And it wasn't Tyvara.

Another woman loomed over him and the stranger, and he recognised her with a jolt. *This* was Tyvara.

But her face was distorted by a savage scowl. She was straining to hold the stranger, who was still making muffled sounds and struggling. Something warm and wet dripped onto his chest. He looked down. It was red, and a trail of it was running down the stranger's side.

231

Blood!

He felt cold all over, then horror filled him with strength and he pushed the stranger and Tyvara off him and scrambled away. The push caused Tyvara's hand to slip from the stranger's mouth and for her to nearly tumble off the end of the bed. As the stranger rolled onto her side, her eyes locked with Tyvara's.

"You! But . . . he has to die. You . . ." Blood leaked from her mouth. She coughed and clutched at her side. Her expression filled with hatred even as she seemed to lose strength. "You are a traitor to your people," she spat.

"I told you I would not let you kill him. You should have heeded my warning and left."

The woman opened her mouth to reply, then tensed as a spasm locked her muscles. Tyvara grabbed the woman's arm.

She's dying, Lorkin realised. *I don't know what's going on, but I can't just let her die.* He sent out magic and surrounded Tyvara, pushing her away, then leapt onto the bed and reached out to the dying woman.

And felt himself and his magic effortlessly countered by another force. It shattered the containment and rolled him off the end of the bed to land on the hard floor. He lay still, stunned. *She has magic. Tyvara has magic. She isn't what she is supposed to be. And . . . ouch!*

"I'm sorry, Lord Lorkin."

He looked up to see Tyvara standing over him. He glanced at the other slave, but she lay still with her back to him. He looked back at Tyvara. *How strong is she?* He eyed her doubtfully. *Is she a Sachakan black magician? But they don't teach women magic. Well, I suppose they might if they need a spy . . .*

"That woman was about to kill you," she told him.

He stared at her. "That wasn't the impression I got."

She smiled, but there was no humour in it. "Yes, she was. She was sent here to do it. You're lucky I arrived in time to stop her."

She's mad, he thought. But she was also a magician of undetermined power. It would be safer to reason with her than try to call for help. And reasoning with her might be more convincing if he wasn't half sitting, half lying on the floor with no clothes on.

Slowly he got to his feet. She made no move to stop him. He saw that the woman she had stabbed was staring up at the ceiling. Or beyond it. *And not seeing anything at all – or ever again.* He shuddered.

Backing up to the set of robes that the slaves had cleaned and left ready for him, hanging on the wall, he took the trousers. Blood had smeared across his chest. He wiped it off onto a cloth the slaves left each night, along with water and a bowl, so he could wash in the morning.

"I gather from your sceptical manner that you don't know of Lover's Death," Tyvara said. "It's a form of higher magic. When a man or woman reaches the peak of pleasure during lovemaking their natural protection against invasive magic falters, and they are vulnerable to being stripped of all power – and their life. Sachakan men know of Lover's Death and are wary of it, but they don't know how to do it. They used to, apparently, but lost the knowledge when they stopped teaching women magic."

"You're a woman," Lorkin pointed out as he pulled his trousers on. "So how is it you know magic?"

She smiled. "Men stopped teaching women magic. Women, however, did not."

"You know how to do this Lover's Death thing, too?" His

notebook and his mother's blood ring lay on the table. He picked up the ring as he reached out to the overrobe, hoping she only saw the latter movement, and held it in his hand as he put on the overrobe. Then he picked up his notebook, slipped it into the internal pocket and dropped the ring in at the same time.

"Yes. Although it's not my preferred method of assassination." She looked at the stranger. Following her gaze, Lorkin considered the corpse. *If Tyvara knows one method of higher magic there's a good chance she knows others. And that she is much, much stronger than me.*

"What are you, really? You're obviously not a real slave."

"I am a spy. I was sent here to protect you."

"By who?"

"I can't tell you that."

"But whoever it is, he or she wants me alive?"

"Yes."

He looked at the dead woman. "You . . . you, er, killed her to save me."

"Yes. If I hadn't found her here with you, *you* would have been the corpse, not her." She sighed. "I apologise. I made a mistake. I thought you were safe. After all, you told me you weren't intending to bed any slaves. I should not have believed you."

He felt his face heat. "I didn't intend to."

"You weren't exactly trying to stop her."

"It was dark. I thought she was . . ." He caught himself. Tyvara wasn't the person he'd thought she was. She was a black magician, a spy, and admitted to having preferred methods of assassination. It might not be a good idea to let her think he found her attractive. *And I'm not sure I do find the person she really is attractive, after all.*

234

Her eyes were darker than ever. They narrowed. "You thought she was what?"

He looked away, then forced himself to meet her gaze. "Someone else. I hadn't woken up properly. I thought I was dreaming."

"You must have interesting and pleasant dreams," she observed. "Now, grab your things."

"Things?"

"Whatever you don't want to leave behind."

"I'm leaving?"

"Yes." She looked at the dead woman again. "When the people who sent her realise she failed to kill you they'll send someone else to finish the job. And they'll send someone to kill me at the same time. It's not safe here for either of us, and I need you alive."

"And D— . . . Ambassador Dannyl?"

She smiled. "He's not a target."

"How are you so sure?"

"Because he's not the son of the man who crossed them."

He froze in surprise. *Was Mother right? She was so sure someone would hold a grudge against me because of what she and father had done.*

She took a step toward the door. "Hurry. We don't have much time."

He did not move. *Do I believe her? Do I have a choice? She knows black magic. She can probably force me to go with her. And if she wants me dead why would she save my life? Unless that was a lie, and she just killed an innocent slave in order to convince me of . . . something.*

Then he remembered the look on the stranger's face when she saw Tyvara. *"But . . . he has to die"*, she'd said. That confirmed that she'd wanted to kill him. *"You are a traitor to your people!"* she'd also said to Tyvara. Did "your people" mean the Sachakan people? Suddenly his mother's concerns seemed much too real. *At least Tyvara seems to want to keep me alive. If I stay here, who knows what will happen? Well, Tyvara believes someone else will try to kill me.*

He was in trouble. But he remembered what he'd decided at the Hearing. Whatever trouble he got into, he had to get himself out of again. Weighing up the choices he had, he settled on what he hoped was the best one.

He glanced around the room. Did he need anything else? No. He already had his mother's ring. He walked over to Tyvara.

"I have everything I need."

She nodded and turned to the doorway, peering out into the corridor.

"So, who was it exactly that you said my father crossed?" he asked.

She rolled her eyes. "We don't have time for me to explain."

"I knew you'd say that."

"But I will, later."

"I'm taking that as a promise," he told her.

She frowned, placed a hand on her lips to indicate silence, then beckoned and quietly slipped out into the dark corridors of the Guild House.

Once Cery would have travelled familiar parts of the Thieves' Road without a light. There had been little danger of encountering a knife in the dark, as only those who had the approval of the Thieves had used the network of passages under the city, and the truce between the Thieves prevented any but approved murders happening on the road.

Now there was no truce, and anyone who dared could travel the road. It had quickly become so dangerous that few did, which, ironically, made the deserted parts safer. And stories of oversized rodents and monsters kept all but the boldest from exploring.

But I still wouldn't travel without a light, Cery thought as he approached a corner. His heart had been beating uncomfortably fast since they had entered the road. He would not relax again until they'd left it. Peering around the turn, he lifted the lamp and felt yet another wave of relief as he saw the tunnel ahead was unoccupied. Then he realised that what he'd assumed was the next turn was actually rubble filling the space. He sighed and turned back to Gol.

"Another blockage," he said.

Gol's eyebrows rose. "It wasn't there last time."

"No." Cery looked up at the ceiling. He winced as he saw the crack where brickwork was separating. "Nobody does any maintenance any more. We'll have to go around."

They backtracked and Cery took a right-hand passage. Gol hesitated before following.

"Aren't we . . .?" the big man asked.

"Getting real close to the Slig City?" Cery finished. "Yes. We better be quiet."

The Sligs had been a group of street urchins who'd found refuge in the underground passages after their area of slums had been lost to new roads and buildings. They'd settled underground, only coming up to steal food. Somehow they'd survived, grown up and bred in the darkness, and now they defended their territory with savage ferocity.

The Thief who operated in the area above Slig City had once tried to gain control of them. His corpse and those of his men had washed out of the sewers a few days later.

After that, people living above had begun leaving food out by known tunnel entrances in the hopes of keeping the Sligs' favour.

At each tunnel entrance, Cery lifted his lamp and examined the brickwork. The Sligs always painted a symbol on the walls around the edges of their territory. Only when he and Gol had moved away from the underworld citizen's domain again did he stop looking for signs of them. Unfortunately, he began to encounter cave-ins and signs of decay again. But soon they'd reached the old entrance to the passages under the Guild.

The entrance had been destroyed after the Ichani Invasion, but Cery had arranged for a new tunnel to be dug. As a precaution, he'd included false entrances and clever deceptions that would lead explorers away again. Cery paused to listen and look for any observers, then slipped through the correct one, Gol following.

"Good luck," Gol said as he stopped beside the niche where he usually waited when Cery made one of his journeys to meet Sonea.

"You, too," Cery replied. "Don't talk to any strangers."

The big man humphed and lifted his lamp up to examine the niche. Brushing away a few faren webs, he sat down on the shelf and yawned. Cery turned away and set off into the passages under the Guild Grounds.

Like much of the Thieves' Road, these passages were in disrepair. They had never been in good condition anyway, except where High Lord Akkarin had made repairs. But the secretive magician hadn't been able to source much in the way of building materials, since it would have aroused suspicion, and had mostly reused bricks from other parts of the maze to patch the walls.

The underlying problems of damp and shifting soil had never been solved.

I'm sure the Guild would rather they were filled in. I'd fix them myself, but if the Guild discovered a Thief repairing their underground passages I don't think they'd be too pleased. I doubt they'd accept the excuse that all I really want is to be able to meet up with Sonea now and then.

Cery's heart was still beating quickly, but more from excitement than fear now. Sneaking into the Guild always gave him a childish thrill. Skirting dangerous areas or cave-ins made Cery's path more complicated than it needed to be, but once he was under the University foundations things improved. The passage from the University to the Magicians' Quarters was the most worrying, as it was the only underground route between the buildings. Its main function was as a sewer, with a maintenance shelf along one side of the ditch. But nobody had maintained it for years, he suspected. Water ran from cracks in the walls and seeped down through the domed ceiling.

One day there'll be a cave-in, and they're going to discover a rather fragrant downside to not servicing their sewer.

Once under the Quarters' foundations, the passage widened a little. Numbers had been carved below rectangular holes in the ceiling. He found the one he was looking for, set his lamp down in a dry spot, then climbed up the wall into the opening.

This was the hardest part of the journey. The openings were at the base of some sort of unused chute system that connected to the roof of the building above. Clean air constantly flowed down them. He had two favourite theories: either it was a ventilation system to keep the sewer air from getting too poisonous, or it was a rubbish disposal system designed not to reek of the sewer below.

The interior was small, but thankfully dry. He climbed slowly, taking his time and resting often. *One day I'm going to be too old to do this. Then I'll have to walk in via the Guild Gates. Or Sonea will have to come see me.*

Finally, he reached the wall behind her rooms. He'd removed a section of bricks long ago, exposing the wood panelling behind. He put his eye to the spy hole he'd drilled into the wood.

The room beyond was dark and empty. But that was the usual situation at this time of night. He carefully and quietly grasped the handles he'd attached to the back of a section of panelling, lifted and twisted.

The panelling squeaked a little as it came free. *I should bring some wax next time to fix that*, he thought. He stepped through the opening, then set the panelling back in place.

It was a matter of some pride and satisfaction to him that Sonea had never seen him enter this way. She insisted on not knowing how he entered or left her rooms. The less she knew, the better for the both of them. It was not mortally dangerous to come here, but the consequences wouldn't be good for her if his visits were discovered, and that knowledge tempered the mischievous delight he felt at reaching her quarters unnoticed.

He made a few deliberate noises, knocking against furniture and stepping on a floorboard he knew creaked, then waited. But she did not emerge from the bedroom. Moving to the door, he opened it a crack. The bed was neat and unused. The room was empty.

Disappointment extinguished the lingering excitement of his journey. He sat down. She had never been absent before. *I never considered she might not be here. What do I do now? Wait for her?*

But if someone else returned with her it would be a bit

awkward. He'd have no time to escape to the chute. And the chute was too uncomfortable a place to wait and watch for her.

Cursing under his breath, he stood up again and quietly searched her furniture. He found what he sought in a drawer: paper and a pen. Tearing a small corner from a sheet of paper, he drew a tiny picture of a ceryni, the rodent that was his namesake, and slipped it under the door to her bedroom.

Then he returned to the panelling and started the long journey home.

The slave that greeted Dannyl at the door of the Guild House was especially quick to abase himself. Too many exciting discoveries were hovering at the fore of Dannyl's thoughts, however, and he did not register what the man said. On the way home from the palace, he had written in his notebook as much as he could of what the king had told him of Sachakan history, but even as he walked down the corridor he remembered something he'd forgotten.

I need to sit down and get it all onto paper. It's going to be a long night, I suspect. I wonder if Achati could arrange a quiet night for me tomorrow . . . what's this?

In the Master's Room a sea of slaves covered the floor, their bodies fanning out from the doorway. The door slave had joined them. It was such a surreal sight he could not speak for a moment.

"Rise," he ordered.

As one the group slowly got to its feet. He saw men and women he did not recognise. Some with robust clothing suited to outdoors work, others with what looked like food stains down their leather aprons.

"Why are you all here?" he asked.

The slaves exchanged glances, then their gazes locked on

the door slave. The man hunched over as if their stares had weight.

"L-Lord Lorkin is . . . is . . . is . . ."

Dannyl felt his heart skip a beat, then start racing. Only something terrible warranted this amount of cowering.

"He is what? Dead?"

The man shook his head and relief rushed over Dannyl. "Then what?"

"G-gone."

The man threw himself on the floor again, then the rest of the slaves followed suit. Irritated, Dannyl drew in a deep breath and made himself speak calmly.

"Gone where?"

"We don't know," the door slave said, his voice strangled. "But . . . he left . . . in his room."

He left something in his room. Most likely a letter explaining why he's gone. And for some reason the slaves think I'll be angry. Has Lorkin taken it into his head to go home?

"Get up," he ordered. "All of you. Go back to what you were doing. No. Wait." The slaves had begun to scramble to their feet. *I might need to question them.* "Stay here. You," he pointed to the door slave, "come with me."

The man's brown face went a pasty colour. He followed Dannyl silently through the Guild House to Lorkin's rooms. Lamps had been lit around the main room, and one still burned in the bedroom.

"Lord Lorkin?" Dannyl called, not really expecting an answer. If Lorkin had told them he was leaving, he wasn't likely to be here. Still, Dannyl walked across to the bedroom door and looked inside.

What he saw made his blood turn to ice.

A naked Sachakan woman lay there, twisted so that her head faced the ceiling but her back was turned toward him. Her eyes staring up at the ceiling blankly. The sheets about her were stained dark red. In places they still glistened wetly. He could see the wound in her back.

Spinning around, Dannyl fixed the door slave with a stern stare. "How did this happen?"

The man cringed. "I don't know. Nobody knows. We heard noises. Voices. After they stopped we came to see." His eyes slid to the corpse, then quickly away again.

Did Lorkin do this? Dannyl wanted to ask. *But if the man says he doesn't know what happened, he won't know if Lorkin was responsible.*

"Who is she?" Dannyl asked instead.

"Riva."

"Is she one of the slaves of this house?"

"Y-yes."

"Is anyone else missing?"

The man frowned, then his eyes widened. "Tyvara."

"Another slave?"

"Yes. Like Riva. A serving slave."

Dannyl considered the dead woman again. Had this Tyvara been involved in the murder somehow? Or had she suffered the same fate?

"Were Riva and Tyvara . . . friendly to each other?" Dannyl asked. "Has anyone seen them speaking?"

"I-I don't know." The man looked at the floor. "I will ask."

"No," Dannyl said. "Bring the slaves to me. Have them line up in the corridor outside and tell them not to speak." The man hurried away. *I suppose they've already had time to collude and think of good alibis or excuses. But they won't be able to modify their story.*

243

He would have to send a message to Ashaki Achati without delay. The slaves belonged to the king. Dannyl wasn't sure if the murder of one of them would be of much concern. But Lorkin's leaving was. Especially if he had been taken against his will. Especially if he'd murdered the slave.

Achati will no doubt question all the slaves himself. He'll probably read their minds. It's possible he'll hide any information he doesn't think I ought to hear. So I must find out everything I can before Achati arrives.

He straightened as a chill ran down his spine. *Is it a coincidence that I was finally invited to the palace the night one of his slaves was murdered here?*

Had Lorkin killed the slave? Surely not. But it certainly looked like it. Was it self-defence? *I should check for evidence either way before the king's men turn up.* Moving into the room, he stared at the body. Aside from the wound, there was a line of red beaded blood along a shallow cut on her arm. *Interesting. That looks like evidence of black magic.* He forced himself to touch the skin of the woman's thigh and search with his senses. Sure enough, the body had been drained of energy. Black magic *had* been used. The relief he felt was overwhelming. *It can't have been Lorkin.*

Then why had Lorkin left? Was he a prisoner of a Sachakan black magician? Suddenly Dannyl felt ill.

When Sonea finds out . . . But would she have to yet? If he managed to track down Lorkin quickly there'd be no bad news to deliver, just a story with a happy ending. He hoped.

He had to find Lorkin, and fast. Sounds from the corridor told him the slaves had arrived for questioning. He sighed. It *was* going to be a long night. But not for the reasons he would have preferred.

PART TWO

CHAPTER 16

HUNTER

Holding the soiled bandages in the air with magic, Sonea sent a flash of heat toward them. They burst into flame and quickly shrivelled into ash. The smell of burnt cloth, mixed with a sickly cooked meat scent, tainted the air. She let the ashes fall into a bucket kept in the room for the purpose, then heated a little scented oil in a dish with magic until the tangy smell covered the less pleasant ones. The clean-up from the last patient finished, she willed the door to the examination room open.

The man who stepped inside was middle-aged, short, and familiar. She felt her heart skip a beat as she recognised him.

"Cery!" she hissed. She cast a quick look around the room, even though she knew nobody was there but her. "What are you doing here?"

He shrugged and sat down in one of the chairs for patients and their families. "I tried your rooms in the Guild, but you weren't there."

"You could have come back tomorrow night," she said. If he was recognised, and someone reported his visit back to the Guild, everyone would know she'd been associating with a Thief. *Though that's not against any rules now.* But it would be seen as suspicious, so soon after she'd pushed to have the rule changed. If it looked as if she was using the hospice as a place to meet Thieves it could endanger all she had achieved here.

Ironically, he was in greater danger of being recognised at the hospice than at the Guild. Sonea doubted that any magicians other than Rothen would remember Cery after all these years, but some of the patients in the hospice might have had dealings with Cery, and they might tell one of the helpers or Healers who she was meeting.

"It's too important to wait," Cery told her.

He met her gaze levelly. His serious expression made him look so different to the young street urchin she had hung out with as a child. He looked haggard and sad, and she felt a fresh pang of sympathy. He was still grieving for his family. She drew in a deep breath and let it out again slowly and quietly.

"How are you getting on?"

His shoulders rose again. "Well enough. Keeping myself occupied finding a rogue magician in the city."

She blinked, then couldn't help smiling. "A rogue, eh?"

"Yes."

Yes, that is *too important to wait.* She leaned back in her chair. "Go on then. Start from the beginning."

He nodded. "Well, it all began when my lockmaker claimed the locks to my hideout were opened with magic."

As he continued, she watched him closely. At any mention of his family he winced as if in pain, and his eyes grew haunted. But each time he spoke of the Thief Hunter his eyes gleamed and his jaw hardened. *This search is as much a way to distract himself from the loss as it is a hunt for revenge.*

Finally he told her, triumphantly, of watching the foreign woman using magic to open the safebox.

248

"A woman," he repeated. "With dark skin like a Lonmar, and straight black hair. From her voice I'd say she was old, but she didn't move like an elderly person. And her accent was foreign, but not one I've heard before. I'd wager she's not from any of the Allied Lands."

"Sachakan?"

"No. I'd have known that one."

Sonea considered his story. There's nobody of that description in the Guild. Cery might have been mistaken, and the woman was a Lonmar. The Lonmars were dark-skinned, and kept their women hidden away, so a Lonmar woman might be so unusual a sight as to seem like she was of a different race. The Lonmars didn't allow their women to be taught magic, however. If she was a natural, and her power had developed spontaneously, the Lonmars would have been forced to teach her to control it. *But after that . . . we're not sure what the Lonmars do with female magicians. We assume they simply forbid the woman to use magic, but it's possible they block her powers. This rogue might have run away in order to escape that fate.*

If that was true, it was strange that she had come to Imardin. Surely she knew that the Guild was bound by the terms of alliance to respect Lonmar's laws regarding female magicians. If they found her they had to send her home.

But perhaps Cery had guessed why she had: books. If she had run away in order to be free to learn and use magic, then Imardin was the place she'd most likely get hold of magical information. *But books on magic can't be cheap. Is she stealing money from the Thieves she kills, or hiring herself out as a killer of Thieves?*

Yet while Cery had said the lock to his hideout was opened with magic, he had not said that his family were killed with it. Perhaps she was only offering magical services, not those of an assassin. Sonea frowned. "How can you be sure this woman and the Thief Hunter are the same person?"

"Either she is, or she's working for the Thief Hunter, or there are two rogues out there. Once you catch her you can read her mind and find out."

"Did you question the seller afterwards?"

He shook his head. "We need him and his shop for another trap." His eyes gleamed. "Only next time you'll be with me and we'll catch ourselves a rogue."

Sonea frowned. "I wish that were possible, but I'm not free to go running around the city these days, Cery. I must ask permission, if I am not going to the hospices."

His shoulders sagged in almost childlike disappointment. He looked thoughtful. "Perhaps if I lured her here somehow."

"I doubt she'll go anywhere near Guild magicians, and hospices are always full of them."

"Unless you arrange for everyone to leave one night, and we put about a rumour that there are books on Healing lying around here."

"I'd have to tell them why, and if I do that I may as well just tell the Guild about the rogue and leave it to them to find her."

"Can't you come up with another reason?"

Sonea sighed. She doubted that Cery cared if he wasn't credited with finding a rogue and helping the Guild to catch her. He only wanted revenge – and no doubt to save himself from being the Thief Hunter's next victim.

I'd like to help him. But the Guild will expect me to pass news about the rogue on to them, and if it is discovered that I didn't it'll be yet another reason for people to distrust me. Her flawless record of trustworthiness since the Ichani Invasion would be tainted by the lie, and people were already so touchy about her past and knowledge of black magic. They would curb her freedom to run the hospices. They'd restrict her to the Guild grounds.

I'm better off passing the information on to the Higher Magicians and letting them deal with it. It doesn't matter if it's me or someone else who finds the rogue, only that she is found. Either way, Cery will have both revenge and safety.

"Do you know where the woman is now?" she asked.

Cery shook his head. "But I know what she looks like, and her appearance is strange enough that I can set others looking for her too."

"Don't let anyone approach her," she warned. "She's clearly in control of her powers, and old enough to have some skill in using them."

"Oh, she's nothing like you were," Cery agreed, his lips stretching into a humourless grin. "You might've wanted to kill a Thief or two all those years ago, but you never got to the point of hunting them down and . . . or . . ." He looked away, his expression suddenly grim.

. . . or killing their families, she finished silently, feeling a pang of sympathy. "I need to think about this, but I'll probably have to tell the Guild and leave the hunt to them."

"No!" he protested. "They'll just bungle it like they did with you."

"Or they'll take what they learned from that experience and tackle this case differently."

He scowled. "A *lot* differently, I hope."

"Are you willing to work with them?" she asked, meeting and holding his gaze.

He grimaced, then sighed. "Maybe. Yes. I guess I have to. Don't have much choice, do I?"

"Not really. Tell me how they can contact you."

Cery sighed. "Could you . . . sleep on it before telling anyone?"

She smiled. "All right. I'll decide before tonight's shift. Either you'll hear from me or the Guild will come knocking at your door."

The kitchen slave's eyes had gone round the moment he'd entered the room and spotted the corpse, and had remained wide through all Dannyl's questions. Yet he answered calmly and without hesitation.

"When did you last see Tyvara?" Dannyl asked.

"Last night. I passed her in the corridor. She was heading for these rooms."

"Did she say anything?"

"No."

"Look any different to usual? Nervous, perhaps?"

"No." The slave paused. "She looked angry, I think. It was dark."

Dannyl nodded and noted the small detail. He had quite a list of them now, but then, he had been interviewing slaves for several hours.

"You said she and Riva knew each other. Did you ever see them arguing? Any odd behaviour?"

"They argued, yes. Tyvara told Riva what to do a lot. Riva didn't like it. Tyvara had no right to. But," the man shrugged, "it happens."

"That some slaves order around others?"

The man nodded. "Yes."

"Did you see them arguing any time yesterday, or hear of them arguing?"

The man opened his mouth to reply, but paused at a soft sound from the doorway. Dannyl looked up to see the door slave hovering nervously in the entrance. The man threw himself to the floor.

"You may rise. What did you come to tell me?" Dannyl asked.

"Ashaki Achati has arrived." The slave was wringing his hands, as he had every time Dannyl had seen him since arriving home.

Dannyl turned to the kitchen slave he was interviewing. "You may go."

Both slaves scurried away as Dannyl rose and tucked his notebook into his robes. He looked around Lorkin's rooms, then strode out of them and made his way to the Master's Room. He arrived just in time to meet Achati.

"Welcome, Ashaki Achati," he said.

"Ambassador Dannyl," Achati replied. "I'm afraid it took some time for your slave to track me down. What has happened? All he would tell me was that it was urgent."

Dannyl beckoned. "Come and I'll show you."

The Sachakan followed Dannyl through the Guild House silently, to Dannyl's relief. The late hour and constant questioning of slaves had begun to take their toll. *But there is still much to do. I won't be sleeping for a while.* He drew a little magic and used it to soothe away the tiredness. *I'll be doing that a few more times in the coming days, I suspect.*

They arrived at Lorkin's rooms. Dannyl led Achati in and to the door of the bedroom. Lamps had burned low, but the body was still clear and shocking to behold.

"A dead slave," Achati said, moving inside and peering at her. "I see why you are concerned."

"To put it lightly."

"Did your . . .?" Achati's gesture took in the rooms.

"No. The body is empty of energy. Whoever killed her used bl— . . . higher magic, which Lorkin has not been taught."

Achati glanced at him, then frowned and touched the dead woman's arm. While the Guild did not want the Sachakans knowing how few Kyralian magicians could use black magic, it didn't require Dannyl to pretend that they *all* did either. It would seem plausible that Lorkin, as a low-status magician, would not yet have been taught it. *It'll be stranger to them that I do not know it.*

"So she has," Achati said, withdrawing his hand with a grimace of distaste. "But this means whoever did kill her had been taught it."

"One of the other slaves, a woman named Tyvara, is missing. I have questioned most of the slaves here and she looks the most likely culprit."

Instead of expressing surprise, as Dannyl expected, Achati looked worried. "You read their minds?"

"No. Guild magicians are not allowed to read minds without the permission of the Higher Magicians."

Achati's eyebrows rose. "Then how do you know they are telling the truth?"

"The slaves were expecting to have their minds read, so they would not have come up with a false story or planned answers before I started questioning them. I had them wait in the corridor in silence, so they could not do so once they realised I wasn't going to be reading their minds. Their stories match, so I doubt they are lying."

The Sachakan looked intrigued. "But what would you learn by questioning them that I wouldn't by reading their minds?"

"Perhaps nothing." Dannyl drew out his notebook and smiled. "But there may be advantages. We won't know until we compare methods."

Achati looked amused. "Shall I read their minds now to test which is better, or do you want to tell me what you have learned?"

Dannyl looked at the corpse. "It would be better if I told you, to save time. Do you agree that this has the look of a spontaneous killing rather than a planned one?"

Achati nodded.

"I've learned that Tyvara and the dead woman, Riva, often argued. Riva appears to have been the subordinate of Tyvara. Riva wanted to be Lorkin's serving slave the day he arrived, but Tyvara took her place. Both women were formerly of Ashaki Tikako's household, and often received messages from slaves there – though each had a separate contact. They did not receive messages from slaves in other households, so I think the most likely place Tyvara would have taken Lorkin is there."

Achati frowned. "If we are to look for them there, we must be sure. Could someone else have taken him?"

"Lorkin had no other visitors. If he was taken against his will, the abductor must be a powerful magician. If not . . ." Dannyl shrugged. "They must be persuasive."

Achati sighed and nodded. "If this Tyvara does know higher magic, it is likely she is no true slave. She must be a spy."

"A spy for whom?" Dannyl asked.

"I don't know." Achati grimaced. "Not the king's, as he would have warned me about her. But if whoever sent her wanted Lorkin dead, he *would* be. If they have taken him from here alive, they must have a purpose for him."

"What purpose?"

"Blackmail, perhaps?" Achati looked thoughtful. "The question is, is the target King Amakira, or the Guild – or both?"

Dannyl smiled wryly. "Must be the Guild. If they sought to embarrass the king, they'd have abducted me. A kidnapped Ambassador has more embarrassment value than a mere assistant."

"But he's not a mere assistant," Achati said, his eyebrows rising. "You didn't believe we were unaware of his parentage, did you?"

Dannyl sighed. "I guess it was too much to hope you hadn't noticed."

"If it eases your mind, we did not think he would be in any danger because of it. In truth, we believed the prospect of his mother taking her rightful revenge if he was harmed was enough to deter foolish acts like this. Though . . ." He stopped, turned back to the dead woman, and frowned as if he'd thought of something.

"Yes?" Dannyl prompted.

The Sachakan shook his head. "There is another group known for abducting people, but they have nothing to gain from taking him and he is not their usual sort of target. No. We will go to Ashaki Tikako's house. If we are in luck your assistant will be found there and be returned to the Guild House before the day is done." He paused. "Though you may want to get rid of the slave's body before then."

Dannyl nodded in agreement. "Not exactly a pleasant welcome home gift. If you are done examining her, I'll get the slaves to do with her whatever they do with their dead."

Since they did not need the new hideout as a trap for the Thief Hunter, Cery had ordered the place to be sealed up. He and

Gol had moved back to his storeroom apartment next to the old city wall.

Cery hadn't said anything to Gol about his conversation with Sonea until the morning. Her response to his news had been so different to what he'd been expecting that he'd needed time to think, to reconsider his plans, and to wonder if he'd regret what he'd agreed to.

"Why isn't she going after the rogue herself?" Gol asked again.

Cery sighed and lifted his shoulders. "She said she wasn't free to go running around the city these days. She can go to the hospice, but not anywhere else without asking first."

Gol scowled. "Ungrateful sods. After all she did to save the city."

Yes, but most Kyralians are scared of her, Cery thought. *They've got her as locked away as well they can without actually putting her in a prison. They don't want to take any risks they don't have to. I can understand that. But it makes things a bit inconvenient for me.*

"So we're going to work with the Guild?"

"We have to." Cery grimaced. "Nobody but us can recognise the rogue. And maybe we can help stop them making a complete mess of things."

Gol's expression told Cery how little he believed that. "What about Skellin? You going to tell him?"

"We still don't have proof the woman is the Thief Hunter, only that she uses magic."

"Which is why you're calling her 'the rogue' now," Gol observed.

"Yes. Until we know for sure she is the Thief Hunter."

Gol crossed his arms. "You're afraid you'll make a fool of yourself."

Cery looked at his friend reproachfully. "I don't want to waste Skellin's time. Or owe him any favours when I don't have to."

"But you said he wasn't what you thought he'd be."

"No." Cery grimaced. "But he's still a Thief and a rot importer. Better men than me and you have done bad things for reasons they believed were good."

"They're the dangerous ones," Gol agreed. "Use family or the pride of a House or protecting the country and anything is excusable."

Cery nodded. "I'd rather be honest with myself when it comes to business. I wanted to be better off than most dwells. Don't want to die a beggar. I'm not pretending I got higher purposes than that."

"So you need money. And to get money you need to be powerful. And unless you're from the Houses, there's no way you're growing powerful by any honest trade."

"It's all about surviving. Which is what I think Skellin is doing. He said he tried importing rot as a way to establish himself as a Thief."

"It worked."

Cery sighed. "It did. And his conscience isn't so bothered that he's got himself out of the trade."

"He said he would, though."

"I'll believe that when I see it. Rot's made him one of the most powerful men in the city. He's got most of the Thieves working for him or owing him favours. I don't think he'd give that up too quick." He shook his head. "I'm not going to risk getting caught up in that if I don't have to."

Gol snorted. "You're too smart to let him talk you into anything, Cery."

Cery looked at his friend and bodyguard. "You think I should tell him?"

The big man pursed his lips. "If somethin's telling you not to, then don't. But if we have trouble finding the Rogue I reckon it'd be interesting to see what Skellin's capable of." He shrugged. "Maybe not much. Or maybe he'd reveal how powerful he really is."

CHAPTER 17

HUNTED

Despite spending several hours in the room, Lorkin's eyes still smarted. The air was thick with the smell of the urine stored in open vats to one side. Tyvara had told him to breathe shallowly to avoid burning his lungs, and to keep his eyes closed. She had also told him, before she slipped away again, that only slaves would enter the room, and to stay quiet.

Time passes very slowly when your every breath sets your throat burning with sour fumes. It also made fleeing into the night far less of an exciting adventure than it had first promised.

Not that I did it for the thrill of it. I do believe it was my only choice. That I was in danger. And still could be.

Was he a fool to believe Tyvara? The only evidence he had that she was telling the truth was the reaction of the slave woman she'd killed.

"You! But . . . he has to die. You . . . You are a traitor to your people."

From that he knew three things: the slave had recognised Tyvara, believed he should be killed, and thought Tyvara a traitor. What had Tyvara said in reply?

"I told you I would not let you kill him. You should have taken the warning and left."

From that he could assume Tyvara had known of the woman's intent and given the slave a chance to abandon her mission. *Or she said it in the hope I'd believe that.* But what reason might she have to deceive him? *Maybe to convince me she had given the woman a chance to leave. That she wasn't as merciless a killer as she seemed.*

One thing was clear. If Tyvara had wanted to kill him, she would have. After all, she knew black magic. She could easily be many times stronger than him, magically.

But what he wasn't sure about was whether it was necessary for him to flee with her. Surely once Dannyl learned what had happened he'd have arranged better protection for them. *But how would he do that? It will take several days for any Guild magicians to get here, and none of them are as strong as most Sachakan magicians. If Mother or Kallen were sent, they would have to strengthen themselves with black magic before they left and that would take more time. As for the Sachakan magicians . . . would any deign to act as bodyguard to a Guild Ambassador's assistant? How could we know they hadn't sent Riva to kill me to begin with?*

As for who wanted him dead, his best guess was the families of the Sachakans his parents had killed during the Ichani Invasion. His mother must be right. Their families must still feel obliged to seek revenge for their relations, despite the fact those relations had been outcasts.

The Higher Magicians were sure there was no danger of that. So were Lord Maron and the other Guild Ambassadors who had lived here. Did those families hide their intentions in the hope that Mother or I would one day travel to Sachaka?

He thought of the ring in his pocket. *Should I try to contact my mother again?* Slaves had been coming in and out of the room constantly. They didn't seem surprised to see him there.

The first time, he'd been about to use his mother's blood ring, and had stuffed it into the spine of his notebook just in time. If they saw it would they suspect he was trying to betray them, and take it away?

What would she say to me? Probably to go back to the Guild House and let Dannyl take care of everything. She'll have no trouble talking the Guild into ordering me home now. He felt a surge of rebellion, but it faded quickly. *She was right*, he reminded himself. *It was too dangerous for me to come here. Yet something tells me going back to the Guild House isn't a safe option right now. If Tyvara saved my life she wants me alive, and clearly that's not where she thinks I should—*

The door to the room opened abruptly, making Lorkin jump. But it was Tyvara standing in the opening. He could not help thinking, as he had done every time he'd seen her previously, that she was alluringly mysterious and exotic. Now, however, she did not stand with her head bowed and gaze lowered. Nor did she throw herself on the floor. Instead she regarded him with amusement, her pose confident and relaxed.

Which is a definite improvement, he decided.

"How are you doing?" she asked, grimacing at the smell.

"Still breathing," he replied. "Though I almost wish I wasn't. Are you going to explain all this to me now?"

She smiled faintly. "Yes. Come out."

He followed her out into the big workroom beyond. Four slave women sat at a large table, watching him with undisguised curiosity but no hint of friendliness. Two were around Tyvara's age, the others were older but it was hard to guess whether their wrinkles were from hard work and sunlight or advancing years. As he looked at them, they glanced away, then straightened and brought their attention back to him. *As if habit made them avoid meeting my gaze at first. Tyvara, though, has to pretend to be a slave. I think . . . I think these women were raised as slaves, while Tyvara was born a free woman.*

"Sit," Tyvara invited, indicating a stool beside the table. As he did, she perched on the edge of another. "I'd introduce everyone but it is always safer to avoid sharing names. I can tell you we are safe with these women."

Lorkin nodded politely at them. "Then I thank you for your help."

The four said nothing, but their eyebrows had risen and they exchanged a few quick looks.

"We are a people known as the Traitors," Tyvara told him. "Several hundred years ago, after Sachaka was conquered by the Kyralians, free women joined with female slaves and escaped to a remote and hidden place. There they built a home where none are slaves and all are equal."

Lorkin frowned. "A society entirely of women? But how do you—"

"Not entirely women." Tyvara smiled. "There are men there, too. But they are not in charge of everything, as they are every-where else in the world."

How fascinating. Lorkin looked at Tyvara closely. *Of course. It's not just that she was born a free woman. She's used to having authority over others.* Then he realised something else. She had always reminded him of someone and now he knew who it was.

My mother! At that thought he felt his stomach sink. *That might not be a good thought to have slip into my mind if we ever . . . no, don't think about it.*

"Any questions?" she asked.

"Why do you call yourselves 'the Traitors'?"

"Apparently we were named after a Sachakan princess who

was killed by her father for being raped by one of his allies. He called her a traitor, and women of the time began calling themselves the same in sympathy."

Lorkin thought about what the dying slave had said. *"You are a traitor to your people."* Did she mean "Traitor"? No, that didn't make any sense. But if Riva had known Tyvara was a spy . . .

"Did Riva know you were a Traitor?"

"Yes."

"Why did she say you were a traitor to your people?"

Tyvara's mouth twitched into a wry smile. "I'm afraid the fact that we don't follow the emperor or the law, and have a habit of interfering in Sachakan politics, means most Sachakans consider us traitors."

"How do you keep Sachakan magicians from finding you all? Surely they have only to read your minds?"

"We have a way of keeping our thoughts hidden from them. They will only see what we want them to see. It means we can have people in the households of powerful Ashaki all through the country."

Lorkin's heart skipped. *Magic I've never heard of!*

"Can you tell me how?"

She shook her head. "We Traitors don't give up our secrets easily."

He nodded. *Something that protects the mind from being read — much like blood gems prevent mental communication between magicians being heard by other magicians.*

"Is it like a blood gem ring?" he asked.

One of the other women laughed. Her eyes met his briefly, then she looked at Tyvara. "This one's smart. You'll have to watch every word."

Tyvara snorted softly. "I know." Then her amusement faded. She sighed, then turned back to Lorkin. "We have to move on from here. This place is too close to the Guild House and some of the slaves there know I had contacts here. You're going to have to give up those pretty clothes and disguise yourself as a slave. Can you do that?"

Lorkin looked down at his robes and suppressed a sigh. "If I have to."

"His face is too pale," one of the younger slave women said. "We'll have to stain it. And we'll need to cut his hair."

An older one looked him up and down. "He's skinny for a Sachakan. But that's better than fat. Don't get many fat slaves." She rose. "I'll get some clothes."

"You'll need a slave name, too," Tyvara said. "How about Ork? It's close enough to your real name that if I call it by mistake people might not notice."

"Ork," Lorkin repeated, shrugging. *Sounds like a monster. My friends back home would find that very funny.* Then he felt a pang of sadness. *They're going to be worried about me when they find out I've gone missing. I wish there was a way — other than contacting Mother through the blood ring — I could let them know I was fine.* He grimaced. *Well, still alive, anyway.*

The older slave had pulled a long rectangle of cloth off a rack where several identical lengths were hanging. She brought it to him along with a length of rope. The women exchanged smirks as he removed his overrobe. He wrapped the cloth around his body and belted it with the rope as instructed, then removed his trousers. He was glad he'd hidden his mother's blood ring in the spine of his notebook. It would have been hard to retrieve it from his robes without it being noticed.

"You can't take that with you," Tyvara said as she saw the notebook.

Lorkin looked down at the book. "Can it be sent back to the Guild House?"

The slave women shook their heads. "Hard to do that without anyone knowing it came from here," one explained.

"It'll have to be destroyed," Tyvara decided, reaching for it.

"No!" Lorkin snatched it away. "It has all my research in it."

"Which no slave would be carrying."

"I'll keep it hidden," he told her. He stuffed it down the front of the wrap.

"And if an Ashaki reads your mind he'll know you're hiding it there."

"If an Ashaki reads his mind, he'll know he's not a slave," one of the older women pointed out, grinning. "Let him keep his book."

Tyvara frowned, then sighed. "Very well, then. Have we got any shoes?"

One of the other women fetched a pair of simple leather shoes that weren't much more than a piece of leather stitched up into a foot-shaped pouch that was bound to the ankle with another, thinner piece of rope. Tyvara nodded approvingly.

"We're halfway there. While our friends here prepare the dye for your skin and cut your hair, I had better tell you how a slave is expected to behave," Tyvara said. "I suspect that's going to be the hardest part for you. How convincing you are may be the difference between survival and assassination."

"I'll keep that in mind," he told her. "It's not something I'm likely to forget."

She smiled grimly. "It can be very easy to forget, when

you're being whipped just because someone has had a bad day. Believe me. I know."

As Sonea walked down the corridor of the Magicians' Quarters, she yawned. The sun had been creeping up over the hill behind the Guild when she had returned, casting a pale glow across the sky. Now it had retreated behind the city, abandoning all to darkness, lamplight or, for the lucky few, magical illumination.

The night shifts at the hospice were the least popular, so she took them whenever she could manage. There were plenty of patients despite the late hours – some of the Healers joked that the night patients were the more interesting ones. She had certainly treated some unique injuries during those shifts. She suspected that a lot more night visitors than those who were forced to admit their profession due to the nature of their illness or injury were involved in business that would scandalise most Guild magicians and their families.

Cery's news had slipped back into her thoughts many times. She felt an unreasonable guilt at not agreeing to assist him in searching for the rogue magician. But she couldn't see how she would be able to without doing so in secret, and once she found the rogue and delivered her to the Guild the truth would be revealed. Her deception would generate more distrust and disapproval. Perhaps enough to persuade the Guild to ban her from working at the hospices.

Still, she hadn't gone straight to Administrator Osen when she arrived at the Guild. Instead she'd decided to sleep on it as Cery had suggested. And now that she was awake, and sleep hadn't brought her any certainty, she had decided to discuss it with Rothen. He had, after all, been the one who had searched for and found her, back when she had been a rogue hiding from the Guild.

Reaching his door, she knocked. She heard a familiar voice inside. The door opened and Rothen smiled as he saw her.

"Sonea. Come in." He opened the door wider, letting her inside. "Sit down. Would you like some raka?"

She looked around the guest room, then turned back to him. "Cery came to see me last night. He's discovered a new rogue magician in the city. A woman in full control of her power. I can't deal with it myself, of course, but . . . do you think the Guild will make a mess of it this time?"

Rothen stared at her in surprise, then looked over her shoulder.

"I'd be willing to bet my family's fortune they'll make as big a mess of it as last time," a familiar voice said.

Sonea's heart sank. She schooled her face and turned to see a man step out of the room that had once been her bedroom, holding one of the many books Rothen now stored in there.

"Regin and I were discussing some trouble among the novices," Rothen said, a note of apology in his voice.

Sonea eyed Regin. *Curse him. This means I will have to tell the Higher Magicians straightaway. Hopefully they'll forgive me for seeking Rothen's advice first.*

"More trouble?" she asked him.

"Oh, there's always some sort of trouble," Regin said, shrugging.

"As for this rogue . . . I agree with Regin," Rothen added. "Though I would not be as pessimistic as he. High Lord Balkan and Administrator Osen would be more subtle in their searching methods, but they don't have the insight, experience and resources that you and I have."

Sonea turned back to him. "How can I hunt for a rogue if I can't move around the city without permission?"

Rothen smiled. "Don't ask for permission."

"But if they find out I've been sneaking around, or failed to report this to the Higher Magicians, or even that I spoke to a Thief, it'll prove right all those people who say I can't be trusted."

"And if you bring in a rogue, the people who matter will overlook that," Regin said.

She crossed her arms. "I'm not going to risk the hospices just so that I can do something that others could do."

"Lady Vinara and the Healers would never let anyone close the hospices," Regin assured her.

"But they might stop me working at them," Sonea countered.

"I doubt it. Even your detractors would have to agree that would be a waste of your talents."

She stared at Regin for a moment, then looked away. He was being far too complimentary. It made her suspicious. Was he urging her to hunt for the rogue in secret in order to reveal it later? *It would gain him nothing, except some sort of petty satisfaction at my downfall.*

"When the time comes to explain what we were doing, I will tell all that I advised and helped you," Rothen said. He looked at Regin. "I'm sure Lord Regin will be happy to do the same."

"Of course. I'll put it on paper and sign it if you wish." There was a slight edge of sarcasm to Regin's voice. *He knows I still don't trust him*, she thought, and felt an unexpected guilt. He hadn't shown a hint of dishonesty or manipulation when she'd worked with him before.

"People will continue to impose restrictions on you so long

269

as you let them," Rothen told her. "You have given them no reason to mistrust you these last twenty years. It's, it's . . ."

"Ridiculous," Regin finished. "I don't see Kallen asking permission to roam around the city, or you sending your lackeys to follow his every movement."

"That's because I don't have lackeys," Sonea retorted. "Or the time to do it myself."

"But if you had either, would you?" Regin asked.

She narrowed her eyes at him. "Probably."

His eyebrows rose. "You think him dangerous?"

"No." She frowned and looked toward the window. "Not dangerous. But one day his . . . his *thoroughness* may do more harm than good."

"Like now," Rothen said. "He has you too well caged and cowed to do what you know you are the best person to do: find this rogue and bring her to the Guild."

She stared at the window. The University lay just outside, and beyond that the city, and a woman who was using magic – possibly to kill. "It will not be like before. Cery said she was older, so she may have many years of using magic behind her. And he suspects she is the Thief Hunter."

"Then it is even more important that we find her quickly," Regin said. "Before she shifts from killing criminals to anyone who gets in her way."

Sonea thought of Cery's family and shuddered. *She may already have done that.* She turned from the window and looked from Regin to Rothen. "But if I openly defy the restrictions to my movements, I'll draw attention and censure before we can find her."

Rothen smiled. "Then it is not entirely our fault we are forced to work in secret. Still, there is no point taking needless risks. As soon as you find out anything, send messages to the both of us. One of us can investigate if you cannot slip away to do it yourself."

Sonea looked at Regin, who nodded. A wave of relief washed over her. It was a compromise. Not a perfect compromise, though. Failing to bring the matter to the Higher Magicians might still be frowned upon, but at least she wouldn't be risking that they'd make a mess of finding the woman themselves. But it did mean Rothen and Regin were going to face disapproval from the Guild when it was revealed that they hadn't passed the information on, either.

Let's hope Regin is right, and it'll be overlooked when they find they've got a captured rogue to deal with.

"I had better go," Regin said. He inclined his head to Sonea. "I will be ready to give my assistance when you require it." He nodded to Rothen, who returned the gesture, then walked to the door and left the room.

Once he had gone, Sonea sat down and let out a sigh. *At least I know the hunt is in the right hands*, she thought wryly. *I have enough to worry about already, with Lorkin in Sachaka and the hospices full of roet users.*

"You look tired," Rothen told her, moving to the side table to prepare sumi and raka for them both.

"I worked the night shift."

"You've been spending a lot of time at the hospices lately."

She shrugged. "It gives me something to do." Then she gave a short laugh. "And now I have even more to do, ferrying information about the rogue to you and Regin."

"The hospices will take care of themselves," he told her. Moving to the chairs, he handed her a cup of steaming raka. "And we'll take care of you."

She raised an eyebrow at him. "You and Regin?"

He nodded. "I told you: he's matured into a sensible young man."

"*Young* man?" Sonea scoffed. "Only in comparison to yourself, *old friend*. He's only a year or two younger than me, with two grown daughters."

"Even so," Rothen replied with a chuckle. "He's improved a great deal from the novice you thrashed in the Arena."

Sonea looked away. "He'd have to, wouldn't he? Couldn't have got much worse." She gave him a searching look. "Can we trust him, do you think?"

He met her eyes, his expression serious. "I believe so. He has always valued the integrity of his House and family, and the Guild. It was the source of his arrogance as a young man and is now his motivation as an adult. It bothers him that so much lawlessness has crept in to all those things. This is another way he can help set things to right. He's sensible enough to realise the best way is for us to do it together, in secret. The Guild may not make a mess of finding the rogue, but there's a chance they will. We can't take that chance."

"You're probably right." Sonea grimaced. "And you had better be right about Regin, because if he wants to make my life unpleasant he certainly has the means to do it now."

The Black Tub bathhouse wasn't as clean as Cery would have liked. It stank of mould and the cheap perfume meant to mask the odour, and the gowns he and Gol had been given bore some interesting repairs and stains. But the place was the only establishment within sight of the pawnshop that they could plausibly linger in, so it needed investigation.

They had been led to a changing room and left there. It

was on the first floor, with cheap undecorated window screens hiding the customers from the street. After changing into the gowns, Gol had slipped out of the room to investigate those next to it and Cery had moved a chair to one of the windows. Cery slid the screen open and smiled in satisfaction as he saw that the pawnshop was within view.

The door opened again, but it was only Gol returning.

"What do you think?"

"There's nobody in the rooms around us, but I can't vouch for upstairs. We can talk, but quietly." Then he grimaced. "It's a bit run down."

"And the service is slow," Cery agreed. "Probably from lack of staff." He indicated the window. "But the view is good."

Gol moved closer and peered outside. "It sure is."

"We should take it in turns. One watching while the other scrubs up."

The big man grimaced. "The water better not be as bad as this place smells." He moved another chair and sat down. "Did our friend say anything about how she intended to do her business?"

Cery shook his head. Sonea's message had been cryptic, saying only that she would be dealing with the matter he had drawn her attention to, thanking him for the information and telling him to send any further news to the hospice. *Clearly she was being cryptic in case the letter was intercepted. If she is dealing with the matter of the rogue then it's unlikely she's told the Guild anything. They wouldn't trust her with the task of finding the woman.*

A knock came from the door. Cery slid closed the screen back across the window.

"Come in," he called.

The same thin young woman who had led them to the

changing room opened the door and stepped inside. She did not meet their eyes.

"The bath is nearly ready. Would you like it warm or hot?"

"Hot," Cery replied.

"Would you like it scented? We have—"

"No," Gol interrupted firmly.

"Do you have a little salt?" Cery asked. He'd heard a salt bath was good for sore muscles, and he was still aching from the practice knife-fight bout he'd had that morning. It was also good for cleaning bad water, too.

"We do." She named a price that raised Gol's eyebrows.

"We'll have it," Cery told her.

The girl nodded politely and left the room. Turning to the window, Cery opened the screen again and glanced outside. The street was busier now.

"Should we convince Makkin the Buyer to help us?" Gol asked. "He's already scared of her so it won't make her suspicious if he acts a bit nervous."

"He's the sort that'll cooperate with whoever he's most scared of," Cery replied. "If he knows she has magic he'll be more scared of her than us."

"She sent him out of the room before she opened the safe. That suggests to me he doesn't know she has magic."

"Yes, but . . ."

Gol hissed. Cery looked at the man and found him staring out of the window.

"What?"

"Is that her? In front of Makkin's shop."

Cery spun back to the window. A stooped woman had stopped in front of the shop. Her hair was streaked with grey. For a moment Cery was sure Gol was mistaken – so much so that he was about to tease him – then the woman turned her head to survey the street. He felt a shiver of recognition.

He looked at Gol. Gol stared at him. Then they both looked down at the wraps they were wearing.

"I'll go," Gol said. "You watch." He leapt over to the pile of clothes he'd removed and hastily began to dress. Cery turned back to the window and watched as the woman entered the shop.

His heart was hammering. He felt every muscle in his body slowly tense, and counted every breath.

"She still in there?"

"Yes," Cery replied. "Whatever you do, don't let her see you're following her. Even if you have to pay someone to—"

"I know, I know," Gol said impatiently. Cery heard him open the door. At the same time he saw the door to the shop open and the woman stepped out.

"She's leaving," he said.

Gol didn't reply. Cery turned to find the big man gone and the door swinging open. He looked back down into the street and caught a glimpse of the woman just before she moved out of view. A moment later Gol appeared. Cery breathed a sigh of relief as his friend and bodyguard headed in the same direction, his steps confident.

Take care, old friend, Cery thought.

"Um . . . sorry for the wait."

He turned to find the bathhouse girl standing in the doorway. Her eyes shifted from him to the window screen then to the floor. Cery closed the screen and stood up.

"The bath is ready?"

"Yes."

"Good. My friend had to leave. Take me to the bath."

Her shoulders drooped at the loss of a customer, then she gestured for him to follow and led him out of the room.

CHAPTER 18

THE TRAITOR

As the slave whimpered, his head squeezed between the large hands of Ashaki Tikako, Dannyl couldn't help wincing. Though Dannyl had never had his mind read by a black magician, if the reaction of this man's slaves was anything to go by, he gathered it wasn't a pleasant experience.

Tikako gave a gasp of anger and frustration and thrust the slave away. The man fell back onto a shoulder, then scrambled away on all fours as his master shouted at him to leave. The slaves kneeling nearby, waiting their turn to be questioned, hunched as the Ashaki's attention turned to them.

There weren't many slaves left. Dannyl had counted over eighty so far. None of them had produced any useful information about Lorkin and Tyvara. They couldn't even confirm if Tyvara had ever spoken to anyone within the estate.

The master's finger jabbed, and a young woman reluctantly came forward, shuffling on knees reddened from long contact with the rough stone pavement. Tikako grabbed her head before she had even settled before him. Her brows knit together, and Dannyl could not help holding his breath and hoping she would prove to be holding the secret to Lorkin's whereabouts, even if that did mean she would probably be killed for not coming forward with the information when her master first demanded it.

After a long pause Tikako stared at her, then with a wordless roar of fury he half lifted, half tossed her away from him. Her eyes flew open as he sent her flying across the room. She crashed into one of the large pottery jugs spaced along the walls, from which pretty, flowering plants spilled. Rising to a sitting position, she blinked slowly, her eyes glazed.

Dannyl bit back yet another curse. *The brutality of these people. They like to think they are so dignified, with all their rituals and hierarchy, but underneath they still are as cruel as the histories have always described them.* After today, Dannyl knew he would not easily forget why the Sachakans were so feared, even when his hosts were being perfectly respectful and well mannered. It was not the power they held that made them cruel, but their willingness to use it to dominate those weaker than themselves.

The girl had not risen to her feet. Nor had any of the other slaves moved to help her. As Ashaki Tikako called another slave, Dannyl slipped away from Ashaki Achati's side and approached her. She blinked at him in surprise, then looked down quickly as he crouched at her side.

"Let me see that," he said. She passively bowed her head as he examined the back of her skull. It was bleeding and starting to swell. He placed a hand against the wound and concentrated, sending magic to heal the wound. Her eyes widened, and her gaze cleared.

"Better?" he asked, as he finished.

She nodded, then leaned closer to him.

"The ones you seek are gone," she told him in a quiet voice.

"He is dressed as a slave now, his skin dyed to look like us. They are taking a cart to the master's country estate to the west."

"Do you mean . . .?" Dannyl began. But she shook her head slowly, as if trying to clear it, and backed away from him.

"Don't waste your power, Ambassador." Dannyl looked up to see Ashaki Tikako smirking at him. "She won't cost much to replace."

Dannyl rose to his feet. "Saving you even a little money is the least I can do after you spent so much time and effort questioning your slaves."

"Without much success, I admit." Tikako sighed and regarded the last five slaves. He beckoned wearily, his anger now turned to resignation.

As the master began to read their minds, Dannyl moved back to Ashaki Achati's side. The man gave him a questioning look. Dannyl shook his head slightly. He couldn't tell Achati what he'd learned within hearing of Tikako. If Tikako learned that the slave had managed to conceal something from his mind-read he would be humiliated. The slave would be questioned again, and possibly killed. That was hardly a nice way to repay her for the information.

Though it is possible it was a decoy. Dannyl frowned. *Why not tell her master when he first asked for information, then? If she did not want him to know, why did she tell me? Is her master working with the woman who abducted Lorkin?*

Whatever the reason, clearly the Sachakan mind-reading method wasn't as thorough as they thought it was. Ashaki Tikako sent the last slave away and turned to Dannyl and Achati. He apologised for failing to find Lorkin. Yet there was a defensive tone to his voice. He felt vindicated. None of his slaves had been hiding fugitives. None had lied about knowing nothing.

Or perhaps they did know, and he pretended to find nothing to protect his pride and honour – or involvement in the abduction.

Achati seemed satisfied, however. He thanked Tikako and told him his assistance would be rewarded. Soon he and Dannyl were walking back to the carriage, farewelling their host and climbing inside. Achati's two slaves, both young men, looked relieved to be leaving.

When the vehicle had rolled out through the gates to Tikako's mansion, Achati turned to Dannyl, his forehead creased with worry.

"I don't know where to go next, I have to confess. I—"

"Westward," Dannyl told him. "Lorkin is dressed as a slave now, and he and Tyvara are in a cart heading for Ashaki Tikako's country estate."

Achati stared at him, then smiled. "The slave girl. She told you this?"

"Yes."

"Your methods of investigation, unlikely as they may be, do appear to be working." The man's smile faded. "Hmm. That means . . . that suggests one of the worst possibilities I have been considering may be the correct one."

"That Ashaki Tikako read this in his slave's mind and did not tell us because he is involved with the kidnapping of Lorkin, or that Sachakan mind-reading methods aren't as effective as they ought to be?"

Achati shrugged. "The first is unlikely. Tikako is related to the king and is one of his greatest supporters. The second has always been the case. You need time and concentration to fully

280

search a mind." He grimaced. "But it is the way of the mind that what it most wants to hide tends to be in its thoughts when it is being read. Tikako should have seen this information. The fact that this girl managed to hide it hints at abilities that she should not have. Abilities that only the members of a particular group of rebels have."

"Rebels?"

"They call themselves the Traitors. They use women slaves to do their spying and to carry out assassinations and abductions. Some – mostly women – believe they are a society made up only of women, because it is women in difficult and unfortunate circumstances they most often take. I suspect it is a rumour to encourage cooperation from their victims, and the real reason for stealing the women is to sell them into slavery, here or in some other country."

Dannyl felt a chill run down his spine. "What do they want with Lorkin, then?"

"I'm not sure. Sometimes they meddle in politics. Usually with bribes or blackmail, but sometimes by assassination. The only gain I can see for them in abducting Lorkin is embarrassing the king." He frowned, thoughtfully. "Unless they want to stir up a war between our countries."

"Surely they would have killed Lorkin if that was their intention."

Achati's expression was grim as he met Dannyl's eyes. "They may still intend to."

"Then we have to find them quickly. Are there many west-leading roads to Tikako's country estate?"

The Sachakan didn't answer. His expression was of distracted puzzlement. "Why tell us?" he said.

"Who?" Dannyl asked.

"The slave girl. Why did she tell you how to find Lorkin if she is a Traitor? Is she trying to put us off the trail?"

"Perhaps the Traitors aren't involved, and want to avoid being blamed for Lorkin's abduction."

Achati's frown deepened. "Well, it is the only clue we have. Decoy or not, we have no alternative but to pursue it."

The road to Tikako's country estate bore a constant stream of traffic, forcing Lorkin to follow Tyvara's advice and not speak in case his Kyralian accent drew attention. He could not ask her where they were going, or question her more about her people, or the people who had tried to kill him. His skin itched from the dye that coated it. She frowned at him disapprovingly if he scratched it, and kicked his ankle gently if he forgot himself and looked directly at the people they passed – even the slaves. This was immensely frustrating, and made the slow pace of the cart, hauled by an ancient-looking horse, almost unbearable.

From time to time he stole a glance at her, noting the tension in her body and the way she chewed at her lip. He could not also help admiring her near-flawless brown skin. It was the first time he'd seen her outside and in sunlight, rather than in the glow of lamp or magical globe light. Her skin had a healthy sheen and he found himself wondering if it would be as warm to touch as Riva's had been. Then the inevitable memory came of Riva's dead, staring eyes and he'd look away.

Tyvara is a dangerous woman to be attracted to, he mused to himself. *But for some reason the mystery that surrounds her, and not knowing how powerful she is, makes her even more alluring. Still, this is not the time to be losing one's wits over a woman. There's a real danger I could end up losing more than my wits.*

It was on the third day of travelling when she finally muttered to him that they were about to arrive at their destination. The sun was hovering just above the horizon. He felt a relief that they wouldn't be sleeping in the wagon again, but it quickly evaporated as she told him what he must do next. They would enter another estate, where he would have to pretend to be a slave. They would eat and sleep there, but she didn't know what they would do after that until she'd made contact with her people.

This would be a more risky test of his disguise. She'd instructed him to say no more than necessary, to keep his eyes to the ground, to obey without hesitation or protest, and to stay in the shadows if he could.

Nodding at a gap in the wall ahead, she told him to steer the cart horse toward it. It was a little odd for a female house slave to be accompanying a delivery slave, so the excuse they had come up with was that she was showing him the route and teaching him to drive the cart because no other slave could be spared. He'd enjoyed the driving lessons, despite not being able to ask many questions for fear of being overheard.

They made it through the gap without mishap, though a corner of the cart brushed one side of the wall. Lorkin looked ahead at the buildings. Figures moved among them – all slaves judging by their clothes and mannerisms. As the cart neared, the slaves stopped to watch for a moment, before continuing with whatever duties they were performing.

"Through here," Tyvara said, pointing to an archway. He directed the cart into a small courtyard. A large slave wearing the headband of a slave master emerged from a doorway and waved at Lorkin to stop.

They pulled up. Conscious of the slave master's stare, Lorkin kept his gaze lowered. Two more slaves stepped out and moved to the horse's head.

"Haven't seen you two before," the man observed.

Tyvara nodded. "I'm Vara. This is Ork. He's new."

"Bit skinny for a delivery slave."

"He'll put on muscle with a bit of work."

The man nodded. "And why are you here?"

"Got to show him the way." She sounded smug. "Nobody else free."

"Hmph." The slave master beckoned and turned away. "The master wants the cart filled now, so you can leave at first light. We don't get fed until it's done."

Tyvara glanced at Lorkin, then shrugged. "Come on then, Ork."

They both climbed off the cart. One of the estate's slaves picked up the reins while another began to undo the harness. Lorkin followed Tyvara into a large wooden room. The smell of reber wool filled the air, heavy and sweet.

"This is the load." The slave master waved at a pile of fleece bundles wrapped in oil cloth that looked twice the size of what the cart should hold. He looked from Lorkin to Tyvara. "You know how to load up a cart?"

"I've watched it plenty of times," Tyvara said. She began describing the order and arrangement. The man nodded and grunted approval. "You've got the gist. I'll check when I get back. If it's wrong," he frowned at Lorkin meaningfully, "you'll have to unpack and repack it right, and that means you'll have to wait until tomorrow for a feed."

"Right," Tyvara said. She looked at Lorkin. "Time to learn something new."

Lorkin was glad that the slave master didn't hang around

to watch, but there were plenty of other slaves coming and going, some pausing to look at him and Tyvara. Thankfully, she did seem to know about packing carts, and had him wedge them together in a self-supporting arrangement. But there were a lot of bundles, and he'd had little sleep during the last few nights. Though he had healed away his weariness each time it started to impede him, it was coming back faster each time.

The bundles were all the same, yet somehow they grew heavier as he worked. He had to toss the last of them up to Tyvara, who was balancing at the top of the pile in the cart. Then he heard footsteps right behind him, jumped in surprise and threw one badly. Tyvara's hands slipped and it dropped, bouncing off the side of the cart. Lorkin stepped backwards to catch it but instead stepped on something.

"Fool!" a familiar voice bellowed. A hand came out of nowhere and whacked Lorkin's head, setting his ears ringing. He pressed a hand to his head and scrambled away. Figuring it would be more slave-like to stay crouched on the ground than to stand up, he hunched his back and waited.

"Don't sit there and sulk. Pick it up and finish the job," the slave master ordered.

Lorkin got to his feet and, bent double and avoiding looking at the man, ran to the last bundle and picked it up. He looked up at Tyvara. She was frowning with worry, but held out her hands to show she was ready. He tossed it and sighed with relief as she caught it and efficiently pressed it into place.

The slave master, apparently having forgiven Lorkin's trampling of him, pressed ropes into his hands and helped them bind the piles of fleeces securely to the cart. When they were done he nodded in approval.

"I'll send the kitchen boy out with food and blankets. You can sleep in the store. Be ready to leave early."

And with that he turned and stalked away. As Lorkin watched the man leave, he caught a movement in the corner of his eye. He resisted the temptation to look for the source. The courtyard was no longer lit by the glow of the late afternoon sky, and the shadows under the verandas were almost impenetrable. Pretending to examine his hands in the fading light, Lorkin looked beyond them and made out a female figure standing within a doorway. She was watching him and Tyvara with narrowed eyes.

"Ork," Tyvara called. He turned to look at her. She was standing beside the cart. "Come help me straighten this up."

He moved to her side. She was tugging at one of the bundles, which appeared to be perfectly positioned.

"My usual contact hasn't appeared," she murmured. "I didn't see another door to the store. Let's stay out here for now."

"There was a woman watching us," he told her. "Did you see her?"

She frowned and shook her head. The crunch of footsteps made her peer around the cart, and she smiled.

"Food!"

Lorkin followed her as she stepped out to meet the boy approaching them. His eyes widened, then he looked down quickly and held out two fist-sized bread buns, still steaming from the oven, and two mugs. The liquid inside the latter quivered as the boy's hand shook.

Tyvara took the food, handing Lorkin his share. As soon as he was divested of his burden, the boy turned, ran back to a door and threw himself inside.

"He was terrified," Lorkin murmured.

"Yes," Tyvara agreed. "And he shouldn't be." She moved back

toward the cart. "And he brought no blankets. Follow me." Passing the cart, she headed for the store. Lorkin followed, taking care not to spill the contents of his mug. A single lamp now lit the room, throwing complicated shadows against the walls. Once inside, she took the mug and bun from him and set it aside, with hers, next to a bucket that smelled strongly of urine.

"We can't eat them," she told him as she began to examine the room. "They could be drugged."

"Drugged?" he looked at the food. "They know who we are?"

"Possibly. Ah! Good. Come here."

"But how could the news have travelled here that fast?" he asked, following her toward the far wall.

The look she gave him clearly showed she thought him an idiot for asking.

"Don't Kyralians use blood rings?"

"Yes, but—"

"Even so, surely you know that travelling on horseback is faster than in a cart."

"Well, yes . . ."

She rolled her eyes, then turned away and slipped behind some boxes filled with wax-stoppered pottery jars. As he followed, he saw a small doorway that had been fixed permanently closed with boards. She glanced at the lamp, then at the boxes of jars. Stepping back, she stared at the boxes. They began to move, swaying precariously as they slid forward to block the view of the doorway.

Then she turned to stare at the boards fixing the door closed, and they began to flex themselves away from the frame.

"Put out the lamp," she ordered without taking her eyes off her work.

Lorkin looked over at the lamp, then drew magic and sent it out, shaping it into a small barrier that starved the flame of air. As the lamp went out and the room filled with darkness, he felt a fresh breeze and turned to see a rectangle of dark blue streaked with orange clouds where the door had been. He took a step toward it, but the sky vanished as Tyvara swung the door to again and he felt her hand press on his chest to stop him.

"Wait," she murmured. "Get out of sight."

Sounds were coming from the main store doorway. Light streaked into the room, moving and spreading as the source drew closer. Then the slave master and the boy entered, followed by a woman. They both stared at the mugs and buns left untouched, then looked around the store.

"They're gone," the boy said.

"They can't have gone far," the woman said. "Should we start searching?"

"No," the slave master said. "Too dangerous. If they are what you say they are, only the master can deal with them, and he's in the city."

The woman looked as if she wanted to argue, but instead nodded stiffly and left the store. The slave master looked around the room again. For a moment he looked as if he might search it, but then he shook his head and headed for the door.

As soon as he was gone, Lorkin felt the breeze again. Tyvara grabbed his arm and pulled him through the doorway. She took hold of both of his arms in a strong grip. He felt his stomach sink as they suddenly began to rise into the air.

Levitation, he thought, looking down at where the invisible force beneath their feet must be. *I haven't had reason to do that in years.*

They stepped off onto the roof of the store. Tyvara crouched and began to creep across it slowly and quietly, keeping below the peak of the roof so that people in the courtyard wouldn't see them. Lorkin followed, wincing at every creak of the wooden tiles. The slave shoes were much quieter than magician's boots, and had surprisingly good grip on the roof tiles.

At the end of the store roof they levitated down to the next building, then the next, and finally to one which provided a good hiding place in the shadow of a large chimney. A loud grinding sound came from below, which would mask any sounds they made.

Perhaps now I can ask her some questions.

"When it's fully dark we'll go back to the road," Tyvara told him.

"And if we encounter anyone?"

"Nobody will look at us closely. Slaves on the road aren't unusual, even at night, whereas if we cut across the fields we become trespassers. Field slaves won't approach us, but they'll report us to their master. Even if we get away before he investigates, anyone paying attention to such reports will know the direction we're travelling in." She sighed. "I was hoping to get further away from the city before this happened."

"You were expecting this?"

"Yes."

"Are your contacts here safe?"

"Yes."

"So . . . they're here, but so are the people who tried to kill me?"

"Yes." She shook her head. "But . . . it's more complicated than that."

He stared at her expectantly, but she said nothing more, only staring out over the fields. *She obviously doesn't want to talk about it. But she can't go hinting that there's more to this than what she's told me without expecting me to pursue it.*

"Why is it more complicated?" he asked, then frowned in surprise at the hard tone in his voice.

She looked at him, her eyes barely visible in the growing darkness.

"I shouldn't . . . but I guess there's no point keeping it secret any longer." She drew in a deep breath, then let it out. "We can't trust any slaves now, not even those that are Traitors. We Traitors . . . we don't always agree with each other. Some of us are divided into groups based on our opinions and philosophy."

"Factions?" he suggested.

"Yes, I suppose they could be called that. The faction that I belong to believes that you are a potential ally and should not be killed. The other . . . doesn't."

Lorkin caught his breath. *Her people want me dead!* He felt a sinking feeling inside, but pushed it aside. *No, only some of them do.*

"My faction has more influence on our people," she told him. "We say that killing you could lead to war between Sachaka and Kyralia. That we should only kill when it is unavoidable. That blaming the child for the actions of the parent is how Sachakans think, not us. But . . ."

She paused, and when she continued her voice had lowered. "But I have done something that may shift that balance." She drew in another breath, and this time it shook slightly. "The woman I killed to save you – Riva – was not an assassin sent by a Sachakan family. She was a Traitor. One from the other faction."

"You lied," Lorkin stated.

"Yes. Even if I'd had time to explain at the Guild House,

you wouldn't have come with me, and you'd probably be dead by now."

Lorkin scowled. *What else has she lied about?* But if all else that she said was true, especially about the Traitors, he understood the deception. *I wouldn't have left with her. I'd have been too confused.*

"When my people find out that I killed her, the other faction will gain support," Tyvara continued. "And from the way things went here I'd say the news has definitely overtaken us. Anyone from the other faction won't help us, and they'll try to stop others helping us. They might try to kill you. They might try to kill us both."

"And the Traitors from your faction?"

"They won't try to kill us, but they may not help us in case that makes them guilty of helping a murderer. Eventually the news will reach Sanctuary and our leaders will override any orders scout leaders in the estates have made. Official orders will be sent out."

Lorkin's head spun with all this new information. Throughout Sachaka there were people – a whole society of them – deciding whether he should be killed or not. He shook his head. *And what did she mean by "blaming a child for the actions of a parent"? What did my parents do to make them so angry?* He had too many questions, and he and Tyvara could be discovered at any moment. Best stick to the more immediate problems. Like how much danger he was in from these Traitors.

"So, if your faction was in control, why did Riva try to kill me?"

Tyvara gave a short, bitter laugh. "She disobeyed her orders. Disobeyed me."

"And nobody knows that, so they think you murdered her?"

291

A pause. "Yes, but even when they find out why I killed her . . . Traitors don't kill Traitors. It's a far more serious crime than disobeying orders. Even my own faction will want me punished for that."

"They'll kill you?"

"I . . . I don't know." She sounded so uncertain, even frightened, that he suddenly had to resist the urge to put his arms around her and reassure her that everything would be fine. But the words would be a lie. He had no idea what was going to happen, where to go, or even where he was. She had dragged him away from all he understood. This was *her* world. She was the resourceful one. Whether he liked it or not, he needed her to be in charge.

"If anyone can get us out of this, you can," he told her. "So what should we do now? Go back to Arvice? Go to Kyralia?"

"We can't go to either. We have Traitors in almost every household in Sachaka. Now that my people know what I have done there will be Traitors watching the Pass." He heard the soft sound of fingers drumming on something. "We can't run away. What we need to do is reach my people – my faction. We will have a chance to explain, and you will be safe. No matter what happens to me, they will protect you." She chuckled quietly. "All I have to do is get you safely across most of Sachaka and to the mountains, without the other faction finding us. Or any Kyralians and Sachakans that are bound to start looking for you."

"The mountains, eh?"

"Yes. And now that it's dark, I think it's time we made a start. We'll drop down by that wall and follow it across to the one that meets the wall that follows the road. Ready?"

He nodded, then grinned ruefully as he realised she couldn't see him.

"Yes," he said. "I'm ready."

The young woman in the examination room had dark shadows under her eyes. In her lap a small baby wriggled, its face screwed up as it howled with almost inhuman volume.

"I don't know what to do with him," the woman confessed. "I've tried everything."

"Let me have a look," Sonea offered.

The mother handed over the child. Taking him into her lap, Sonea examined him thoroughly, both by touch and sight and with magic. To her relief there was no sign of injury or disease. She sensed a more ordinary disturbance, however.

"He's fine," she assured the girl. "Just hungry."

"Already?" The girl's hand went to her chest. "I can't seem to make enough—"

Abruptly the door opened and Healer Nikea slipped into the room.

"Sorry to interrupt," she said, looking at the young woman apologetically. Then her eyes rose to meet Sonea's. "There's a messenger here for you. He says it's urgent."

Sonea felt her heart skip a beat. Was it Cery? She rose and handed the baby back to his mother. "You had better send him in. Could you take this young woman to Adrea." She looked at the mother and smiled. "Adrea is an expert at dealing with production problems and food alternatives. I wish I'd known her when my son was born. She'll help you out."

The young woman nodded and followed Nikea out of the room. The door closed behind them. Sonea stared at it as she waited for Cery. When it finally opened, however, it was a large man who entered the room. He looked familiar, and after a moment she remembered who he was.

"Gol, isn't it?" she asked.

"Yes, my lady," he said.

She smiled. It had been a long time since anyone had called her "my lady" instead of "Black Magician". "What news?"

"We've found her," the big man said, his eyes widening with excitement. "I tracked her back to where she lives, and now Cery's keeping an eye on her until you can come get her."

Sonea felt her heart skip again, but then her stomach sank. *I won't be getting her. I have to send for Rothen. And Regin.* Could she simply neglect to summon Regin? *No, if the rogue is a strong magician she might overcome Rothen. Perhaps even kill him. Better that two magicians confront her rather than one. Oh, I wish I could go with him! But if I'm going to have to trust Regin with the knowledge that I've withheld information about a rogue, then he needs to get his hands dirty, too.*

"How long have we got?" she asked.

Gol shrugged. "I don't know, but if we're lucky she's gone to bed."

"I need to send for some help. Two magicians are better than one in this situation." She took a piece of paper and quickly scrawled the words "Northside" and "Now?" on it, then folded it and wrote Regin's name and title on the back. Then she wrote the same message to Rothen. "Give these to Healer Nikea – the one who brought you in."

Gol took the notes and slipped out of the room.

When the door opened again, Sonea expected it to be Gol returning. Instead it was Healer Nikea. As the young woman approached, she met Sonea's eyes, then looked away, and immediately Sonea's skin began to prickle. *She's going to ask me what all this is about. Maybe she's recognised Gol, or found out that he works for a Thief. I doubt she's going to scold me, but Nikea's not the sort to let anything she disapproves of go unmentioned and ignored.*

"Ah . . . I wanted to say . . ." the young woman began, rubbing her hands together with uncharacteristic nervousness.

"Yes?" Sonea prompted.

"Whatever it is you're doing, I know it's got to be for a good purpose." Nikea straightened. "If you need someone here to . . . to 'cover your tracks', as they say, you can rely on me. And some of the other Healers, too. We'll tell people you were here if you need to go out."

Sonea realised her mouth had dropped open in surprise, and she quickly closed it.

"How many of you think this?" she managed to ask.

"Four of us. Sylia, Gejen, Colea and myself."

Amused, Sonea suppressed the urge to smile. "You've discussed this already?"

Nikea's gaze was steady. "Yes. We weren't sure what was going on, if anything. But we all thought it had to be important, and that we were willing to help."

Sonea felt her face begin to heat. "Thank you, Nikea."

The girl shrugged, then backed away to the door. "Of course, we'd love to know what is going on, if you can tell us." She touched the handle, then looked back hopefully.

Sonea chuckled. "When I can, I will."

Nikea grinned. "I'll send the next patient in."

"Thank you. Again."

As the door closed behind the Healer, Sonea couldn't help grinning. *Seems not all the Guild thinks I'll turn into a crazed black-magic-wielding murderer the moment I'm out of their sight.* The Healers' trust was touching. Perhaps she could risk leaving the hospice, after all. It would be safer for Rothen and Regin. While there had been no hint that the rogue was a black magician, things could turn very nasty if it turned out she were.

And Sonea had to admit, the idea of sneaking around the city with Cery again filled her with both nostalgia and excitement. It wouldn't be fair if Rothen and Regin got to have all the fun, while she had to sit and wait for news.

CHAPTER 19

IN HIDING

As Gol had warned, the area of the city the rogue lived in was surprisingly respectable, and not the sort where anyone could loiter and remain inconspicuous. She rented the basement of a shoemaker's shop and home. All of the street's buildings had a shop at ground level and accommodation for the shopkeeper upstairs.

Cery had sent some of his people out to visit local shops to see if he could watch for the woman from within one of them. One reported overhearing a shopkeeper say his neighbour was away visiting his wife's family in Elyne, and a few picked locks later Cery was sitting in the absent shopkeeper's first floor guest room, relaxing in a comfortable chair next to the street side window, watching night fall and lamp-lighters setting the street aglow with light.

He'd also sent people to watch the rear entrance to the shoe-maker's home. The basement was accessible not just via the shop above it but through a sunken back door. Regular reports assured him that she hadn't left.

Gol was taking longer than he ought to, though. *Did I misunderstand Sonea's message? She said she would be dealing with "the matter" and that I should send information to the hospice. Well, I've done that.*

A door opened downstairs and he tensed. The footsteps of two or three people thumped up the staircase. Were they his people, or the shopkeeper and his family returning? He moved quickly, concealing himself behind the open door where he could hopefully slip out of the room unnoticed if he needed to. In case they should notice him, he slipped a hand into his coat to where he kept his most visually impressive knife.

"Cery?" a familiar voice called.

Gol. Letting out a sigh of relief, Cery stepped out from behind the door to find his bodyguard and two people wearing long concealing cloaks nearing the top of the stairs. He recognised Sonea. Cery narrowed his eyes at the other man. There was something familiar about him. As the trio came into the light, Cery felt an old memory spring to life.

"Regin," he said. "Or is that Lord Regin now?"

"It is," the man replied.

"It always was, Cery," Sonea reminded him. "But calling novices 'Lord' or 'Lady' always feels a bit premature. Lord Regin and Lord Rothen have volunteered to assist me in catching the rogue, which could prove vital if I am unable to sneak away unnoticed from the hospice at some point."

"If luck is with us, you won't have to slip away again," Cery told her. "So is Lord Rothen coming?"

She shook her head. "He didn't see the point, if I was going."

Cery watched Regin follow Sonea into the room. *From what I remember, Sonea didn't like this man much when she was a novice. He made things bad for her.* But when Cery had met Regin during the Ichani Invasion, the young man had volunteered to be the bait that drew a Sachakan magician into Sonea and Akkarin's trap. It had been a brave move. Had the timing been wrong – and it nearly had been from what Cery recalled – Regin would have had all magic and life drained from him.

If he hadn't known better, Cery would never have believed the man he was examining had been the prank-playing, mischief-making novice Sonea had complained about. Lord Regin's face appeared set into a permanent expression of seriousness. Though his build had the healthy weight of someone who'd lived a privileged life, the lines between his brows and around his mouth spoke of worry and resignation. *But there's intelligence in those eyes*, he noted. *He's no less dangerous than he was as a novice, I'd wager. Still, Sonea trusts him enough to recruit him for this.* Then he looked at her and saw the wariness in her posture as she glanced at her magician helper. *Or maybe she has no choice. I'd better ask her about him, as soon as I have a chance to chat to her alone.*

"So where is our rogue?" Sonea asked.

Cery moved to the window. "In the basement of the shoemaker across the street."

She peered outside. "How many entrances?"

"Two. Both watched."

"We should split into two groups then. One magician in each."

Cery nodded in agreement. "I'll go with you in through the front door. Gol can take Regin around to the back. We'll meet in the basement, where you'll do whatever it is you do." He looked at the others. They nodded. "Any questions?" Glances were exchanged, then heads shook. "Let's go then."

They filed back down the stairs. Cery explained and demonstrated a few signals that he and Gol would use as warnings or to signal a retreat, then they stepped outside. It was full night now. The lamps cast circles of light on the ground. Gol led Regin away toward the back entrance. Cery and Sonea waited to give them time to get into place, then walked across the road to the shoemaker's shop.

Climbing the steps, they approached the front door. Cery produced an oil dripper and quickly smeared the door hinges. Then he drew picks from within his coat. Sonea said nothing, her face in shadow, as he worked the lock open. *I guess she could do this with magic – possibly faster than I can. So why don't I suggest it? Am I showing off?*

The lock clicked softly. Cery slowly turned the handle, bracing as the latch sprung free. He pulled the door open, relieved when it made only a soft groan. Sonea stepped inside, then waited as he closed the door behind them.

It was dark in the shop and as his eyes adjusted he was able to make out rows of shoes lined up on shelving, and a work table. Opposite the door was a narrow staircase leading down, and another leading up. According to his spies, the shoemaker was asleep upstairs. *And about to get a rude wake-up.*

Sonea moved to the stairs and looked at the treads leading down. She shook her head, then beckoned to Cery. As he approached, she grabbed his arm and pulled him close. Staring at her in surprise, he realised that in the dim light she looked like the young woman he'd once helped hide from the Guild so many years ago. She wore the same intent, worried expression.

Then he felt himself rising in the air and all thought of the past fled from his mind. He looked down. Though he could feel something beneath his feet, he couldn't see it. Whatever it was, it was carrying him and Sonea down the staircase.

I guess this means there's no risk of creaking treads betraying us.

300

A sparsely furnished room appeared as they neared the floor of the basement. Dazzling light filled the space as a glowing ball appeared above Sonea's head. Cery looked for the bed, found it, then felt a surge of disappointment. It was unoccupied.

A door opened and they both spun about, then sighed as they saw Regin and Gol enter the room. Both frowned as they saw the rogue was nowhere in sight.

"Search," Sonea said. "But carefully."

They each chose a wall, examining the furniture, looking under the bed, opening cupboards.

"This room isn't being used," Regin observed. "The clothes in this cupboard are dusty."

Cery nodded and nudged a basin with soiled cups, bowls and cutlery in it. "And these dishes have been dirty for so long they're mouldy."

"Aha!" Gol exclaimed quietly. All turned to see him gesturing at the wall. A section of bricks sat at an angle to the rest, swivelling aside as he pressed on one end. Behind was a dark space. Cery crossed to it and sniffed at the air inside.

"The Thieves' Road," he said. "Or a passage to it."

Sonea chuckled. "Not two entrances after all. I'm surprised you didn't check for subterranean ones."

Cery shrugged. "It's a new street. When the king demolishes the old ones, he makes sure the Road goes too."

"He wasn't thorough enough this time," she said. Coming closer, she ran a hand over the brickwork. "Or perhaps he was. This is new – hardly any dust or cobwebs on it. Should we see where it leads?"

"If you want to explore, go ahead," Cery told her. "But this isn't my territory. I can't enter without permission. If I trespass," he shrugged, "the Thief Hunter will have one less Thief to do in."

"Does this passage suggest our rogue is working with the local Thief?" Regin asked.

Sonea looked at Cery. "If she is the Thief Hunter, then I doubt it. But if she's not, then she'd have skills a Thief would find very useful."

In other words, she thinks this proves that the rogue isn't the Thief Hunter, Cery thought.

Regin peered into the tunnel, his expression intent. He looked as if he might move inside, but then he stepped back and straightened.

"I suspect she's long gone. What do you recommend we do next, Cery?" he asked.

Cery glanced at the magician in surprise. A magician asking him his opinion was not something that happened often. "I agree that you're unlikely to find her in the tunnels." He reached out and turned the bricks back into place. "If she doesn't notice that we invaded her room she might continue using it to access the tunnels. We should make sure everything is exactly how we found it. I'll put a watch on this place and let you know if she returns."

"And if she does notice?" Regin asked.

"Then we'll have to hope another bit of luck leads us to her again."

Regin nodded, then looked at Sonea. She shrugged. "Not much else we can do for now. If anyone can find her again, Cery will."

Cery felt a flush of pleasure, followed by a niggling anxiety that she might be wrong. He had spotted the rogue by chance. It might not be so easy to find her again. The four of them moved around the room quickly, making sure everything was in order, then left the way they had come. Sonea relocked the front door with magic. They slipped out the back way. Once in the main street again, they exchanged glances but remained silent. The two magicians raised hands in farewell before they walked away. Cery and Gol returned to the empty shopkeeper's house.

"Well, that was disappointing," Gol said.

"Yes," Cery agreed.

"Do you think the rogue will come back?"

"No. She'll have had something set up to tell her if anyone came visiting."

"So what do we do next?"

"Watch and hope I'm wrong." He looked around the room. "And find out when the owner of this place is due back. We don't want to scare him and his family half to death at finding a Thief in his house."

The slave master looked surprised to see Dannyl and Ashaki Achati, before he threw himself to the ground at their feet. His surprise was not because a powerful Sachakan and Kyralian magician had come visiting. The estate had been expecting them, or someone, to arrive.

"You came faster than we hoped," the big man said when Achati explained that they were looking for an escaped female slave and a Kyralian man dressed as a slave.

"You have seen the pair I described?" Achati asked.

"Yes. Two nights ago. One of the slaves thought they were people we'd been warned about, and when we came to question them they had run away."

"Did you search for them?"

"No." The man bowed his head. "We were warned they were magicians, and that only magicians could catch them."

"Who gave you this warning?"

"The master, in a message."

"When did the message arrive?"

"A day before the pair arrived here."

Achati glanced at Dannyl, his eyebrows raised in disbelief. *So if Ashaki Tikako didn't send the message, who did?* Dannyl felt his heart skip a beat. *The Traitors. They must be very organised to get messages like this out to the country estates so quickly.*

"How long ago did you send your message warning your master of their appearance here?"

"Two nights ago – straight after they disappeared."

Achati turned to Dannyl. "If he is on his way he won't arrive for another day, even if he rides rather than taking a carriage. I'm afraid we'll have to wait. I don't have the authority to read the minds of another man's slaves."

"Do you have the authority to question them?" Dannyl asked.

The magician frowned. "There is no custom or law preventing me. Or you."

"Then let's question them."

Achati smiled. "We'll do it your way? Why not?" He chuckled. "If you do not mind, I would like to watch and learn from you. I would not know what questions to ask that might trick a slave into revealing more than he or she wanted to."

"There really isn't any trickery involved," Dannyl assured him.

"Which do you want to question first?"

"This man, and anyone who saw Lorkin and Tyvara. And most of all, the slave who saw them and thought they might be the people they'd been warned about." Dannyl drew out his notebook and looked at the slave master. "And I need a room – nothing fancy – where I can question them alone without others overhearing."

The man looked from Dannyl to Achati uncertainly.

"Arrange it," Achati ordered. As the man hurried away, the Sachakan magician turned to smile crookedly at Dannyl. "You really must learn to phrase your requests as orders, Ambassador Dannyl."

"You have the greater authority here," Dannyl replied. "And I am a foreigner. It would be rude of me to assume I could take control."

Achati looked at him thoughtfully, then shrugged. "I suppose you are right."

The slave master returned and then led them into the building to a small room that smelled of grain. The floor was covered in a fine dust patterned with the sweeping grooves of a broom. Particles hung in the beams of sunlight streaming in from a high window. Two chairs had been placed under the window.

"Well, it's definitely not fancy," Achati said, not hiding his amusement.

"Where would you suggest we question them?" Dannyl asked.

Achati sighed. "I guess it would be presumptuous if we'd questioned them in the Master's Room, and guest rooms would have made it obvious we aren't in charge here. No, I suppose this is an appropriate setting." He moved to one of the chairs and sat down.

Dannyl took the other seat, then ordered the slave master to enter. The man related how two slaves had arrived with an empty cart, the male apparently new but lacking in muscle for a delivery slave, and the woman there to show him the route. While they'd loaded the cart one of the kitchen slaves had suggested to him that the pair might be the people they'd been warned to watch out for. She suggested drugging their food, as they would be less dangerous asleep.

At the mention of drugged food, Dannyl had to hide his dismay. Fortunately Lorkin and Tyvara hadn't fallen for the trap. They'd slipped away.

He then questioned the woman who had suspected the pair weren't who they said they were. As she entered the room, Dannyl noted that her gaze was sharp, though she gave him only one quick look before bowing her head and prostrating herself. He told her to get up, and she kept her gaze lowered.

Her explanation matched the slave master's, including the contents of the message warning of two dangerous magicians posing as slaves.

"What made you think they were the people you'd been warned about?" Dannyl asked her.

"They were as described. A tall man with pale skin and a shorter Sachakan female."

Pale skin? Dannyl frowned. *The slave master didn't mention Lorkin's skin, and surely it would have been unusual enough for the man to notice. Wait . . . didn't the woman I healed at Tikako's home say Lorkin's skin had been dyed?*

Had the dye worn off, or was this woman feeding him the information she thought he expected?

"Tall, short, male, female – none of these things would make them stand out from other slaves surely. What made you notice they were different?"

The woman's gaze, fixed on the floor, flickered. "The way

they moved and talked. Like they weren't used to following orders."

So not the pale skin. Dannyl paused, writing down her answer as he considered what to ask next. Perhaps it was time to be more direct.

"A slave I spoke to a few days ago thought the woman was a Traitor and that they mean to kill the man she has abducted. Do you think it likely they will kill him?"

The woman was very still as she answered.

"No."

"Do you know of the Traitors?"

"Yes. Every slave does."

"Why do you believe it is unlikely the Traitors intend to kill the man?"

"Because if they wanted him dead they would have killed him, not abducted him."

"What do you think they intend to do with him then?"

She shook her head. "I am only a slave. I do not know."

"What do other slaves think the Traitors will do with him?"

She paused and her head lifted slightly before bowing again, as if she resisted the urge to look at him.

"I've heard some say," she said slowly. "That the woman is a murderer. That the Traitors want you to find them."

Dannyl felt a chill. Tyvara had killed a slave. What if that slave had been the Traitor, not Tyvara?

"Who said this?" he asked.

"I . . . I can't remember."

"Are there any slaves who are more likely to say this sort of thing than others?"

She paused then shook her head. "All slaves gossip."

After a few more questions, he knew he would not get

anything more out of her. She'd said all she wanted to say, and if she was withholding information he would not get it out of her voluntarily. He sent her away.

I'd wager she does know more. And then there's the description of Lorkin's pale skin. She wanted me to be sure Lorkin was here. Which makes sense if this rumour that the Traitors want me to find Tyvara and Lorkin is true.

But it could be a decoy. Still, the slave he'd helped at Tikako's home had spoken the truth. Tyvara and Lorkin *had* come to his country estate.

What if the Traitors did want him to find the pair? *Then they'll make sure we find them. Though I can't imagine Tyvara will let us capture her without a fight. And we'll have to be prepared for any reaction from Lorkin. It's possible she's convinced him to accompany her — perhaps even seduced him — and he'll resist being rescued.*

He wanted to believe Lorkin was more sensible than that, but he had heard the gossip in the Guild that the young man had a weakness for pretty, smart women. Being the son of Black Magician Sonea and the late High Lord Akkarin didn't mean the young man had any of his parents' wisdom, either. Those characteristics could only come with experience. With making mistakes and choices, and learning from the consequences.

I just hope this isn't a serious mistake, and that the consequences are the kind he can learn from, not ones that will lead to me spending the rest of my life in Sachaka for fear of what Sonea might do to me if I ever return to the Guild.

Lorkin would have thought that a male and female slave walking along a country road in the middle of the night would raise suspicion, but the few slaves they had passed had barely glanced at them. A carriage had overtaken them once, and

Tyvara had hissed something about it probably containing a magician or Ashaki, but all she'd had him do was scamper off the road and keep his gaze lowered.

"If anyone asks, we've been sent out to work at Ashaki Catika's estate," she'd told him. "We're both house slaves. We're travelling at night because he wants us there by tomorrow evening and that means walking night and day."

"Ashaki Catika is known for that sort of cruelty?"

"All Sachakan magicians are."

"Surely there are one or two good magicians."

"There are some who treat their slaves better than others, but ultimately enslaving another person is cruel, so I wouldn't call any of them good. If they were good, they'd free their slaves and pay those willing to stay and work for them." She glanced at him. "As Kyralians do."

"Not all Kyralians are kind to their servants," Lorkin told her.

"At least those servants can leave and find a new employer."

"They can, but it is not as easy as it sounds. Servant positions are in high demand and a servant who quits may find it hard to get work elsewhere. Households tend to hire servants from the same family over servants they don't know. Of course, a servant can try other work, like a trade, but they will be competing with families who have practised that trade for generations."

"Do you think slavery is better then?"

"No. Definitely not. I am only saying the alternative isn't easier. How well do Traitors treat their servants?"

"We are all servants. Just as we are all Traitors," Tyvara explained. "The term isn't like 'Ashaki' or 'Lord'. It is a word for a people."

"But not a race?"

"No. We are Sachakans, though we don't often call ourselves that."

"So even magicians do the tasks of servants? They clean and cook?"

"Yes and no." She grimaced then. "At first that was how it was supposed to be. We would all do the same work. A Traitor might clean dirty dishes one moment and then vote on important decisions, like which crops to plant, the next. But it didn't work. Some bad decisions were made because people who were not smart or educated enough to understand the consequences chose badly.

"We started a range of tests designed to find out what a person's talent was and to develop it, so the best person would end up taking on the tasks that required their skills. Though that meant we weren't all doing the same things any more, it was still better than slavery. So long as the tasks required for maintaining our home and feeding our people were met, nobody was forced to do a certain job, or prevented from doing something they were talented at, because of their family status or class."

"Sounds wonderful," Lorkin remarked.

She shrugged. "It works most of the time, but like all systems it's not perfect. There are some magicians who would rather spend their time complaining and manipulating others than wasting their magic on tilling the fields or heating kilns."

"Most Guild magicians would agree. But we do work for the people in other ways. Maintaining the port. Building bridges and other structures. Defending the country. Healing the sick and in—"

The look she cast him had stopped the words in his throat.

It began as a savage glare, then turned into a troubled frown, and then she turned away.

"What is it?" he asked.

"Someone's coming," she said, looking into the shadowed road ahead. "Anyone we pass could be a Traitor. We shouldn't be talking. Someone might overhear us and realise who we are."

The approaching figure turned out to be another slave. From then on Tyvara would not speak, telling him to be quiet if he attempted to start another conversation. As the sky began to lighten, she began scanning the surrounding area as she had done the previous morning, eventually moving off the road to where some thin trees barely screened a field wall.

They'd hidden among some dense, prickly bushes the previous day. These trees weren't going to provide the same cover, however. Tyvara was staring at the ground. Lorkin felt a vibration, then heard a strange tearing sound followed by something between a thump and a popping noise. A cloud of dust rose up beyond the wall and the air filled with the smell of grit and dirt.

Before their feet a hole appeared.

"In you go," Tyvara said, gesturing toward the hole.

"In there?" Lorkin crouched and peered into the darkness. "Are you hoping to bury me alive?"

"No, foolish Kyralian," she snapped. "I'm trying to hide us both. Get inside before someone sees us."

He put his hands on either side of the hole and let his legs dangle inside. There was no floor that he could reach. The prospect of falling into darkness didn't appeal, so he created a spark of light within the space. It illuminated a hollow space under the ground, the curved floor not far below his feet. He let himself drop, then crouched to avoid scraping his head on the "ceiling" as he moved further inside.

The hollow was globe-shaped, mainly situated below the wall. Two holes showed circles of brightening sky above the field, one that he had entered and another that he guessed had been the exit for the dirt. The inside of the hollow was no doubt restrained from falling in and burying him by Tyvara's magic.

She dropped and slid in beside him, immediately folding herself down into a sitting position facing him. The space was small for two people, and her legs brushed up against his. He hoped the flash of interest this stirred in him didn't show somehow. Her eyes flickered up to meet his, then she sighed and looked away.

"Sorry for snapping at you. It can't be easy for you to trust me."

He smiled ruefully. *The trouble is, I want to trust her. I should be questioning every move she makes, especially after what she told me the other night. Well, I would, but when I get her talking something happens and she goes all silent on me again.* She was watching him, her expression apologetic. *Maybe I should try again.*

"That's fine. But it's not the first time I've annoyed you tonight. What did I say, when we were discussing servants and the Traitors at the beginning of the night, that bothered you?" he asked.

Her eyes widened, then her mouth thinned into a line of reluctance. He thought she wasn't going to answer, but she shook her head.

"I'll have to explain eventually." She grimaced and looked down at her knees. "Many years ago my people noticed that one of the Ichani that roam about the wasteland had a strange

312

slave. A pale man, possibly a Kyralian." Her gaze flickered up to meet his, then away. "Your father."

Lorkin felt a chill run across his skin. Though he had heard the story before, his mother had always been reluctant to talk about this part of his father's life.

"They watched for a long time and eventually realised that the slave was a Guild magician," Tyvara continued. "This was unusual, as you may know already, as Sachakans don't tolerate slaves knowing magic. If a slave develops powers naturally they will kill him, or her. Enslaving a foreign magician – especially a Guild magician – was extraordinary and dangerous. But this was no ordinary Ichani. He was cunning and ambitious.

"As my people watched, they guessed that your father did not know higher magic. Then, one day, the daughter of the leader of my people fell terribly ill and soon it was clear she was dying. Our leader had heard of the Guild's skills in healing with magic. We've tried for many years to discover the secret for ourselves, without success. So our leader sent one of us out to meet your father and make an offer." Tyvara's face darkened. "She would teach him higher magic in exchange for Healing magic."

She looked up at him. Lorkin stared back at her. His mother had never mentioned that his father had agreed to exchange anything for black magic, nor had anybody else in the Guild.

"And?" he prompted.

"He agreed."

"He can't – couldn't – do that!" Lorkin blurted.

Tyvara frowned. "Why not?"

"It's . . . it's a decision only the Higher Magicians can make. And then probably only with the approval of the king. To give such valuable knowledge to another race . . . a people not of the Allied Lands . . . is too risky. And there would have to be something given in exchange."

"Higher magic," she reminded him.

"Which they would never have accepted in exchange. It is . . ." He caught himself. Revealing that black magic was forbidden would reveal the Guild's greatest weakness. "It was not his decision to make."

Tyvara's mouth set in a disapproving line. "Yet he agreed to the offer," she said. "He agreed to come to our home and teach us Healing – something he said that could not be taught in a moment, as higher magic can be. So he was taught higher magic and he used it to kill his master. Then he disappeared, returning to Imardin and breaking his promise. Our leader's daughter died."

Lorkin found he could not meet her accusing gaze. He looked at the ground and picked up a handful of dirt, letting it fall between his fingers.

"I can see why your people are angry with him," he said lamely.

She drew in a deep breath and looked away. "Not all of them. One of my people travelled to Imardin later, when it was clear the brother of your father's former master was preparing to invade Kyralia. She discovered that this Ichani had been sending spies into Imardin for some time, and that your father was killing them off in secret. It could be that your father returned home because he discovered the threat from his master's brother."

"Or he assumed you understood he had to persuade the Guild to allow him to teach you Healing before he could return."

She looked at him. "Do you think that is true?"

Lorkin shook his head. "No. He could not have told them about you without revealing that he had . . ." – *he had learned black magic* – ". . . he had been enslaved here."

"He broke his promise out of pride?" Her tone was disapproving, though not as much as he would have expected. Perhaps she understood why his father had been reluctant to tell his tale.

"I doubt that was the only reason," he said. "He did reveal the truth when it was needed. Or most of the truth, as it turns out," he added.

"Well," she said, shrugging. "Whatever the reason, he didn't keep his promise. Some of my people – the faction I mentioned the other night – want you punished for it." She smiled crookedly as he looked at her in horror. "Which is why Riva was sent to kill you, against our leader's orders. But the majority of us hold to the principle that we are better than our barbaric Sachakan cousins. We do not punish the child for the crimes of the parent."

Lorkin sighed with relief. "I'm glad to hear that."

She smiled. "Instead we give them a chance to make amends."

"But what can I do? I am a mere Ambassador's assistant. I don't even know higher magic."

Her expression became serious. "You could teach us Healing."

They stared at each other in silence. Then she looked down.

"But, as you just pointed out, you haven't the authority to give us that knowledge."

He shook his head. "Is there anything else I can do?" he asked apologetically.

She frowned, her eyes fixed on the dirt wall as she considered.

"No." Her mouth twisted into a grimace. "This isn't good. We have kept the other faction from gaining popularity by promoting the idea that you could give us what your father promised. When my people realise that you can't give them Healing they will be disappointed. And angry." She bowed her head. "Perhaps it would be better if I didn't take you there. Perhaps I should send you back home."

"Don't you need me there to help prove that Riva tried to kill me against orders?" he asked.

"It would help my case."

"Would going to Sanctuary to speak on your behalf improve my standing among your people?"

She frowned and looked at him. "Yes . . . but . . ."

As Lorkin considered that, he felt conflicting emotions. *I was hoping to see her home and learn about her people – and find out what they know about stones with magical qualities. What will happen to her if I don't go there? She killed one of her own people to save me. Though Riva was disobeying orders, they may still punish Tyvara. Perhaps even execute her. It doesn't seem right to run away home when she might die for saving my life. And I don't much like my chances of getting home – on my own or with Dannyl's help – with black-magic-wielding Traitors all over Sachaka trying to kill me.*

"Then I will travel with you to Sanctuary."

Her eyes widened and she gazed at him. "Are you sure?"

He shrugged. "I am an Ambassador's assistant. Perhaps not an actual Ambassador, but it is still my role to assist in establishing and maintaining friendly relations between Kyralia and Sachaka. If it turns out that there's a part of Sachaka we've been failing to establish friendly relations with, it is my duty to ensure that part is not ignored or neglected."

She was staring at him now, mouth open, though whether from surprise or disbelief or because he'd sounded like a complete idiot he wasn't sure.

"And since my predecessor made such a bad impression on your people it is even more important that I do what I can to improve their view of the Guild and Kyralians," he continued. Then he felt a giddying rush of inspiration. "And discuss the possibility of negotiating an exchange of magical knowledge, this time with the appropriate parties and processes involved."

Tyvara's mouth snapped shut and, for a moment, she regarded him with an intensity that he could only meet with a hopeful and foolish smile. Then she threw back her head and laughed. The sound echoed in the hole and she smacked a hand over her mouth.

"You are mad," she said, when her shoulders had stopped shaking. "Fortunately for you it's a madness I like. If you truly wish to risk your life coming to Sanctuary, whether to defend me or try to persuade my people to give you something in exchange for what they already feel they are owed . . . then I selfishly feel I shouldn't try to dissuade you."

He shrugged. "It's the least I can do. For you saving my life. And for your people saving my father's. Will you take me?"

"Yes." She smiled grimly. "And if you help me then I will do all I can to help you survive when you get there."

"That would be appreciated, too."

She looked as if she would say something else, but then looked away. "Well, we have to get there first. It's a long walk. Better get some sleep."

He watched her curl up, tucking one arm under her head; then he lay down. It was impossible to find a comfortable position on the curved floor, and eventually he copied her, curling up on his side with his back to her. He could feel the heat from her body. *No, don't think about that, or you'll never get to sleep.*

"Could you turn the light out?" she murmured.

"Can I dim it instead?" The prospect of being underground in complete darkness did not appeal at all.

"If you must."

He reduced the spark of light until it barely illuminated the two of them. Then he listened to the sound of her breathing, waiting for the slow, deep rhythm of sleep. He knew he was far too conscious of her body so close to his to fall asleep himself. But he was very tired . . .

Before long he had drifted into strange dreams, in which he walked along a road of dirt so soft he had to wade through it, while Tyvara, being lighter and more nimble, barely stirred the soil and was getting further and further ahead . . .

CHAPTER 20

ALLIES AND ENEMIES

In the street below, on the other side, a man stopped and looked up at the window. Cery resisted the urge to shrink back out of sight. It was too late to avoid being seen, and the motion would confirm he should not be there.

"Uh, oh," Gol said. "That's the shopkeeper from next door."

"Looks like he's worked out his neighbour has some un-invited guests."

The man looked away, down at the ground. After a moment his shoulders straightened and he strode across the street toward the shop. A loud rapping followed.

Gol rose. "I'll get rid of him for you."

"No." Cery stood up and stretched. "I'll take care of it. Stay here and keep watch. What's his name, again?"

"Tevan."

As Gol sat down again, he muttered something about it all being a waste of time. *He's probably right*, Cery thought. *The rogue won't be coming back. But we may as well watch because we'll look right fools if we're wrong and she does come back. And we have no other clues to follow.*

He walked out of the room and entered the stairway, descending to the ground floor. Pushing through the door to the storekeeper's shop, Cery looked around with interest. They'd been using the back door, so he hadn't been in here before. The room was full of fine ceramic bowls. He blinked and looked closer, then chuckled. They were all toilet basins, as finely painted and sculpted as vases or dinner ware.

Through the frosted glass door he could see the next-door shopkeeper's hunched silhouette. The man had probably promised to keep an eye on his neighbour's shop and house, and felt obliged to confront these trespassers. He was probably worried that he would regret it, too.

The front door was locked and there was no key in it or in any obvious hiding place close by. Cery was amused to find he had to pick the lock. Once unlocked, he opened the door, smiled at the shopkeeper and effected the sort of cultured accent merchants liked to use to impress rich customers.

"The shop is closed, I'm sorry." Cery pretended to give the man a second look. "But you know that, don't you? You're . . . Tevan? You run the shop next door, correct?"

The man was of average height and carried the excess weight of a middle-aged man who hadn't been forced to skip a meal in a long time − if ever.

"Who are you and what are you doing in Wendel's house?" he demanded.

"I am Wendel's cousin, Delin, and I am borrowing his house for the week."

"Wendel doesn't have a cousin. He has no family. He told me."

"Second cousin, by marriage," Cery explained. "He didn't tell you I was staying here?" He frowned in mock puzzlement. "I suppose it was decided very late."

"He didn't. It's not something he's likely to neglect to tell

me, either." Tevan narrowed his eyes, then took a step backwards. "I'm calling on the Guard. If you're lying you'd better
get out while you have the chance." The man turned and took
a step away.

"The Guard's like to get you and Wendel more rub than I
ever will," Cery said, dropping the accent and letting a little
slum drawl colour his words. "Crawling all over this place
breaking things looking for proof we were here, then saying
you made it up. Let's sort this out ourselves."

Tevan had stopped, and now he looked at Cery with a worried
frown.

"I only need be here for a week, maybe less," Cery told him.
"Wendel won't see a sign I've been here. I'd pay him rent if he
was about, but since he's not here . . ." He reached into his coat,
allowing the hilt of a knife to flash into sight briefly, and drew
out a cap of gold coins he kept there for moments like these.

The man's eyes widened. "A week?" he repeated. He looked
transfixed by all the gold.

"Or less."

Teran's gaze rose to Cery's. "Rent's high around here."

"Your house would be cheaper," Cery replied.

Tevan swallowed. He looked at the coins again, then nodded.
"What's your going rate?"

"Half a gold per day," Cery replied. He slipped the cap back
into his coat. "You'll find 'em dropped by your back door after
I'm gone."

The man nodded, but his mouth was set in a thin line of
disbelief. Still, he didn't voice his doubts. Instead he looked
across the road.

"You're watching something," he said. "Or looking for
someone. Anything I can help with?"

"Hoping to get rid of me sooner?" Cery asked. A look of confusion entered the man's eyes. *No, perhaps he thinks he's found another way to turn a profit.* "Well, if you've seen anything suspicious going on over there . . ."

Tevan frowned. "There's a foreign woman keeps odd hours. The shoemaker says she rents his basement. We've never worked out what she does for a living. Too old and ugly to be whoring around, I'd have thought. My wife's seen her at the market on Freeday mornings with the spice and herb sellers. We think maybe she . . ." – he leaned closer and lowered his voice – "unburdens young women of unwanted situations."

Cery felt his heart skip, but kept his expression blank. Tevan looked at him expectantly.

"Not my line of interest," Cery said, shrugging. "Anything else?"

The man shook his head. "Supposed to be a clean, honest area, this one. If anything is going on it's well hidden." He paused. "Is something going on?"

Cery shook his head. "Nothing you'd want to know about."

"Right." Tevan stepped away again. "Good luck then."

"Good night."

The man nodded, then turned away and headed for the shop next door. Cery closed the door and locked it, then jogged upstairs, taking the stairs two at a time. At the top he paused to catch his breath. His heart hammered in his chest.

"What's wrong?" Gol asked.

"Nothing. Not . . . as young . . . as I used to be," Cery panted. He returned to his chair. "I should get out more often. Any sign of our rogue?"

"No."

"Anyone pay much attention to the neighbourly exchange downstairs?"

"Not much."

"Good. One of us needs to go to the Freeday market tomorrow. To the spice sellers."

"Oh?"

"Our rogue apparently visits them regularly."

"That's Skellin's territory."

Cery cursed. Gol was right. While some Thieves did not mind others doing a little snooping around in their territory without permission – so long as the snooping wasn't on their operations – others definitely did. Cery would wager that Skellin was the latter kind.

"I doubt he'd deny you permission," Gol said.

"Yes, but to get permission I'd have to explain what I'm doing. And then he'd know I didn't seek his help in finding someone I thought might be the Thief Hunter, when I said I would."

"Just tell him the truth: you're not sure it is, and you didn't want to bother him until you had proof."

"If he thinks there's a chance I'm right, he'll want to help us search for her," Cery pointed out.

"We could do with the help," Gol replied.

Cery sighed. "We could. But what will Sonea think of us involving another Thief?"

Gol gave him a serious look. "She won't care, so long as the rogue is caught."

"What will Skellin think of having to work with the Guild?"

"He won't have any choice." Gol smiled. "And from what you said about his interest in magicians, he might be thrilled at the chance."

Cery regarded his friend thoughtfully. "You want me to ask for Skellin's help, don't you?"

Gol shrugged. "If this woman is the Thief Hunter, I want her caught quick. The sooner she's gone the safer you'll be."

"And you."

The big man spread his hands. "Is it wrong to want that?"

"Hmph." Cery looked outside and saw the first of the lamp-lighters stride into sight. It was growing dark already. "Not at all. Once Skellin learns the Thief Hunter might be a magician, he'll realise he has no choice but to work with the Guild. He's not going to be able to catch or kill her himself."

"So you'll go see him?"

Cery sighed. "I guess I have to."

Since Achati had not told Ashaki Tikako of his intention to visit his country estate, as it would have meant pointing out the humiliating fact that the man had not read his slave's mind properly, he did not want to impose further by staying there for the night. Instead, he and Dannyl travelled further down the road to another estate, owned by an elderly Ashaki, and requested a meal and beds in the name of the king.

The old man and his wife were clearly unused to company and played host and hostess reluctantly. But custom dictated that they could not refuse the king's representative. Achati took pity on them, eating sparingly and quickly, and the couple were happy to oblige when he indicated that both he and Dannyl were tired and would appreciate an early night.

Once settled in the guest rooms, they did not go to bed straightaway, but sat and discussed what they had learned.

"If the Traitors want us to find Lorkin, we'll find him," Achati said.

"You believe they have that much power and influence?"

The Sachakan grimaced as he nodded. "Unfortunately, yes. They have evaded us for centuries. Many previous kings have tried to flush them out, or find their base, but the Traitors have only grown better at what they do. King Amakira has said to me we could be better off leaving them alone, as they may grow weaker if they have nothing to strive against."

Dannyl chuckled. "He may be right, but I doubt it."

"Why is that?"

"Without conflict killing them off and taking up their time, they will raise families. They may grow weaker in fighting skills, but greater in numbers."

Achati frowned thoughtfully. "Eventually there will be too many mouths to feed. They will starve." He smiled. "So maybe the king is right after all."

"Only if the Traitors remain hidden."

"You think they'll be forced to come out? To come begging for food?"

"Or they'll choose to reveal themselves in other ways. How strong is your army?"

Achati snorted derisively. "Most likely a hundred times bigger and stronger than theirs. We know their base is in the mountains, where the land is harsh and infertile. They could not feed a population to match the rest of the country, so I doubt their army is the same size or larger than ours."

Dannyl nodded in agreement. "Which is why they use cunning, secretive methods. I wonder . . . do you think they could overthrow the country merely by assassinating and manipulating the right people?"

Achati's expression became serious. "It is possible, but if they could have done it before now, surely they would have."

"The perfect opportunity may not have presented itself yet. It may require some new and extraordinary factor."

Achati's eyebrows rose. "Like the chance to abduct the son of a powerful Guild magician?"

"Do you think that would be extraordinary enough?"

"No." He shook his head and smiled. "Manipulating Kyralia and Sachaka into a war would be too risky. What if Kyralia won? What if we resisted their manipulations, joined forces and attacked the Traitors together? The Guild may prove better at hunting them than we are." He paused. "Which reminds me. Has the Guild responded to the news of Lorkin's abduction yet?"

"No," Dannyl looked away. *I'm not going to be able to put this off any longer. Achati will start wondering why they're taking so long.* "That reminds me – I should check on their progress."

"I'll leave you to it." Achati rose. "It's late and I should get some rest. Tell me what they say in the morning."

"I will."

As the door to the Sachakan's room closed, Dannyl reached into his robe and drew out Administrator Osen's blood ring. He stared at it, running through his mind all the ways he'd considered phrasing the bad news, and choosing what he hoped was the best.

Then he slipped on the ring.

As Sonea opened the door to her rooms, she was surprised to find Administrator Osen standing outside with one hand raised ready to knock. The startled look on his face faded and he straightened.

"Black Magician Sonea," he said. "I must speak with you."

"It's lucky we caught you before you left for the hospices," another voice added.

She turned to see Rothen standing behind and to one side of the Administrator. At once she felt her stomach sink and her heart start to race. *There's that look again. Something's happened to Lorkin . . .*

"Come in," she said, stepping back and beckoning impatiently.

Osen strode inside, followed by Rothen. She closed the door and turned to stare at the Administrator expectantly. He regarded her soberly.

"I must inform you that your son has . . ." Osen paused and frowned. "I'm not sure what to call it. It appears Lorkin has been abducted."

Sonea's legs lost all strength and she felt herself sway a little. Rothen took a step toward her, but she gestured for him to stop. She drew in a deep breath, forced herself to stand firmly and turned back to Osen.

"Abducted?" she repeated.

"Yes. By a young female magician posing as a slave. Ambassador Dannyl believes there is a possibility your son went willingly, but he's not certain of it."

"Ah." A traitorous and seductive relief trickled through Sonea. *Women. Why is it always women with Lorkin?* She felt her heart slow to a calmer rhythm. "So this is more of a matter of social impropriety than impending and certain death?"

"We certainly hope so. But it is more complicated than that. It seems we are not the only people with an underground, secret and not entirely lawful society, and they may be involved."

"Criminals?"

Osen shook his head. "Ambassador Dannyl described them as rebels. They call themselves the Traitors. It is rumoured that they are all women." Osen's eyebrows rose, hinting that he thought this unlikely. "They are also magicians – black magicians. The woman who abducted Lorkin is one. She killed another slave the same night and drained her of power. Dannyl is not sure whether the abductor is the Traitor and the slave just got in her way, or the dead slave was a Traitor and the abductor is not. Either way, the Traitors have indicated that they want her and Lorkin found, and apparently they have such influence that this makes the likeliness of that happening very good."

Sonea took a moment to absorb that. "So when was Lorkin taken away?"

"Three nights ago."

Sonea's heart stopped. "Three nights! Why wasn't I told immediately!"

"You are being told immediately." Osen smiled wryly. "When I impressed upon the new Ambassador that he only contact me in the gravest of emergencies, he took me far too seriously. He expected to find Lorkin quickly, and only told me of the situation tonight."

"I'll kill him," she muttered, moving away to pace the room. "If this woman is a black magician – do they have any other kind over there? – how is Dannyl going to force her to give Lorkin back?"

"He has the assistance of the Sachakan king's representative."

"What if she doesn't want to be found? Who knows what she'll do to survive? Threaten to kill Lorkin?" Sonea stopped, suddenly out of breath. She felt as if her lungs weren't expelling as much air as she was drawing in. Her head was starting to spin. Grabbing the back of a chair, she forced herself to breathe slowly. When her head had cleared she turned to Osen. "I have to go there. I have to be there when they find him."

Osen's expression had been open and sympathetic. Now it closed in and became hard.

"You know you can't do that," he said.

She narrowed her eyes at him, feeling a deep fury rising. "Who would dare stop me?"

"The Guild must have two black magicians present at all times," he reminded her. "The king will never allow you to leave Imardin, let alone Kyralia."

"This is my *son*!" she snapped.

"And the Sachakan king might not appreciate us sending – or allowing – you into his country," Osen continued, "making a politically dangerous situation worse, and implying his people can't sort something like this out for themselves."

"And what if they ca—"

"Lorkin isn't stupid, Sonea," Rothen interrupted quietly. "And neither is Dannyl."

She stared at him, struggling to hold back a surge of hurt and anger that he was arguing against her. *But if Rothen doesn't think I should go . . .*

"I don't believe Lorkin would have gone with this woman if there hadn't been a good reason."

"What if that reason was he had no choice?" she argued.

"Then we must trust Dannyl. You know he would have told us straightaway if the situation was truly grim. If Lorkin is a hostage, then you will not be able to do more for him than Dannyl. Dannyl has experience at negotiation. He has the help of the Sachakans." His voice hardened. "If you barge in there you could make the situation much worse, not just for Lorkin but for Kyralia and Sachaka."

Suddenly she felt weak and drained. Helpless. *What is the use of all this power if I can't use it to save my own son?*

But perhaps he doesn't need saving, a faint voice said somewhere in the back of her mind.

Osen sighed. "I'm afraid I must forbid you to leave, Black Magician Sonea. Or to speak of this to anyone but myself, the king, High Lord Balkan and Lord Rothen."

"Not even Akkarin's family?"

He shook his head. "Not even them. As Lorkin's mother you have a right to know what is happening, and I will keep you informed of the situation. I will be discussing ways that we may assist Lord Dannyl with High Lord Balkan tonight, including sending someone to help him. If we do that, I will let you know as many details as it is safe to reveal."

You had better, she thought. "I will look forward to regular reports," she said stiffly.

He gave her a long, thoughtful look. "Good night, Black Magician Sonea."

She followed him to the door, opening it with magic. Before he stepped out, he nodded politely to her. Then he was gone and she shut the door on the sound of his footsteps striding away down the corridor.

She turned to Rothen.

"I'm going anyway," she told him, then headed for her bedroom. A small trunk sat upon the clothes cabinet. She lifted it with magic and set it on the floor.

"You won't be let back in a second time," Rothen told her, from the doorway.

She moved to the cupboard and opened it. It was full of black robes. "I don't care. I'll find Lorkin, then we'll go travelling. It'll be their loss, not mine."

"I didn't mean the Guild. I mean the country. The Allied Lands."

"I know. There are lands beyond the Allied ones, you know."

"Yes. But while the Guild can train another black magician to replace you, you will not find another Guild to replace it. *You* may not care about that, but will Lorkin?"

She was still staring at the robes. They were not what a magician ought to wear when casting off the shackles of the Guild. She wasn't sure what a magician ought to wear when rebelling and storming out of the country, only that these were definitely not appropriate. But they were all she had.

I can't believe I'm worrying about clothing right now!

"You need to find the rogue, Sonea."

"Regin can find her."

"Cery doesn't trust him."

"I don't blame him," she muttered. "Cery will have to make do."

Rothen sighed. "Sonea." His voice now had a fatherly, stern tone.

She crossed her arms, put on her best don't-mess-with-me-I've-faced-worse-than-you-and-won stare, which made novices flinch and magicians reconsider their words, and turned to face him. "*What?*"

As always, he remained unaffected.

"You know you can't go," he told her. "You know you will more likely make Lorkin's situation worse than better, and that after this is over he'll need a safe, secure Guild to return to – *with his mother in it.*"

She stared at him, then cursed.

"Why are you always right, Rothen?"

He shrugged. "I'm older and smarter than you. Now, you and I need to discuss and make less obvious and destructive

331

plans. For a start, I think we should send someone to Sachaka to act on our behalf."

"Who?"

He smiled. "I have a few people in mind. Come sit down and I'll tell you."

CHAPTER 21

WELCOME ASSISTANCE

The stream did not look healthy, even in the soft light of approaching dawn. A mere trickle winding sluggishly along a shallow ditch, it was fringed with green slime and smelled of mould and rotten vegetation. Tyvara was unperturbed. She dropped into a squat and scooped up a palmful of water.

Lorkin watched her stare at it for a moment, then gulp it down.

"You'll make yourself sick," he told her.

She looked up at him. "Don't worry. I'm stripping it first."

"Stripping?"

"Drawing out all the life within it. It's still gritty with sediment, but that's unpleasant, not dangerous. This is much faster and more efficient than what you do, since I'm taking energy, not using it. Are you going to drink? We can't be sure when we'll find water again."

Lorkin looked at her hands, still dirty from the water. "I thought blood was the only substance magic can be drawn through."

She smiled and scooped up more water. "You know that humans and most animals have a layer of magical protection that naturally sits about the skin?"

"Yes."

"To reach past it you must break it, and the simplest way is by cutting the skin. Naturally that results in bleeding, so people think the blood is essential. It isn't." Her voice grew husky as she spoke. It had been too long since they'd found water. She paused to stare at the liquid cupped in her hands, then drank, before looking up at him again. "There are tiny forms of life in water – you can sense it even when you can't see it – and they're what make you sick. But they don't seem to have a layer of protection, so it's easy to draw their energy. You wouldn't want to rely on such a feeble source, though." She looked down. "Plants seem to have a weaker protection than animals. It's possible to draw their power without cutting them, though it is slow and there's so little to gain you wouldn't bother." She reached for another palmful of water.

Lorkin sighed and sat down. He drew magic and gathered up a cup's worth of water from the stream, holding it within an invisible globe of force. The liquid was cloudy and un-appealing. Sending out more magic, he heated the water until it boiled.

In Healing classes, where purifying water was taught, he'd been told it was best to boil the water for several minutes. But soon Tyvara had finished drinking and was watching him expectantly, obviously anxious to move on. He stopped heating the water and let it cool to a temperature he could bear to touch and drink. Thankfully by then the grit in the water had settled to the bottom, and he was able to scoop the cleaner water from the top. A few gulps later he was done, and they rose to their feet. Rays of sunlight were streaking through the tops of the trees that surrounded them. He hadn't realised dawn had been so close.

"Where next?" Lorkin asked.

"Into the forest. I thought you'd appreciate sleeping above ground.

He grimaced. Though they'd slept in a hole underground each day for several days, he had grown no more comfortable with the knowledge that he was one magical barrier away from being buried alive. "I certainly would."

"Come on then."

Stepping off the road, she led the way into the trees, and Lorkin followed. At first he stumbled over obstacles, dodging branches that Tyvara pushed out of her way which then sprang back at him, his thin shoes catching on rocks and the uneven ground threatening to unbalance him. It took all his concentration to avoid tripping over. Tyvara drew further and further ahead, until she noticed he was falling behind and stopped to wait for him to catch up.

"Have you ever been in a forest before?" she asked.

"Yes. There's one in the Guild Grounds, but it has pathways."

"Ever left Imardin before this?"

"No."

"Why not?"

Because my mother isn't allowed to leave the city. But he couldn't tell her that without explaining why, and he wasn't supposed to reveal how few Kyralians knew black magic or how it was regarded.

"Never had reason to."

She shook her head in disbelief, then turned and continued through the forest. This time she appeared to choose her steps more carefully, and their path became much easier. Then he realised that it *was* a path. A very narrow path, but clearly someone or something had come this way often enough to wear a track in the undergrowth.

"Have you been here before?" he asked.

"No."

"So you don't know where this path goes."

"It's an animal track."

"Ah." He looked down and his heart skipped a beat. "So why are there shoe prints?"

Tyvara stopped and looked back to where he was pointing.

"The forest belongs to the Ashaki who owns this land. There will be slaves harvesting the wood, or hunting the animals that live here." She frowned and looked around them. "I suppose this is as far as we can risk going. We should split up – but stay close enough that you can see and hear me. Look for thick vegetation. Or a hollow in the ground we could cover. If you find anything, whistle to me."

He headed off to the right of the track. After roaming about for a while he found a place where a huge tree had fallen long ago. All that was left of the tree was a massive stump. Roots splayed out like protective arms, and thick, low bushes had grown around the disturbed soil. Guessing there would be a hollow where the roots had once been, he pushed through the bushes. A hole, half as deep as he was tall, remained.

Thick vegetation and a hollow, he thought with satisfaction. *It's perfect.*

Turning to look for Tyvara, he saw her walking twenty or so strides away. He whistled, and when she looked up he beckoned. She headed over to him and pushed her way through the bushes. Stopping at the edge of the hole, she examined it with interest. She sniffed the air.

"Smells damp. You first."

Lorkin drew magic, created a barrier in the shape of a disc, and stepped onto it. He lowered himself into the hole. The soil beneath the barrier was soft, and flattened as he reached the bottom. Removing the barrier, he felt himself start to sink further. The soil wasn't just soft, but waterlogged. Muddy water welled up and into his shoes. One foot touched firm ground but the other kept going, and he threw out his arms and tried to step sideways to catch his balance.

But the mud held him firmly. He fell backwards and landed with a splash in a sticky, smelly mire.

The forest echoed with Tyvara's laughter.

Looking up at her, Lorkin smiled ruefully. *She has a great laugh*, he thought. *As if she doesn't often laugh, but when she does she relishes it.* He waited until she had stopped, then patted the mud beside him.

"Come on down. It's damp, but much softer than those holes in the ground," he told her.

She chuckled a little more, shook her head, then opened her mouth to speak. But something caught her attention. She looked up, then cursed quietly.

"You!" a voice called. "Come here."

She did not look at Lorkin, but hissed words out between her teeth.

"Ashaki. He's seen me. Stay hidden. Stay here."

Then she walked away, disappearing through the bushes. Lorkin pushed himself up into a crouch. He listened carefully, and heard the tinkle of a horse's harness somewhere behind him. Behind the fallen tree.

Moving to the mass of roots, he straightened and peered through them. A Sachakan man was standing beside a horse, staring at something below him. His clothing was not the decorated garb of an Ashaki, but it was well made and more practical for riding.

Then Lorkin saw the knife on the man's belt. His mouth went dry.

"Get up," the Ashaki said.

From the ground before him, Tyvara rose. Lorkin fought the urge to rush after her. *She's a magician. A black magician. She can look after herself. And probably more easily if she doesn't have me to protect at the same time.*

"What are you doing here?" the man demanded.

Her reply was meek and quiet.

"Where's your water bottle? Your supplies?"

"I put them down. Now I can't find them."

The man regarded her thoughtfully. "Come here," he said finally.

She took a step closer, her shoulders stooped. Lorkin felt his heart freeze as the man placed his hands either side of her head. *I should stop this. He'll learn who we are. But why would she let him read her mind? Surely once she knew what he intended she would have fought him off?*

After a moment the man let her go.

"Seems you are as stupid as you say. Follow me. I'll take you back to the road."

As the man turned away to mount his horse, Tyvara glanced back at Lorkin and smiled. The triumph in her expression blew away his earlier alarm. He watched as she meekly followed the man away into the forest. When they were no longer in sight Lorkin turned and sat down on one of the thicker lower roots of the tree.

"Stay hidden. Stay here," she said. *I guess she means she'll come back once the magician has led her to the road and gone on his way.*

338

He looked up at the position of the sunlight streaming between the trees and decided that, if she wasn't back within what he estimated was an hour, he'd set out in search of her.

It was a long hour. Time dragged by. Sunbeams raked the undergrowth with excruciating slowness. As the mud dried, he scratched and brushed it off his skin and clothes. He tried to stop himself imagining what might happen to her, if the magician discovered who and what she was. He tried not to worry that the magician would find out he was here, come back for him and . . .

"Good to see you know how to follow orders," a voice said behind him.

He whirled about to find her standing on top of the stump, smiling down at him. Heart pounding in his chest, he watched her step out into thin air and float down to hover in front of him.

"How did you do that?" he asked.

She frowned and glanced at the shimmering disc of magic just visible beneath her feet. "Same way you did."

"Not levitation. Stopping him from reading your mind."

"Ah. That." She rolled her eyes. "Don't you remember me telling you we have a way of making mind-readers see what we want them to see?"

He thought back to the first place they'd hidden, and of the other slave women. "Ah. Yes, I do. Some sort of blood gem, right?"

She smiled. "Might be. Might not be."

Blood gem. Lorkin's heart skipped. *I could have used Mother's ring while she was gone, but I forgot all about it!* He'd been too concerned about Tyvara. He cursed under his breath.

"What is it?" she asked.

He shook his head. "What if it had been me he'd spotted? My mind he'd read?"

"I'd have stopped him." She shrugged. "While it's always best to avoid confrontation, that isn't always possible."

"You'd fight him? Wouldn't that draw attention to us?"

"It might." She waved a hand at their surroundings. "But we're well hidden. I'd try to finish him off quickly."

"You'd kill him?"

"Of course. He'd come after us if I didn't."

"And when his body was discovered, someone else would come after us. Wouldn't it be better overall if I could hide my thoughts?"

She chuckled. "Even if I was prepared to give the Traitors another reason to be angry with me, even if I thought we couldn't reach Sanctuary without me revealing this secret to you, I couldn't do it. I simply don't have the materials or the time."

He felt his heart skip. "It's like a blood gem, isn't it?"

She rolled her eyes again. "Lie down and go to sleep, Lorkin."

He looked down at the mud, then up at her in disbelief.

"I was only joking, when I said it made a soft bed."

She sighed and waved a hand at him.

"Stand back."

He obeyed, sitting back on his former perch and, guessing what she planned to do, lifting his feet and soggy shoes out of the mud. Soon the air above the sludge began to mist. For a while they were bathed in hot steam, then the air cleared and he saw that only cracked, dried earth remained. Tyvara stepped off the disc of magic under her feet onto the hardened ground. She tapped her foot.

"Get some sleep while you can," she said. "I'll wake you in a few hours, then you can watch. I don't think our host will return any time soon, but he clearly likes taking rides around his estate. We had better keep an eye out for him."

Sighing, Lorkin lay down on the hard ground, and tried to do as she suggested.

A gentle autumn rain began to patter down on the garden at Sunny House, but the small stone shelter Cery and Skellin were sitting within kept them dry. Gol stood nearby, blinking rain out of his eyes as he watched Skellin's bodyguard standing on the opposite side of the shelter. They were alone, the locals keeping indoors in the drab weather and the owner of the land mumbling to himself in another corner of the garden.

As Cery finished his brief description of what he and Gol had seen from the roof of the pawnshop, Skellin looked thoughtful.

"A woman, eh? Did you get a good look at her?"

Cery shrugged. "It was dark and we were watching from above, but I reckon I could pick her again. She's got dark skin and hair. About this tall . . ." Cery held out a hand to indicate.

"Now that you know she has magic, how do you plan to catch her?"

"Oh, I only have to find her." Cery shrugged. "It's up to the Guild to capture rogue magicians. Which is just as well, because if she is the Thief Hunter neither you nor I have a hope of stopping her."

Skellin's eyes flashed with interest. "You're working for the Guild!"

"*Helping* the Guild. If I was working for them I'd expect to be paid."

"You're not being paid?" Skellin shook his head and his expression became serious. "I suppose there are other benefits. When

I heard about your family I figured you'd be looking for revenge. Your search for the murderer turned into a search for the Thief Hunter and now your search for the Thief Hunter has turned into a search for a rogue magician."

"It's been a wild few weeks," Cery replied.

"I hope you'll forgive me pointing out you've got a little off track."

Cery nodded. "It still may turn out that the three are the same person. I guess we'll find out once we've caught her."

"If you can get the truth out of her."

Cery opened his mouth to remind Skellin that black magicians were able to read the minds of unwilling subjects, then thought better of it. No point giving away that nugget of information until he had to. "Are you interested in helping us find her?"

The other Thief pursed his lips as he considered, then he nodded. "Of course I am. If she turns out to be a rogue magician at least I'll have had the chance to make a few friends in the Guild. If she turns out to be the Thief Hunter it will be a boon to us all." He rubbed his hands together. "So tell me: where did you last see her?"

"We saw a woman coming out of the pawn-dealer's shop that looked like her, so I sent Gol after her." As Cery described the basement the woman had used, and the underground tunnel leading away from it, Skellin frowned.

"I didn't know there were passages there," he said. "The rebuilding was supposed to have destroyed them. But I guess if you have magic it would be easy and fast to build yourself a new one."

"I'm a little behind on the borders. Whose territory is it currently part of?"

Skellin grimaced. "Mine, actually." He met Cery's surprised gaze, then smiled crookedly. "Do you know what's going on in every corner of yours at all times?"

Cery shook his head. "Probably not. I don't have many areas where so much rebuilding has gone on, either. One of the other shopkeepers said she'd been seen in the nearby market, buying herbs."

"I'll check it out," Skellin told him. "And see if any of my contacts have heard of a woman like you describe lurking around. Sounds like she'd be the sort to stick to herself. Which, of course, always makes a person stand out. If I hear anything I'll let you know. We can set a trap for her and send for your Guild friends."

Cery nodded. "And I'll let you know if I track her down."

"I'll hold you to that," Skellin said, smiling. "I don't want to miss out on my chance to meet a few Guild magicians." His eyebrows rose. "One of them wouldn't happen to be your famous childhood friend, would it?"

"It might be. But if you want to meet Sonea, you only have to visit one of the hospices."

"Then I'd have to pretend to be sick." Skellin shrugged. "And I don't think she'd like me taking the place of someone who needed her help."

"No. Probably not. So you never get sick?"

"Never."

"Lucky you."

Skellin grinned. "It's been pleasant talking to you again, Ceryni of Northside. I hope we will meet again soon, and that I have good news for you."

Cery nodded. "Looking forward to it. Safe journey home."

"You, too."

The other Thief turned to his bodyguard and strode away. Stepping out from the shelter, Cery drew his collar in close to keep out the rain and walked over to Gol. The big man said nothing at first, falling into step beside Cery as they headed back. Then, when Sunny House was far behind them, he asked how the meeting had gone. Cery went over the details.

"I didn't know Skellin's territory stretched that far," Gol interrupted.

"Neither did I," Cery replied. "It's been too long since we found out where the boundaries were."

"I can find out for you."

"I was hoping you'd say that."

Gol chuckled. "Of course you were."

Why hasn't he used the ring?

Sonea rose from her chair and paced to the window. Sliding across the paper screen, she stared out over the Guild and sighed. Perhaps Lorkin hadn't found the blood ring among his possessions. Perhaps it was still at the Guild House in Arvice, deep in his travelling chest.

That thought left her uneasy. With Dannyl and Lorkin both absent from the Guild House, was it possible a snooping slave might find the ring? If it fell into the wrong hands . . . she shuddered. One of the Sachakan Ichani who had invaded Kyralia twenty years ago had caught Rothen and made a gem from his blood, then used it to send Rothen mental images of all his victims. If Lorkin's abductor found the ring and used it to send her images of her son being tortured . . .

Her heart froze. *I don't think I could bear it. I'd agree to their*

*demands, no matter what they were. Rothen is right. It would make
the situation worse if I were there. I only hope, if they find the ring,
they realise the maker is too far away for it to be effective as a tool
of persuasion.*

She paced away from the window, circling the room. Her
shift at the hospice wouldn't begin for another few hours. The
Healers there had grown bolder since offering to conceal her
absence if she needed to venture into the city. They had grown
almost annoyingly protective of her, pestering her with questions about how much sleep she was getting if she arrived
early for a shift or stayed later.

*But if Cery finds the rogue, it'll be easier and faster for him to
contact me at the hospice. I wish he* would *contact me. Chasing after
this woman would at least keep me busy enough to stop fruitlessly
worrying about Lorkin for a while.*

At once she felt the deep pit of anxiety in her stomach open
up and thoughts of what might happen to her son threatened
to spill out. She forced her mind elsewhere. *The rogue,* she
thought. *Think about the rogue.*

It had been only a few days since their failed attempt to
catch the woman, but it felt like far longer. She considered
the passage entrance they'd found. If the woman had access to
the Thieves' Road did that mean she had links to a Thief? It
would have done once, but the old rules and restrictions were
no longer in place in Imardin's underworld.

Another possibility disturbed her. If the woman had access
to the Thieves' Road, did she know about the tunnels under
the Guild?

A knock at the main door interrupted Sonea's thoughts. She
rose and hurried toward it. Perhaps it was Rothen. Maybe he
had news of Lorkin. Even if it were someone else, at least

they'd provide some distraction from her thoughts. A small twist and push of magic unlatched the door and swung it inward.

Regin stood outside. He inclined his head politely.

"Black Magician Sonea," he said.

"Lord Regin." She hoped her disappointment didn't show in her face.

"Have you heard anything?" he asked, lowering his voice.

"No."

He nodded and looked away. It struck her then that it was unexpectedly considerate of him to stop by and enquire about Lorkin, and she felt guilty for the hostility she felt toward him. She opened her mouth to thank him, but he continued on without realising she had been about to speak.

"I've made some enquiries and they've led to a few small ideas," he said, then shrugged and looked at her. "Probably not worth the trouble and they may clash with your friend's plans, but I thought I should share them with you."

My friend's plans? Suddenly Sonea understood. He was not talking about Lorkin, but about Cery and the hunt for the rogue. She shook her head. *Of course, he doesn't even know about Lorkin. I'm such a fool . . .*

"No?" Regin took a step back, seeing her shake her head. "I can come back another time if it is more convenient."

"Yes – come in. I'd like to hear your ideas," she told him, beckoning and moving aside. He looked at her questioningly, then smiled faintly and stepped past her into her main room. She gestured to the chairs, inviting him to sit down, then closed the door with magic.

"Sumi?" she asked.

He nodded. "Thank you." He watched her move to a sideboard where she kept a tray containing the sumi-making utensils. "I thought you didn't like sumi."

"I don't, but it's growing on me. Raka makes me a bit edgy these days. Tell me about your ideas."

As he began explaining, she carried the tray to the chairs and started making the hot drink. She forced herself to listen. He had met with a few of the magicians he suspected of having links to underworld traders, having befriended them a few months earlier in order to gain information for the Hearing.

Regin grimaced. "They were quite pleased about the result of the Hearing. Changing the ban from associating with criminals to working for them means they can help out their lowlife friends without censure — so long as they don't get paid for it in any obvious way." He sighed. "They're quite pleased with us, which at least has the advantage that they're still happy to talk to me. And to complain about a certain foreign magician receiving money in exchange for using magic."

"Foreign, eh?" Sonea handed him a cup. "Cery said the rogue is foreign."

"Yes." Regin's expression became thoughtful, his head tilting slightly as he considered her. "The law against anyone outside the Guild learning and practising magic isn't always a practical one. It has worked only because the Allied Lands all agreed to it. But what of magicians from other lands? If they set foot on Allied soil and happen to use magic, they immediately break a law. That hardly seems fair."

"Or practical," Sonea agreed. "The king and Higher Magicians have been discussing this for years now. Of course, we are hoping that Sachaka will eventually join the Allied Lands and their magicians will become members of the Guild and bound by our laws. Achieving the first may be difficult, since they'd have to give up slavery. The second, in comparison, seems impossible."

"The other alternative is to change the law."

"I doubt the Guild would want to relinquish its control of magicians, especially foreign ones."

"They've only ever been concerned with controlling those living in the Allied Lands," Regin said. "But *visitors* from other lands might be allowed to enter them without the obligation to join the Guild."

"With some time restriction to their visit, I hope."

"Of course. And no trading of magic for profit."

Sonea smiled. "Can't have the Guild getting any poorer."

Regin chuckled. "If the reactions of my magician friends with dubious connections are anything to go by, no foreign magician would gain permission to trade for long."

"Do they know where this foreign magician is?"

He shook his head. "I could set them digging for information, if you think it won't clash with Cery's plans."

She sipped her cup of sumi and considered, then nodded. "I'll ask him. In the meantime it won't hurt if they keep their ears open and pass anything on to you."

Regin grimaced and set down his empty cup. "It'll only hurt my sense of good taste. They're hardly the sort of company I like to keep. Their idea of entertainment is . . ." His nose wrinkled. "Crude."

Sonea kept her expression neutral. Regin had always been a snob. But then, there were plenty of magicians from the Houses, and not just the lower classes, whose liking for intoxication, whores and gambling were well known and disapproved of. *Like some of Lorkin's friends, it seems*, she thought, remembering the young magicians found in a playhouse. *Maybe Lorkin is better off away from Imardin.*

Then the whole painful truth about his adventures in Sachaka flooded back, and she winced. Rising, she moved the sumi utensils and empty cups back to the side table.

"Hopefully Cery will find her soon, and you won't have to deal with them," she said. Turning back to Regin, she was relieved to see he'd taken the hint and risen to his feet. "Thank you for coming by."

He inclined his head. "Thank you for hearing me out. I'll let you know as soon as I have any further information." He turned to the door and, as she opened it with magic, walked out.

She closed the door, leaned on the back of a chair and sighed. *A few minutes' distraction, at least. Is it too soon to go to the hospice?* She looked at the mechanical timepiece that Rothen had given her last year. *Yes.*

Sighing again, she went back to pacing the room and worrying about her son.

CHAPTER 22

A REUNION

After one night at the old Ashaki's home, Achati and Dannyl had travelled north-west for half of a day, then stopped at the estate of Achati's cousin, Ashaki Tanucha. Though not much younger than the previous host, Tanucha was clearly a far wealthier and more sociable man. His much younger wife, in her middle years, only appeared at dinner and was otherwise busy looking after their seven children, including five boys.

"Seven! I know it's more a city man's viewpoint, but it seems a touch irresponsible," Achati said to Dannyl quietly when they retired to the guest rooms after dinner. "Only one can inherit. He must find occupation for the rest. The daughters will be married as best can be arranged, of course. But the sons . . ." He sighed. "Landless and dependent on their brother, as will be their sons – if they can attract wives at all." He shook his head. "This is how Ichani come to be."

"They rebel against their brothers?"

"Against the whole country. It is better that younger sons are not trained in magic, but it is rare for a parent who loves his child to withhold that knowledge, since it means the younger son will have such low status."

"Younger sons are more likely to become magicians in Kyralia," Dannyl told him. "Magicians are not supposed to involve themselves in politics, and it's considered better if the son destined to become the head of the family is the one with political influence."

Achati nodded thoughtfully. "I think I like your way better. It gives power to both older and younger sons."

They spent the next day riding around Tanucha's estate, and the evening in eating and talking. Afterwards Achati and Dannyl chatted late into the night. The next day they slept late, then explored Tanucha's library, which was disappointingly small and neglected. Though the rest was welcome, Dannyl could not relax. When they retired to the guest rooms for the second night he asked Achati when they would be moving on.

"That depends on the Traitors, doesn't it?" Achati replied as he reclined on the pillows in the central room.

"Surely we're not going to wait around for them to deliver Lorkin and Tyvara to us?" Dannyl said, sitting down on one of the stools. He could not get used to lying about on the floor as the Sachakans did.

"Why not? If we keep moving they may not know where to find us. Or we may end up travelling in the wrong direction – away from those who are bringing them to us."

Dannyl frowned. "I'm not sure why, but I can't picture these Traitors turning up at the front gate of Tanucha's estate with Lorkin and Tyvara in chains. They wouldn't reveal themselves like that."

"Then how do you think they'll do it?"

Dannyl considered. "If I were them . . . I'd lead us to Lorkin and Tyvara. I'd leave us clues or directions – as they have already – so that we will eventually cross paths with the pair."

"Have they left us any clues or directions lately?"

"No," Dannyl admitted. "But they haven't told us to stay put, either."

Achati laughed. "I am growing very fond of you, Ambassador Dannyl. You have a unique mind." He turned to one of his slaves, a handsome young man who attended to most of his needs, while the other slave's role appeared to be to do heavy work and drive the carriage. "Get us some more water, Varn." The slave picked up a pitcher and hurried away.

"Of course, telling us that they want us to find Lorkin could still be a decoy," Dannyl said.

"So if it was, then where would we go next?"

Dannyl shook his head and sighed. "I don't know. If the Traitors did want the girl and Lorkin to evade us, where would they take them?"

"To their mountain home."

"And which direction has the pair been heading?"

"The mountains."

"Presumably they are ahead of us." Dannyl looked up at Achati. "That is the direction I would go."

Achati nodded, then raised an eyebrow in warning. "We don't know where their home is," he reminded Dannyl. "Only that it is in the mountains."

"I haven't forgotten that. Have you ever used trackers?"

"Occasionally. When we had a confirmed Traitor to follow."

"And it failed because?"

"The tracks always stop." Achati shrugged. "The Traitors are not fools. They know how to erase signs of their passing. Which is not hard when your land is mostly bare rock and you can levitate."

Dannyl frowned, then shook his head. "If the Traitors wanted us to stop and stay put, or change direction, they'd have let us know."

"This whole journey and all the clues we've followed could have been a ruse," Achati pointed out. "Designed to keep us busy and heading in the wrong direction."

"Then it doesn't matter if we keep going. They've already made fools of us. But if there's a chance they haven't, and we're on the right track, then I'm willing to risk being made a slightly bigger fool by continuing toward the mountains. It's worth it, for the chance we'll find Lorkin."

Achati regarded Dannyl thoughtfully, then nodded. The slave returned and handed him the pitcher. "Then we'll leave. Will the morning be soon enough?" He refilled his goblet but paused to wait for Dannyl's answer.

Dannyl looked at the man, noting signs of reluctance. *I shouldn't push him too far*, he thought. He nodded. "Of course. But early in the morning would be best."

Achati sighed, nodded, then drained his goblet. "I'll send a slave to inform Tanucha we'll be moving on, and request some supplies for the journey. There are fewer estates out by the mountains, and they don't tend to be that prosperous. We'll also need some magical support. I'll contact the king and ask him to send some locals to help us." With a grunt, he rose to his feet. "Don't wait for me. Go to bed. This could take some time."

Magical support. Contacting the king. Dannyl felt a twinge of apprehension. *He really does think these Traitors are dangerous.*

"Ashaki Achati?" Dannyl said.

The man turned to look back at him. "Yes?"

Dannyl smiled. "Thank you."

Achati's frown disappeared and his eyes warmed with good humour. "I think I could get to like Kyralian ideas of manners." Then he turned and disappeared through the door to his room.

Lorkin opened his eyes. The sky was streaked with orange clouds. He frowned. He'd been dreaming, but he couldn't remember anything of the dream. Something had woken him. He had that unpleasant, disorienting feeling of being disturbed. Of being wrenched awake before he was ready.

He felt something move against him, and his heart was suddenly pounding.

Lifting his head he saw that Tyvara had fallen asleep. Sitting up against the wall of the old ruin, she had sagged sideways against a protruding stone, and bent her right leg instinctively to avoid toppling sideways. Her knee had come to rest on his arm.

Her skin was wonderfully warm – a stark contrast to the cold ground beneath him and the growing chill of approaching night. Though Sachaka was warm during the day, the evenings could be surprisingly cold.

What should I do? If I move she'll wake up. But she's supposed to be keeping watch, and it's nearly time for us to head off anyway. She needed the sleep, though. She'd been taking longer shifts keeping watch at night, despite him arguing that she could trust him to share the burden. He didn't have the heart to tell her he could Heal away the weariness. It would be insensitive, considering what his father had promised the Traitors, then failed to deliver.

The cold air told him that she had also let fall the magical shield protecting them, so he put up one of his own, then warmed the air inside it. Keeping still so he didn't disturb her, he watched her sleeping. The dark circles under her eyes and the little frown creasing her forehead bothered him. But being able to look at her closely without disturbing or embarrassing her . . . he could appreciate the feminine curve of her jaw and the exotic tilt of her eyes, the curve of her lips . . .

Which twitched, and he quickly looked away.

He felt her hastily throw up a shield as she woke up and realised she'd dropped hers, so he drew his own in to surround himself. Listening to her draw in a deep breath, then yawn, he considered the ruins they were hiding within. Though Tyvara had been here before, she didn't know anything about their history. High on a rocky hill, they overlooked the intersection of the road they had been following where it met another. As the sun had risen, just after they'd arrived, he'd been able to pick out details of the mountains, which before had been only a hazy, uneven line of blue-grey at the horizon. Below them was mostly level farmland, broken here and there by plantations of trees or game forests, and criss-crossed by low walls.

"How far away are we?" he had asked.

"Three or four more nights walking to the foothills, then several more to climb into the mountains."

Now he looked at the area surrounding the hill, checking for signs of life.

"Mind if I have a look around?" he asked as Tyvara rose to her feet and stretched.

She looked up at the sky, which was now a deep scarlet, but the night was not quite dark enough for continuing their trek. "Go ahead. Just keep out of sight of the road."

"I will."

They'd sheltered within an open square of walls. He rose

and headed for one of the gaps, intending to have a closer look at the outside of the building.

A woman stepped into the gap.

He skidded to a halt. The woman was dressed as a slave, but her demeanour was all wrong. She was smiling at him, but the smile was not friendly. She took a step toward him, her eyes narrowing. Instinctively, he strengthened his shield.

His instinct proved correct. The woman's nose wrinkled with concentration, and his shield vibrated violently as magic battered it. The air between them shimmered. He backed away.

The woman's stare was cold and intent. He had no doubt she meant to kill him. Fear set his heart pounding. He felt a growing urge to run. *Which would be sensible*, he thought. *She's got to be a Traitor, which means she's a black magician, which means she's a lot stronger than me.*

But before he had even finished that thought, Tyvara stepped past him. The woman's gaze shifted to her. He felt a giddy rush of relief. Tyvara stopped a step in front of him and he felt her shield envelop his own. Though the battering stopped, he kept his shield strong within hers, in case her own faltered.

"Stop this, Rasha," Tyvara said.

"Only if *you* do," the woman replied.

"Do you swear you will not strike at me or Lorkin?"

"I swear I will not strike you. But he," the woman's gaze shifted back to him, "must die."

Lorkin shivered. But he also noted that the woman had stopped striking at Tyvara.

"The queen ordered that he was not to be killed."

"She has no right to tell us we cannot have our revenge," Rasha hissed.

"Ishira was the first to die."

The woman's eyes flashed with anger. "First or last, what does it matter?"

"She was my playmate. Do you think I didn't miss her? Do you think I didn't grieve?"

"*You don't know what it's like to lose a child!*" the woman shouted.

"No," Tyvara replied, an edge to her voice. "But I would consider the queen an example of how to live with the loss, not those who would murder someone else's child for their parent's mistakes or crimes."

Rasha stared at Tyvara, her face a mask of hatred. "Not everyone can be so forgiving. Not of that. And not of you murdering one of your own people." The woman's eyes gleamed. "You're wasting your strength protecting him. Let me have him."

"Once you kill him, what will you do with me?" Tyvara sounded remarkably calm, Lorkin noted. But she stood braced as if she expected another attack any moment. *She's trying to keep the woman talking. Well, I hope she is. She could also be about to start bartering my life for her own.*

"You're coming back to Sanctuary with me. All Traitors need to know that the queen would rather one of our own died than the son of the man who killed her daughter."

"Actually, the queen would rather people obeyed her orders. Then nobody would get killed," a high voice said. "It's quite a reasonable order, and good for everybody."

Rasha stepped to the side and turned in one movement. Another woman dressed as a slave stood within the gap, leaning against the wall in a deliberately nonchalant pose.

"Chari," Tyvara said, relief and warmth in her voice.

The newcomer gave them all a cheerful smile, then stepped into the building with all the poise of a young Kyralian woman making a grand entrance at a ball or party.

"I have fresh, shiny orders from the queen," she told them. "Lord Lorkin is not to be harmed. Tyvara is to be brought to Sanctuary to be put on trial for the murder of Riva." She turned to Rasha. "Since I outrank you, this little task falls to me. You had better run along, before your master realises you're gone and sends a whipping party after you."

Rasha stared at Chari for a moment, then she hissed and stalked through the gap in the wall. The snap and crack of the woman pushing through the spiny bushes covering the hill could be clearly heard.

Chari turned to regard Tyvara. "You're in *so* much trouble."

Tyvara smiled. "Thanks for stepping in. How'd you know where we were?"

The young woman shrugged. "I didn't. I was keeping an eye out for you, of course, but I didn't think you'd come here. It's the most obvious hiding place in this area. What were you thinking?"

Tyvara shrugged. "I don't know." She rubbed her face, her weariness suddenly plain to see. "We'd done so well . . . I thought maybe people were assuming we wouldn't head for Sanctuary."

Chari shook her head. "It's just as well I was keeping an eye on Rasha. She's head watcher at the estate next to mine and she's been sweating on catching you. When I heard she'd gathered together a group and was heading out to get you I slipped away and followed."

"A group?" Tyvara frowned. "Where are the others?"

"Fortunately for you, she told them to wait so she could go

358

on ahead and knock off your new friend here." Chari glanced at Lorkin and smiled. "I got to them first and told them to go home."

"*I outrank you*", Lorkin recalled her saying to Rasha. *She's obviously a fairly powerful Traitor. And if they have ranks then they aren't as equal as Tyvara says.*

"Well . . . thank you for that." Tyvara paused. "So what are *you* going to do with us?"

Chari did not answer. She looked down, pursed her lips and walked a few steps closer. She stopped a few steps away, then looked at Tyvara searchingly. "Is it true?"

"Yes."

Chari nodded and sighed. "Riva was a troublemaker. If anyone was going to give you reason, she would."

Tyvara shook her head. "If there had been any other way . . ."

"Well, good for you for not denying it. What are your plans?"

"To go home and sort this out."

Chari's gaze shifted to Lorkin and moved from his head to his feet and back again. "What about him?"

Lorkin decided to ignore that he was being discussed as if he wasn't there. He inclined his head politely. "Honoured to meet you, Chari of the Traitors."

The woman grinned and walked over to face him. "I like him. Honoured to meet you, too, Lorkin of the Guild."

"He has offered to return with me, to speak in my defence at the trial." Tyvara's words were quiet.

Chari's eyebrows rose. "And are you wanting to go with her?" she asked of him.

"Yes."

Her expression became both approving and appraising.

"You're a brave man. Are you going to give us what your father didn't?"

"We'll discuss that when we get there," Tyvara replied before he could respond.

The young woman chuckled. "I'm sure you will. Of course, that's not what's supposed to happen," she told him. "You're supposed to be returned to Arvice. We're certainly not meant to bring you back to our secret home. I'll have to get permission for that."

"How long will that take?" he asked.

Chari considered. "Six or seven days. We can shorten that by meeting Speaker Savara at the tanners' huts." She glanced at Tyvara. "Savara was Tyvara's mentor – and mine – and is one of our leaders. If you still want to come to Sanctuary, you'll have to talk her into taking you."

"How would I best do that?"

Chari shrugged.

"With your usual charm and enthusiasm," Tyvara told him. "Don't make any promises, though. My people will regard them with suspicion, if they believe them at all. You only need to mention you are willing to consider making amends for your father's betrayal, not specify how."

He nodded. "I can do that."

Tyvara smiled. "I'm looking forward to watching you try."

"As am I," Chari said. She looked down at his shoes. "How are your feet?"

"Well used."

"Fancy a cart ride? We have a load of feed headed for one of the outer estates tomorrow. I'm sure there's room for two more slaves."

Lorkin looked at Tyvara. "We can trust her?"

She nodded. "Chari is an old friend of mine. We trained together."

He smiled at Chari and inclined his head. "Then I accept. In fact, it sounds like an offer too good to refuse."

"Then don't." Chari smiled brightly. "I can offer you more comfortable beds at my estate than a bit of dirt in an old ruin. And," she leaned toward Lorkin and sniffed, "a bath."

Lorkin looked toward Tyvara. She was frowning.

"What's wrong?" he asked.

She shook her head. "Nothing." Sighing, she looked at Chari. "Are you sure Lorkin is safe at your estate?"

The young woman grinned. "The master's a sweet old drunk. I make all the decisions there, including which slaves he buys. There's not one slave there I didn't approve of, and the few times Speaker Sneaky has tried to get one of her girls in I've found them somewhere else to be."

Tyvara shook her head slowly. "You're going to be a very scary woman if you ever decide to take a place at the Table."

"You can bet on it." Chari grinned. "So you'd better stay on my good side. And you'll have a better chance of that if you have that bath. Come on. Let's get home before the master misses me."

"She wouldn't ask to meet you if there wasn't good reason," Gol said as he hurried after Cery.

"Is that supposed to make me feel better?" Cery retorted.

"Well . . . all I'm saying is she's a sensible girl."

"I'd much rather she was *not* sensible with *no* good reason to see me." Cery scowled. "If she's sensible and has a good reason then there's a better chance something bad has happened."

Gol sighed and said nothing more. Cery wove past boxes and tubs of rotting food in the alley. *At least I know that Anyi is still alive*, he thought. Gol had occasionally tried to find her, and Cery had been pleased that he'd failed – and tried to tell himself it was because she'd succeeded in hiding rather than because her corpse had never been found or recognised.

Near the end of the alleyway he stopped and hammered on a door. After a short pause, the door swung inward and a man with a scarred face ushered them inside. A familiar woman stepped out of a side door to meet them.

"Donia," Cery said, managing a half-smile. "How's business?"

"The usual," she said, the corner of her mouth lifting into a wry smile. "Good to see you again. I've got the rooms set the way you like. She's waiting up there."

"Thanks."

He and Gol climbed the stairs. Worry made him edgy, and he couldn't help glancing through doorways and around corners for signs of ambush. Though Cery did not think Donia would betray him willingly, he never discounted the chance that someone would remember they had been friends in their youth, and set a trap for him in her bolhouse. Or spy on him. He always had Donia empty the top-floor rooms either side of and below the one he held meetings in, so nobody could eavesdrop.

Reaching the door of the same room he had met Anyi in last time, he was amused to see her sitting in the exact position he had been in during the previous meeting. Keeping his expression neutral, he followed Gol inside. The big man looked around the room, then closed the door. Cery looked closely at his daughter.

There were dark circles under her eyes and she appeared to be even thinner, but her gaze was sharp and unflinching.

362

"Anyi," he said. "I'm glad to see you've kept out of trouble."

The corner of her mouth twitched. "It's good to see you're still alive, too. Any luck catching my brothers' murderer?"

He felt a familiar wrench of grief. "Yes and no."

"Which means what?"

Cery suppressed a sigh. Her mother had disliked evasive answers, too.

"I've been tracking someone, but I won't be sure if it is the right someone until I catch them."

She pursed her lips, then nodded. "Why have you let brazier houses open in Northside?"

He blinked in surprise. "I haven't."

"You don't know about them?" Her eyebrows rose and her attention shifted to Gol. "*He* doesn't know?"

"No." Cery glanced at Gol. "But we do now."

"You'll shut them down?"

"Of course."

She frowned. "But you won't do it yourself, will you? Not in person."

He shrugged. "Probably not. Why do you ask?"

"One opened next to where I was staying. It's why I'm not staying there now. Nasty, nasty people. I heard them talking to the previous owner. The walls are pretty thin so it wasn't hard to listen in." Her eyes narrowed. "They told the man they were going to take his house and shop. They said if he told anyone they'd do things to him and his family. There was a woman with a strange accent – nothing I've ever heard before. She said something and then the bootmaker yelled. When his wife got home after they'd gone, I heard him telling her what had happened. He said they'd hurt him with magic." Anyi looked at Cery intently. "Do you think that's possible, or did they trick him?"

363

Cery stared back at her. *If this is the rogue . . . if it is the Thief Hunter . . . is she worming her way closer to Skellin by working for his rot-sellers?* "A strange accent," he repeated.

"Yes."

"Did you get a look at her?"

"No. But there have been rumours of rogue magicians in the city for years. It kind of makes sense if they're foreigners. Magicians from countries outside the Allied Lands aren't going to be part of the Guild." She paused, then shrugged. "Of course, she could've been faking it."

Cery nodded approvingly. "You were right to leave. Better to assume she has magic and get out of there. Have you got another hiding place?"

She scowled. "No. I had a few, but they've all been spoiled in one way or another." She looked up at him. "You're doing okay, from the look of it."

"I'm not sure how much of that is because of what I've done, or sheer luck," he admitted.

"Still, with the money and contacts you have, you must have a better chance than me."

Cery shrugged. "They do help."

"They do, do they? Well, how about I come and stay with you, then? Because hiding doesn't earn me any money, and I've used up all mine – as well as my contacts."

As Cery opened his mouth to protest, she leapt to her feet.

"Don't go telling me I'd be safer away from you. Nobody but you and Gol know we're related and I have no intention of making it public gossip. I'm not going to be with you all the time because I'm your daughter." She straightened and put her hands on her hips. "I'm going to be there as your body-guard."

Gol made a choking noise.

"Anyi—" Cery began.

"Face it, you need one. Gol's getting old and slow. You need someone young. Someone you can trust as much as him."

Gol's choking became a spluttering.

"Youth and trustworthiness aren't all that a bodyguard's gotta be," Cery pointed out.

She smiled and crossed her arms. "You don't think I can fight? I can fight. I've even had some training. I'll prove it."

Cery bit back the sceptical remark he would normally have made. *She is my daughter. We haven't exchanged this many words in years. I'll gain nothing by dismissing her. And . . . perhaps she does have a little of her father's talent.*

"Well, then," he said. "How about you do that? Show me how old and slow Gol is."

He nearly laughed aloud at the expression on his bodyguard's face. Gol's look of hurt and dismay changed to wariness as Anyi turned to face him and dropped into a crouch. There was a glint of metal in one hand. Cery hadn't seen her reach for the knife. He noted the way she held it and nodded in approval.

This could be interesting.

"Don't actually kill him," he told her.

Gol had recovered from his surprise now, and was drawing closer to Anyi with the careful, well-balanced steps that Cery knew so well. He slowly drew out a knife. The big man might not be fast on his feet, but he was as solid as a wall and knew how to use an adversary's momentum and weight against him. Or her.

Anyi was edging closer as well, but Cery was pleased to see she wasn't rushing in. She was circling Gol though, and that wasn't good. A bodyguard ought to keep him- or herself between an attacker and the person they were supposed to be protecting. *I'll have to teach her that.*

Cery caught himself and frowned. *Will I? Should I even keep her near me, let alone put her in a position where she is more likely to be attacked? I should give her money and send her away.*

Somehow he knew she would not be content with that. Whether he sent her away or let her stay with him, she would want to be *doing* something. *And she has no place to hide. How can I send her away?*

But she was tenacious. If he sent her back out into the city — especially if he gave her some money — she would find new places to conceal herself. *Or she will decide she can't stand being cooped up any more and throw all caution to the wind.*

A flurry of movement drew his attention back to the fight. Anyi had attacked Gol, he noted. Again, not the best move for a bodyguard. Gol had neatly dodged her knife, caught her arm and used her lunge to propel and twist her to the floor behind him. She gave a yelp of protest and pain as he held her arm behind her back, stopping her from rising.

Cery walked forward and prised the knife out of her hand, then he stepped back.

"Let her up."

Gol released her and backed away. He met Cery's gaze and nodded once. "She's fast, but she has some bad habits. We'll have to retrain her."

Cery frowned at the man. *He's already decided I'm going to keep her!*

Rising to her feet, Anyi narrowed her eyes at Gol, but said nothing. She glanced at Cery, then looked at the floor.

"I'll learn," she said.

"You have a lot to learn," Cery told her.

"So you'll take me on as a bodyguard?"

He paused before answering. "I'll consider it, once you've been trained right, and if I think you're good enough. Either way, you're working for me now, and that means you must do what I tell you. No arguments. You obey orders, even if you don't know why."

She nodded. "That's fair."

He walked over to her and handed back the knife. "And Gol's not old. He's close to the same age as me."

Anyi's eyebrows rose. "If you think that means he's not old, then you really do need a new bodyguard."

CHAPTER 23

NEW HELPERS

Healer Nikea stepped into the examination room as the last patient Sonea had seen left – a woman who was trying, unsuccessfully, to give up roet. Sonea had Healed the woman, but it had made no difference to the cravings.

"There's something I need to show you," Nikea said.

"Oh?" Sonea looked up from the notes she had been taking. "What is that?"

"Something," Nikea said. She smiled, and her eyes widened meaningfully.

Somehow Sonea's heart managed to skip a beat and then, straight after, sink to her stomach. If Cery had merely sent a message, Nikea would have delivered it. This meaningful look suggested that more than a note had arrived, and Sonea suspected that "something" was Cery.

He knew she didn't like him coming here. Still, there had to be a good reason for him doing so.

Rising, she stepped out of the room and followed Nikea down the corridor. They entered the non-public part of the hospice. A pair of Healers stood in the hallway, heads close as they talked in whispers. Their eyes were on a storeroom door,

but shifted to Sonea as she appeared. They immediately straightened and inclined their heads politely.

"Black Magician Sonea," they murmured, then hurried away.

Nikea led Sonea to the door they'd found so interesting and
opened it. Inside, a familiar figure sat on a short ladder, between
rows of shelving filled with bandages and other hospice supplies.
He stood up. Sighing, Sonea stepped inside and pulled the
door closed behind her.

"Cery," she said. "Is it good news or bad?"

His mouth twisted into a wry smile. "I'm good, thanks for
asking. How are you?"

She crossed her arms. "Fine."

"You seem a bit cranky."

"It's the middle of the night, yet for some reason we have
as many patients as we get during the day, nothing I try cures
roet addiction, there's a rogue magician loose in the city, and
instead of telling the Guild about it I'm risking the little
freedom I have by working with a Thief who insists on visiting
me in a public place, and my son is still missing in Sachaka.
I'm supposed to be in a good mood?"

Cery grimaced. "I guess not. So . . . no news on Lorkin?"

"No." She sighed again. "I know you wouldn't have come
here if there wasn't a good reason, Cery. Just don't expect me
to be all calm and relaxed about it. What's the news?"

He sat down again. "How do you feel about another Thief
helping us find the rogue?"

Sonea stared at him in surprise. "Is it anyone I know?"

"I doubt it. He's one of the new lot. Faren's successor. Name
is Skellin."

"He'd have to have a lot to offer, for you to consider it."

Cery nodded. "He does. He's one of the most powerful

Thieves in the city. He has a particular interest in the Thief Hunter. Asked me a while back if I'd keep him informed if I picked up anything. He knows the rogue may not be the Thief Hunter, but feels it's worth tracking her down to find out."

"What does he get out of it?"

He smiled. "He'd like to meet you. Sounds like Faren told him stories, so he's got a hankering to meet the legend."

Sonea made a rude noise. "So long as he doesn't have the same ideas Faren had about how useful I could be to him."

"I'm sure he does, but he'll not be expecting you to have them, too."

"Does he have a better chance of finding the rogue than you?"

Cery grew serious. "She did a favour for a rot-seller that set up shop in my area until I put a stop to it. Skellin controls most of the trade, so I'm hoping that he can trace the—"

"The Thief we're working with is the main source of roet?" Sonea interrupted.

Cery nodded, his nose wrinkling in distaste. "Yes."

She turned away. "Oh, that's just wonderful."

"Will you accept his help?"

She looked at him. His gaze was hard and challenging. Yet what had he said? *". . . set up shop in my area until I put a stop to it"*. Perhaps he did not like what roet did to people any more than she did. But he had no choice but to work with people like Skellin. *"He's one of the most powerful Thieves in the city."* If the rogue was working for a roet seller then it made sense for her and Cery to trace her through the contacts of the Thief importing it. Then something else occurred to her. Perhaps the rogue was addicted to the drug, and the seller was forcing her to use her magic in support of his criminal activities in order to get it.

Sonea rubbed her temples as she considered. *I'm already breaking a whole lot of rules and restrictions. Ironically, this will not make things any worse, as far as the Guild is concerned. It will only feel worse to me.*

"Go ahead and recruit him. So long as he realises that meeting the legend does not involve anything more than us both being in the same place once and having a nice chat for a reasonable length of time – and so long as you feel it is necessary to involve him – then I have no argument against it."

Cery nodded. "I do think we need him. And I'll make sure he understands you're not for hire."

Climbing out of the carriage, Dannyl and Achati turned to take in their surroundings. The road they had been travelling northwards along ended where it met an east- to west-running thoroughfare. A stream ran alongside the new road. Hills surrounded them, rocks jutting out from wild vegetation.

"We'll wait here," Achati said.

"How long, do you think?" Dannyl asked.

"An hour, maybe two."

Achati had arranged for the group of local magicians, who would provide magical support, to meet them at the junction. They were bringing a tracker. He'd explained that, if they got as far as the mountains and had to leave the road, the risk of being attacked by the Traitors would increase dramatically.

The Sachakan turned and spoke to his slaves, instructing them to bring out food for him, Dannyl and themselves. As the two young men obeyed, Dannyl found himself thinking, not for the first time, that Achati treated his slaves well. He almost seemed fond of them.

As they ate the small, flat pastries that they'd been given at the last estate, Dannyl looked at the hills again. His gaze was drawn to the rocky outcrops. He frowned as he noticed how some were more like piles of boulders. In places, these boulders fitted together much too well to be natural.

"Is that a ruin up there?" he asked, turning to Achati.

The man looked where Dannyl was pointing, and nodded. "Probably. There are a few in this area."

"How old are they?"

Achati shrugged. "Old."

"Do you mind if I have a look?"

"Of course not." Achati smiled. "I'll signal to you if the others arrive."

Finishing the pastry, Dannyl crossed the road and set off up the slope. The hill was steeper than it had looked from the carriage, and by the time Dannyl reached the first pile of boulders he was breathing hard. Examining the pile, he decided it was part of a wall. For a while he moved across the slope, finding more sections of wall and resting to catch his breath. When he had recovered he decided to see what this fortification surrounded, and headed uphill.

The vegetation grew thicker and taller the closer he got to the summit. He caught his sleeve on a prickly shrub, managing to tear the material, after which he gave such plants a wide berth. It was easy enough to dry cloth with magic, and even remove some stains, but mending tears was beyond him. It might be possible to re-join the fine threads somehow, but it would take time and concentration.

He realised with dismay that while he could see remnants of more walls ahead, they peeked out of a mass of tangled, prickly bushes. He created a magical shield so he could push past them. There was a flat section at the top, within the low walls that were all that was left of a building, but other than that there was nothing to see but weathered stones.

I'm not going to learn anything here, he decided. *Not without digging all this up.* He looked out over the fields below, noting the mountains in the distance. To the west dark clouds lurked, suggesting a break in the dry, sunny weather they'd enjoyed since leaving Arvice. He could not guess how long it would take for the rain to reach them. Leaving the building, he headed back to the road.

A little way down the slope the vegetation parted and he had a clear view of the carriage and road below. Achati was sitting in the narrow doorway of the vehicle. As Dannyl watched, the handsome slave called Varn knelt before the magician and held out his hands, palm upward. Something in Achati's hand caught the light.

A knife.

Dannyl's heart lurched and he stopped. Achati lifted the highly decorated blade that usually sat in its sheath at his side and lightly touched the slave's wrists. He sheathed the knife and grasped the man's wrists with both hands. Dannyl watched, his heart racing. After only a short pause, Achati let the slave go.

I guess this means Varn is Achati's source slave, Dannyl thought. He realised his heart was not racing with fear. *More like excitement. I just witnessed an ancient ritual of black magic.* Magic had passed from slave to master. And it hadn't involved anyone being slaughtered. It had been remarkably serene and dignified.

The young man did not stand up, but drew closer to his master. Instead of keeping his gaze lowered as he usually did, he looked up at Achati. Dannyl stared, fascinated by the man's expression. *If I'm not imagining things at this distance, I'd say it was adoring.* He smiled to himself. *I guess it would be easy to love a master that treated you well.*

Then the slave smiled and stepped *very* close to Achati. The magician placed a hand on the young man's cheek and shook his head. He leaned forward and kissed Varn on the lips. The slave moved away again, still smiling.

Dannyl realised several things at once. Firstly, that the next thing both of the men were likely to do was glance around themselves to see if anyone had seen them. He looked away so that they didn't catch him watching them and continued down the slope. Secondly, that the slave didn't just love his master – he *loved* his master. And thirdly, that the way Achati had caressed the young man's face suggested there was more to his ownership of Varn than having a slave for pleasure.

Is this the only way it works here? he wondered. *What of men of similar rank?*

But he did not have time to consider it. As he broke free from the dense vegetation, he stopped to look down the road toward the west, and saw five men and a cart not far along it. They would reach the junction soon. Dannyl hurried down the hill and stopped on the road, beckoning as Achati saw him. The Sachakan rose to his feet and walked over to join him.

"Excellent timing, Ambassador Dannyl," he said, squinting at the figures in the distance. "Did you find anything up there?"

"Lots of thorny plants," Dannyl replied ruefully. "I'm afraid your friends are about to meet a shabby Kyralian."

Achati looked down at Dannyl's torn robe. "Ah, yes.

Sachakan vegetation can be as prickly as its people. I'll get Varn to mend it for you."

Dannyl nodded in gratitude. "Thank you. Now, is there anything in particular I should say or do in greeting our new companions?"

Achati shook his head. "When in doubt, let me do the talking."

The farm cart was big and moved slowly. It was piled high with bales of stock feed, its load strapped down securely with many ropes. Four gorin hauled it – the first Lorkin had seen of the big animals in Sachaka. The driver was a short, silent male slave who occupied the only seat on the vehicle.

The other three passengers rode in a cave within the bales. Gaps between the bales that formed the roof allowed some air to get into the narrow space, but the walls were tightly packed. Three small packs were stowed at one end, which Lorkin assumed were full of food and supplies for the journey into the mountains. Chari and Tyvara were sitting either side of him on a seat of bales running along the gap, which meant he had to turn his back on Chari to look at Tyvara, and vice versa.

Chari nudged his arm with her elbow. "More comfortable than walking, right?"

"Definitely. Was this your idea?"

She waved a hand dismissively. "No, we've been doing this for centuries. Got to move slaves about somehow."

He frowned. "Won't any Traitors seeing a cart like this suspect there's someone travelling inside, then?"

Chari shrugged. "Yes, but unless they've got a good reason, they won't approach us. Especially not during the day. Slaves don't stop other estate's carts. None of their business. If an

Ashaki saw them doing it, they'd think it odd and investigate." She frowned. "Keeping you hidden has the added benefit of preventing confrontations like the one you had with Rasha. I have the authority to stop Traitors like her – don't worry, not all of us want you dead – but dealing with it would delay us. If other Traitors do suspect you're in here, they'll rightly assume it wouldn't be without the knowledge of other Traitors. This is not something you could ever arrange on your own."

"And let's not forget the people searching for Lorkin," Tyvara added. "Ambassador Dannyl and the king's representative, Ashaki Achati."

"Those two?" Chari waved a hand dismissively. "We've arranged for them to be sent off track, next time they go snooping around an estate." She smiled. "They could ride past us and never know we're here." She looked up at the bales above them. "Though, it can get a bit stuffy on hot days. Good thing you two had a bath last night, eh?"

Lorkin nodded and looked down at himself. The last of the dye had washed off his skin. He patted the clean slave wrap. "Thank you for the new clothes, too."

She looked at him and grimaced. "We'll have you out of them and into proper clothes soon."

"I never thought I'd say it, but I miss my Guild robes," he lamented.

"Why didn't you like them before?"

"Because every magician wears them. It gets a bit boring. The only change you get is when you graduate from a novice to a magician – unless you become one of the Higher Magicians, and most of them only wear a different colour sash."

"A novice is a student, right? How long do they stay novices for?"

"All new entrants to the Guild are novices. They spend about five years in the University before they graduate."

"So what sorts of magic do you learn at the University?"

"At first a range of things," he told her. "Magic, of course, but also non-magical studies like history and strategy. Most of us turn out to be better at something, and eventually we get to choose which of the three disciplines we'll follow: Healing, Warrior Studies or Alchemy."

"What did you choose?"

"Alchemy. You can tell which of us are Alchemists because we wear purple. Healers wear green and Warriors wear red."

Chari frowned. "What do Alchemists do?"

"Everything that Healers and Warriors don't do," Lorkin explained. "Mainly it involves magic but sometimes not. Ambassador Dannyl, the magician I came here with and am supposed to be assisting, is a historian, which doesn't involve magic at all."

"Can you choose two disciplines? Be an Alchemist and a Warrior – or an Alchemist and a Healer? Or—"

"We already know this, Chari," Tyvara interrupted.

Lorkin turned to regard her. She looked at him apologetically. "We're taught about the Guild along with the culture of many other lands during our training," she told him.

"Yes, but I didn't pay much attention at the time," Chari replied. "It's so much more interesting when it comes from an actual Kyralian magician."

Lorkin turned back to find her looking at him expectantly. "You were saying?" she prompted.

He shook his head. "No, we can't choose more than one discipline, but we all get a basic education in the three."

"So you can Heal?"

"Yes, but not with the skill and knowledge of a fully trained Healer."

Chari opened her mouth to ask another question, but Tyvara cut in before she could speak.

"You can ask questions in return," she told Lorkin. "Chari may not be able to answer some of them, but if you let her do all the asking she'll interrogate you all the way to the mountains."

He looked at Tyvara in surprise. Throughout their journey from Arvice she had been reluctant to answer his questions. At his stare, her lips pressed into a thin line and she shifted her gaze to Chari. He turned to look at the other woman. Chari was regarding Tyvara with amusement.

"Well, then," she said, turning to Lorkin. "What would you like to know?"

Though there were hundreds of things he wanted to know about the Traitors and their secret home, and Chari seemed much more receptive to questions, he suspected that Tyvara's habit of secrecy would soon have her stopping him and Chari talking at all. Was there anything he could safely ask about the Traitors, when so much information about them was secret?

I definitely shouldn't ask how they block mind-reading. Though I still suspect it involves a process similar to making a blood gem. Suddenly he remembered the references to a storestone in the records he'd read for Dannyl.

Was there any risk in mentioning the storestone? It wasn't as if he knew where to find it, or how to make one, so he wouldn't be putting a weapon into the Traitor's hands if he talked about it.

"Remember how I said that Ambassador Dannyl is a historian?" he asked.

Chari nodded.

"He's writing a history of magic. We've both done a bit of research here in Sachaka. Dannyl is more interested in filling the gaps of our history – how the wasteland was created, or when and how Imardin was destroyed and rebuilt. I'm more interested in how old kinds of magic worked."

He paused to gauge their reaction. Chari was watching him intently, while Tyvara regarded him with one eyebrow raised, which he took to indicate interest and a little surprise.

"When I was taking notes for Dannyl I found a reference to an object called a storestone," he continued, "that was kept in Arvice after the Sachakan War. It was clearly a thing of great power. It was lost a few years after the war – apparently stolen by a Kyralian magician. Do you know anything about it?"

Chari looked at Tyvara, who shrugged and shook her head.

"I don't know about that one, but I know a bit about store-stones," Chari told him. "Anyone would guess from the name that they are stones that store power. Which would be very useful. But they're rare. So rare that individual stones were once given names and their histories recorded as if they were people. All the ones we've heard of were destroyed long ago. It's probably over a thousand years, probably more, since the last one existed. If this storestone existed just after the Sachakan War, it is the most recent record of one. So you didn't know about it until recently?"

He shook his head.

She looked thoughtful. "Then either the thief hid it much too effectively, or it was broken. You said Imardin was destroyed and rebuilt?"

"Yes."

"Breaking a storestone is supposed to be dangerous. It releases the power within it in an uncontrolled way. Maybe that's what destroyed Imardin."

Lorkin frowned. "I suppose that's possible." He considered the idea. *I've always doubted that the Mad Apprentice could have been powerful enough to cause that much devastation, but what if he had the storestone?*

"We could ask the record keepers at Sanctuary," Chari said. "About older storestones, that is. I doubt they know anything about Imardin's history."

"Queen Zarala might," Tyvara said.

Chari's eyebrows rose. "I suppose if she lets him into the city, she'll want to check him out."

"She will." Tyvara eyed him with a strange, smug amusement. "Definitely."

Chari chuckled and turned to Lorkin. "Are you sure you want to come to Sanctuary?"

"Of course."

"Tyvara has told you that it's run by women, hasn't she? Men can't go bossing people about. Even magicians like you."

He shrugged. "I have no desire to boss anyone about."

She smiled. "You're such a reasonable man. I always thought Kyralians were arrogant and dishonest. I guess you can't all be the same. Tyvara wouldn't be taking you there if you were. And it's so sweet of you to come all this way and risk your life for Tyvara."

"Well, she did save my life."

"That's true." Chari reached out and patted his arm lightly. "Honourable and good-looking. I reckon you'll do well. My people will change their minds about Kyralians once they meet you."

"Yes, in no time we'll be exchanging gifts and swapping recipes," Tyvara muttered dryly.

Lorkin turned to look at her. She met his eyes briefly, then looked away, frowning. *She's not happy about something*, he thought. His heart skipped a beat. *Does she think Chari is going to betray us?*

"So tell me more about the Guild," Chari said behind him.

Tyvara rolled her eyes and sighed. Relief and amusement replaced apprehension. She was simply irritated by Chari's chatter. *Well, I hope that's it. I wish I could talk to her.* They'd not had a private moment together since Chari had found them.

He felt a stab of frustration. *I wish I could talk to many people. Mother and Dannyl for a start.* He thought of the blood gem still hidden in the spine of his notebook, tucked into his clothing. He'd had no chance to use it without revealing it to Tyvara. And now Chari was with them, there would be even less opportunity to use it. Perhaps he should have let Tyvara know he had it. *But it is my only link to the Guild. If I'm going to chance losing it, I must wait until the risk is unavoidable. And if I'm going to negotiate any sort of trade or alliance between the Guild and Traitors, I'll need a way to communicate between them.*

In the meantime, he might as well do his best to establish good relations between his country and the Traitors. Turning back to Chari, he smiled.

"More about the Guild? What would you like to know?"

CHAPTER 24

THE ALLIES YOU NEED

Sunny House was living up to its name. Warm sunlight bathed the garden and ruins, setting the more colourful flowers glowing in a sea of green vegetation. Skellin was waiting for Cery in the same shelter they had met in last time, his guard standing nearby.

Gol stopped, as far from the shelter as the other guard was. Cery walked on, resisting the urge to turn and look behind, but not because of his friend and bodyguard. As always, he'd arranged for some of his people to follow and watch, ready to help if he needed them, or warn of approaching danger. He called them his "shadow guard". Only this time there was a new face among the familiar ones.

Anyi. She was learning fast. She was quick and agile, and a bit too reckless at times. It had turned out though that the risks she took were more often out of ignorance than foolishness, and she was taking in his and Gol's instruction with reassuring enthusiasm and intelligence. Ordering her to follow and watch was the safest way to let her feel she was doing the job she wanted, without risking revealing her identity to anyone or putting her in real danger.

Yet the streets they'd passed through were never completely

safe, and he couldn't help worrying that some stupid thug would try something with her, and it would lead to a fight.

As Cery reached the shelter, Skellin rose to greet him.

"What do you have to tell me, friend?" the other Thief asked.

"Some news I heard the other day."

The story of the rot-seller and his foreign, female helper brought a frown to the man's exotic face. Cery lied about the source of the information, saying that it was a washerwoman who'd overheard the conversation. Better to keep Anyi's name out of this.

"Hmm," was all Skellin said. He looked displeased. Perhaps even angry.

"I also informed my friend that you would like to meet her," Cery added. "She agreed to it."

Skellin's gaze lightened and he straightened his shoulders. "Did she?" He rubbed his hands together and smiled. "Well, that's something to look forward to. As for your rather bad news ... I will look into it." He sighed. "It does not look good, does it? First she is seen in my territory, now she is working for my rot-sellers."

"Unless they're someone else's rot-sellers."

The other Thief's mouth twitched into a crooked smile. "Which would make it even worse news. I'll let you know what I find out." His voice had gained a harder, almost threatening edge. *That's more like what I'd expect from a man with his power and trade*, Cery thought.

Cery nodded. They spoke polite farewells, parted and headed in different directions. *After all the effort I have to put into getting here, these meetings always feel too brief. But sitting and chatting to Skellin doesn't appeal either. I'm not sure why. Probably because I'm always waiting for him to try getting me to sell rot for him.*

Gol joined him and they set off into the city. Sunny House was several streets behind when a figure stepped out of a doorway and walked toward them. Cery tensed, then relaxed as he recognised Anyi, then tensed again as he realised she was disobeying his orders. She wasn't supposed to approach him until they were back at the hideout.

Maybe she needs to warn me of something.

Anyi nodded to him politely, her expression serious, then fell into step beside him.

"So," she said, her voice low. "You got a good reason to be working with the King of Rot?"

Cery glanced at her, amused. "Who calls him that?"

"Half the city," she replied.

"Which half?"

"The lower half."

"I'm from the lower half, so why haven't I heard of it?"

She shrugged. "You're old and out of touch. So. Have you got a good reason?"

"Yes."

They walked in silence for several paces.

"Because I hate that man," she added suddenly.

"Oh? Why is that?"

"We had no rot here until he came along."

Cery grimaced wryly. "If he hadn't brought it, someone else would have."

She scowled. "Why don't you sell it?"

"I have standards. Pretty low standards, but that's to be expected. I'm a Thief."

"There's a big difference between what he does and what you do."

"You have no idea what I do."

"That's true." She frowned. "And I'm not in a hurry to find out. But . . . why don't you deal in rot?"

He shrugged. "Rot makes people unreliable. If they lose interest in making a living they don't want loans. If they can't work they can't pay back the loans. If they're broke, they can't buy things. If they die they're no good to anyone. Rot isn't good for business – unless it *is* the business. And if it was no worse than bol I'd be lining up to trade in it."

Anyi nodded, then let out a long sigh. "It sure does make people unreliable. There was . . . I had a friend. We worked together, were going to . . . do things together. My friend helped me out when you told me I had to hide.

"But we started to run out of money a lot faster than we should have. I knew my friend took rot, only enough to relax and sleep. When it ran out, my friend disappeared off to get more. I went next door to talk to the neighbour's wife, so I was out when my friend returned. With two thugs. I heard them talking. My so-called 'friend' was going to sell me out."

Cery cursed. "Did he know why you were hiding?"

"Yes."

"So the thugs know, too."

"I guess so."

Cery glanced at Gol.

"They probably wanted to sell Anyi on to someone better positioned to use her against you," the big man said. "Her boyfriend will have only wanted fast money."

"So there are two thugs out there who know too much," Cery said. He turned to Anyi. "Would you like this former friend killed?"

She looked at him sharply. "No."

He smiled. "Would you mind if I had the thugs killed?"

Her eyes widened, then narrowed. "No."

"Good, because I would have them killed whether you minded or not, but I'd rather be certain we got the right ones, and that'll be easier if you can pick them for us."

She nodded. Then she looked at him sidelong. "You know, nobody uses that old slum slang any more. 'Pick' is so old-fashioned."

"I'm an old-fashioned kind of man." They turned into a wider street, which was full of vehicles and people and noise. He lowered his voice. "Just so you know, the reason for today's meeting is to find the person who you were hiding from."

Anyi paused in scanning the street to glance at him. "Guess that's a good reason to be talking to the King of Rot. Can I watch when you kill the murderer?"

"No."

"Why not?"

"Because I won't be killing her. I doubt I could if I tried."

"It's a woman? Why can't you kill her?" She sent him another quick look, this time full of confusion. He chuckled.

"Don't worry. I'll explain when the time is right."

I bet Regin wishes he was here, Sonea thought as the young female Healer was led to the front of the Guildhall. The woman wasn't one of the Healers who worked at the hospices, so Sonea did not know her well. Lady Vinara had explained that she was from one of the city's less powerful Houses – a younger daughter sent to the Guild in order to gain prestige, and Healing for the family without charge.

The Healer had been overheard relating how she had used magic for a smuggler, and, when the information had been reported, she'd been summoned to a Hearing by the Higher Magicians. Rumours claimed that the smuggler was her cousin.

It was the first time anyone had been accused of breaking the new rule against magicians working for criminals.

It's going to be interesting to see how the Higher Magicians deal with this. Regin will be itching to know what is decided. I expect he'll pay me a visit tonight, to find out the details.

She realised the prospect didn't bother her that much. Though she could never completely relax in Regin's company, he seemed genuinely concerned about the new rule and how it affected the welfare of magicians. And, of course, he was keen to find the rogue. But he didn't drone on about it, like some magicians might, and never outstayed his welcome.

Because he's a man who'd prefer to take action than whinge about something.

She stilled in surprise. Had she just found something admirable in Regin's character? Surely not.

Of the rogue, there had been no news. Most nights Sonea worked at the same hospice in Northside, knowing this would make it easier for a messenger from Cery to find her. But no messages had come since he'd visited personally to tell her he was enlisting the help of another Thief.

Below her, Administrator Osen turned to the Higher Magicians.

"Lady Talie is charged with breaking the new rule forbidding a magician to be involved in or benefit from criminal activity," he told them. "We are to decide if this is true and, if so, how she is to be punished." He turned to look at a pair of magicians standing to one side. "I call on Lord Jawen to speak as witness."

One of the pair, a middle-aged Healer, stepped forward. He was frowning and the way he was trying not to look at Lady Talie made it obvious that he was uncomfortable about speaking against her.

"Please tell us what you heard," Osen said.

The man nodded. "A few nights ago I was gathering cures from a storeroom when I heard voices at the rear of the room. One of the voices belonged to Lady Talie. I heard her say, quite clearly, that what was inside some boxes wasn't legal. Well, that attracted my attention, and I stopped to listen. She went on to say that she didn't want to know what was in them. That she moved them, Healed a man then went home." His frown deepened. "And that someone was stupid for thinking something so big and heavy could be moved by one man."

"What did you do then?" Osen asked.

Jawen grimaced. "I left the room and went on working. I needed time to think about what to do. A few hours later I decided I had to tell Lady Vinara what I'd heard."

"That is all you overheard?"

"Yes."

"Then that is all for now." As the man retreated to his former position, Osen turned to the young Healer. "Lady Talie, please come forward."

She obeyed. Her mouth was pressed into a thin line, and there was a crease between her brows.

"Please explain to us what Lord Jawen overheard."

Talie drew in a deep breath and let it out again before answering. "He has the gist of it," she said. "I did move a box that was probably full of illegal goods – though I don't know that for sure. When Lord Jawen overheard me, I was worried if this meant I'd broken a rule or law, and was asking a friend what she thought."

"How did you find yourself in a situation where you might question the legality of your actions?"

She looked at the floor. "I was tricked. Well, not tricked . . .

but I didn't feel like I could refuse." She paused to shake her head. "What I mean is, someone I wish I didn't know took me to that place where the boxes were, saying a person was hurt and needed my help. He wasn't lying, actually. One of the boxes had fallen on top of a man and his thigh bone had been crushed. I had to lift the box off him so I could Heal him. Once I'd done that they took me home."

Sonea felt a pang of sympathy. The young woman clearly could not have left the injured man in his predicament. She shouldn't have gone with the smuggler in the first place, of course, but she wasn't asked to do anything criminal. *Yet, while Healing isn't a criminal activity, moving a box of illegal goods might be considered so.*

"So your only action was to move one box and Heal a man?" Osen asked.

"Yes."

"And you don't know for sure that the goods inside were illegal."

She grimaced and shook her head. "No."

"Did you receive any payment for your help?"

"He tried to give me something but I refused to take it."

"Is that all you can tell us?"

She paused, then cast a doubtful glance at Lady Vinara. "I'd have Healed that man anyway. And moved the box off him. I couldn't have left him like that."

Osen nodded then turned to the Higher Magicians. "Any questions for Lady Talie or Lord Jawen?"

"I have one for Lady Talie. Has this man asked favours or services of you before?" Lord Garrel asked.

"No."

"What is your connection to him, then?"

Talie looked at Osen and bit her lip. "He has done work and favours for my family, though it was years ago before anyone knew he was involved in anything illegal."

"Could you take someone back to the place these goods were stored?"

"No. He made sure the carriage windows were covered. When we arrived the carriage was inside a big room. And even if I did know where it was, I doubt the goods are still there."

Sonea smiled at that. The young Healer was probably right. But by saying so, she had suggested she knew more about smuggling than a magician from a House ought to.

No more questions came, so Osen sent Lord Jawen and Lady Talie out of the hall. When they were gone, Lord Telano sighed.

"This is ridiculous," he said. "She only did what any Healer ought to do. She shouldn't be punished for that."

"She wasn't paid," Garrel added. "She didn't benefit from it. I see no wrongdoing here."

"The rule forbids involvement in criminal activity as well as benefiting from it," Vinara pointed out. "But I agree. Moving a box is hardly involvement in crime."

"Still, we ought to be discouraging magicians from having anything to do with such people," Lord Peakin said.

"Which, as we established recently, is too difficult to enforce and apparently unfair to some Guild members," Garrel reminded him.

"Has she clearly broken a rule?" Osen asked.

None of the magicians answered. Several shook their heads.

"Does anybody believe she should be punished?"

The question received the same response. Osen nodded. "Then, unless anybody disagrees with me, I will declare she has broken no rule. I will also let it be known that Lord Jawen acted correctly in reporting what he heard, and state that tests of the new rule are beneficial and to be encouraged. We don't want anyone taking today's decision as an indicator that doing favours for dubious characters will always be overlooked."

"Do you think Lady Talie would agree to identify this man and confirm his activities for the Guard?" Rothen asked, looking back at Lady Vinara.

"I imagine she would be reluctant," Vinara replied. "If he had enough influence to force her to this store, then he may have enough to prevent her speaking against him. I will ask her, but only if the Guard does require her help."

"If she agrees and a conviction is achieved, it will discourage criminals from taking advantage of magicians," Osen said. He called the young Healer back in and told her their decision. She looked relieved.

And perhaps a little annoyed to have been put through this, Sonea observed. Osen announced the meeting over and the Higher Magicians began to leave. As she reached the floor of the hall, she found Rothen waiting for her.

"What do you think?" he murmured to her.

"I think the new rule is going to be ineffective at keeping magicians and criminals apart," she replied.

"But in the past someone of her status would never have been reported, not even if what she'd done was clearly wrong."

"No, but there is nothing to stop that sort of bias returning as magicians realise the limitations of the new rule. I won't be convinced it's an improvement unless the degree of harassment of lower-class-origin magicians lessens."

"Do you think she would have helped the injured man if

there was no incentive to please the man who asked her to?"

Sonea considered the question. "Yes, though not without some disdain."

He chuckled. "Well, that's an improvement on the past anyway. Thanks to your hospices, it's no longer thought of as acceptable to deny Healing because the patient can't afford it."

She looked at him, surprised. "Things have changed that much? But surely Vinara hasn't stopped charging patients who come to the Healers' Quarters."

"No." He smiled. "It's more of an attitude change. It's not, well, *healerly* to ignore anyone you stumble upon who is in great need. That is, if they are injured or dying – not if they've got a hangover or the winter cough. It is as if the ideal for a Healer to aspire to is now someone who has Vinara's clever-ness and your compassion."

She stared at him in disbelief and dismay.

He laughed. "I'd love to come to the end of my life knowing I'd made a change for the good, but despite all my work I don't think I will. But now I see how uncomfortable it makes you, I wonder if I should be grateful for that."

"You *have* made a difference, Rothen," she protested. "I'd have never become a magician if it were not for you. And what is this talk of your life ending? It's going to be years – decades – before you need to start planning a gravestone to outdazzle everyone else's."

He grimaced. "A plain one will do just fine."

"That's good, because by then there'll be no gold left in the Allied Lands except what's on magicians' headstones. Now, that's enough talk of death. Regin is, no doubt, pacing outside my door wanting to know how we decided, and I'd like to get that little interview over with so I can get some sleep in before tonight's shift."

Nine men now rode on either side of Achati's carriage each day – four Sachakan magicians, their source slaves and one of the grey-skinned Duna tribesmen from the north, who had been hired as a tracker.

Dannyl had been acutely aware that these powerful men had left their comfortable homes and joined the search based on a mere guess that Lorkin and Tyvara were heading for the mountains, and that the Traitors would continue working toward the pair being captured. If he was wrong . . . it would be embarrassing at the least.

If the four magicians doubted Dannyl's reasoning, they hid it well. They and Achati had discussed their plans in a way that had included Dannyl, but made it clear he was not in charge. He decided it was best to accept that, to seek their advice on everything and go along with their plans, but always make it clear he was determined to find his assistant and would not easily be persuaded otherwise.

One had asked the Duna tribesman, Unh, if he thought Lorkin and Tyvara were heading toward the Traitor home. The man had nodded and pointed toward the mountains.

The tribesman rarely spoke, and if he did he used as few words as possible to get across his meaning. He wore only a skirt of cloth on top of which a belt was strapped, hung with little drawstring bags, strange carvings and a small knife in a wooden sheath. At night he slept outside, and though he accepted food brought to him by the slaves he never spoke to them or ordered them about.

I wonder if all his people are like this.

"What are you thinking?"

Dannyl blinked and looked at Achati. The Sachakan was regarding him thoughtfully from the opposite seat in the carriage.

"About Unh. He has so few possessions and seems to need so little. Yet he does not behave like a poor man or beggar. He is . . . dignified."

"The Duna tribe have lived the same way for thousands of years," Achati told him. "They are nomads, constantly travelling. I suppose you would learn to keep only what you most needed if you had to carry it all the time."

"Why do they travel so much?"

"Their land is constantly changing. Cracks open up and leak poisonous fumes, molten blackrock from the nearby volcanoes spills over the land or scorching ash falls on it. Every few hundred years or so my people have tried to take their lands, either by force or by establishing towns and claiming the land by settling on it. In the first case the Duna vanished into the dangerous shadows of the volcanoes, and in the latter they simply traded with the settlers and waited. It soon becomes clear that crops won't grow consistently and animals die there, and each time my people have abandoned the villages and returned to Sachaka. The Duna returned to their old ways and . . ." Achati stopped as the carriage turned, and looked out of the window. "Looks like we have arrived."

They passed low white walls, then a pair of open gates. As soon as the carriage stopped, Achati's slave opened the door. Following his companion out, Dannyl looked around at the estate courtyard and the slaves lying, face-down, on the dusty ground. The rest of the magicians, their slaves and the Duna tribesman dismounted, and Achati stepped forward to speak to the head slave.

I wonder how many of these slaves are Traitors, Dannyl thought. At each estate they'd stayed at, with the permission of the owners, the Sachakans had read the slave's minds. Many believed that some of the country estates run by slaves, and a few by Ashaki, were actually controlled by Traitors, and were secret training places for spies.

This estate was run by an Ashaki. Dannyl's helpers had decided it was the safest one in this area to investigate. Even so, the thought that they might be in a place effectively controlled by Traitors sent a small shiver of excitement and fear down Dannyl's spine. If the slaves were all Traitors, did that mean they were also magicians? If they were, they outnumbered the visitors.

But even if they were all spies and black magicians, they would need a strong reason to attack a group of visiting Ashaki. The inevitable retaliation would force them to abandon their hold on the estate.

The head slave took them all to the Master's Room. The Ashaki owner, an old man with a limp, greeted them warmly. When they explained why they were there, and that they needed to read the minds of his slaves, he agreed reluctantly.

"It is likely there are Traitors among my slaves," he admitted. "Considering how close we are to the mountains. But they seem to have a way of hiding it from their thoughts." He shrugged, suggesting that he'd given up on finding them.

After an hour, all the slaves but a few field workers had been read. The Ashaki visitors retired to the guest rooms, where they lounged on cushions and discussed what they had learned, after first sending away the slaves sent to attend to them.

395

"A female slave from another estate visited last night," one of the Ashaki said. "She wanted food for four people."

Another nodded. "A lone woman was seen arriving and leaving by one of the field workers. She took food to a stock cart."

"We heard about this stock cart last night," Achati said. "Is it the same one? Is it unusual for a cart to be travelling this way?"

"It's not unusual for more prosperous estates to sell feed to less fertile ones at the foot of the mountains."

"They are in the cart," stated a new voice.

All looked up to see Unh standing in the doorway. He looked oddly out of place indoors, Dannyl noted. *Like a plant which you know will die from lack of sunlight.*

"A slave told me," the man said. He turned and walked away.

The Ashaki exchanged thoughtful looks. None of them questioned Unh's claim, Dannyl noted. *What reason would the tribesman have to lie? He is being paid to find Lorkin and Tyvara.*

Achati turned to Dannyl. "You were right, Ambassador. The Traitors do want us to find them, and they have finally given us directions."

CHAPTER 25

THE MESSENGER'S NEWS

While not as sturdy as the boots the Guild had provided for Lorkin all his life, the simple leather shoes slaves wore made little noise. The pack he carried had seemed too small and light to contain enough supplies at first, but the weight of it appeared to have grown since he'd first shouldered it. Tyvara had taken the lead, walking with steady, measured steps as the way became more steep and difficult. Chari followed behind Lorkin, uncharacteristically quiet.

They'd told him to avoid using magic in any obvious way, now that he was in territory patrolled by the Traitors. If they'd detected the barrier he'd raised both to protect himself and keep the air around him warm, they must have decided it wasn't an obvious use of magic, as neither had commented on it. Though they had assured him that the Traitors would not attack him while he was with two of their people, he wasn't about to gamble his life on it. Not after their encounter with Rasha.

They'd left the cart and the road a few hours before, and were travelling on foot across hills and valleys that grew rapidly more steep and stony. Neither woman spoke. Lorkin found he missed Chari's chatter and constant questions. Tyvara had grown more withdrawn the further they travelled. Her frowns made him feel vaguely guilty, but he wasn't sure why.

She's heading toward judgement by her people for killing one of their own, which wouldn't be happening if she hadn't saved my life.

Abruptly, Tyvara slowed and he pulled up short to avoid stumbling into her. Looking past her shoulder, he saw that, beyond a rise ahead, a group of people were standing before two small huts. They were watching as he, Tyvara and Chari approached.

The huts were small and old and circled by a low fence. From the eaves hung animal skins, and several hide stretchers leaned against the walls, but none of the people gathered outside looked like hunters. All wore simple clothing made of fine cloth. Most were women. He noted two men standing among them and felt a mild surprise. After all that Tyvara and Chari had said about their people, he'd almost come to expect to see no men at all.

A hundred or so paces from the waiting group, Tyvara stopped. She turned to look at Lorkin, frowning as she considered something.

"I can speak for you, if you want," Chari offered.

Tyvara scowled at her. "I can speak for myself," she snapped. "Stay here." Turning on her heel, she stalked toward her people, leaving Chari and Lorkin to exchange a look of bemusement.

"Have you two fallen out over something?" he asked.

Chari shook her head and smiled. "No. Why do you ask?"

"She hasn't behaved as if the two of you are friends."

"Oh, don't worry about that." Chari chuckled and turned to look at the group. "She's just jealous. And she doesn't know it."

"Jealous of what?"

Chari gave him a lofty look. "You really don't know? I've always wondered how it was that men in the rest of the world are in charge, when they're so perpetually thick."

He snorted softly. "And I'm curious to know how Traitor women stay in charge when they're just as inclined to communicate by indirect hints and innuendo as women everywhere else."

She laughed. "Oh, I like you, Lorkin. If Tyvara doesn't wake up to herself and—" A voice called out and she immediately grew serious. She gave him a crooked smile. "Looks like it's time to introduce you."

He followed her across the remaining distance to the waiting Traitors. Tyvara watched them, her brow creased with a worried frown. Chari did not look at her friend, but fixed her attention on a middle-aged woman with grey streaks in her long hair.

"Speaker Savara," she said respectfully. She gestured gracefully toward Lorkin. "Lorkin, assistant to Guild Ambassador Dannyl, of the land of Kyralia."

The woman nodded. "*Lord* Lorkin," she said. "If I am correct."

"You are, indeed," he replied, inclining his head. "An honour to meet you, Speaker Savara."

Savara smiled. "It is polite of you to say so, after all you have been through." She drew in a deep breath. "First, I wish to convey from the queen, but also heartfelt from myself, an apology for the disruption, fear and threat to your life that you have endured due to the Traitors. Whether Tyvara's actions are deemed justifiable or not, you have been put through a great deal and for that we feel responsible."

It did not seem like a good moment to be defending Tyvara, so he nodded. "Thank you."

"If you wish to rejoin the Guild Ambassador, we can have you safely delivered into his protection. I can also arrange for guides to take you back to the Kyralian border. Which would you prefer?"

"Again, thank you," Lorkin replied. "I am aware that there will be a trial to judge Tyvara's actions and I would like to speak in her defence, if that is possible."

Savara's eyebrows rose, and a murmur of surprise and interest went through the rest of the gathering.

"That would mean taking him to Sanctuary," someone said.

"The queen would never agree to it."

"Unless we hold the trial outside Sanctuary."

"No, that would be too dangerous. If there was an ambush we'd lose too many valuable people."

"Nobody is going to ambush us," Savara said firmly.

She looked back at her people and they fell silent. Turning back to Lorkin, she considered him thoughtfully. "It is an admirable thing you wish to do. I will think on it. How much does the Guild know about us?"

Lorkin shook his head. "Nothing. Well, they've heard nothing from me, anyway. I haven't communicated with anyone there."

"And what of the Guild magician here?" He has been following you since you left Arvice. With surprising accuracy."

"I haven't communicated with Dannyl either," Lorkin told her firmly. "But I'm not surprised he is searching successfully. He is clever and unlikely to give up." He paused as he realised the truth of his words. Was Dannyl smart and determined enough to follow him all the way to Sanctuary?

"He's had plenty of help from Traitors, no doubt," Tyvara muttered.

Savara looked at her. "You have explained the likely price for entering the city?"

Tyvara paused, then looked down. "No. I was hoping we'd find a way around that."

The Speaker frowned, then sighed and nodded. "I'll see what I can do. Rest and eat."

With that, the group scattered, some moving into the huts, some sitting on rough, narrow wooden benches that Lorkin had assumed were a crude fence. He, Chari and Tyvara moved to one of the seats and shrugged out of their packs. A young woman dressed as a slave brought them small cakes laced with tart berries. She smiled when he thanked her.

"Lorkin," Tyvara said.

He turned to her. "Yes?"

"You should take up Savara's offer. Go back to Kyralia."

"Not to Arvice?"

She shook her head. "I don't trust the . . . the other faction. They might try to kill you again."

"And how are you going to prove that they've tried it before?"

Her lips pressed into a thin line. "I'll let them read my mind."

He heard Chari draw in a sharp breath. "You can't," she hissed. "You promised the . . ." She looked at Lorkin, then bit her lip.

Tyvara sighed. "We'll find a way around it," she told Chari. She turned to Lorkin. "The price Savara spoke of . . . if you come to Sanctuary there's a good chance you won't be allowed to leave again. Would you be willing to stay there for the rest of your life?"

He stared at her in disbelief. *The rest of his life? Never see Mother or Rothen or his friends again?*

"You haven't told him this before?" Chari asked, her tone shocked and disbelieving.

Tyvara flushed and looked away. "No. I couldn't send him back to Arvice. Someone would have tried to kill him. I knew once I found someone from our faction he'd be safe."

"Faction?"

"Lorkin came up with the term. I mean those of us who agree with the queen, and Savara, on . . . most things."

Chari nodded. "Not a bad term, really." She looked at him. "We've been avoiding calling ourselves anything, because it would mean there was a split within the Traitors, and if we named the two sides it would only encourage people to, well, take sides." She turned to Tyvara. "They might not want Lorkin to stay, since he is one of the reasons for the split."

"Nobody from the other side will trust him enough to let him go once he knows the city's location. And few from our side will, either."

"Then we cover his eyes and make sure he can't find it again."

Tyvara sighed. "We all know how well that worked last time."

"Last time it was a Sachakan, and he was a spy," Chari pointed out. "Lorkin is different. And how is Sanctuary ever going to form alliances and trade with other nations if we never let visitors into and out of the city?"

Tyvara opened her mouth, then closed it again. "It's too soon for that," she said. "We can't even trust each other, let alone foreigners."

"Well, we have to start some time." Chari sniffed and looked away. "You bring him all this way, and now you want him gone. I think you're too scared of being responsible for someone."

Tyvara's head snapped up and she glared at her friend. "That's—" But she stopped herself. Her eyes narrowed. Rising, she stalked away, sitting down again several strides away. Chari sighed.

"Don't worry," she told Lorkin. "She isn't always this grumpy." She looked at him and smiled. "I mean it. When she's not worried silly, she's smart, funny and quite lovable. And apparently quite good under the rug, as we say here." She winked, then grew serious. "Though choosy. Not any and every man for our Tyvara. Don't worry about that."

He gazed at her in surprise at this sudden and unexpected flow of personal information, then looked down and hoped his amusement and embarrassment weren't obvious. *So, here's yet another way Traitor women are different to Kyralian women.* He thought back to some of the women he'd taken to bed over the last year. *Well, maybe not that different, but certainly more open about it.*

Though why Chari was trying to reassure him . . .

Suddenly, he understood what Chari had been hinting at. She thought there was something romantic going on between him and Tyvara. His heart skipped a beat. *Well, there has been, in a regretfully one-sided way.* Since he'd first met Tyvara he'd found her alluring and attractive. The night he'd nearly been murdered he'd thought it was her in his bed, and the thought had pleased him a great deal.

Chari seems to think it isn't one-sided. Is she right?

He stole a glance at Tyvara. She was standing again, staring in the direction she, Chari and he had arrived from, her brows knit with worry. He turned to see what she was looking at. Two women were running up the path. As they passed, Lorkin heard them panting with exertion.

They disappeared into a hut and a moment of tense silence followed as all watched and waited, then Savara strode out followed by a handful of Traitors and the two women. She said something and the globe lights immediately dimmed to a faint glow.

"We must all leave immediately," she said. Her eyes skimmed over the assembled faces and settled on Lorkin. "The magicians tracking Lord Lorkin are heading this way, and there are now six of them, including the Kyralian. Divide yourselves into three groups. Each will take a different route away from here. Tyvara, Lorkin and Chari, you should come with me."

Lorkin rose and hurried over to her. "If I talk with Ambassador Dannyl I am sure I can persuade him to call off the search."

She shook her head. "You may persuade him, but you won't persuade the others if they think they might catch us this time. There is also a man with them – a tracker – who might succeed where others have failed." She smiled grimly. "I am sorry. The offer is appreciated, but it is too great a risk."

Lorkin nodded. Around him people were hastily picking up and packing away all signs of their presence. One began to sweep the ground, but Savara stopped her.

"There's no point hiding all trace of ourselves. We want them to either split up or follow the wrong trail." She looked Lorkin up and down. "Find someone with similar sized feet as his and get them to swap shoes."

Soon the Traitors had formed three groups of near equal size. Savara ordered them to travel without hiding their trail until morning, then head for Sanctuary using the usual precautions. All murmured farewells to the other groups, then departed. Lorkin followed as Savara's group began to climb the steep side of the valley, his mind shifting between wondering if his suspicions about Tyvara were true, itching to know what Savara's decision would be, and worrying that Dannyl and the Sachakans would catch up with them.

And if they did, what would the Sachakans do? What would the Traitors do? Would it end in a fight? He didn't want anyone dying because of him. *Well, anyone else*, he amended.

If it came to a fight, what should he do? Would he have to choose between joining Dannyl in order to prevent a battle and siding with the Traitors so he could help save Tyvara from execution?

Too slow, Cery's twist did not bring him out of the way far enough or fast enough to avoid the knife pushing into his ribs. He heard Anyi give a little huff of triumph.

"Good," he said, resisting a smile as he let go of her and stepped away. "You've got the hang of it now."

She grinned and swapped the wooden practice knife back to her left hand.

"Though you aimed a little high," he told her. "You're used to practising with Gol, I suppose."

"I'd have still cut you," she pointed out.

"Yes, but your knife might have caught on my ribs." Cery patted his lower chest where her knife had pressed. "Which is not one of the five weak spots. Eyes, throat, belly, groin, knees."

"Sometimes it's better to smash an attacker's knees and run than try to stab him in the heart," Gol said. "The heart can be hard to reach. Ribs might skew your aim. If you miss, he can come after you. If you get his knees, he can't. And he mightn't be expecting it."

"A stab to the guts will kill slowly, too," Cery said. "Not much fun, but enough time to try and get you back for it."

"And you shouldn't kill unless ordered to," Gol added.

"I should get you practising with shorter people."

"And younger ones," Anyi said. Gol gave a snort, and she turned to him. "Come on. You're both not as fast as you used to be, and if anyone's gonna send somebody after you they're not going to get some old assassin out of retirement to give you a sporting chance."

Gol chuckled. "She's got a point."

A tapping came from the door and they all turned to face it. They were in one of the upper-storey rooms of a bolhouse Cery owned, known as the Grinder. It was a place where he could meet the people of his territory who had requested an audience. Business had to be maintained, and that meant making himself available now and then. As with all his places, there were plenty of escape routes.

Cery nodded to Gol, who strode over to open the door. The big man paused, then stepped aside. In the entrance stood a squat, solid man, who had worked for Cery for years.

"A messenger's here to speak to you," he said. "From Skellin."

Cery nodded. "Send him in."

Gol took up a position to the left of Cery, arms crossed in his typical protective pose. Anyi's eyes narrowed, then she walked past Cery to stand at his right. As he looked at her, she stared back defiantly, daring him to challenge her. He smothered a laugh.

"Did I say the lesson was over?" he asked, looking from her to Gol. His bodyguard blinked, then looked at Anyi. "Get back to work," Cery ordered.

He watched them walk back to where they had been practising. Gol said something, to which Anyi shrugged, then dropped into a fighting crouch. *Good*, Cery thought. *If Skellin's messenger reports that I have a new, female bodyguard, I may as well have him report on her skills as well. I can't hide her forever. If anyone picks that I'm keeping someone hidden they'll assume there's a reason and start asking questions.*

Still, his skin pricked as a figure moved into the doorway. It was one thing to know one's loved ones were in danger because of who you were, but quite another to actually put them in a position that involved no small amount of risk.

Skellin's messenger was lean and tall, with the constant tense poise of a runner. His eyes met Cery's and he nodded politely. Then his gaze snapped to Gol and Anyi, the latter having just launched herself in an attack. Gol countered it deftly, but she darted gracefully out of his reach.

As Cery had expected, a spark of interest lit the messenger's gaze, but there was more than just professional assessment in his expression. Suddenly Cery regretted having Anyi and Gol return to practising. It took a great effort to keep his face composed and posture relaxed.

"You have a message for me?" he asked.

"You are Cery of Northside?" the man asked, though his voice held no doubt. It was a formality.

"Yes."

"Skellin said to tell you that he has found the quarry and is setting a trap. If you bring your friends to the old butchery in Inner Westside when the sun sets tonight, they can take possession of their new pet."

Cery nodded. "Thank you. We'll be there. You may go."

The man gave a slight bow, then left. Gol walked over to the door and closed it, before turning to regard Cery soberly. "You've only got a few hours."

"I know." Cery frowned. "And my friend won't be at her place of employment yet."

"They'll send a message on to the Guild."

"The Guild?" Anyi repeated. She gave Cery a hard look. "What is going on? Is this the thing you couldn't tell me about yet?"

Cery and Gol exchanged a look. The bodyguard nodded once.

They'd discussed since the meeting with Skellin when to tell Anyi the whole story. If they told her about the rogue – and in particular that they suspected she was the Thief Hunter and the killer of his family – she'd want to come along and see the woman captured. If he ordered her to stay behind she would probably disobey him, figuring she'd wear whatever punishment he gave her for it. Assuming he discovered she had disobeyed him.

It wasn't that she made a habit of defying him, but with something this big she'd make an exception. He would too, in her place.

He could, instead, simply not tell her about the rogue, but there was still a good chance she'd slip away and follow him just to find out. Again, it was what he would have done.

So he and Gol had decided their only choice was to involve her in the capture by giving her a relatively safe job to do. Once again she would be one of his shadow guards. This time she would have to know the nature of the quarry they were chasing. There would be no rushing in to fight this enemy if things went wrong. Fighting magicians with knives was pointless and suicidal.

"Yes, the Guild. It is time you knew what we're dealing with," Cery told her. "There are three things you will learn from tonight: even the most powerful Thief has limitations, it pays to have friends in high places, and there are some things best left to magicians."

There was a long pause between when Sonea knocked on the door of Administrator Osen's office to when it finally swung open. Osen's gaze was slightly distracted as he ushered them in.

"Black Magician Sonea, Lord Rothen," he said hesitantly. "I've called you here because Ambassador Dannyl and the Sachakans who have volunteered to help him are close to catching Lord Lorkin and his abductors."

Sonea's heart stopped, then lurched into a racing beat. She opened her mouth to ask him . . . what? What to ask first? Where was Lorkin? Did the Sachakans understand that they weren't to kill him?

"How long until they do?" Rothen asked.

"Dannyl can't say exactly. Half an hour. Maybe less. You had better make yourselves comfortable."

Osen sat down behind his desk, and she and Rothen used magic to move two of the room's armchairs to the front. Osen's gaze slid to the distance.

He is linked to Dannyl by a blood ring, she guessed. *What can he see?* She wanted to demand that he describe everything he saw in detail, but instead took a deep breath and let it out slowly.

"You said 'abductors'," she pointed out. "Is there more than one?"

Osen paused and his gaze shifted to somewhere far beyond the office walls.

"Yes. Several Traitors. Unh thinks eight."

"Unh?"

The Administrator's gaze focused on her with difficulty. "A Duna tribesman. He's tracking for them. Apparently he's quite good at it. Wait . . ." His expression shifted and became eager. "They got a look at them. Just a glimpse . . ."

He was silent, staring at the desk without seeing it for a painfully long moment. Sonea realised she was gripping the arms of her chair. She forced herself to let go and folded her hands in her lap instead.

"Ah." Osen's shoulders dropped with disappointment.

"What?" Rothen asked. Sonea glanced at him. He was leaning forward, his eyes wide.

Osen shook his head. "He's not there. Not in that group. They're following the wrong trail – wrong people." He sucked in a breath, held it, then sighed. "There were three trails, apparently. They thought he was with one of them, but they were wrong. They're going to have to go back and try another trail."

Sonea let out a sigh of frustration. Rothen groaned and leaned against the back of his chair. Silence filled the room. Nobody spoke. Osen's gaze had shifted to the distance again. Rothen was rubbing his forehead.

Then all jumped at a loud knock at the door.

Osen waved a hand. The door opened and a Healer stepped inside. The young man looked at Sonea, smiled and hurried toward her, holding out a slip of paper.

"Forgive the interruption, Administrator," he said. "I have an urgent message for Black Magician Sonea."

She took the paper from him and nodded in reply as he bent into a shallow bow. He hurried from the room. When the door closed she looked down at the note, then unfolded it.

Your friend in the city says his friend has found the thing you're after. You have to be at the old butcher's building in Inner Westside by sunset. Bring your other friend.

If she'd been in a better mood she would have laughed at the vague and rather silly language. But this was the last thing she needed. How could she race off into the city to catch the rogue when Lorkin could be found at any moment?

A hand passed before her eyes and plucked the message from her. Her heart skipped, but it was only Rothen. He scanned the note, looked at her and narrowed his eyes in thought.

"How long until they backtrack to where the trail split?"

"A few hours," Osen intoned, his gaze still fixed on far-away things.

"And then a few more before they travel as far down the next one. Shall we leave you to follow their progress, and return later?"

"Of course." Osen snapped out of his trance and looked at them in turn. "I'm sorry. These blood stones are remarkably involving of the attention. I should have Dannyl take off the ring until he is close to finding Lorkin again." He waved a hand. "Go."

Rothen rose, then looked at Sonea. She stood up reluctantly. *How can I leave now? But it'll be hours before they catch up with Lorkin. I can't sit here waiting while the rogue escapes. And if we don't turn up and Cery confronts the rogue by himself, he might get hurt.*

She forced herself to move, following Rothen to the door, then out into the corridor. Long shadows striped the Guild grounds outside the University doors. The Healer was waiting for her, smiling nervously as she noticed him. Rothen beckoned to the man.

"Has anyone contacted Lord Regin?" he murmured.

The young man frowned and shook his head. Rothen turned to Sonea. "Sunset is not far off. You had better go now. I'll find Regin and send him to meet you at the hospice."

Hospice. Of course. I can't go straight to Inner Westside. Must maintain the ruse, in case this doesn't work. That means we really don't have much time . . .

The urgency of their mission seized her at last, and she shooed Rothen away. "Tell him to go straight there." She turned to the Healer. "Did you come by carriage?"

He nodded. "It's waiting outside for you."

"Good man." She smiled and rubbed her hands together. "Let's go, then."

CHAPTER 26

A LONG NIGHT

It was Unh who had noticed the scatter of stalks beside the road, which he said might be feed that had spilled from a cart when it had stopped there. The local Ashaki hadn't wanted to investigate, eager to chase after the cart, but Achati had sided with the tribesman, jokingly reminding them that Unh hadn't been hired so that they had someone to ignore.

The tribesman found the tracks of three people wearing slave shoes – a man and two women – leading away from the road.

"I see this print at the last place," Unh told them, pointing to a slight depression in the sandy ground. "The shape is longer and thinner than Sachakan foot, and there a hole under the heel."

They had all been impressed with Unh. Now, hours later, they were not so pleased with him. After finding the tracks, they'd sent the carriages and horses on to the next estate with Achati's driver, and continued on foot. At the tanner's huts, they'd followed one of the three clear trails leading away. They'd been in a hurry because the sun was dipping toward the horizon, but it had made the tracker's job harder. Long shadows, then twilight, made it difficult for him to make out the finer details of the footprints and other signs he was following. The Sachakans resisted creating a light for him, as it would make them visible from a distance in this exposed landscape. Nobody had been concerned, however, as the trail was still clear enough for them to follow it.

It was with a surge of triumph that Dannyl had spotted the figures in the distance. But the feeling hadn't lasted long. It turned to dismay as he realised Lorkin was not among them.

Much cursing had followed. The Traitors they'd tracked were too far ahead to be caught and questioned, because doing so would take too much time, so Dannyl and his Sachakan helpers had hurried back to the huts. By then it was night, and creating a light for the tracker was unavoidable. To direct the light where he needed it they had to follow closely behind Unh, and several times they wound up trampling the signs he was looking for. It made the process of picking up the trail slow and difficult, so when Unh had lost the trail completely a few hours later, Achati decided they should camp for the night and continue after the sun rose.

The slaves dropped their burdens with obvious relief. But though they were obviously exhausted, their masters were more demanding than usual. The Ashaki groaned and complained, and had their slaves rub their legs and feet. At first Dannyl was puzzled, then he remembered that the one kind of magic the Sachakans didn't possess knowledge of was Healing. While he had been soothing away the aches and pains and blisters of walking, they had no choice but to suffer.

I hadn't realised how much of an advantage it is to us. It could be a significant one, if our countries were ever to fight each other, or another enemy. If we both have to trek to meet our foe, the Sachakans will be the only ones sore and tired from the effort.

414

The Duna tribesman abruptly rose and announced he was going to try locating the trail again. Achati looked at the others, saying that someone should go with him to keep them both shielded. Dannyl stood up.

"I'll go. Unless you need me here?"

The magician shook his head. "Go. Keep your shield strong and don't go too far. The Traitors may be watching us. They may not dare to kill anyone, but if they injured one or some of us we'd have to split up or slow down."

Following Unh out of the camp, Dannyl created a globe light and set it hovering ahead of the man. He stayed several paces back and tried to step wherever the tribesman did so that he couldn't possibly be trampling on any tracks but Unh's. The distance between them made keeping both within a shield challenging.

The Sachakans had camped in a bowl-like hollow between two ridges. Unh made his way around the shorter arm of one ridge, keeping his eyes to the ground. After several paces he squatted and stared at the ground, then looked up at Dannyl and beckoned.

Dannyl closed the distance between them, then looked where Unh was pointing.

"See here," the man said. "That stone has been stepped upon, then pushed back into the dirt. You can see the direction the stepper was going by the way there is a groove at the front, and a tiny mound at the back."

It was rather obvious now that the man had pointed it out.

"How do you know it was a human and not an animal?"

Unh shrugged. "I don't. It would have to be a big animal though, and most of those were hunted out long ago."

He rose and went looking for more signs of passage. Dannyl

415

followed, concentrating on holding the shield, directing the globe light, and walking only where the tribesman did. They stopped again and again, Unh pointing out a thread of cloth caught on one of the few stunted trees, some human hair, and some distinct footprints in a sandy area. Then he spent a long time examining the ground, and Dannyl used the opportunity to look around, trying not to imagine figures watching them in the darkness. He glanced to the side and felt a shiver run down his spine.

"Is that a cave?" he asked, pointing at a crack in the steep slope to one side.

Unh rose and approached the gash of darkness in the rock slowly. He continued to scan the ground, his head nodding from it to the crack and back again.

"Nobody went this way," he said. He touched the side of the opening. "This happen not long ago."

He beckoned and Dannyl hurried over. They peered into the darkness. Dannyl drew magic and created another light, which he sent inside. Stones filled the base of the crack, sloping downward then levelling off. The sides of the opening continued for a short way, then ended in darkness.

"There a bigger space inside. Want to look?" Unh asked.

Dannyl glanced back toward the camp, which was not far out of sight, then nodded. Unh grinned, an expression at odds with his usual dignified aloofness. A thrill of eagerness went through Dannyl, not unlike the excitement he'd felt so long ago when exploring the Allied Lands with Tayend.

Unh gestured to the opening. "You first."

Dannyl chuckled. Of course. He was far more likely to survive if they happened to surprise a wild animal, or Traitors.

The floor was loose gravelly rock, and he half slid down

into the space. Looking around, he saw only darkness and the hint of walls all around. He paused as Unh slid down to join him, then he increased the strength of the light . . .

. . . and ducked as walls of glittering gemstones shone back at him. A sound echoed in the room, and he realised he had let out a wordless exclamation of fear.

No relentless strikes came. He was breathing heavily, his heart hammering in his chest.

"You seen something like this before," Unh stated. He was regarding Dannyl with interest.

Dannyl looked at him. "Yes." No point denying it. His reaction had been nothing less than obvious.

"This not dangerous."

The man spoke with certainty and authority. Now it was Dannyl's turn to look at his companion with curiosity.

"You know what this is?"

Unh nodded and looked around, his expression knowing and happy. "Yes. These stones have no power. They have not been raised to have power. They are natural. Safe."

"So . . . the stones in the place I was in before were made to be dangerous?"

"Yes. By people. Where was this place?"

"In Elyne. Beneath an ancient ruined city."

Unh nodded again. "A people once lived in the mountains here. They knew the secret of the stones. But they are gone. All things end." He shook his head. "Not all," he corrected. "A few secrets Duna kept."

"You *know* how to make gemstones with magic in them?"

"Not me. Some of my people. Trusted ones." His expression darkened. "And Traitors. Long ago they came and made a pact. But they broke it and stole the secrets. That is why I

417

help the Sachakans, even after what they do to my people. The Duna not forgiven the Traitors."

"Do the Traitors know how to make caves like the one in Elyne?" Dannyl asked. If he'd known that, he'd never have entered this one like some child exploring for fun.

"No," Unh replied. "Nobody knows that. Even the Duna forget some things."

"That's one thing probably best forgotten."

"Yes." Unh grinned. "I like you, Kyralian."

Dannyl blinked in surprise. "Thank you. I like you, too."

The man turned away. "We get back to camp now. I found trail."

It was much harder to get out of the cave than into it, with the stones sliding out from under their feet, but the tribesman set his toes into the rough surface of one side of the crack and climbed out that way. Dannyl created a small disc of magic under his feet and levitated out. Unh seemed to find this very funny.

The walk back to camp was much quicker, since Unh no longer needed to stop and examine the ground. Dannyl was relieved to find that the magicians had let their slaves go to sleep, sprawled on the ground behind them. They were drinking some sort of liquor from the ornate cups each had brought with them. Dannyl accepted a measure of the fiery liquid. He only half listened to their conversation about an Ashaki's son who had no skill as a trader and was going to ruin his family.

His mind kept returning to the fear that had coursed through him when he'd seen the walls of gemstones. *I never even thought to wonder the worth of them as mere jewels, even after I calmed down. Hmm. I don't think I did last time, either. But then, I was rather distracted . . .*

418

A memory flashed through his mind of waking up utterly drained of power. Of Tayend, and the realisation of what he'd been hiding from himself for most of his life. That he was a "lad". That he loved Tayend.

He felt a wave of sadness. *A pity we had to change so much. Instead of growing around each other like that romantic notion of couples being like entwined trees, we became uncomfortably tangled, competing for water and soil.*

He snorted softly. Such sentimental imagery was more the taste of Tayend's poet friends. He looked at the Sachakans and Unh. They'd find such notions foolish, though in quite different ways.

Do the Traitors know of the cave? Unh said the crack was recent. I doubt the Sachakans do. From what I recall, the Duna's main trade is selling gemstones. I wonder if Unh plans to come back with some of his people and harvest them before the Traitors discover them.

Then he recalled what Unh had said. The Duna knew how to make gemstones with magical properties. It was hard to imagine that a people like his could have access to such rare knowledge, yet live a simple, nomadic life.

Maybe it's not all that simple, after all.

How was it that the Traitors could have such power, but have never left their hidden city? Clearly there were limitations to the gemstones. Maybe they had to be fixed to a surface, in a cave, in great numbers, in order to be an effective weapon.

The records of the storestone did not say it was fixed to anything. If it had been, removing it would have made it worthless. So why bother chasing after the thief?

Lorkin would be very interested to know what he'd learned tonight. But Lorkin was with the Traitors . . .

. . . and the Traitors had knowledge of magical gemstones.

Dannyl caught his breath.

Suddenly he understood something that was going to cause him considerable awkwardness with the men he was with, the Sachakan king, the Guild and, not the least, Lorkin's mother.

Suddenly he understood there was a good chance Lorkin did not want to be found.

Not long after dawn, Savara had called a halt on a high, exposed ridge. The way had grown steeper and more rugged through the night, and all of the Traitors in their group had used tiny, faint lights hovering close to the ground to illuminate the way. After posting guards and sending out scouts, she told the rest of the group to settle just beyond the crest of the ridge, out of sight, and try to sleep.

"Our pursuers are several hours behind us now," she said. "They'll have to stop to rest, too, and they're not as used to moving about in such rough territory as we are. We'll continue on after sunset."

The rest of the Traitors wore small packs like the ones Lorkin, Tyvara and Chari had carried since leaving the cart. He now discovered what the rolled-up bundles of thick fabric were. They were unrolling them for use as a mattress. He'd assumed they were some sort of blanket. But it made sense they'd carry a mattress over a blanket: magicians could heat the air but they couldn't make the ground any softer.

Certainly not around here, he thought as he stretched out next to Chari and Tyvara. The area was all rock and stones, with the occasional twisted tree. Hearing footsteps, he turned to see Savara approaching and quickly got up again.

"I've considered your proposal and consulted with the queen," she told him. *Via a blood ring, no doubt*, he thought.

"If you still wish to accompany us to Sanctuary she will allow it. But she will not be the one to decide if you will be permitted to leave again. That decision will be made by vote, which makes it likely you will have to stay. Many Traitors will fear you will reveal the location of the city if we let you go."

Lorkin nodded. "I understand."

"Take some time to think about it," she said. "But I will need your decision before we leave tonight."

She moved away, climbing to the top of the ridge and sitting in the shadow of a large boulder. *Keeping watch*, Lorkin decided. He lay down again, despite knowing he wouldn't be able to sleep with such a decision to make.

"Nobody would think badly of you if you went home," a voice said nearby.

He rolled over to see Chari watching him, one arm beneath her head as a pillow.

"This other faction – the one that sent someone to kill me – will they try it again if I go to Sanctuary?" he asked.

"No," she answered without hesitation. "One of our queens decided long ago that there can be no such thing as assassination in Sanctuary. I think a few of our people decided that if it was a good political tool outside of Sanctuary it would be so inside it too. In Sanctuary, murder is murder, except when it's execution, which is the punishment for murder."

Lorkin nodded. *Which is what Tyvara is facing.*

"Is there any chance a Traitor will want to read my mind?"

"They'll all want to get a look inside that head of yours. But they aren't allowed to unless you agree to it. Forcibly reading someone's mind is also a serious crime. It would make us too much like the Ashaki."

421

"So if I refuse . . . surely they will want to check if I've got good intentions before letting me into the city."

"They'd love to. But laws are laws. Some of them are a little crazy. Like how the queen can decide if an outsider is allowed into the city, but not if they can leave again."

"If I can't leave, what will be expected of me then?"

"To follow our laws, of course." She shrugged. "Which includes contributing to the work of the city. You can't expect to be fed and have a bed to sleep on if you don't help out in some way."

"Sounds fair."

Chari smiled. "Any more questions?"

"No." Lorkin rolled onto his back. "Not yet, anyway."

He'd done a lot of thinking since they'd joined Speaker Savara and her companions and learned that he might not be able to leave Sanctuary. In that time he'd listed reasons why he should and shouldn't go there. The list of reasons not to was short:

I came to Sachaka to assist Dannyl, not go off on adventures of my own – even if those adventures might lead to a beneficial alliance for the Guild.

He didn't have the authority to negotiate an alliance. But he only needed to get the Traitors to the point of wanting to negotiate and then arrange for a Guild magician with the authority to meet them. Like Dannyl.

Mother will not like it.

But this was a decision for him to make, for himself. Still, thinking of her he felt both longing and guilt. He did not like the thought of never seeing her again. Or never speaking to her. He still hadn't had a chance to use her blood ring without revealing its existence to anyone. If he entered

Sanctuary, would he be searched? Would the Traitors take the ring off him if they found it? If they were so suspicious of him that they wouldn't let him leave Sanctuary, they certainly wouldn't want him using a magical device that allowed him to convey everything he knew to the Guild.

He was beginning to think that he should use it soon, even if just to reassure his mother. And then find a place to hide it.

Retaining the ring is another reason not to go to Sanctuary. It's only a small reason, though. And one I can remove.

There were many more reasons to go than not, however. First, there was Tyvara. He could not contemplate abandoning her. If he didn't speak on her behalf at the trial, she might be executed. She had saved his life, and might die for it. Which would make it entirely his fault.

Even if I knew she would be fine, the thought of never seeing her again . . . His chest tightened and his heart began to beat faster. He frowned. *There is more to this than an obligation to help her. I like her. A lot. I couldn't abandon her, even if she doesn't have the same feelings for me.*

He thought about what Chari had hinted at. "*Not any and every man for our Tyvara. Don't worry about that.*" The woman believed that Tyvara found him attractive. But Tyvara wasn't behaving that way. She seemed determined to repel him, frowning and scowling when he talked to her, and trying to talk him into going home. Each time she did, Chari assured him that Tyvara felt guilty for not telling him earlier about the price for entering Sanctuary, and didn't want him sacrificing his freedom for her sake.

But if I let her talk me into going home, she'd have not only saved me, but possibly sacrificed her own life for me. I can't let that happen.

Tyvara wasn't the only reason he ought to go to Sanctuary. To have come so far, got so close to these Traitors, and not attempt to set up negotiations between them and the Guild would be a waste of a great opportunity. He doubted that strangers often had the chance to enter Sanctuary and make such proposals. Even if the Traitors didn't like the idea, at least he'd have put it into their minds.

But how realistic was it to hope that a people so secretive would, one day, decide to trade with the Guild?

Well, if they want Healing knowledge they'll have to.

It was possible that the Traitors would decide it was safer to reject Healing and remain hidden to the world, keeping him trapped in Sanctuary. But it was worth the risk.

He had to admit, he did feel a nagging obligation to atone for his father's betrayal. Though he would never give them Healing knowledge without the permission of the Guild, he could work toward gaining that permission. He felt like he owed the Traitors that much.

And if all goes to plan, we'll get something in return. Perhaps only this ability to block mind-reading, but I have a feeling they have more to offer than that. I'm sure the mind-blocking is done with some sort of gem like the blood stones. That could be a whole new area of magic to be explored.

There was no way the Guild would agree to a trade with the Traitors while they had Lorkin imprisoned. Eventually, if the Traitors wanted Healing knowledge, they would have to let him go. In the meantime . . . Chari had mentioned records. Having been hidden away for several centuries, the Traitors must have historical information that Dannyl had never encountered before. Records that might lead to the rediscovery of ancient magic. Magic that the Guild could use for its defence.

Assuming that such magic does exist, can be used for defence, and I ever manage to get the information to the Guild.

Lorkin sighed. Perhaps he was being too optimistic, thinking that one day the Traitors would ally themselves with the Guild and the Allied Lands, and he would regain his freedom. Maybe it was wishful thinking.

Yet the Traitors were much better people than those that ruled the rest of Sachaka. They hated slavery, for a start. They counted all as equals, men and women, magicians and non-magicians.

They also had an incredible amount of influence over the country through their spies. He had to admit, the possibility of them taking over Sachaka one day was appealing. He had no doubt the first thing they would do is abolish slavery. He doubted they'd give up black magic, though. Still, it would be a big step toward Sachaka becoming one of the Allied Lands.

How can I give up and go back to Arvice, after all I've seen there? The slaves, the awful hierarchy based on inheritance and black magic. The Traitors' society can't be worse than that.

So many reasons to go to Sanctuary. So few to go back to Arvice.

He hadn't realised he'd stood up until he found himself on his feet. The feeling of determination and decisiveness was exhilarating. He stepped past dozing women and walked to where Savara leaned against the rock wall, her eyes closed.

"I'll come to Sanctuary," he told her, guessing that she wasn't asleep.

Her eyes flew open and snapped to his. She stared at him, her gaze disconcertingly intelligent. He found himself thinking that she must have been quite a beauty in her youth.

"Good," she said.

"But you're going to have to let me deal with Ambassador Dannyl," he added. "He's not going to give up. If you'd met my mother you'd understand why. Eventually he'll either find Sanctuary or you'll have to kill him. I rather like him, and would appreciate you not killing him. And if you did, there would probably be consequences that would not be good for the Traitors."

"How will you persuade him to stop following you?"

He smiled grimly. "I know what to say to him. I'll need to speak to him alone, though."

"I doubt the Ashaki will let you go, if they see you."

"We'll have to lure him away from them."

She frowned as she considered this. "I think we can arrange that."

"Thank you."

"Go sleep. We'll have to let them catch up with us again, so we may as well get some rest in the meantime."

He walked back to his mattress and found Tyvara sitting up, glaring at him.

"What?" he asked.

"You had better not be thinking there is more between you and I than there actually is, Kyralian," she said in a low voice.

He stared at her, feeling doubts starting to creep in. She stared back, then abruptly turned away and lay down with her back to him. He settled onto his mattress, feeling worry starting to eat at him.

Perhaps this is a one-sided thing . . .

"Don't worry," Chari whispered. "She always does this. The more she likes someone the more she pushes them away."

"Shut up, Chari," Tyvara hissed.

Lying on the hard ground, Lorkin knew that sleep was going

to be impossible. It was going to be a very long day. And he was beginning to wonder if there might be a significant downside to living in a city of women like these.

As Regin related the final stages of the Ichani Invasion, Sonea cursed Cery again and tried not to listen. After leaving the Guild, she and the Healer who had brought the message had hurried to the hospice by carriage.

So many hours have passed since then, it feels like something that happened yesterday.

There had been a delay, she remembered. A Healer new to the hospice had pinned her down with questions about protocol. Sonea had told the man that he could ask such questions of any Healer there, and some of the helpers, but he didn't seem to trust them. By the time Sonea extracted herself, Regin was there, waiting for her.

He arrived in a covered cart used to transport supplies to his family home. She had felt strangely out of place, riding in the back of an old cart, the both of them using empty crates as seats. But it was a smart move. They would attract too much attention if they arrived in a Guild carriage.

He'd also brought some threadbare old coats to wear over their robes. For that she was immensely grateful, and a little ashamed that she hadn't considered how they were going to disguise themselves.

Well, I had a lot on my mind. A lot more than Regin knows. And while Cery knows about Lorkin's abduction, I haven't had a chance to tell him that Dannyl is in the midst of tracking Lorkin down right now.

When they arrived at their destination, a man had walked up to them and told them their host was waiting for them –

just knock on the last door to the left down that alleyway. They'd entered the old butchery building, whose owner had been forced to move his business away when the area had grown more prosperous and finicky about its neighbours. It was used as a storehouse.

The sun was setting when we arrived. I was worried we were too late. I needn't have rushed.

They'd been ushered into a surprisingly well-furnished room. An extraordinary-looking man had risen from one of the expensive chairs to bow to them. He was dark like a Lonmar, but with a distinct reddish tone to his skin, and strange, elongated eyes that put her in mind of drawings of the dangerous predatory animals that roamed the mountains.

He had no accent, however. He introduced himself as Skellin and offered them a drink. They'd declined. She assumed Regin was as reluctant to muddle his senses before a possible magical confrontation as she was.

Maybe I should have had that drink.

Skellin was clearly excited to meet them. When he had finally stopped exclaiming about being in the presence of real magicians – and the famous Black Magician Sonea herself, he told them of his history. He and his mother had left their homeland – a land far to the north – when he was a child. Faren, the Thief she had once agreed to use magic for in exchange for hiding her from the Guild, had raised him to be his heir. He remembered little of his homeland, and considered himself a Kyralian.

Sonea had begun to warm to him at this point, though she hadn't forgotten that he was an importer of roet. Cery had arrived at last and Skellin grew serious. He explained his trap. The rogue, he had learned, worked for a roet seller who bought his supply from a worker in this building. They were due to pick up some more. But the timing was never sure. Sometimes they dropped by early in the evening, sometimes late. Skellin had men ready to tell him when she and the seller arrived. They had only to wait.

And wait we have, she thought. *For hours and hours. All I want to do is get back to Osen and find out if Dannyl has caught up with Lorkin yet.*

Instead, she and Regin had been urged to tell stories about the Guild. Skellin knew how she had become a magician, but not how Regin had come to join the Guild. Even though Regin's story was hardly exciting or unusual, it clearly intrigued Skellin. He then wanted to know how their learning in the University was structured. Of the rules that they had to follow. Of the disciplines and what they involved.

It grew less pleasant when he urged them to describe the Ichani Invasion. "You must have amazing tales to tell," the Thief had said, grinning. "I wasn't there, of course. My mother and I hadn't arrived in the country yet."

Regin had saved her from revisiting the more painful time in her past by taking over the storytelling at that point. She wondered if he had guessed how difficult it would be for her. Either way, she felt even more gratitude toward him.

That's three things I have to thank him for tonight, she thought. *The cart, the coats and saving me from reliving some unpleasant memories. I had better . . .*

A knock at the door interrupted her thoughts. Skellin called out, and a lean man in black clothes opened the door.

"They're here," the man said, then backed out of the room again.

Sonea sighed with relief as quietly as she could manage. They all rose to their feet. Skellin looked at them in turn.

"Leave your coats here, if you wish. Nobody but my people and the rogue will see you." He smiled. "I'm looking forward to seeing those famous powers of yours at work. Follow me."

They filed through another door into a long corridor. Windows at the far end glowed faintly.

It's nearly dawn. We've been up all night! She felt a stab of apprehension. *Has Dannyl found Lorkin yet? What if Osen sent someone to get me and they discovered I'm missing? Even if he hasn't, my allies at the hospice will have found it hard to stop the new Healer from looking for me to ask yet more questions.*

Someone must have noticed my absence by now.

But if they had, it would not matter. When she and Regin returned to the Guild with the rogue there would be no more concealing her venturing outside of the hospices. If Rothen was right, nobody would care. Everybody's attention would be on the discovery that a magician who not only wasn't a member of the Guild but had actively been working for criminals had been living in the city.

If he was wrong, things were going to get very unpleasant for both of them.

CHAPTER 27

THE TRAP IS SPRUNG

As Cery had followed Skellin, Sonea and Regin out of the room he'd made a mental note to apologise to Sonea, once they were alone, for the long night she had endured. Perhaps it was only because he'd known her for so long that he'd detected how uncomfortable she'd been with Skellin's questions about the Ichani Invasion.

Though I'd have thought anyone clever enough to become a Thief as powerful as he was, in such a short time, would realise that she'd hardly want to talk about the battle that led to the death of the man she loved.

Cery had felt an overwhelming gratitude to Regin for taking over at that point and saving Sonea from telling the story, or refusing to. The irony of that wasn't lost on him. Regin was not a person he'd have ever expected to thank for being considerate.

At the end of the long corridor they climbed stairs to the upper floor of the old building. Skellin led them to a closed door. He paused as he took hold of the handle and looked at Sonea and Regin.

"Ready?"

The two magicians nodded.

Skellin opened the door and stepped through, then moved aside quickly as if eager not to be caught between the magicians and their quarry. Cery followed Sonea and Regin into a room filled with crates, lit with lamps set around the room. Four people had turned to see who had entered. Three were men and one was a woman wearing a cloak, the hood up and shadowing all but the dark skin of her chin and jaw. Two of the men looked unconcerned and unsurprised at the interruption. The third man looked from Skellin to the magicians, his gaze dropping to their robes. He looked shocked and frightened.

But the woman's reaction was the most dramatic. She backed away, then raised her arms as if to ward off a blow. The air vibrated faintly. Sonea and Regin exchanged a knowing look. *That was some sort of magical attack*, Cery guessed. The magicians turned their attention back to the woman. She yelped in surprise and tucked her arms in against her sides.

Or is that an involuntary movement? Cery thought. *She looks as if something invisible is wrapped around her.*

The magicians paused as if waiting for something, but nothing happened. Sonea glanced at Regin again, then walked over to the woman.

"What is your name?" she asked.

"F-Forlie," the woman answered, her voice trembling.

"Did you know, Forlie, that all magicians in the Allied Lands must be members of the Magicians' Guild?"

The woman swallowed audibly and nodded.

"Why aren't you a member?" Sonea asked. There was no accusation in her voice, just curiosity.

The woman blinked, then her head turned toward Skellin. "I . . . I didn't want to."

Sonea smiled, and while it was a reassuring smile there was a sadness to it. "We have to take you to the Guild now. They won't harm you, but you have broken a law. They'll have to decide what to do with you. If you cooperate it will be better for you in the long run. Will you come with us quietly?"

Forlie nodded. Sonea reached out a hand to her. Whatever force Sonea or Regin had kept her arms fixed against her body with was removed and the woman's shoulders relaxed. Tentatively, she reached out to take Sonea's hand. The two of them walked over to Regin. Everyone in the room breathed a sigh of relief. Skellin looked pleased, Cery noted. Sonea and Regin looked grim but also relieved. Forlie . . .

Cery frowned, then walked over to the woman and tugged off her hood. He felt a shock as he saw her face.

"This isn't her. This isn't the rogue."

There was a pause, then Skellin coughed. "Of course it is. She used magic, didn't she?" He looked at Sonea and Regin.

"She did," Regin agreed.

"Then there must be two rogues," Cery said. "It might've been dark when I saw her, but Forlie doesn't look anything like the woman I saw doing magic."

"She has dark skin and she is the right age. You only saw her from above. How can you be so sure?"

"The shape of her face is all wrong." The woman's skin was lighter, too. She had Lonmar bloodlines, he guessed, and their typical physique. But the woman he'd seen in the pawnshop had an entirely different build. "She's too tall." And too meek to my family's killer.

"You didn't tell me this before," Skellin pointed out.

Cery looked at him. "I guess I didn't think it was worth

going into detail, if there was only one woman using magic in the city."

"It would have been useful to know." For a moment a scowl crossed Skellin's face, then he sighed and shrugged. "Well, I guess it'll still be useful. You can identify the other one for us."

Looking at Sonea, Cery saw she was shaking her head in dismay. He remembered how concerned she was that she might be discovered wandering about the city without permission. Once she brought this rogue to the Guild, they would know she'd defied their restrictions.

"Is this going to be a problem for you?" he asked.

"We'll make sure it isn't," Regin replied firmly. "But it may be a problem for you. Once word gets out that we have caught this w—" He glanced at the woman. "Forlie," he corrected. "The other rogue will be more cautious. She will not be so easy to find."

"Not that she was in the first place," Skellin added.

Regin looked at the Thief. "Will you assist us again?"

"Of course," Skellin smiled.

As the magician's gaze shifted to him, Cery bowed. "As always."

"Then we'll be waiting for your next message," Sonea said. "In the meantime, we need to get back to the Guild as quickly as possible." Her eyes flitted away. Following her gaze, Cery saw that the light of dawn was filtering through windows all around the room.

"Yes. Go," Skellin said. He waved a hand dismissively at the three men still standing over by the crates, watching with bemused expressions. "Continue your work," he said to them. "Now, let me escort you out," he said to the magicians. "Come this way."

Forlie said nothing as she walked with the magicians and

Thieves. They backtracked down the stairs, along the wide corridor, and into the room they'd spent most of the night in. The magicians retrieved their coats and stepped into the alley outside. Skellin wished them all well and said he would be in contact as soon as he had something to tell them. At the end of the alley, Cery stopped.

"Good luck and all that," he said to Sonea. "I'll be in touch."

She smiled. "Thanks for your help, Cery."

He shrugged, then turned away and strode to where Gol was waiting, concealed in the shadows of a doorway opposite the old butchery building.

"Who was that?" the big man asked, stepping out to meet Cery.

"Black Magician Sonea and Lord Regin."

"Not *them*." Gol rolled his eyes. "The woman."

"The rogue."

"No she isn't."

"Not our rogue. Another one."

"You're joking with me?"

Cery shook his head. "Wish I was. Seems we're still on the hunt for our rogue. I'll explain later. Let's get home. It's been a long night."

"Sure has," Gol muttered. He looked back. Following his gaze, Cery saw that Regin and Sonea were still standing by their cart.

"That's odd. Sonea was in a hurry to get back," Cery said.

"This whole thing has been odd from the start," Gol complained.

He's right, Cery thought. *And nothing more odd than Forlie herself. The way she looked at Skellin when Sonea asked her a question . . . as if looking to him for instruction.*

435

There was no doubt about it. Something wasn't right. But they had caught a rogue magician. Maybe not the rogue magician he suspected had something to do with the death of his family, but at least there was one less rogue available for hire by unscrupulous characters like himself. Life in the city's underworld was dangerous enough without magicians hiring themselves out.

Though it would be handy having one to call on now and then. It might make finding my family's killer a lot easier.

One thing he was sure of, though. The other rogue would not be so easy to catch.

Lorkin sat down on a dried-out old log and waited. Somewhere ahead, several Sachakan magicians and their slaves, a Duna tribesman, and one Kyralian Ambassador were making their way toward him. Somewhere behind him, Tyvara and Chari waited. And all around him, Traitors were taking positions ready to spring the trap they'd planned.

He was alone.

Despite Speaker Savara's air of confidence, he knew what they were planning was dangerous. She wouldn't tell him how they planned to separate Dannyl from his companions. She'd said nothing when he'd asked if they were planning to kill anyone. He assumed they weren't, because they seemed anxious not to give the Sachakan king reason to enter their territory, and the obligation to retaliate or seek revenge for Ashaki deaths would certainly provide that.

Savara had told him he would not have much time. Once the Ashaki realised Dannyl had been deliberately separated from them they would be determined to find him. And if Lorkin was still with Dannyl, he'd be captured.

Lorkin sighed and looked around at the bare, rocky land-scape. He hadn't been alone in weeks. It would have been a nice change, if it weren't for the circumstances. But he doubted he was unobserved.

If it weren't for that, I'd try contacting Mother.

The blood ring was now a worrying burden. It wouldn't surprise him if the Traitors searched him before or just after he arrived in Sanctuary. Though they did not treat him as if he posed much of a threat, he wouldn't expect them to trust him completely.

And when they do, they'll find Mother's ring. It's too obvious that something has been stuffed into the spine of my notebook. They'll investigate. They'll find it and take it off me in case I let her know where I am. Do I trust them to keep it safe?

He wasn't prepared to take the risk. So far he'd come up with only two solutions: hide it somewhere, or give it to Dannyl. He'd decided on the latter.

Wait a moment . . . that means I can use it now. It won't matter if anyone sees me and works out what I'm doing. He'll have it, and he'll take it away with him.

He was surprised at the relief that flooded through him, but not at the sudden reluctance that came afterwards. While he wanted to explain what he was doing to his mother, and reassure her he was fine, she was going to take some persuading.

Still, he had to try. And he didn't have much time.

Reaching inside his clothes, he took the notebook out. A bit of pushing and digging later, he had the ring. He took a deep breath, then slipped it on a finger.

—*Mother?*

—*Lorkin!*

437

Relief and worry filtered through to him like muffled music.

—*Are you all right?* she asked.

—*Yes. I don't have much time to explain.*

—*Well . . . get to it then.*

—*Someone tried to kill me, but I was saved by a woman who is a member of a people called the Traitors. We had to leave Arvice because it was likely someone would try to kill me again. Now we're heading toward the secret city she comes from. I'm going with her, but there's a good chance they won't let me leave the city in case I tell people where it is.*

—*Do you have to go?*

—*Yes. She wasn't supposed to kill the person who tried to kill me. If I don't speak in her defence they might execute her for murder.*

—*She saved you and now you want to save her.* She paused. *That's fair, but is it worth being imprisoned?*

—*I think I can change their minds. But it might take a while. In the meantime . . . the Guild doesn't know anything about them. I want to learn as much as I can. They have magic we've never seen before.*

—*The magic you went to Sachaka for in the first place.*

—*Maybe. I won't know until I get there.*

She was silent for a long moment.

—*I can't stop you . . . You had better be right about talking them into letting you go. Otherwise I'll come fetch you myself.*

—*Give me a few years first. And lots of warning.*

—*Years!*

—*Of course. You can't change a whole society overnight. But I'll try to make it sooner.*

—*Well . . . you had better remember to put on the ring now and then.*

—*Ah, that's going to be a problem. I suspect they'll search me.*

If they find a blood ring, they'll take it off me. They're very keen to keep their city's location a secret, and considering what the rest of Sachaka is like I don't blame them. I'm going to give it to Dannyl.

—You haven't spoken to Dannyl yet?

—No. But I will soon. I have to stop him following me, or the Traitors will have to kill him. I don't suppose you could get Osen to tell him to stop?

—Not right now. I'm in the city.

A movement caught Lorkin's eye.

—I have to go.

—Good luck Lorkin. Be careful. I love you.

—I love you, too.

He slipped the ring off and stood up. The movement he'd seen was a Traitor slowly making her way along the top of a ravine. Her attention seemed fixed on something below. Lorkin's heart skipped a beat.

Dannyl had better be holding a strong shield.

Ahead, Unh was casting about, moving in different directions then returning to the same spot. He shook his head, turned and beckoned to Dannyl. For some reason, the tribesman was more inclined to speak to Dannyl now, whenever there was something to report.

"Tracks stop here," the man said, pointing to the ground. He looked up at the rock wall that loomed over them on one side. "We try there?"

Dannyl looked up and judged the distance. The top of the wall wasn't too far away. Drawing magic, he created a disc of force beneath their feet. He took hold of the man's upper arms, and the man did the same with his. They had done this many times already that day, either rising up to the top of a ridge or wall, or dropping down to a ledge or into a valley.

This close, the tribesman smelled of sweat and spices, a combination that was not entirely pleasing, but not too unpleasant, either. Concentrating, Dannyl lifted the disc upward, bearing them with it.

The rock wall rushed past, then fell away as they passed the top of it. There was a narrow ridge along the top. Dannyl moved them to the middle of this before setting them down. Beyond, the high peaks of the mountains cut the sky to a jagged edge.

"If magicians can do this, why don't they fly over the mountains and find Traitor city?" Unh asked.

Dannyl looked at the man in surprise. The man hadn't questioned his ability until now. "Levitation takes concentration," he replied. "The further from the ground you are, the more concentration it takes. I'm not sure why. But the higher you go, the easier it is to become disorientated, and the further you have to fall."

The man pursed his lips, then nodded. "I see."

He turned away and began searching the ground. Moments later he gave a huff of satisfaction. He leaned over the precipice, looking down at the Sachakans, who were staring up in puzzlement.

"Trail goes here," he called. Then he set off along the ridge.

Dannyl waited and watched as the Sachakans took it in turns to levitate themselves and their slaves up the rock face.

"We're getting further in," one of the Ashaki said, looking around. "Has anyone gone this far before?"

"Who knows?" another answered. "We've been trying to find them for centuries. I'm sure someone must have."

"I doubt we've got that close to them," a third pointed out. "They'd have tried to stop us by now."

Achati chuckled and brushed dust off his clothing. "They won't risk that our Kyralian friend might get hurt. Attacking us wouldn't bother them, but they don't dare kill a Guild magician in case it motivates our neighbours into helping us rid Sachaka of our Traitor problem."

"We'd better stick close to the Ambassador, then," the first Ashaki said. Then he lowered his voice. "Though not so close that we have to endure the stink of our tracker."

The others chuckled. Dannyl looked beyond them to see that Unh was standing a hundred strides or so away, beckoning to him. It was obvious the tribesman preferred his assistance to the Sachakans'. *I can't blame him. Though I have to admit, the man doesn't smell too good. Still, I bet I don't either, after walking through the mountains for days without a bath or a change of clothes.*

He caught up with Unh and they continued on. Soon they had to levitate down the other side of the ridge, then up two more walls. Every time, Unh found the trail again. Time passed and soon the sun was dropping ever closer to the horizon. They entered a narrow ravine. Unh hesitated at the entrance, then indicated Dannyl should walk beside him.

"You keep magic shield on," he said. "Keep it strong."

Dannyl followed the man's advice. He felt the skin down his back crawl as he and the tribesman slowly walked down the middle of the ravine. He glanced back to see the Sachakans following, their expressions grim. They were casting suspicious glances up at the ravine walls.

After several hundred paces the walls began to retreat and the ravine floor widened. Ahead, it became a small valley. Unh let out a breath and muttered something.

Then a crack and a boom shook the air. The sound came from behind them. Dannyl and Unh spun about, then threw up their hands as stones pattered against the barrier that protected them. They backed away. A fog of dust had filled the ravine.

Slowly it settled to reveal a huge pile of rocks.

Where are the Sachakans? Are they buried? Dannyl took a step forward, but a hand caught his arm. He turned to Unh, but the man wasn't looking at him. He was looking toward the valley. Following his gaze, Dannyl saw a lone figure walking toward them. His heart skipped a beat.

Lorkin!

"They'll be fine," the young magician said. "They had strong barriers. It won't take long for them to haul themselves out, then to work out how they're going to get through to you, so I can't stay long." He smiled and stopped a few paces from Dannyl. "We need to talk."

"We certainly do," Dannyl agreed.

Lorkin looked healthy. He was even a little tanned. He was wearing slave's clothes, yet he looked strangely comfortable in them. Perhaps only because he'd been wearing them for several days now.

"Let's sit down," Lorkin said. He moved to a low boulder and sat. Dannyl found another rock to sit upon. Unh remained standing. The tribesman watched Lorkin with a cautious, knowing expression.

Abruptly all sounds in the ravine were silenced. Dannyl guessed that Lorkin had created a barrier to prevent their conversation being overheard. *Overheard by Unh, or others as well?*

"You must have many questions," Lorkin said. "I'll do my best to answer them."

Dannyl nodded. Where to start? Perhaps where it had all started to go wrong.

"Who killed the slave in your room?"

Lorkin smiled wryly. "The woman I've been travelling with. She saved my life."

"Tyvara?"

"Yes. The one you found dead in my room tried to kill me. Tyvara said that others would try to finish the job, and offered to take me somewhere safe."

"Who wants you killed, and why?"

Lorkin grimaced. "That's kind of complicated. I can't tell you who, but I can tell you why. It's because of my father. But not because he killed any Ichani. Because of something else he did. Or rather, something he *didn't* do. Do you remember how someone helped him escape Sachaka by teaching him black magic?"

Dannyl, nodded.

"Well, that person was a Traitor. He agreed to give them something in return, and he never did. In fact, it was something he was not authorised to give, but I guess he was desperate to go home and would have agreed to anything." Lorkin shrugged. "I need to sort that out with the Traitors. And . . . there are other things. I have to tell them what happened with Riva – the slave Tyvara killed – or Tyvara will be charged for murder and executed. So I need you to stop following me."

"How did I know you were going to say that?" Dannyl said, sighing.

"They'll kill you if you don't." Lorkin's expression was more serious than Dannyl had ever seen before. "They don't want to. I don't think they want to kill the Sachakans either . . . well, they'd love to kill them, I suspect, just not here and now. They know that the more people they have to kill to keep their location secret, the more people will try to find them."

Dannyl nodded. "So you want me and Unh to pretend we lost the trail."

"Yes. Or whatever you need to say to end the search."

Somehow I don't think it'll take much to convince the Sachakans, after this, he thought, looking at the rocks blocking the ravine. *What about Unh? I guess he'll follow orders. But maybe the truth will suffice. If I decide we don't need to find Lorkin, will the Ashaki keep searching?*

Then Dannyl remembered the gemstones. He looked at Lorkin closely.

"This isn't just because of your father and this woman, is it?"

The young magician blinked, then smiled.

"No. I want to know more about the Traitors. They don't have slaves, and the way their society is structured is completely different to the rest of Sachaka. I think they may have forms of magic we've never heard of – or haven't seen in thousands of years. I think they might be good people to establish friendly ties with. I think . . . I think that we need to get on their good side, because one day we might be dealing with *them* instead of the people ruling Arvice now."

Dannyl cursed. "If it comes to a war, don't take sides," he warned. "If they lose, you may not be immune to the consequences."

"I wouldn't expect to be." Lorkin shrugged. "I do realise the problems that would cause for the Guild. For now it would be better if everyone acted as if I'd left the Guild. I'm not sure how long I will have to stay here." He frowned. "There's a chance they won't let me leave in case I tell others how to find them. I've explained all this to Mother, by the way."

"Oh. Good." Dannyl heaved a sigh of relief. "Do you realise how much I dreaded telling her about your disappearance?"

"Yes." Lorkin chuckled. "Sorry about that." The amusement left his face and he grimaced. He looked down and uncurled the fingers of one hand. On his palm lay a blood ring. He held it out to Dannyl with obvious reluctance. "Take it. I don't dare carry it any longer. If they found it on me it would hardly encourage them to trust me and I don't want to risk it falling into other hands."

Dannyl took the ring. "It's Sonea's?"

"Yes." A movement caught their attention. Dust rose from the pile of rocks behind them. Lorkin's gaze flickered to them, and he stood up. "I have to go."

At the movement, Unh turned to look at them. Once more Dannyl remembered the cave full of gemstones.

"My friend here – he's from the Duna tribes, by the way – told me something interesting the other day. He said that his people have knowledge of how to make gemstones like those in the Cavern of Ultimate Punishment."

Lorkin's eyes brightened with interest.

"He also said," Dannyl continued. "That the Traitors stole that knowledge from his people. You might want to keep that in mind. Your new friends may not be without a few nasty traits."

The young magician smiled. "Who is? But I will keep that in mind. It is interesting information. Very interesting." His eyes narrowed for a moment, then he looked at Dannyl and grasped his upper arm. "Goodbye, Ambassador. I hope your new assistant is more useful than I've proven to be."

Dannyl returned the gesture. Then he jumped as sound

returned. Lorkin moved away, pausing to say something to the tribesman as he passed. Dannyl rose and moved to Unh's side and they watched the lone magician stride away.

"What did he say to you?" Dannyl asked when Lorkin finally moved out of sight.

"He said, 'You're the only one in danger'," Unh replied. "He means the Traitors fear I may lead you to their city."

"Not without the help of a magician, I suspect."

The tribesman looked at him and smiled. "No."

"So we'd better get you out of here sooner rather than later. How about we levitate over that pile of rocks and see if any of our Sachakan companions have dug themselves out yet?"

"Is a good idea," the tribesman agreed.

When she had finally left Skellin, Sonea had simultaneously wanted to scream in frustration and cheer in relief.

By now, not only could Dannyl have found Lorkin, she'd thought, *but there could have been a battle, funerals for the dead arranged, and a victory celebration held. Osen must have progressed from wondering where I am to discovering I haven't been at the hospice all night to ordering Kallen to start strengthening himself ready to hunt me down.*

And all for nothing. Well, not *nothing*. They had found one rogue. Just not the one they were looking for.

But at least she was away from Skellin, she'd reasoned, and headed back to the Guild at last. Then something happened that negated all her desire to rush back for news. She'd heard Lorkin's voice in her mind. And felt hints at what he'd been feeling.

It had been very enlightening.

She'd forgotten how effective a blood ring could be at conveying

446

the mind of the wearer. In a short time she had not only learned that Lorkin was alive, but that he did not fear for his life and was full of hope. Though he was not entirely certain how the people he was with would treat him, in general he respected them and believed they were benevolent. He was smitten with the woman who had rescued him, but the obligation he felt toward her was not entirely based on lust or fondness.

Ah, Lorkin. Why does there always have to be a woman involved?

Lorkin was as safe as she could hope, considering the situation. She'd rather he was home, and she did not like the possibility these Traitors would not let him leave their city, but he had decided to risk that and there was nothing she could do to stop him.

At least he's a long way from the people who tried to kill him.

She'd got into the cart feeling much better. But before they had travelled far, Forlie had begun to groan and hold her head and stomach. A quick check told Sonea the woman was particularly susceptible to carriage sickness, so they had been forced to tell the driver to slow down.

She wondered if Lorkin had met Dannyl yet. And if Osen was now looking for her, to tell her the good news.

The cart slowed even further. Outside, someone was shouting, and the driver began shouting back. Sonea exchanged a frown with Regin as the vehicle stopped. Forlie began to whimper with fear.

They all jumped as someone began hammering on the side of the cart.

"Black Magician Sonea," someone called. A young woman, Sonea guessed. "You have to come out. You've got the wrong woman."

Sonea moved to the rear flap of the cart's cover. She pulled it aside. The street beyond was empty but for a few people in the distance. A knocking came from the side of the cart again.

"I work for Cery," the woman said. "I—"

"We know she's the wrong rogue," Sonea called out. "Cery told us."

A slim young woman appeared, hurrying around the cart to scowl at Sonea.

"Then . . . you didn't . . . you don't know . . ." The girl stopped and took a deep breath. "You're letting the other rogue go, then?"

Sonea stared at her. "Not if I can help it."

"Well . . . I know where the real rogue is. I was watching you and Cery from the roof of one of the other buildings and saw her turn up to do the same. I think she's still there."

Regin uttered an oath. Sonea turned to look at him.

"Go," he said. "I'll get Forlie to the hospice and come back."

"But . . ." *But what if the woman has already left? My absence from the hospice might not have been noticed. If it hasn't, I'll be able to keep hunting for her. But if I get out of the cart and I'm seen . . .*

"You should go," she told Regin. "If I go and I'm recognised, the Guild will stop me hunting for h—"

"*You* must be the one to catch her." Regin stared at her, his gaze intense and his expression unexpectedly angry. "People need to see you do it. They need to remember that you're more than a Healer. That restricting you to that is a *waste*." He pointed out of the cart. "*Go!* Before she gets away!"

Sonea stared at him for a moment, then pulled the flap wide and jumped out onto the road. Her coat flared open and the young woman's eyes widened as she saw the black robes beneath. Sonea took the hint and buttoned the coat up. "What's your name?"

"Anyi." The girl straightened. "Follow me." The girl broke into a jog, heading back toward the old butchery.

"Have you told Cery?" Sonea asked.

The girl shook her head. "I couldn't find him."

They moved into a maze of alleys, jogging from shadow to shadow. Sonea realised her heart was beating fast with a strange mix of long-forgotten excitement and something more primal. *I'm like a hunter about to catch its prey*, she thought. Then she remembered how it had felt to be hounded and frightened, sought by powerful magicians, and she sobered. *Still, this woman is no untrained child. Why was she watching us? Did she know about Skellin's trap?*

She must have known about it. How had she found out? Had she sent Forlie in her place? Close to the old butchery, Anyi entered an alleyway. At the far end Sonea could see a busy main road.

"She was on the roof of this building," she said. "There's a spot out of sight around here where you can climb up—"

The girl had been about to dive into a small, dead end side alley, but suddenly checked her stride then backed away from the entrance.

"*That's her!*" she hissed, pointing.

Her finger pointed upward. Sonea looked up, caught a movement and felt a chill run down her spine. She drew magic and threw up a shield around them. A woman was slowly levitating down into the side alley. She disappeared into the shadows.

"Can you trap her in there?" Anyi asked.

The sound of footsteps suddenly broke out, coming rapidly closer.

"Only one way to find out," Sonea replied. She looked at

Anyi. "Go back. When Regin returns, bring him here. I might need assistance."

Anyi nodded and raced away. Sonea adjusted her shield to allow the girl out. When she turned back, the woman was about to emerge from the side alley.

Sonea stepped forward and threw up a barrier to block the woman's way.

Surprise, shock and dismay crossed the woman's dark face. Then her strange, angular eyes narrowed. A force hammered against the barrier. It was no test strike, but a full blast that was stronger than Sonea expected, and at the same time another strike flashed toward her. The barrier wavered and fell before she had a chance to strengthen it.

The woman dashed out of the dead end alley and ran toward the main road. Sonea ran after her, throwing out another, stronger barrier to envelop her, but the woman smashed this down with a violent blast. A moment later, the rogue was among the people moving up and down the road beyond.

Sonea reached the alley entrance. She saw the woman pause and turn to look at her, well within the flow of traffic. Seeing the distinctive red-brown skin, she knew why Cery had been so sure that Forlie was not the woman he'd seen. As Skellin's face flashed through Sonea's memory, she felt a chill run down her spine. Same reddish dark skin. Same strange eyes. *This woman is of the same race!*

A smile stretched the woman's lips. A dangerous, triumphant smile.

She thinks I won't dare use magic with all these people around, and she is right. I also don't want to risk harming her. Though it would certainly make matters simpler for the Guild if the woman got herself killed.

450

To deserve that fate, she'd have to do much worse than be a rogue magician working for roet-sellers as a blackmailer. Like killing Cery's family.

We need her alive to find out if she's guilty or knows who is. We also need her alive so we can find out where she came from, and if there are more magicians like her. And find out why she was watching us catch Forlie.

And it would be much harder for Sonea to gain forgiveness for not obeying rules if her disobedience had led to her killing someone.

Sonea drew magic. Lots of magic. She had no idea how long she could hold the woman for. Despite knowing how to take power from magicians and people and even animals, and store it away until needed, Sonea had not done so for over twenty years. She was forbidden to unless ordered to do so by the Higher Magicians.

She was no more powerful than she had been before she had learned black magic. No more powerful than she had been as a novice.

But she had been an exceptionally powerful novice.

With the magic she had gathered, Sonea sent power over the heads of the people passing between her and the rogue, and surrounded the woman in a globe of force. At once the woman began striking in all directions, but though her attacks were powerful, Sonea had expected them to be so, and kept the containment barrier strong. The flash and vibration of magic sent people scattering away from the woman. Sonea shrugged out of the old coat and tossed it aside. When people recovered enough to stop and watch, she did not want them wondering why she had been wearing it.

The black cloth of her robes stirred in a breeze as she stepped out of the alley entrance and walked toward the rogue. She heard exclamations, from either side, where crowds of onlookers were no doubt gathering, but kept her attention on the woman. The rogue snarled and increased her attack on the barrier. Sonea strengthened it further, trying not to worry at how rapidly she was using her reserves of magic.

How long can I keep this up? How long can she *keep it up?*

A sound broke out from either side. Sonea did not realise what it was at first, then as she did her concentration nearly faltered from amazement.

The crowd was cheering.

Through the sound came a different sort of shout. In the corner of her eye she saw someone approaching. Someone wearing purple.

"Need some help?" a young male voice asked.

An Alchemist. Not one she knew, however.

"Yes," she said. "Come through."

Letting him into her barrier, she held out a hand to him. "Send me your magic."

"The old-fashioned way?" he asked, surprise in his voice.

She laughed. "Of course. I think we can manage one rogue between us."

He took her hand, and she felt magic flow into her. She channelled it to the containment barrier. The Alchemist called out, and she realised another magician was approaching. This time a Healer. As the woman took Sonea's other hand, Sonea almost expected the rogue to give up. But the foreign woman fought on.

Yet her strikes were growing weaker and weaker. Sonea felt an unexpected pity as the woman threw all her strength at the barrier until her attack finally faltered. The rogue's shoulders drooped. She looked haggard and resigned.

Letting go of her fellow magicians' hands, Sonea glanced at them.

"Thank you."

The Alchemist shrugged, and the Healer murmured something like "of course". Sonea turned her attention back to the rogue. She closed the distance between them, taking slow measured strides. The Alchemist and Healer paced beside her, staying within her shield. The rogue regarded Sonea sullenly as she stopped before her.

"What is your name?" Sonea asked.

The woman did not answer.

"Do you know the law regarding magicians in the Allied Lands? The law that states that all magicians must be a member of the Magicians' Guild?"

"I know it," the woman replied.

"Yet here you are, a magician who is not a member of the Guild. Why is that?"

The woman laughed. "I don't need your Guild. I learned magic long before I came to this land. Why should I bow to you?"

Sonea smiled. "Why indeed?"

The woman glowered.

"So," Sonea continued. "How long have you lived within the Allied Lands?"

"Too long." The woman spat on the ground.

"If you don't like it, why do you stay?"

The woman stared balefully at Sonea.

"What is the name of your homeland?"

The rogue's lips pressed together stubbornly.

"Well, then." Sonea brought the barrier around the woman in closer. "Whether you like it or not, the Magicians' Guild is bound by law to deal with you. We're taking you to the Guild now."

Anger contorted the woman's face and a new blast of power pounded the barrier surrounding her, but it was a weak attack. Sonea considered waiting until the woman tired, then decided against it. She shrank the barrier around the woman, then used it to nudge her to the centre of the road. She began pushing the rogue firmly but gently forward. The Healer and Alchemist fell into step beside her.

And in this way, through streets lined with curious onlookers, they escorted the second rogue found that day to the Guild.

CHAPTER 28

QUESTIONS

The blindfold over Lorkin's eyes itched, but each of his arms was being held by a Traitor.

"We're stopping," one of the women said, gently pulling him to a halt. "Now we're going up again."

The other woman let his arm go and he took the opportunity to scratch. He braced himself and felt his stomach lurch as they began to rise. After several heartbeats he felt the unevenness of the ground under his feet again. The woman tugged him into motion.

"Be careful, the ground slopes here. Duck your head."

He felt a sudden coolness and guessed that they'd moved from sunlight into shadows. That wasn't all. There was moisture in the air, and a faint smell of rotting vegetation or mould. His guide stopped.

"There's stairs now, descending. Four of them."

He found the edge with his toe, then cautiously stepped downward. The steps were wide and shallow, and from the way sounds were echoing he had entered a cave or room. The trickle of water came from a few strides away.

"It's all flat from here."

That wasn't strictly true, he could tell as he walked. The

ground was smooth, but there was a definite gradual incline. He listened to the sound of the group's footsteps, and the flow of water. If they made any turns, they were too large and slow for him to detect.

The sound of wind, vegetation rustling and distant voices came from somewhere ahead. A few more strides and, from the way the noise surrounded him, he knew he was now outside. He felt the warmth of sunlight on his face and a breeze on his skin. He heard someone say Savara's name.

Without warning, the blindfold was removed and he found himself blinking into the brightness of the midday sun. Before his eyes had adjusted, the Traitor who had been guiding him tugged at his arm, indicating he should continue walking.

Savara led the group, walking along a pathway beside tall, swaying stalks. He realised this was the edge of a crop, the large seed heads peeking out from the topmost leaves. The path ascended steeply and he found himself staring out over a wide valley.

Steep cliff walls rose on either side, meeting at the ends of the valley. Fields filled the floor, each at a different height, like disturbed tiles, but all level. The tiers of green stepped down to a long, narrow lake at the valley's lowest point. *Not one corner wasted*, he thought. *How else can they feed a whole city of people? But where are the buildings?*

A movement up on the nearest cliff wall answered that question. Someone was looking out of a hole in the rock face. A moment later he realised that the entire wall was riddled with holes, from one end of the valley to the other.

A city carved into the rock. He shook his head in wonder.

"It was already here when we found the valley," a familiar voice said, from beside him.

He looked at Tyvara in surprise. She had barely said a word to him since they'd joined Savara's group.

"Of course, we've made it much bigger," she continued. "A lot of the old part collapsed and had to be replaced sixty years after the first Traitors settled here."

"How deep does it go?"

"Mostly it's only one or two rooms deep. Think of it as a city half the size of Arvice, but more elongated, and tipped on its side. We have tremors here now and then, and parts collapse. Though we've got a lot better at judging if the rock is safe before making new rooms, then strengthening them with magic, people feel more comfortable living close to the outside."

"I can understand how they'd come to feel that way."

He could see, now, that part of the base of the wall was broken by sturdy archways, through which people were entering and leaving the city. Elsewhere there were smaller, more widely spaced openings. The arches suggested a formal, public entrance, and he was not surprised when Savara headed for them.

But not long after, she was forced to stop. A crowd had begun to gather. Many of the people were staring at him. Some were clearly curious, but others looked suspicious. Some were glaring in anger, but not just at him. Their attention was also on Tyvara.

"Murderer!" someone called out, followed by sounds of agreement here and there. But a few people frowned at the accusation, and some even voiced a protest.

"Move out of the way," Savara ordered, her tone firm but not angry.

The people blocking the path obeyed. Lorkin read respect

in their faces when they looked at Savara. *She is definitely a Traitor to get on the good side of*, he thought, as the group followed their leader to the arches and into the city.

A wide but shallow hall supported by several rows of columns spread before them.

"Speaker Savara," a voice called. "I'm glad to see you've returned safely."

The voice belonged to a short, round woman, who was walking toward them from the back of the hall. Her words had been spoken in a lofty tone. Savara slowed to meet her.

"Speaker Kalia," Savara replied. "Have the Table assembled?"

"All but you and I."

Lorkin felt something nudge his arm. He looked down at Tyvara. She mouthed something, but he could not make it out, so she leaned closer.

"*Other faction*," she whispered. "*Leader.*"

He nodded to show he understood, then gave the woman a closer look. *So this is the one who ordered me killed.* She was older than Savara, possibly older than his mother, if the roundness of her face was smoothing out the lines a woman her age might normally have. The sharpness of her eyes and the set of her mouth contradicted her soft demeanour. They gave her a mean expression, he decided. But maybe his perception was skewed by the knowledge she'd wanted him dead. Maybe other people found her appealing and motherly.

Kalia's gaze swept over the other members of Savara's group and her nose twitched. Lorkin realised that the slave garb he and some of the others wore now looked out of place. *Like the costume it is.* Savara turned to two of her companions.

"Take Tyvara to her room and guard the doors."

They nodded, and as they looked to Tyvara she stepped forward to join them. Without glancing at him or saying a word, she strode away. Savara looked at another of her people.

"Find Evana and Nayshia and have them replace Ishiya and Ralana as soon as possible." She looked at the last two women. "Go. Get some rest and proper food."

As the women left, Savara turned to Lorkin. "I hope you're ready to answer a lot of questions."

He smiled. "I am."

But as she and Kalia fell into step either side of him, leading him out of the hall and into a wide corridor, he realised he did not feel ready. He knew that there was a queen here, but it was suddenly clear that Tyvara and Chari had neglected to tell him how power was divided below the level of royalty. He knew the women flanking him were Speakers, but he had no idea exactly how they fitted into the hierarchy, and he was feeling a fool for not asking.

Savara asked if a Table had been assembled. I'm guessing they don't mean furniture. They're both part of it, so I assume it's some sort of group like the Higher Magicians. With someone directing the formalities and ceremonies, as Administrator Osen does at Guild meets.

Light in the corridor was subdued, but bright enough to illuminate the way. There was colour to it – colour that shifted and changed. He looked around, seeking the source, and realised that it came from bright points of light embedded into the roof.

Gemstones! Magical gemstones! He tried to make out their shape as he passed, but they were too bright to look at directly. They left spots floating before his vision, so he forced himself to avert his eyes.

The corridor was not long, and Savara and Kalia led him

through a wide doorway into a large room. A curved stone table had been set at one end. Four women sat along the length of it, with two empty seats waiting. At the far end of the table sat a grey-haired woman, who had the same tired look about her that Osen always seemed to have.

She's the Traitors' version of the Administrator, I'd wager.

At the closer end was another chair, larger and studded with gemstones, and empty. The rest of the room was a large wedge shape, fanning out from the table. The floor had been carved into steps, on which cushions had been neatly spaced. *For an audience, though there's nobody here today.*

Savara directed him to stand before the table, then she and Kalia took their seats.

"Welcome, Lorkin of the Magicians' Guild of Kyralia," the tired woman said. "I am Riaya, Director of the Table. These are Yvali, Shaiya, Kalia, Lanna, Halana and Savara, Speakers for the Traitors."

"Thank you for allowing me into your city," he replied, bending in a slight bow that he directed at them all.

"I understand you have come to Sanctuary willingly," Riaya said.

"Yes."

"Why?"

"Foremost, to speak in defence of Tyvara at her trial."

"And why else?"

He paused to consider how to begin. "I understand that my father made a promise to your people that he should not have. If I can, I would like to settle that matter."

The speakers exchanged glances. Some looked sceptical, others hopeful.

"Is that your only other reason?"

Lorkin shook his head. "Though I was only an assistant to the Guild Ambassador to Sachaka, I know that part of the role – part of the reason for having Ambassadors in the first place – is to seek and maintain peaceful links with other peoples. The Traitors are a part of Sachaka, so if we do not seek links with them we are neglecting an important section of the country. Even the little I know about the Traitors tells me that your values are more compatible with those of the Allied Lands. You reject slavery, for instance." He took a deep breath. "If there is a chance that a beneficial link might be established between us I feel obliged to explore the possibility."

"What possible benefit would there be for us in such an alliance?" Kalia asked, her tone full of disbelief.

Lorkin smiled. "Trade."

Kalia gave a sharp, humourless laugh. "We've already sought honest trade with your kind, and regretted it."

"You refer, of course, to my father," he said. "I was told that Traitors agreed to teach him black magic in exchange for Healing magic? Is that correct?"

The seven women frowned.

"Black magic?" Riaya repeated.

"Higher magic," Lorkin explained.

"Then that is true," Riaya said.

Lorkin shook his head. "Only the Higher Magicians of the Guild, with permission from the leaders of the Allied Lands, could have made that decision. It was not my father's right to offer you such knowledge."

The women began to exclaim and speak all at once and, though Lorkin could not make out what all of them said, the general opinion was clear. They were angry, yet also puzzled.

"Why would he make the promise? Did he intend to break his word?"

"It's obvious why he did what he did," Lorkin said. "He was—"

But Kalia and the woman beside her were still talking, agreeing with each other – from the bits he caught – on how Kyralians weren't to be trusted.

"Let him speak," Riaya said, her voice cutting across theirs. The two women quietened. Kalia crossed her arms and looked at him with haughty expectation.

"My father was desperate," Lorkin reminded them. "He had been a slave for many years. He knew his country was in danger. He probably felt his personal honour did not matter in the face of his country's safety. And after years of . . . being a slave, how much dignity would you have left?"

He stopped as he realised he was allowing too much emotion to enter his words. "I have a question for you," he said.

"You don't get to ask us questions," Kalia sneered. "You must wait until—"

"I would like to hear this question," Savara interrupted. "Would anyone else?"

The rest of the women paused, then nodded.

"Go on, Lorkin," Riaya urged.

"I was told your people had known my father was a slave for some time before you offered him this trade. Why did you wait until it was of advantage to you to offer that help? Why did you require such a high price for helping him, when you rescue your own people from such tyranny all the time?"

His last words were drowned in protests.

"How dare you question our generosity!" Kalia shouted.

"He was a man and a foreigner!" another exclaimed.

462

"The queen's only daughter died because of him!"

"And hundreds more could have been saved if he'd kept his word."

His gaze slid across their angry faces and he suddenly regretted speaking out. He needed to charm and woo these women, not anger them. But then his eyes met Savara's. He saw her nod approvingly.

"Will you give us what your father promised?" Kalia demanded.

Instantly, the women quietened. They stared at him intently. *They want Healing so badly*, he thought. *Why wouldn't they? The desire to be protected from injury, disease and death is a powerful one. But they don't realise how powerful the knowledge is. The advantage it gives over an enemy. How it can be used to harm as well as help.*

"I am not authorised to do so," he told them. "But I am willing to help you gain it, through negotiating an exchange with the Guild and the Allied Lands."

"An exchange?" Riaya frowned. "For what?"

"For something of equal value."

"We gave you higher magic!" Kalia exclaimed.

"Yes, you gave my father black magic," Lorkin pointed out. "It is not new to the Guild, nor would they consider it a suitable exchange for Healing."

Lorkin had expected more protest at this, but the women had fallen into thoughtful silence. Savara regarded him with narrowed eyes. Was that suspicion he read in them?

"What do we have that would be considered of equal value?" Riaya asked.

He shrugged. "I don't know yet. I only just got here."

Kalia sighed loudly. "There is no point wasting time and

energy fantasising about trades and alliances. Sanctuary's location is a secret. We can't have foreigners coming and going, for trade or otherwise."

Riaya nodded. She looked at the women, then at Lorkin.

"We are not yet in a position to consider such matters as trade with the Guild. Did Savara warn you that you would not be allowed to leave if you came to Sanctuary?"

"She did."

She turned to the speakers. "Do any of you see reason why this law should not apply to Lorkin?"

All shook their heads. Even Savara, he noticed. He felt his stomach sink.

"Do you accept this?" Riaya asked him.

He nodded. "I do."

"Then you are now subject to the laws of Sanctuary. So you had better find out what they are and pay them the respect they deserve. This meeting is over." Riaya looked at Savara. "Since you brought him in you are charged with ensuring he is obedient and useful."

Savara nodded, then stood up and waved a hand to indicate he should follow. As they walked out of the room, Lorkin felt a strange gloom settle on him. He'd known there would be a price for following Tyvara to Sanctuary. Though he was prepared to accept it, a part of him still rebelled.

And then he remembered what Riaya had said. *"We are not yet in a position to consider such matters . . ."* Not yet. That did not mean "never". It might take years for them to gather the strength and courage to venture beyond their mountains, but they would have to, if they wanted what the Allied Lands had to offer.

Although if they did steal gem magic from the Duna tribes, he found himself thinking, *then I had better be very careful they don't try to do something similar to me.*

Anyi's hand reached out to caress the fine leather of the carriage seat, then trace the gold inlay set into the edge of the seat's wooden base. Looking down at the floor, Cery noted, with amusement, that the Guild symbol – a Y within a diamond – had been created with different inlayed timbers, all which had been polished to a rich shine.

"We're here," Gol said, his voice hushed with awe.

Cery looked out of the window. The Guild gates were swinging open. The carriage slowed as it passed through, then sped up again to take them to the front of the University. It stopped before the steps and the driver jumped down to open the door for them. As Cery climbed out, a figure in black robes emerged from the building.

"Cery of Northside," Sonea said, grinning at him.

"Black Magician Sonea," he replied, bending in an exaggerated bow. Her eyes crinkled with amusement. "This is Anyi," he told her. "And you know Gol."

Sonea nodded at his daughter. "I didn't realise you were *that* Anyi," she murmured. "But then, I hadn't seen you since you were no taller than my knees."

Anyi bowed. "Let's not spread that about," she said. "I'm Cery's bodyguard, nothing more."

"And that's all that the Guild will know," Sonea assured them. Sonea looked up at Gol. "You've got no taller since the other day, I'm glad to see."

The man sketched a hasty bow. He opened his mouth and closed it again, clearly too overwhelmed by his surroundings to think of a witty reply.

"Come inside." Sonea beckoned and started climbing the steps. "Everyone is looking forward to hearing your stories."

Catching the dryness of her tone, Cery looked at her closely. He had been both pleased and dismayed by her summons to the Guild to identify the rogue, but she'd assured him that she had only referred to him as an old friend. There was a chance some of the older magicians would remember him from twenty years before, and knew he'd become a Thief but it was a slim one. But it was worth the risk if it meant his family's murderer was found.

He also understood she was worried that the Guild would restrict her freedom more now they knew she had been roaming about the city without permission. The fact that she'd been associating with a Thief would not make things any better for her, despite the fact that this was no longer against any Guild rules.

While the hunt for the rogue was over, the matter was hardly settled as far as the Guild was concerned.

"How has the meeting gone so far?" he asked.

"There has been lots and lots of arguing," she began.

"Of course."

"Worse than usual. I always suspected that if a magician from beyond the Allied Lands wanted to live in one of our countries it would bring our laws into question. But I always assumed it would be a Sachakan magician."

"Has the rogue told you anything about where she came from?"

"No. She's refusing to speak. So is Forlie, though I think that's more out of fear than stubbornness."

They reached the top of the stairs and she led them through the entry hall full of impossibly delicate spiralling staircases that Cery remembered from his last visit, over twenty years before. Gol and Anyi both gazed around, their mouths open in astonishment, and Cery had to smother a chuckle. Sonea did not hesitate, but led them into a wide corridor. This finished at the huge Great Hall that contained the old building that was the Guildhall. A building within a building. Cery didn't think Gol and Anyi's mouths could open any wider.

"Will you read her mind?" Cery asked Sonea.

"I expect we will eventually. That's part of what the arguing has been about. Since we don't know anything about the place she came from we don't know if reading her mind without her permission would be taken as an unforgivable abuse."

"But you can't find out where she came from without reading her mind," Anyi said.

"No."

"And that's why we're here. You need proof she did something illegal."

Sonea had reached the doors of the Guildhall, which were slowly opening. She looked at Anyi and smiled crookedly.

"Yes. More than just using magic in self defence."

As the doors swung wide, Cery caught his breath. The hall was full of magicians. It was a sight he suspected few non-magicians could see and not feel awed and intimidated. Especially when they considered all the magical power these magicians held.

Looks like they're doing a good job of replacing the numbers they lost during the Ichani Invasion, he noted. The tiered seats on either side were full, but the rows of chairs in the centre of the room were empty. *Which are for the novices*, he recalled.

That's good. There's likely to be more people from the low end of town among them, who might recognise me.

Sonea strode forward, black robes swirling. Following her, Cery glanced at Gol and Anyi, walking on either side of him. Both were averting their eyes from the watching magicians, keeping their gaze fixed on the scene ahead of them.

A magician in blue robes stood waiting at the far end of the room. *The Administrator.* This was a different man to the one Cery remembered wearing those robes long ago, before the Ichani Invasion. He was older than that man had been.

Behind the Administrator were more tiered seats. *The Higher Magicians.* Cery examined the faces. Some looked familiar, some did not. He recognised Rothen, the magician who had guided Sonea through her early years in the University. The old man met Cery's gaze and nodded once.

Two women stood before the Higher Magicians. Cery recognised Forlie, who looked frightened out of her wits. The other woman turned to see who was approaching and Cery felt his heart skip.

Yes, that's her.

As she glared at him, Cery's blood went cold. In the dim light of the pawnshop attic, he hadn't seen her too clearly, though enough to recognise her when he saw her the next time. And when he'd seen her in the street outside the shop, it had been at a distance. But here, under the bright glow of many magical globe lights, he noticed something he'd not had the opportunity to see before.

She had the same strange eyes as Skellin's. They were of the same race.

That's not something the Guild needs to know, he decided. *Skellin would not appreciate me directing the Guild's attention in his direction. Though I doubt Sonea failed to notice the similarity. She probably hasn't told anyone because that would mean revealing she had enlisted the help of a Thief . . .*

As Sonea stopped before the Higher Magicians, Cery, Anyi and Gol bowed. She introduced him and his bodyguards and explained that Cery was the friend she had spoken of, who had first seen the foreign rogue and brought the matter to her attention. As she finished, the Administrator looked at Cery.

"Firstly, the Guild offers its thanks for your assistance in capturing these rogue magicians," he said. "Secondly, we thank you for helping us today." He gestured to the two women. "Do you recognise either of these women?"

Cery turned to Forlie. "I had not seen Forlie until a few days ago, when she was caught." He gestured to the other woman. "This one I saw a few months ago. Gol and I were after a murderer, and the clues we'd got led us to spy on a shop owner and his customer – this woman. We saw her use magic to open a safebox."

The rogue was still staring at him, and as his gaze shifted to her she narrowed her eyes.

"Do you think this woman is the murderer you sought?"

Cery shrugged. "I don't know. Magic was used in the murder. She has magic. But I have no proof that it was her."

The Administrator's attention moved to Gol. "You were there the night your employer spied on this woman."

Gol nodded. "I was."

"Was it as he described? Were there any details you noticed that he didn't?"

"He got it straight," the big man said.

Now the Administrator looked at Anyi. "And were you there?"

"No," she replied.

"Have you observed this woman performing magic?"

"Yes. I first put eyes on her an hour or so before S— . . . Black Magician Sonea caught her. She was watching Forlie being caught. I thought it a bit odd. Then I saw her using magic to kill some birds that were making so much noise fighting they might've drawn attention to her. I knew she had to be a rogue, too, so I went to get Black Magician Sonea."

The Administrator looked thoughtful, then regarded Cery, Anyi and Gol in turn. "Is there anything else you can tell us about either of these women?"

"No," Cery replied. He glanced at his daughter and bodyguard. They were shaking their heads.

The Administrator turned to regard the Higher Magicians. "Any questions?"

"I have one," the magician in white robes said. He must be the High Lord, Cery recalled. Sonea had told him the High Lord's robes had been changed to white after it was decided the Black Magicians should, logically, wear black. "Have you ever seen anyone with the same physical characteristics as this woman?" The man gestured toward the rogue. "Aside from her gender, of course."

"Maybe once or twice," Cery replied.

"Do you know where those people came from?"

Cery shook his head. "No."

The magician nodded, then waved a hand at the Administrator to indicate he had no more questions. Relieved, Cery found he was looking forward to leaving this place. He might be a powerful man in the city's underworld, but he was not used to being scrutinised by so many people. *A Thief works best unnoticed. Better to be known by reputation than by being the centre of attention.*

"Thank you for your assistance, Cery of Northside, Anyi and Gol," the Administrator said. "You may now leave."

Sonea ushered them out again. Once the Guildhall doors had closed behind them, Cery let out a sigh of relief.

"Did that help?" Anyi asked.

Sonea nodded. "I think it will. They now have witness accounts of the woman breaking the law. The only magic she used within sight of magicians was arguably in her defence, when I captured her and took her to the Guild."

"So if she has broken the law it is excusable to read her mind?"

"It was already." Sonea smiled grimly. "But now they won't feel so bad about it."

"Will you do it?" Cery asked.

Her smile vanished. "It'll either be me or Kallen. I suspect they'll choose Kallen, since he's had much less involvement in the search and hasn't been disobeying rules."

Cery frowned. "Are they going to give you trouble for that?"

"I don't *think* so," she said, her brow creasing with worry. "Kallen doesn't seem too pleased. He hasn't had the time to raise the matter so far, but he will eventually. Nobody else has brought it up, but I'm sure someone will." She sighed and took a step back toward the hall. "I had better return. I'll let you know what happens." She paused, then smiled. "Oh, and Lorkin contacted me. He's alive and well. I'll tell you all about it another time."

"Great news!" Cery said. "See you then."

She waved, then pushed one of the doors open wide enough to slip through. Cery looked from Anyi to Gol. "Let's see if the carriage is waiting for us."

They grinned, and followed as he set off back to the front of the University.

When Achati, Dannyl, the other Ashaki and Unh reached the road, they found that the slaves they had sent ahead had the carriage and horses ready and waiting for them. The Ashaki helpers turned to face Dannyl and bid him farewell.

"You have our sympathy," one of them said. "It must be annoying to have your assistant seduced away from you."

"Yes," Dannyl replied. "But at least I know he went willingly and is in no danger – or doesn't believe himself to be. And . . . I apologise for his behaviour again. He led you all into danger unnecessarily."

Another shrugged. "It was worth it for the chance to finally attempt to do something about them, or find their base, even if it led to nothing."

"But . . . surely you could not have followed the Traitors much further without them being forced to kill you," Dannyl said.

The Ashaki exchanged glances, and suddenly Dannyl understood their apparent lack of concern. They did not want to admit that they had been hopelessly outnumbered, or had failed in their task, so they pretended otherwise. In truth they had been well aware and fearful of the risk they had been taking. It would be rude to make them say so aloud, however.

"Well, Ashaki Achati tells me we got further into their territory than anyone has managed to go before," he said, putting pride and admiration into his tone.

The Ashaki smiled and nodded.

"If you change your mind about retrieving your assistant, let us know," the more talkative of them told him. "The king would not have much trouble gathering together a small army for the purpose. We are always looking for an excuse to weed them out."

"That is good to know," he assured them. "And much appreciated." He turned to look at Unh. "I know he has good trackers to call upon, too."

The tribesman inclined his head slightly, but remained expressionless. The Sachakans said nothing, then the quieter of them cleared his throat. "What do you think the Guild will do about Lord Lorkin?"

Dannyl shook his head. "I don't know," he admitted. "But they'll have to send me a new assistant. Hopefully they'll be better at choosing one than I was."

The Sachakans chuckled. Then the talkative Ashaki rubbed his hands together. "We had all best be on our way, then."

So farewells were uttered and the Sachakans rode away. Unh nodded once at Dannyl, which was somehow more meaningful a farewell than the Sachakans'. The group's passing stirred up dust as they left. Dannyl and Achati climbed into the carriage and Achati's two slaves took their positions on the outside. The vehicle jolted into motion, and began swaying gently as it rolled along the other road.

"Now this is better," Achati said. "Comfort. Privacy. The promise of regular baths."

"I'm definitely looking forward to a bath."

"I suspect our helpers are as keen to get home, despite the fact that they didn't get a chance to rid Sachaka of a few Traitors."

Dannyl winced. "I apologise again, for causing so much discomfort and risk for no reason."

"It wasn't for no reason," Achati corrected. "You were obliged to search; I was obliged to help you. A young man could have been in danger. The fact that he wasn't made our journey no less important."

Dannyl nodded in gratitude for the Sachakan's understanding. "I suppose I'm apologising on Lorkin's behalf. I'm sure if he'd been able to tell us of his decision earlier he would have."

"He may not have decided what he was going to do until just before he spoke to you." Achati shrugged. "It was not a wasted trip. In fact, it has been educational, both in how Kyralians think and how *you* think. I made assumptions about your determination to find your assistant, for example. I thought it might . . . go beyond mere loyalty to a fellow magician and Kyralian."

Dannyl looked up at Achati in surprise. "You thought we were . . .?"

"Lovers." The man's expression was serious now. He looked away. "My slave is young, good-looking and quite talented. He adores me. But it is the adoration a slave feels for a good master. I envied you your assistant."

Unable to stop himself staring at Achati in surprise, Dannyl searched for an appropriate answer and found none. Achati chuckled.

"Surely you knew this much about me."

"Well . . . yes, but I'll admit I was a bit slow to notice."

"You were preoccupied."

"I gather you weren't making any great assumption about me?"

Achati shook his head. "We make sure we know everything we can about the Ambassadors the Guild sends our way. And your choice of companions isn't exactly a secret in Imardin."

"No," Dannyl agreed, thinking of Tayend and his parties.

Achati sighed. "I can buy myself a companion – in fact I have done so many times. Someone beautiful. Someone well trained in pleasing a master. I might perhaps find someone intelligent and witty enough to converse with, even be lucky enough to be loved by that slave. But there is always something lacking."

Dannyl watched Achati closely. "What is that?"

The man's mouth twisted into a lopsided smile. "Risk. Only when you know the other could easily leave you, do you appreciate when he stays. Only when it's not easier on them to like you than not, do you appreciate it when they do."

"An equal."

Achati shrugged. "Or near enough. For a companion to be truly equal to me would restrict my choices too much. As the king's envoy I am one of the most powerful men in the country, after all."

Dannyl nodded. "I've never had to consider such differences in status. Though I suppose I might have, if my companion was a servant."

"But a servant can leave."

"Yes."

"Do servants make good conversation?"

"I suppose some might."

Achati flexed his shoulders, then relaxed. "I enjoy our conversations."

Dannyl smiled. "That's just as well. You've only got me to talk to between here and Arvice."

"Indeed." The other man's eyes narrowed. "I think I'd enjoy more than just conversation with you."

Once again, Dannyl was speechless. Surprise was followed

by embarrassment, then was overtaken by curiosity, and not a little flattery. *This Sachakan – who had just pointed out he was one of the most powerful men in the country – is actually propositioning me! What should I do? How do you turn someone like him down without being impolite or causing a political repercussion? Do I even want to?*

He felt a shiver go down his spine. *He's younger than me, but not by many years. He's good-looking in a Sachakan kind of way. He's good company. He's nice to his slaves. But oh, such a liaison would be politically dangerous!*

Achati chuckled again. "I don't expect anything of you, Ambassador Dannyl. I only express a view. And a possibility. Something to think about. For now let's keep to conversations. After all, I would hate to have ruined our friendship by suggesting anything that you are uncomfortable with."

Dannyl nodded. "As I said, I'm a bit slow."

"Not at all." Achati grinned. "Otherwise I wouldn't like you so much. You've been preoccupied. Focused on one goal. That distraction is gone. You can think of other things. Like how long it will take for the Guild to choose and send you a new assistant."

"I'm not sure anyone will be willing to volunteer for the position, after what happened to Lorkin."

Achati chuckled. "You may be surprised. Some might come in the hopes of being snatched away to a secret place ruled by exotic women."

Dannyl groaned. "Oh, I hope not. I certainly hope not."

CHAPTER 29

ANSWERS, AND MORE QUESTIONS

Sonea sat back in her seat and waited for the Higher Magicians to stop procrastinating.

She had tried to prevent bringing Cery into the Guild, but once it was known that others had helped her and Regin find the rogues, the Guild's habit of exploring all sides to a situation had made it unavoidable. She had told them Cery was an old friend, not that he was a Thief. A few might make the connection to a Thief named Cery who had helped her and Akkarin during the Ichani Invasion, but most would have forgotten that detail in history. Those that preferred to ignore her part in the defeat of the invaders wouldn't have paid attention to the names of her helpers, and the few who didn't understood, she hoped, why she wanted to avoid too much attention being drawn to her old friend.

It was only Kallen, who paid too much attention to her already, who might make the connection and speak of it. But he was, if anything, discreet. He would not announce it to the entire Guild. He would consult with other Higher Magicians.

What annoyed Sonea was that bringing Cery in had proved nothing they didn't already know. The woman was obviously a rogue. She had used magic in front of hundreds of people, including the Alchemist and Healer who had helped Sonea capture her. She had also used it in a vain attempt to resist the magicians who had taken her to her temporary prison, the Dome.

But the Guild, and most likely the king, were worried about offending a foreign land. Especially when they weren't sure which land they might be offending.

Earlier in the meeting, an advisor of the king had brought maps and described some of the distant lands on them. The woman remained silent, refusing to answer when asked where she was from. The advisor had made a few guesses based on her appearance. If he was right, she made no sign.

"I cannot see any other option," High Lord Balkan said, and there was a note of finality in his tone. "We must read her mind."

Administrator Osen nodded. "Then I call on Black Magician Kallen and Black Magician Sonea to descend to the floor. Black Magician Kallen will read the mind of the unnamed rogue and Black Magician Sonea will read Forlie's mind."

Though she had been expecting this, Sonea felt a brief disappointment. There were many answers she would like to have from the foreign woman that she couldn't ask Kallen to search for. Like whether the woman had killed Cery's family.

Following Kallen down the stairs, she kept her gaze on Forlie. The woman had gone pale, and stared at Sonea with wide eyes.

"I'll tell you everything," Forlie blurted out. "You don't have to read my mind."

"Stupid woman," a strangely accented voice said. "Don't you know they can't read your mind if you don't want them to?"

Sonea turned to regard the foreign rogue, and realised that all of the magicians had done the same. The woman glanced from face to face, her expression changing as she read amusement and pity. Doubt and then fear crept into her eyes as Kallen stopped in front of her.

As he reached toward her, his arms were slapped away by magic.

Not wanting to watch the struggle, Sonea turned her attention back to Forlie, who flinched.

"I'm not a magician," the woman said, looking from Sonea to the Higher Magicians. "I was made to lie. They said . . . they said they'd kill my daughter and her children if I told you." She sucked in a shuddering breath, then burst into tears.

Sonea put a hand on her shoulder. "Do you know where they are?"

"I . . . I think so."

"They don't know you have told us anything yet. We'll go get your children before they find out."

"Th-thank you."

"I'm afraid I do have to check that you're telling the truth. I promise you, mind-reading doesn't hurt. In fact, you won't feel anything. You won't even know I'm there. And I'll be as quick as I can."

Forlie stared at Sonea, then nodded.

Reaching out to gently touch the woman's temples, Sonea sent her mind forth. Fear and anxiety washed over her as she touched the woman's mind. She let herself waft into Forlie's thoughts, which were of her daughter and two grandchildren, and the men who had taken them. Sonea recognised the man who had blackmailed Forlie – he was the roet-seller who had been with Forlie when she was captured.

Remembering that moment, Sonea recalled the magical force she'd felt come from Forlie. Someone else must have sent it. Perhaps the real rogue, watching them through the windows.

—*Who used magic when we found you?*

—*I don't know.*

—*Where are your daughter and grandchildren now?*

A maze of alleys and makeshift houses flashed into Sonea's mind, then settled on one house in particular. Forlie's family were in one of the remaining poor areas of the city.

—*We'll find them, Forlie. We'll punish the people who did this.*

Opening her eyes, Sonea withdrew her fingers. Forlie's expression was hopeful and determined now.

"Thank you," she whispered.

Turning to the Higher Magicians, Sonea related what she had learned. "I recommend that one or more of us go with Forlie to free her children as soon as possible."

There were many nods of agreement. A small noise drew their attention to the foreign woman. Her face, caught between Kallen's hands, expressed a mixture of surprise and dismay.

All watched in silence, and when Kallen finally released her Sonea heard a collective sigh of relief. Kallen stepped back, then turned to face the Higher Magicians.

"Her name is Lorandra," he announced. "She is from Igra, the land beyond the great northern desert. It is a strange place, where all magic is taboo and punishable by death. Yet those who watch for and punish magicians are magicians themselves. They steal the children of those they execute in order to maintain their numbers." He shook his head in amazement at this hypocrisy and cruelty.

"Lorandra learned magic as a young woman and was forced to flee her country with her newborn son. They managed to

480

cross the desert to Lonmar, then travelled through Elyne to Kyralia. Here they were taken in by a Thief, who protected them in exchange for magical favours. The Thief eventually adopted the boy and made him his heir. He trained the boy in crime, while his mother trained him in magic."

Kallen looked at Sonea and frowned.

"The son's name is Skellin, one of the Thieves that Black Magician Sonea and Lord Regin enlisted to help them find the rogue. Of course, he did not want them finding his mother, so he arranged for Forlie to be caught in her place. He even used his own magic to make it look as if she had attacked them."

He looked back at the Higher Magicians. "Skellin has been sending his mother out to kill off rival Thieves since he came to power. Through murder and alliances he intended to make himself king of the city's underworld."

Sonea's heart skipped a beat. *This woman is the Thief Hunter!*

Kallen paused and his frown deepened. "And he imported roet to help bind people to him. Not just the poor but the rich as well. And magicians. He seemed to think we would be easy to manipulate once we'd all been introduced to the drug."

A murmur of voices rose as the magicians began to discuss what they'd learned. Sonea caught dismissive remarks about Skellin's delusions, but a chill had run down her spine at the mention of roet. She thought of Stoneworker Berrin, whose addiction she had tried and failed to Heal away. If roet addiction could not be Healed, and Skellin knew it, then his grand plan might have succeeded.

"What *are* you?" the foreign woman said. She was staring at Kallen. Her eyes slid to Sonea. "And *you*?"

Sonea answered the question with a small smile. Skellin and his mother were magicians, but clearly they weren't black magicians. *That's something to be grateful for. Hopefully we can assume Igra isn't a land of black magicians, too. We don't need another Sachaka to worry about.*

Administrator Osen now turned to face the hall and raised his arms. Voices quieted to a near silence.

"We now know the truth. One of our captives is innocent, the other is a murderess and a rogue. We have another rogue in our city to find and deal with. Lorandra will be imprisoned. Forlie is free to go. Certain actions must be taken immediately, so I must end this meeting now."

The hall filled with the sound of hundreds of magicians standing up and bursting into conversation. Osen strode over to Sonea.

"Take Forlie and find her children quickly," he ordered quietly. "Before Lorandra thinks to inform Skellin of her betrayal."

Sonea stared at him in surprise, then nodded. *Of course. She only has to communicate with him mentally to tell him what happened here.* "I'll take Lord Regin as backup, if that is acceptable."

He nodded. "I'll send Kallen after Skellin once they're safe."

She felt her heart warm with appreciation. Osen might be cold toward her, but he wasn't a man without compassion for others. As he walked away, she looked around the room and found Regin standing by one of the stairs, watching her. She beckoned to him.

"Is that appropriate?"

Kallen's voice reached her over the chatter and footsteps of the Higher Magicians. She looked over to see him frowning at Osen.

"If you can rouse the support of the majority of Higher Magicians to oppose her going in the next few minutes, I'll consider sending someone else."

Kallen glanced at the magicians filing out of the building, then at Sonea, and his lips thinned.

"It's your decision," he said. "Not mine."

As Regin reached her side, Sonea smiled to herself, enjoying a moment of triumph. If Osen now trusted her enough to send her into the city, perhaps the rest of the Guild would forgive her for breaking the rules so often in recent weeks.

"Care to assist me in my next assignment?" she asked Regin.

His eyebrows rose and he almost managed a smile. "Always."

She hooked an arm around Forlie's. "Let's go find your family."

Lorkin was not completely sure how long had passed since he'd been put in the room. It had no window, so he had no sunlight to track the time of day. He'd shifted from travelling at night and sleeping during the day when with Tyvara to the opposite when travelling with Chari, so he couldn't judge what time it was by when he grew sleepy. Nor could he judge it by hunger, as he'd been eating whenever opportunity came rather than at regular times.

The meals that were brought to him seemed to follow a pattern, so he was counting the days that way. A simple meal of grainy sweet mush and fruit was followed a few hours later by a larger meal with meat and vegetables. Then after another interval a light meal of flat bread and a cup of warmed milk was served. It was basic food, but wonderful after the scavenged fare he'd had for the weeks he'd been travelling with Tyvara.

He'd been told he had to stay there until Tyvara's trial. Two and a half days had passed so far, he guessed. He'd kept himself entertained by reading his notebook, and writing observations about everything he had learned about the Traitors so far. He also listed questions he would seek the answer to, when he was free to do so. Each time food was brought, Lorkin glimpsed the Traitor keeping guard on his door. Always a woman, but not always the same woman. Were there no male magicians? Or none willing to guard him? Or did they not trust a man to guard another man?

He'd spent a lot of time sleeping, too. Though he'd been able to Heal away soreness and weariness, it was always better to let the body regain its energy and health through natural means.

Light came from a gemstone set into the ceiling. He'd got a closer look at it by standing on the bed. It was too bright to stare at for long. He'd reached up to it, finding it didn't give off any heat. The surface was faceted, like stones in jewellery.

Had it naturally formed the shape, or had a human carved it? Would it go on glowing forever, or eventually fade?

Unanswered questions were gradually stacking up in his mind and his notebook.

He wondered how he was supposed to find out about Sanctuary's laws, as Riaya had suggested. Was he meant to ask for someone to teach him? What would happen if he knocked to get the guard's attention, then asked for a teacher?

He thought about that for some time. Before he could gather the determination to try it, he heard voices outside. He sat up and turned to face the door as it opened.

A woman he'd never seen before looked him up and down. "Lord Lorkin," she said. "You're to come with me."

The atmosphere in the city was different now, he noted. More people were about, and many looked as if they were standing around waiting for something. When they noticed him they stared at him with curiosity, but the expectation in the air was clearly for something else.

The trial of Tyvara? he wondered. *Well, why else would they come and get me?*

His assumption was proved correct when they arrived at the same room in which he'd met the Table of Speakers. The same seven women were seated at the curved table, but this time the gem-encrusted chair was occupied. An old woman sat there, watching him thoughtfully.

The rest of the room was filled with people. The stepped seating was full and many more men and women stood around the walls. Opposite to the entrance was a smaller door that he hadn't noticed last time. Within it stood Tyvara and two other women. There was a feeling about the room that this meeting had already been going for some time. He wished he could tell how well it was going.

"You don't bow to Queen Zarala," his guide murmured into his ear. "You put a hand to your chest and look at her until she nods at you. Now, go stand in front of the Table and answer their questions."

He did as she instructed. The queen smiled and nodded as he made the hand-over-heart gesture. Her attention shifted to Riaya.

"Lord Lorkin, former assistant to Guild Ambassador to Sachaka, Dannyl," the Director said, her voice filling the room. "You came to Sanctuary in order to speak in Tyvara's defence at this trial. That time has come. Tell us how you came to meet Tyvara."

"She was a slave at the Guild House."

"Where you would have met Riva as well."

"I didn't meet Riva until the night she died."

Riaya nodded. "How did Riva come to be in your room that night?"

Lorkin bit his lip. "She slipped in while I was asleep."

"And what did she do?"

"Woke me up." He pushed aside reluctance at having to describe how. "By getting into my bed and . . . er . . . being a lot nicer to me than was required."

A faint smile touched Riaya's lips. "So you were not in the habit of bedding slaves, then?"

"No."

"But you didn't send her away."

"No."

"What happened then?"

"The room lit up. I saw that Tyvara had stabbed Riva."

"And then?"

"Tyvara explained how Riva had intended to kill me." He felt his face warm. "With a kind of magic I'd never heard of before. She said if I stayed at the Guild House, others would attempt to assassinate me."

"You believed her?"

"Yes."

"Why?"

"The other slave – Riva – said something." He thought back. "She said: 'he has to die'. It was obvious that she was referring to me."

Riaya's eyebrows rose. She looked at the six women and the queen, then turned back to Lorkin.

"What happened then?"

"We left and went to an estate — to the slave quarters. The slaves there were helpful. But at the estate we went to next, the slaves had set a trap for us. They tried to drug us. After that we didn't trust anyone — until we met Chari."

Riaya nodded, then turned to the Table.

"Any questions for Lord Lorkin?"

The first woman nodded. Lorkin recalled their names from the last meeting. *Yvali, I think.* She fixed Lorkin with a direct stare.

"Did you ever bed Tyvara?"

"No."

A murmur went through the audience. It sounded like a protest, Lorkin noted. Yvali opened her mouth to ask another question, then thought better of it. She looked at the others.

"Did Tyvara kill anybody else while you were travelling together?" Lanna asked.

"Not as far as I know."

"Why did you not head for Kyralia?" Shaiya asked.

"Tyvara said that it was the obvious thing to do, so we'd find assassins waiting for us."

"What did you give Ambassador Dannyl after you persuaded him to stop following us?" Savara asked.

Lorkin looked at her in surprise, but not at the sudden change of subject. If she had seen this, why hadn't she asked him before now? Her expression was impossible to read. He decided it would be best to tell the truth.

"My mother's blood ring. I knew it was likely it would be taken from me when I got here, and I don't think she would have liked it falling into unfamiliar hands."

A low murmur filled the room, but quickly subsided.

"Did you use it at any time after Tyvara killed Riva?"

"No. Tyvara didn't know I had it . . . I think." He resisted glancing in her direction.

"Do you have any other blood rings?"

"No."

Savara nodded to indicate she had no more questions.

"Will you consent to a mind-read to confirm the truth of your words?" Kalia asked.

The room fell utterly silent.

"No," Lorkin replied.

Muttered words and exhalations followed. He met Kalia's gaze and held it. *How stupid does she think I am? If I let anyone read my mind they'll go looking for the secret to Healing, and then I can forget about ever leaving this place.*

No more questions came. Riaya exchanged glances with all of the women at the table, then looked at Lorkin.

"Thank you, Lord Lorkin, for your cooperation. Please stand over by the entrance."

He nodded to her respectfully out of habit, then to the six women and to the queen in case his gesture would be taken as giving inappropriate favour to the Director. Spotting near the entrance the guide who had taken him to the room, he walked over to stand by her.

She eyed him thoughtfully, then nodded.

"That was well done," she murmured.

"Thank you," he replied. He looked across the room to Tyvara. She was frowning, but as he met her gaze she gave him a strained smile.

"We will now deliberate," Riaya announced.

As the eight women around the table began to talk, the audience broke into noisy chatter. Lorkin tried to pick conversations out of the voices, but could not make out more than the occasional phrase. The leaders around the table had clearly set a magical barrier against noise around themselves. So instead of listening, he examined the people in the room in the hope of learning what he could before he was returned to the window-less cell.

There were many couples sitting on the stairs, he noted, but all others were women. Those standing around the walls were mostly male, however. The clothing of all was simple. Some of the Traitors were dressed in practical trousers and tunics, while others wore long belted shifts in finer cloth. He was surprised to see that both women and men wore these long shifts.

The colour of the cloth ranged from undyed to deep colours, but none were vivid or bright. He guessed it was hard to bring dyes into the city, and with limited space to grow crops, priority would be given to plants that produced food.

Though he tried to keep his attention focused on the audi-ence, he could not help glancing at Tyvara from time to time. Every time he did so, he found her watching him. She did not smile again, however. She looked thoughtful. And worried.

Finally, Riaya's voice rose over the noise in the room.

"We have finished deliberations," she announced.

The room quietened. Riaya looked at the other women at the table, then turned to regard Tyvara.

"You offered to allow Speaker Halana to read your mind. We have explored all other avenues as required by law, but I can see no other way to confirm your claims. Please come forward and remove the mind block."

From the audience came low voices and whispers. Lorkin thought back to a snippet of conversation between Chari and Tyvara, from the journey into the mountains. Tyvara had said she would let the Traitors read her mind. Chari had been shocked. *"You can't,"* she had hissed. *"You promised . . ."*

Promised what? To who? Lorkin watched as the woman who had saved his life walked with head high to stand before her leaders. He felt his heart lighten with a rush of sudden, giddy affection. *She is so proud. So beautiful.* Then he felt a familiar doubt and annoyance spoil the moment. *I wish I knew whether Chari is right or not about Tyvara's regard for me. If she is wrong I don't want to make a fool of myself trying to win over Tyvara. But if she is right . . . if Tyvara likes me . . . but makes a habit of pushing away those who admire her . . . do I have the determination to keep pursuing her?*

Every part of him was sure he did.

Stopping in front of the Table, Tyvara held out her left hand. She paused, then grimaced. Lorkin blinked in surprise and horror as blood began to drip from her palm. She kneaded the base of her thumb, then held up something too tiny for him to see. She let it drop on the table.

I was right, he thought. *The mind block* is *an object similar to a blood gem.*

The leaders wore expressions of grim sympathy. He watched Halana stand up and reach out to Tyvara, who bent forward a little. The older woman took hold of Tyvara's head and closed her eyes.

A long pause followed in which all watched the pair expectantly. When Halana drew her hands away at last, she said nothing. She sat down. Tyvara picked up the mind block and backed away from the table.

"What have you learned?" Riaya asked.

"Everything Tyvara has told us is true," Halana said.

A collective sigh went through the room. Riaya placed her hands on the table.

"Then it is time to cast our votes." She looked at Tyvara, then the audience. "We have concluded that Tyvara did not need to kill Riva. She should have pushed Riva away from Lorkin, or otherwise separated them. But we also acknowledge that there was no time, upon discovery of the crime taking place, for deliberation. Tyvara acted in order to ensure the wishes of the queen were met, and to prevent a situation that might lead to a threat to Sanctuary and increased danger to our people in Sachaka." She paused and looked at the Speakers. "Should Tyvara be executed for the murder of Riva?"

Of the six women sitting behind the table, two held their hands up. The rest held their hands out, palm facing downward. Lorkin assumed that since Kalia had her hand up, that signal was for the affirmative.

"Four against, two for," Riaya said. She looked at the audience. To Lorkin's surprise, they were making one or the other gesture. "The majority against," Riaya declared. She looked to the queen, who now held out her hand, palm down. "The answer is 'no'."

Hands dropped. Riaya looked pleased, Lorkin noted.

"The death of a fellow Traitor is a serious matter," she continued. "And no matter the reason for it, penalties must be applied. Tyvara must remain in Sanctuary for the next three years, after which she may take a position as scout or watcher and work to regain the responsibilities she had before. During those three years she is to dedicate one day of each six to the benefit of Riva's family." Riaya's gaze returned to Tyvara. "Do you accept this judgement?"

"Yes."

"Then it is decided. You are free to go. This trial is concluded and the laws of Sanctuary upheld. May the stones keep singing."

"May the stones keep singing," the audience replied.

The room filled with movement as all rose to their feet. Lorkin watched Tyvara. She was looking at the floor. She gave a little shake of her head, then looked up at Savara. The older woman smiled with approval. Then one of her eyebrows rose in query and her gaze shifted to Lorkin. He blinked, then saw Tyvara roll her eyes, turn and stride to the door at the far side of the room. He could see Chari standing there. The young woman was grinning. She looked across to him and winked.

Someone tugged at his sleeve. The guide smiled at him.

"I'm to take you to your quarters next." Her smile widened. "Your new quarters."

He felt his heart, in the process of sinking, lighten. "It wouldn't happen to have a window, would it?"

She gestured for him to follow her. "No. But you'll have some company, and you're free to come and go as you please – so long as you don't leave Sanctuary, of course. I'm Vytra, by the way."

"Pleased to meet you, Vytra."

She chuckled. "You Kyralians have funny ways," she said. "So polite."

"I can be rude if you want."

She laughed. "That would be a shame. Now, on the way I should give you a few tips on how to get along with people here."

Listening carefully, Lorkin followed the woman out into the city.

Cery watched his daughter thoughtfully. She wasn't doing well in her lessons today, but then Gol had also made some uncharacteristic blunders. Both were still too wound up from their morning visit to the Guild to focus fully on the training session.

They shouldn't be letting that affect their concentration, he thought. *I guess I'm going to have to make sure I can protect myself, if my bodyguards are ever treated to a glimpse of the life of the rich and powerful again.*

A knock at the door drew everyone's attention. They were back at the Grinder Bolhouse, and Cery's people had been sent out to inform those who had requested a meeting with him that they could see him now.

At a nod from Cery, Gol strode to the door and opened it a crack, before pulling it open. The man standing in the corridor outside had the same awed look on his face that Anyi and Gol had worn for hours after their visit to the Guild.

"Black Magician Sonea, Lord Regin, two women and two children to see you," he said.

"Send them up."

The man nodded and hurried away. Anyi and Gol stood and grinned at each other.

"Well, come on. Take your places," Cery ordered.

They hurried over to stand on either side of his chair. Gol struck a pose that looked more ridiculous than imposing. Anyi flexed her fingers as she always did when nervous. Shaking his head, Cery sighed and waited.

The sound of footsteps grew louder, then the room seemed to fill with magicians' robes. Sonea's black ones first, then Regin's red. Following the pair and looking very plain and meek came Forlie and a younger woman. The latter was carrying a small girl in one arm, and a slightly older boy clung to her other hand.

Anyi and Gol bowed awkwardly, but with enthusiasm.

"Cery," Sonea said, then she nodded to his daughter and friend. "Anyi and Gol. Thank you for coming to the Guild. I tried to prevent it, but the Guild, when it is investigating something as serious as a rogue magician, tends to be overly thorough."

"That's fine," Cery replied. He turned to Gol. "Bring them some chairs."

The chunky old chairs that normally sat in the centre of the room had been moved to one side to allow room for training sessions. Gol took a step toward them, but Sonea raised a hand to stop him.

"I'll do it."

Anyi, Forlie and the other woman gaped as the heavy chairs rose and floated to the middle of the room, arranging themselves in a square incorporating Cery's seat. Gol merely grinned in knowing satisfaction. He'd seen plenty of magic back when Cery had been working for the former High Lord.

"We came to tell you the results of our investigation," Sonea said as she sat down. "And to ask a favour."

"A favour?" Cery rolled his eyes in mock exasperation. "Here we go again."

She smiled. "Yes. Can you find Forlie, her daughter and her grandchildren a safe place to hide?"

Cery looked at the women. They smiled back at him tentatively. The younger woman had not let go of either child as she'd sat down. The girl was in her lap, and the boy was sitting on the arm of the chair.

"They're in danger?"

"Yes. She was set up to take the place of Lorandra – the real rogue."

"But you have the real rogue . . . don't you?"

"We do. And we don't." Sonea paused and considered him for a moment. "Lorandra is Skellin's mother."

Cery felt a chill rise up from somewhere behind his chair and flow through all his body. His heart began to thump in his chest. *Skellin's mother. That's why he was annoyed to learn that I'd seen the rogue fairly clearly and hadn't told him. It would have told him his ploy of setting up Forlie wouldn't work. Well, it would have failed anyway because he didn't know that some of the Guild's magicians can read minds.*

"I can't imagine he's a very happy man at the moment," Cery said dryly.

Regin chuckled. "No. Unfortunately for us all, he evaded the magicians sent to capture him, so we now have a rogue on the loose who knows we're after him."

Cery stared at him. "*Skellin* is a magician?"

Sonea nodded. "Which is why we need you to help Forlie. He blackmailed her by taking her daughter and grandchildren and threatening to kill them. We're hoping he's too busy hiding himself from us to worry about seeking revenge on her, but we'd rather not take that risk."

Cery looked at Forlie and shrugged. "Of course I'll help her."

"You'll want to take some extra precautions yourself," Regin added.

Cery smiled at the man's understatement. *He's far more likely to seek revenge on me for the capture of his mother than on Forlie. Maybe I should see if another Thief will take care of her for me. Someone who doesn't like Skellin . . .*

"There's more," Sonea said. "Lorandra is – was – the Thief Hunter. Skellin sent her out to kill off his rivals. He had big plans for himself. He wanted to become king of the under-world. Was going to use roet to keep everyone – even the Guild – in line."

When Cery thought about how powerful Skellin had already become, that did not seem as impossible as it sounded. *How many people did he already have control over? I'm going to have to be very careful who I choose to trade with now.*

"Do you know if Lorandra killed Cery's family?" Anyi asked.

Cery felt his heart shrink. He glanced at his daughter, appreciating her asking the question to save him from having to, but dreading the answer.

Sonea grimaced. "I don't know. I wasn't the one who read her mind, and I would have to have asked publicly for Kallen to find out."

Which would have revealed more about me than I'd have liked.

"I'll try to find out," she promised. "Even if she didn't kill them, if her part was only to break into your hideout using magic, she'll know who did. Or who ordered it."

"Skellin most likely," Regin said. "Unless she did occasional work on the side for other customers."

"At least we know Skellin can't have been the actual killer," Gol said. "He was talking with Cery at the time."

Anyi made a small humming noise. "It doesn't make sense. Why send someone to kill another Thief's family at the same time as inviting them to become an ally?"

They all fell silent for a long moment, frowning in thought.

"Maybe Lorandra knows," Gol suggested.

Cery shook his head, puzzled. "Well, I do know one thing for sure. We've got another rogue to catch."

"If he's still in Kyralia," Regin said.

"Oh, he's still here," Cery assured them. "He hasn't spent

all that time and effort on his little empire to scamper off somewhere else. No, there are people here, rich and poor, who'll fall over themselves to help him, some because they have to, many because they'll benefit from it. He won't have that anywhere else."

Sonea nodded. "His influence over the city is already dangerously strong, but I suspect if he's removed his empire will fall. We have to find him." She looked at Cery. "Will you help us again?"

He nodded. "Wouldn't want to miss the fun."

She smiled, then stood up. Regin followed suit. "We must get back to the Guild. Thank you for taking care of Forlie and her family."

Cery looked at the woman, who was watching him expectantly. "I'll find somewhere safe for you all. Where is their father?" Both women scowled so fiercely Cery couldn't help but laugh. "Never mind about that then." He turned back to Sonea and ushered her to the door. "I bet you attracted a lot of attention on the way here."

She laughed ruefully. "Yes. And the customers downstairs will be talking about it for months."

"Might not be a bad thing," Regin said, following her out of the door. "It will remind people who might be considering helping Skellin that you have powerful friends."

"Well, it wouldn't hurt if they thought you were still here. It will give us time to make plans before we leave. The more private way out goes through the kitchen and the side door."

"We'll go that way, then. Thanks for your help," Sonea said. "And take care of yourselves."

"I always do," he called after them, as they strode down the corridor to the stairs. Closing the door, he turned back to regard the remaining occupants of the room. Looking at the children made his heart ache, and he pushed painful memories away. "Gol, take Forlie's family downstairs and see if they're hungry."

"Right," Gol replied. He beckoned, and they followed him out of the room. Cery returned to his chair and let out a sigh.

He looked at Anyi. She was frowning. It was not a worried frown, but a puzzled one.

"What is it?" he asked.

She looked at him, then away again. "Remember that magician at the Guild who was dressed the same as Sonea."

"Yes. Black Magician Kallen."

"He looked familiar. I didn't recognise him at first because of the robes."

"You've seen him without robes on?"

She looked up at him and laughed. "Not in the way you just put it. I didn't get much of a look at what he was wearing the time I saw him."

"What was he doing?" he asked.

A crease appeared between her brows, then her forehead smoothed and her mouth opened in a circle of revelation. "Ah! That's it. I went with my friend one day to get rot. Not for me, of course." Her eyes flicked up to his, serious and concerned. "In the middle of the dealing a carriage pulled up. The man inside wanted rot, and didn't want to wait. I got a look at his face."

"Kallen?"

"Yes."

"Are you sure?"

"Oh, yes." Her eyes twinkled. "I take special note of anyone who looks like they might be doing something they shouldn't."

Cery snorted. "That'd be nearly everyone in the city."

She grinned. "And in particular if it looks like what I learn about them might be useful some time," she amended. "Do you think Sonea would be interested? Lots of magicians take rot, I've heard."

"Oh, I think she'll find this interesting," Cery told her. "I think she'll find this *very* interesting. It'll be a good excuse to sneak into her hospice again. Or maybe I'll wait until I have something useful to tell her about Skellin." He looked at Anyi and grimaced. "We're going to have to be real careful who we trust. Skellin has a lot of friends, and I doubt I'm one of them now. We've got to help find him without getting ourselves caught. Things are going to get wild."

Anyi nodded, then smiled and rolled her eyes. "How many times do I have to tell you? Nobody says things like 'wild' any more."

EPILOGUE

With a final push of magic, Lorkin swept the last of the dust, hair, food scraps and unidentifiable particles into a small pile, then went to fetch a basket to dump it in.

A few weeks had passed since he'd taken up residence in the men's room. It was a large room, filled with rows of narrow beds. Most were empty now, but from the possessions tucked under their frames it was clear nearly all had regular occupants. Though he knew most of the regulars' names, there were a few who stayed for three or four days then disappeared for a few more that he'd not yet been introduced to.

"These beds are for men who don't want to stay with their family any more, and who haven't paired with a woman," Vytra had told him. "There isn't space for everyone to have their own room."

"Are there women's rooms?" Lorkin had asked.

"Sort of." She had shrugged. "Sometimes friends and sisters share rooms."

At first he'd been a novelty to the male Traitors, subjected to plenty of questions about Kyralia, how he had come to Sanctuary, and what he planned to do there. The latter he could not answer to their satisfaction. He could hardly tell them about his interest in Tyvara, and they scoffed at his plans to negotiate links between their people and the Allied Lands.

"You're a magician," one had pointed out. "Surely you'll be given something to do that involves magic."

Despite Savara's assurance to the other Speakers that she'd find him work to do, he hadn't been set any task or duty yet. So the men had given him the job of keeping their room tidy. They'd been surprised to discover he didn't know how to, and were impressed that he'd had servants to do such menial tasks for him in the Guild. It didn't get him assigned to any other task, however. They gave him some rough instructions, then left him to work it out for himself.

He'd asked plenty of questions in return, learning about the rules and laws of Sanctuary, including those subtle ones about manners and fairness that people set and stick to in order to reduce the conflicts that arise when living in close contact with each other.

As Chari had warned, Sanctuary was ruled by women. But while men were blocked from the highest positions of power, they were involved in all other activities in the city. The founders had decided that Sanctuary would be foremost a place where women were in charge, but beyond that it must be a place where people were equal. Lorkin was impressed to find that men had more freedom and respect here than women did in Kyralia. He'd been worried that Traitor society may be the opposite. It made him appreciate, in ways he'd never considered before, how unfair Kyralian society actually was to women. Though it was a lot better than some other societies – like Lonmar's. And the rest of Sachaka's.

Still, there were some notable ways that women were favoured over men here. Men were taught magic, but not black magic. Only women knew how to prevent a pregnancy, and all children belonged to them.

In the small storeroom off the main room – in which, he noted, even there, gemstones were set into the ceiling to provide illumination – Lorkin found what he was looking for. He grabbed a tightly woven basket from a stack and checked it for holes.

"It's going to happen soon, I say."

The voice was male and came from the main room. Lorkin hesitated.

"No," another man answered. "It could take years yet before we're ready."

"But they've doubled the battle training sessions. We have more scouts out there than ever before."

"And we've got hundreds of gems still only half grown. No war is going to happen until they mature, and that's going to take months, if not a year." The man sighed. "I'm hungry."

War? Lorkin looked at the basket, knowing that if he hovered here and one of the men came into the store to get something to eat they'd know he'd been listening. He forced himself to walk out of the room, then straighten and smile as he saw them. They looked at him in surprise.

"Greetings," he said, despite knowing they found the term of welcome odd. "You're back early. Can I get you anything?"

The two men glanced at each other, then the one who'd said he was hungry started toward the store. "No, but thanks for offering."

Lorkin began sweeping the rubbish into the basket. It was not easy getting the dust particles from the flat floor into the circular woven vessel, and he was concentrating so hard that he lost track of where the other men were.

"Lorkin," a sharp, female voice said close behind him.

He froze. Which was better than visibly jumping, he decided as he recognised the voice. Straightening, he turned to smile politely at the woman.

"Speaker Kalia," he replied.

She looked him up and down. He was wearing the simple trousers and tunic that the other men favoured – those that did not prefer the shift that both men and women wore.

"Follow me," she said.

She turned on her heel and strode toward the door. Putting the basket down, he hurried after her. He glanced at the two men, who both grimaced in sympathy.

Kalia walked quickly for someone with short legs and a plump body. Lorkin found he took one step for every two of hers, yet she did not appear to tire. He imagined that anyone seeing them both would know instantly who was in charge. *Definitely not me. Ah, how low I've sunk since leaving home . . .*

Her pace and expression didn't invite conversation, but this woman had wanted Tyvara executed. He was not going to let her intimidate him. Or, at least, he wasn't going to let her know he was intimidated.

"Where are we going?" he ventured.

"Somewhere you can be put to work at more appropriate duties than cleaning your room." She glanced at him; her eyes were sharp and calculating. "Here in Sanctuary we try to give people tasks to suit their temperament and talents. I'm not sure if the task I have for you will suit your temperament, but it definitely will suit your talents."

Somehow she managed to quicken her pace even further, hinting that no more conversation was welcome. When they reached a large archway she stopped, her breathing a little laboured. She drew in a deep breath and let it out, gesturing at the contents of the large room beyond.

As in the men's room, there were rows of beds. But instead of being empty at this time of day, plenty of these were occupied, with men, women and children. Familiar smells reached Lorkin's nose, along with some he did not recognise.

The smells of sickness and medicines.

His stomach sank, but not at the presence of so many sick people. Instead, it was at the realisation that the Traitors had found the best way to avenge themselves on him for his father's betrayal. And to test his own resolve to teach them Healing only if they gave something equally important in return.

"This is the Care Room," Kalia told him. "You'll be working for me from now on."

GLOSSARY

ANIMALS

aga moths – pests that eat clothing

anyi – sea mammals with short spines

ceryni – small rodent

enka – horned domestic animal, bred for meat

eyoma – sea leeches

faren – general term for arachnids

gorin – large domestic animal used for food and to haul boats and wagons

harrel – small domestic animal bred for meat

inava – insect believed to bestow good luck

limek – wild predatory dog

mullook – wild nocturnal bird

quannea – rare shells

rassook – domestic bird used for meat and feathers

ravi – rodent, larger than ceryni

reber – domestic animal, bred for wool and meat

sapfly – woodland insect

sevli – poisonous lizard

squimp – squirrel-like creature that steals food

yeel – small domesticated breed of limek used for tracking

zill – small, intelligent mammal sometimes kept as a pet

PLANTS/FOOD

anivope vine – plant sensitive to mental projection

bellspice – spice grown in Sachaka

bol – (also means "river scum') strong liquor made from tugors

brasi – green leafy vegetable with small buds

briskbark – bark with decongestant properties

cabbas – hollow, bell-shaped vegetable

chebol sauce – rich meat sauce made from bol

cone cakes – bite-sized cakes

creamflower – flower used as a soporific

crots – large, purple beans

curem – smooth, nutty spice

curren – coarse grain with robust flavour

dall – long fruit with tart orange, seedy flesh

dunda – root chewed as a stimulating drug

gan-gan – flowering bush from Lan

husroot – herb used for cleansing wounds

iker – stimulating drug, reputed to have aphrodisiac properties

jerras – long yellow beans

kreppa – foul-smelling medicinal herb

marin – red citrus fruit
monyo – bulb
myk – mind-affecting drug
nalar – pungent root
nemmin – sleep-inducing drug
nightwood – hardwood timber
pachi – crisp, sweet fruit
papea – pepper-like spice
piorres – small, bell-shaped fruit
raka/suka – stimulating drink made from roasted beans, originally from Sachaka
shem – edible reed-like plant
sumi – bitter drink
sweetdrops – candies
telk – seed from which an oil is extracted
tenn – grain that can be cooked as is, broken into small pieces, or ground to make a flour
tiro – edible nuts
tugor – parsnip-like root
ukkas – carnivorous plants
vare – berries from which most wine is produced
whitewater – pure spirits made from tugors
yellowseed – crop grown in Sachaka

CLOTHING AND WEAPONRY

incal – square symbol, not unlike a family shield, sewn onto sleeve or cuff
quan – tiny disc-shaped beads made of shell
undershift – Kyralian women's undergarment
vyer – stringed instrument from Elyne

COUNTRIES/PEOPLES IN THE REGION

Duna – tribes who live in volcanic desert north of Sachaka
Elyne – neighbour to Kyralia and Sachaka and once ruled by Sachaka
Kyralia – neighbour to Elyne and Sachaka and once ruled by Sachaka
Lan – a mountainous land peopled by warrior tribes
Lonmar – a desert land home to the strict Mahga religion
Sachaka – home of the once great Sachakan Empire, where all but the most powerful are slaves
Vin – an island nation known for their seamanship

TITLES/POSITIONS

Apprentice – Kyralian magician under training, and who has not been taught higher magic yet
Ashaki – Sachakan landowner
Ichani – Sachakan free man or woman who has been declared outcast
Lady – wife of a Kyralian landowner
Lord – Kyralian landowner, either of a ley or a city House, or their heir
Magician – Kyralian higher magician ("Lord" used instead if magician is a landowner)
Master – free Sachakan
Village/Town Master – commoner in charge of a rural community (answers to the ley's lord)

OTHER TERMS

the approach – main corridor to the master's room in Sachakan houses

blood gem – artificial gemstone that allows maker to hear the thoughts of wearer

earthblood – term the Duna tribes use for lava

kyrima – a game played by magicians to teach and practise strategic skills in battle

master's room – main room in Sachakan houses for greeting guests

slavehouse – part of Sachakan homes where the slaves live and work

slavespot – sexually transmitted disease

storestone – gemstone that can store magic

LORD DANNYL'S GUIDE TO
SLUM SLANG

blood money – payment for assassination

boot – refuse/refusal (don't boot us)

capper – man who frequents brothels

clicked – occurred

client – person who has an obligation or agreement with a Thief

counter – whore

done – murdered

dull – persuade to keep silent

dunghead – fool

dwells – term used to describe slum dwellers

eye – keep watch

fired – angry (got fired about it)

fish – propose/ask/look for (also someone fleeing the Guard)

gauntlet – guard who is bribeable or in the control of a Thief

goldmine – man who prefers boys

good go – a reasonable try

got – caught

grandmother – pimp

gutter – dealer in stolen goods

hai – a call for attention or expression of surprise or inquiry

heavies – important people

kin – a Thief's closest and most trusted

knife – assassin/hired killer

messenger – thug who delivers or carries out a threat

mind – hide (minds his business/I'll mind that for you)

mug – mouth (as in vessel for bol)

out for – looking for

pick – recognise/understand

punt – smuggler

right-sided – trustworthy/heart in the right place

rope – freedom

rub – trouble (got into some rub over it)

shine – attraction (got a shine for him)

show – introduce

space – allowances/permission

squimp – someone who double-crosses the Thieves

style – manner of performing business

tag – recognise (also means a spy, usually undercover)

thief – leader of a criminal group

watcher – posted to observe something or someone

wild – difficult

visitor – burglar

ACKNOWLEDGEMENTS

The writing of this book was blissfully free of the stresses and distractions that made the previous one so difficult to complete, and so these acknowledgements are short and sweet.

Thanks to Paul.

A big cheer to the Orbit team, especially Darren Nash and Joanna Kramer, who have always been patient and delightful to work with even during times of frustrating technical glitches. An extra nod of appreciation to the local Orbit team and especially Adele, Amy, Linda and Todd, who took me on signing tours of bookshops in their respective Aussie cities and were such great company.

A special thanks to Marianne de Pierres for launching *The Magician's Apprentice* with style, and statistics even I was amazed to hear.

Thanks, as always, to Fran and Liz, and all the agents around the world, doing the hard part for me.

And the feedback readers: Donna, Nicole, Jenny, Mum and Dad.

Finally, as always, to the readers. May you never run out of good books to read.